Born in the UK, **Becky Wicks** has suffered with interminable wanderlust from an early age. She's lived and worked all over the world, from London to Dubai, Sydney, Bali, NYC and Amsterdam. She's written for the likes of *GQ*, *Hello!*, *Fabulous* and *Time Out*, a host of YA romance, plus three travel memoirs—*Burqalicious*, *Balilicious* and *Latinalicious* (HarperCollins, Australia). Now she blends travel with romance for Mills & Boon and loves every minute! Tweet her @bex_wicks and subscribe at beckywicks.com.

Juliette Hyland began crafting heroes and heroines in high school. She lives in Ohio, USA, with her Prince Charming, who has patiently listened to many rants regarding characters failing to follow their outline. When not working on fun and flirty happily-ever-afters, Juliette can be found spending time with her beautiful daughters, her giant dogs, or sewing uneven stitches with her sewing machine.

Also by Becky Wicks

Tempted by Her Hot-Shot Doc
From Doctor to Daddy

Also by Juliette Hyland

Unlocking the Ex-Army Doc's Heart

Discover more at millsandboon.co.uk.

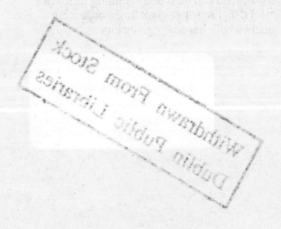

ENTICED BY HER ISLAND BILLIONAIRE

BECKY WICKS

FALLING AGAIN FOR THE SINGLE DAD

JULIETTE HYLAND

MILLS & BOON

First Published in Great Britain 2020
by Mills & Boon, an imprint of HarperCollins*Publishers*
1 London Bridge Street, London, SE1 9GF

Enticed by Her Island Billionaire © 2020 Becky Wicks

Falling Again for the Single Dad © 2020 Juliette Hyland

ISBN: 978-0-263-27982-5

MIX
Paper from
responsible sources
FSC™ C007454

This book is produced from independently certified FSC™ paper
to ensure responsible forest management.
For more information visit www.harpercollins.co.uk/green.

Printed and bound in Spain
by CPI, Barcelona

ENTICED BY HER ISLAND BILLIONAIRE

BECKY WICKS

MILLS & BOON

To my rock star boyfriend Konrad,
who is by now quite used to long periods of
keyboard tap-tap-tapping before I stop and ask him
worrying questions like, 'How much do you think
a facelift would cost on a remote island near Bali?'
#grateful

CHAPTER ONE

MILA RICCI SWIPED at her thrashing hair as the waves jumped and frothed around the speeding boat. The exclusive transfer by Dr Becker's private yacht from Bali to the island of Gili Indah wouldn't have been quite as bumpy as this, she mused, as a tourist shrieked behind her, but she'd missed it. She'd been advised by an elderly lady with a twinkle in her eyes to sit on the roof of the tourist boat for the next best thing.

The tree-dotted hills in the far distance were pale swathes of varying greens, shrouded by a thin veil of fog in the morning light. The island looked like a painting—just as Annabel had once described it.

Gathering up her red dress, Mila copied the backpackers next to her and dangled her legs over the edge of the roof, resting her arms on the railings. It didn't seem entirely safe by the standards she was used to at home in Britain, but she wasn't worried.

Travelling in potential peril had been standard practice during her time in the Army—especially out in Afghanistan. A few bumpy waves were nothing compared to the time she'd had to take a convoy in the middle of the night and go past the place where the insurgents had burned the bodies of the soldiers they'd shot dead on the bridge.

The direct route to the nearest air station had been just

eight miles straight, but they'd gone over a hundred miles around it to escape. Two of the trucks had broken down in the first hour. She'd hitched a ride on another truck and they'd hidden in the sand dunes, listening to the mortar rounds being fired at the vehicle they'd just fled.

Mila rubbed her face. She was tired. She was thinking too much about the past. She couldn't be further from a war zone now if she tried. This was a new start. There was nothing to fear on a paradise island…except maybe a tsunami.

She rolled her eyes at herself at the thought. Why did she always fear the worst?

You know why, she reminded herself. *Because you can't always prepare for the worst, even when you think you can.*

On the deck, an Indonesian man was playing with a rescued baby monkey. Mark would've got a kick out of that, she thought now, acknowledging the stab of guilt that told her she hadn't ended things with him too well.

She'd been so busy wrapping things up before she'd left the London hospital where she'd devoted herself to her work since leaving the Army. She'd barely had a moment even to think about him since she'd broken things off. He was a good man, but maybe a little too soft for her. He didn't know how to handle her.

What was it Mark had said before he'd left her flat? *'You don't need a man right now anyway, Mila. You need to figure out who you are.'*

He was probably right about that. She hadn't come home from Afghanistan the same person. She'd learned quickly out there who she really was. She was part of a team and she couldn't fail. She was eyes, ears, instincts. She was ready for the worst—always.

She could still hear the whirring rotors of the helicopters infiltrating the hot, sticky night air. When she least wanted to she could conjure up the smell of dust and the acrid stench of wet blood on inconceivably terrible wounds. The agonised moans of broken soldiers still made it into her dreams some nights.

It had been more than her twenty-four-year-old self had known how to handle at the time she'd been deployed, though she'd never admitted that to anyone. It had only been after her twin Annabel's death, eight years later, that she'd truly fallen apart.

Mila watched two Australian lads making faces at the monkey, but she wasn't really paying attention. She was dreading the anniversary of her sister's death all over again. It was almost three years ago now since the accident.

She'd been home on leave for a few weeks when it had happened. Annabel had been trying to lift her spirits, keeping her one step ahead of depression after her latest posting to Afghanistan. But for all of Mila's Army training, and everything she'd endured in combat, she'd still frozen on the spot when she'd come across her mother's twisted, unrecognisable car, smashed just like the motorbike Annabel had hit before wrapping the car around a tree.

Those wasted seconds she'd spent, willing the steel of the car to unwind, willing the clock to go back, might have been the difference between her sister's life or death. The worst thing had happened and she hadn't been prepared. She'd failed to get Annabel out alive.

'There they are!'

Mila blinked as a voice shrieked excitedly behind her. A backpacker in a red football shirt was pointing at the islands, coming ever closer to them. They were headed for the largest of those several small bumps in the ocean, which jutted like camel humps ahead of them.

Adrenaline spiked in her veins. She willed herself not to think about Afghanistan, or the accident. But she knew Annabel would be here too; she was everywhere.

Annabel had actually come to Gili Indah without her years ago. She and her twin had planned the trip together, but Mila had come down with an unfortunate case of laryngitis just before the flight. She could still remember that crackly phone call from her twin.

'You've got to see it one day, Mila! The most beautiful mountain views...the blue of the water...it's unreal! And there are loads of hot men here. You're missing out, I can tell you.'

Was it a coincidence that this opportunity to spend the next couple of months or so at the prestigious Medical Arts Centre there—or the MAC, as it was known—had appeared in her online searches, just last month?

The MAC hadn't been there at the time of Annabel's visit, six and a half years ago. It would have been a mere gleam in the eye of its founder, the billionaire Dr Sebastian Becker. He'd left his whole celebrity surgeon lifestyle behind in Chicago only three years ago, to set up this exclusive facility.

Mila watched the monkey peel its own banana, its tail wrapped around one of the Australian guys' forearms.

What was he like? she mused. This man Dr Becker?

Her friend Anna back at the hospital in London had told her a little about him, but only what she'd garnered from watching him on TV.

The Becker Institute—Dr Becker's revered plastic surgery practice in Chicago—was the base for a globally popular reality TV show focused on the lives of its patients and their various cosmetic surgery procedures.

Dr Becker had only starred in one season, with his brother Jared Becker, before leaving the show to concentrate on building the MAC. Anna had said he'd really left because the media circus had got too much for him. Something about an ex-girlfriend, threats, scandal...

Mila had stopped her there. She hated listening to gossip. And it had felt wrong to poison her mind about a man she'd never met—especially a man who was doing such remarkable work.

Dr Sebastian Becker had pioneered what was now the world's leading method of scar tissue surgery, blending the newest innovative laser treatment with a simplified but highly effective surgical procedure. This was the first time he'd offered an opportunity for another experienced surgeon to come to the clinic for a short-term placement and observe his techniques.

It had sounded fascinating to her—the chance to learn something new at his exclusive private island clinic—and she hadn't hesitated to hand in her notice at the London hospital.

Indonesia was surely bound to be a far nicer setting than an overwhelmed city hospital or a military hospital in the Middle East. She was done with all that. She'd come for something completely different—a new focus, a change of pace, even if it was only temporary.

She couldn't even recall what Dr Sebastian Becker looked like, or the name of the TV show he'd so briefly starred in. She'd never had much time for TV, and she didn't ever bother with social media. Hopefully the man was agreeable, at least; they'd be working in pretty close proximity.

Mila smoothed her red sundress and held her hair back as the wind wrestled with it. She wished she could have asked Annabel what to expect from this place beyond the gorgeous guy she'd met when she had been here. What had she said his name was? Bas...or something like that?

Sebastian Becker hauled the last remaining tank out of the water and eyed the speedboat heading his way. He reached down to help the first of his dive group back onto the boat. Getting them all on board before the next intake of tourists whipped up the water was imperative if he didn't want his students flailing in opposite directions within seconds.

'Give me your hand.'

Gabby, a British woman in her early twenties, pushed her mask down to her neck and grinned up at him from the water. 'I'll give you whatever you need.'

He helped her up the ladder and she fell against his chest, heavy and wet in her tank and vest.

'Sorry,' she muttered, so close to his face he could feel her breath on his skin.

She wasn't sorry. This girl had been flirting with him all morning.

He helped the others up. Checking his students were seated and had disposed of their flippers in the right place, he yelled, 'Ketut, start the engine!' and bounded up the three metal rungs to the roof.

Alone, he unzipped his wetsuit, letting the thick wet fabric unfold around his middle. The sun sizzled on his skin.

Maybe tonight, when the last scheduled surgery was done, he'd take Gabby out for a drink, somewhere with candles and a sandy floor. She'd be gone in a day or two. Why not give her something to talk about, once her plane deposited her back into her boring existence?

Those had been her words this morning, not his.

'My life is so boring compared to yours. I should stay here and just go scuba diving all day with you...what do you think?'

He hadn't encouraged her. Why tell a stranger that he wasn't only a scuba diver, either? Why tell a tourist he would never see again that he was actually living here because he'd pioneered a way of operating on the facial scarring of accident victims which minimised their scars often to near invisibility?

He thought back to last week, satisfied. Lasers were incredible things. Trevor Nolan, a forty-two-year-old wedding singer from Dakota, had grappled with his young son to prevent a firework going off in his face and the poor guy had taken the hit himself. After six months of surgery and a month of crowdfunding by his friends he come to him at the MAC for what all the medical journals were calling 'revolutionary treatment.'

Trevor had left with his chin almost the shade of the rest of his face, instead of raw red and stretched in scars. Best of all, he could sing for people again without it hurting.

'Mr Diver Man, come down here!'

Gabby was calling him from below. He stayed put. The sun at this time of the day was perfect. Not too hot. He liked to soak it up while he could, before he put his hospital scrubs back on.

Sebastian assumed most people visiting the island's clubs and bars and dive shops didn't even know the MAC was on the other side of it, and if they did most of them didn't know what happened there.

He always let word of mouth bring his clients in now. He wasn't famous on Gili Indah. He wasn't followed and he was barely recognised. It was too small an island and he was too out of context, he supposed—a world away from the Institute in Chicago and all those cameras.

He still had to be careful on the mainland of nearby Bali, though.

He'd left the hugely successful *Faces of Chicago* show back home. He'd left Klara behind, too, he told himself, furrowing his brow at the horizon. Now all that mattered was his team, and having his patients walking away looking and feeling better than when they'd arrived.

The speedboat was close now. A few faces stood out—locals, friends. And lots of new arrivals. But none for the MAC. *His* staff came in on *his* boat.

All but Dr Ricci, he remembered suddenly, raking a hand through his hair. She'd missed her transfer, which wasn't uncommon—the traffic on the mainland was a nightmare.

He stood, scanning the other boats around the bay. He'd been too swamped at work to search online and put a face to the name of his latest employee, but he knew she'd worked in trauma on deployment with the Army in Afghanistan, so she was likely looking to add a new scar treatment string to her bow.

He considered what it must be like to spend months in a war zone, seeing soldiers with their limbs blown to shreds. All those gunshot wounds, severed bones and bombs exploding…

Some of the things he'd had to fix himself had been far worse than Trevor Nolan's chin after his battle with a rocket in his backyard. But to be in a war zone—that was something else.

The boat jolted and he heard a tank flip downstairs. He shot back down the ladder. This woman, Dr Ricci, must be some kind of special breed. What was she looking for, exactly, here on such a remote island?

He set the tank upright again and watched Gabby make a show of resting her bare pink toes on it to keep it in place. Ketut threw him a look from behind the wheel, and Sebastian took a seat as far away from her as he could.

Was Dr Ricci running from the horrors of war and looking for peace, like he had been? But he'd been running from the media explosion after starring in the TV show and from the guilt that had racked him over what had happened to Klara. Hardly the same thing.

Sebastian realised he was scowling at the horizon, thinking about Klara again.

He couldn't have known what would happen after filming started. No one could have anticipated so many photographs, so many camera lenses zooming in on his every move, in and out of surgery. All those headlines and subheadlines…the crazy stories people had sold or made up about them just to get their clicks in.

Letting cameras into his surgery had invited the whole damn media circus in—which had squeezed every last remaining shred of joy out of his relationship with Klara.

All she had ever wanted to do was be with the kids at her kindergarten school and live a simple happy life with him. She had been so broken by the invasion of her privacy, and everything people had said about them both as a couple, that at the end she'd left without saying goodbye.

He put a hand down to the ocean spray and let his thoughts about her go—like he did every time he went diving. Diving was a workout for his brain…a place to switch off from other thoughts. It was only when he was on the surface that the memories came back.

He knew Klara wasn't in Chicago any more. She'd already got married—someone she'd met in Nepal. He didn't know where she was now, but he was happy for her. Sometimes.

Right now he would much rather be living here, somewhere beautiful, fixing Trevor Nolans and kids with burns the size of basketballs on their cheeks, than go back to having camera flashes and the paparazzi's car tyres screeching in his wake, and performing endless boob jobs in Chicago. Although he wished he could see his family more often—especially his brother Jared and Charlie… He smiled thinking of his nephew.

The tourist boat slowed. A line of excited people craned

their necks from the roof to the turquoise shallows. Everyone was in awe of the colour of the water here.

A slender woman in a bright red sundress had her hand on her brown hair, trying her best to tame it, and a memory flickered across his mind.

He lifted his sunglasses and squinted to see better.

She was leaning on the railings now, elbows out. Her sundress was catching her ankles in the wind. He gripped the side of the boat even as Gabby tickled his calf with her toes. It looked *exactly* like her. Must be six or seven years ago now… A British woman dancing drunken pirouettes on the sand, back when he'd been here for the first time— long before he'd even had the idea to build the MAC.

What was *she* doing back here?

Mila's eyes followed the diver right until his boat rocked out of sight. His abs were like a digitally enhanced ad for a diving school. She'd seen men like that at military hospitals, trained for fighting but battered and blue. Never this colour. The diver's skin was a warm shade of caramel—as if he'd earned that tan with a life outdoors over a long, long time.

Her boat bobbed in the shallows as people leapt from the sides onto the sand. Mila followed, taking the ladder down. She hoisted her sundress further up her legs as an eager Indonesian boy no older than eight or nine helped her down into an inch of crystal-clear water.

'*Terima kasih!*' she told him. She'd already mastered a few basics.

The warmth of the sand rose to meet her toes in her flip-flops and she breathed in the scent of the air. Flowers… maybe jasmine…or was that an incense stick? The local market on a dusty path ahead told her she wasn't exactly in Robinson Crusoe territory.

Mila stood still. When was the last time she'd stood in

the ocean? Probably back in Cornwall, about twenty years ago. She'd been with her mum and Annabel, and they'd bought Cornish pasties and prodded jellyfish in the sand. That had been a good day.

'Can I help you, miss? You need room?'

The kid in front of her now looked about seventeen, and he seemed to want to deny her the pleasurable personal moment of feeling her feet in the ocean for the first time in twenty years. He waded over purposefully and helped drag her case away from the shore.

She studied his tattooed wrists as he flashed a ring binder at her, showing coloured photographs of accommodation options. 'Oh, no, thank you. I have a hotel for tonight.'

'I have better one!' He flicked to a page with a photo of a shack on it. It looked basic, to say the least.

'Tomorrow I move to the MAC,' she explained, wading onto the beach. Tiny bits of coral prodded at her heels and toes.

Mila took her case back quickly. She had probably divulged too much information already. It was never good to trust strangers on a first encounter unless in a medical situation. Besides, she already knew Dr Sebastian Becker kept a low profile.

He encouraged his staff to do the same.

For protection, when it comes to our clients' anonymity.

He'd written that in a welcome email.

'Taxi?' she said in vain as a horse and cart trotted past her on the dusty street.

'Watch out!'

The teenager was back. He caught her elbow and yanked

her to the side of the path just as another horse and cart rattled past at full speed. It almost struck her.

'Thank you, I'm fine.'

She picked up her fallen sunglasses. She wanted to tell him she could take care of herself but she refrained. He was only being chivalrous and she *had* been caught off-guard. She hadn't slept in almost two days.

Frazzled and sweating, she wheeled all her worldly belongings along the thick, dusty, potholed concrete that constituted a street.

Street food vendors were mixing noodles and jabbing straws into coconuts. Girls were swigging beer, pedalling bicycles in bikinis. The salty air was already clinging to her forehead. No one else offered to help her but that was OK. She'd done this before, in worse places. She just hadn't imagined the island would be this crowded...

Through the jet lag she remembered that she'd come in on a tourist boat, to the tourist side of Gili Indah. The MAC was on the west side. That part of the island was exclusive territory—just for patients and staff. She couldn't wait to dive into a swimming pool. She just had to wait until tomorrow...

Mila was about to hail the approaching horse and cart when a noise from the shore made her stop in her tracks. A shriek. Someone thrashing in the waves.

Squinting through the throng, her eyes fell on a girl a few metres behind the speedboat. She saw the yellow dive boat she'd seen before, from the water. Something must have happened.

'Snake!' Gabby screamed. 'It bit me! Ow, it hurts! Sebastian, help!'

'OK...it's OK. Let's get you back to shore.'

Sebastian looped an arm around her waist, turning his

head in all directions, looking at the shallows. Where was the snake?

One minute Gabby had been heading back from the boat right next to him, after their second dive, the next she'd been toppling over in her half-undone wetsuit.

He made a grab for her mask and fins before they were swept out of reach, and threw them to another guy in their group.

'There it is!' Gabby sounded horrified.

He followed her pointing finger to the thin, yellow and black stripy body of a sea snake. It wriggled past him, heading for the deep beyond the reef.

Sebastian tried to wade faster. Gabby's face had turned pale. She wasn't making this up.

'Where did it bite you?' He kept his voice controlled, not wanting to panic her. Her head was heavier every time it landed on his shoulder.

'On my foot…my foot!' She was sobbing now, barely able to breathe.

'Ketut!' he yelled.

Gabby's legs seemed to crumple underneath her on the sand. He caught her before she could fall and lowered her gently to her back on the sand. She was whimpering now, trying to clutch at his arm. Her face was almost white.

A frenzy of people crowded around. Some were even snapping the scene with their cameras.

'Get back,' he ordered gruffly, as the familiar surge of contempt for this kind of privacy invasion consumed him. 'Ketut!' he called again.

But someone else was already sprinting over.

'I'm a doctor—how can I help?'

The lady in red from the boat. The British tourist. It was definitely her…the woman from a few years ago. Speechless, he watched as she dropped to her knees.

'Snake bite,' she noted out loud, before he could explain. She put a hand to Gabby's ankle.

'Yeow!' Gabby clamped her hand around his wrist in a death grip.

Easing her fingers away, he helped his new partner adjust the bitten leg and support it on an upturned rock.

'We need pressure immobilisation,' she told him—as if he didn't know.

She started pulling things from her bag. Her sunglasses were pushed high on her head, sweeping back the kind of thick honey-brown hair he'd bet smelled good wet, right after she showered...

He caught himself, racking his brain for her name.

They hadn't done more than flirt a little back then. If his memory served him right there had been no chemistry between them whatsoever. She'd been a drinker, he hadn't, and she'd been intent on partying every night until she dropped.

But he never forgot a face. Had she really forgotten his?

'Do you know what to do?' she asked him.

Her wide-set eyes were a vivid blue in the sun, over high, freckled cheekbones.

'There's anti venom at the clinic,' he said.

'At the Medical Arts Centre?'

He lost his voice for a second. Up close, he smelled the coconut waft of her sunscreen.

'No, the other one—the Blue Ray Medical Clinic on the strip.'

Didn't she recognise him at all? Was it even her? But, yes, it had to be. Her eyes, her face...they were all so familiar. He just couldn't remember her name.

'What will you do to me?' Gabby cried out.

'You need to keep as still as you can,' he said. 'Stop the venom circulating.'

The Brit…what *was* her name?…raised an eyebrow. Her blue eyes gave his body a swift appraisal in his wetsuit.

'You're a doctor?'

'You could say that.' He watched her pull an elastic bandage from her bag. 'The clinic's next to the Villa Sunset Hotel. It wasn't here before.'

'Before…?'

Her hands worked quickly, wrapping the elastic bandage around Gabby's leg with deft efficiency, starting from her toes, moving swiftly up to her thigh.

He sprinted to the restaurant right by the harbour. Their fence was made up of pieces of piled-up driftwood—just the right size for a splint.

'Use this,' he said, dropping back down next to her.

'Perfect—thanks.'

She was impressively fast. She *looked* like the girl he'd met before, but she sure as hell wasn't *acting* like her. Her red dress was catching dirt but she didn't look as if she cared or even noticed as they loaded a sobbing Gabby into the back of a cart. His eyes lingered on the curve of her shoulder as one strap fell down to her arm. She caught his eye and yanked the strap up.

'Come with me, *please*,' Gabby begged him.

The Brit answered instead. 'I'll go with you. We need to take the pressure off your leg as much as possible in this cart, though. Can you work with me on that?'

'I'll try.'

'I'll help you.'

She was good with her patient. Sebastian helped her arrange the leg, waiting for any hint that she might remember him.

'The driver knows where to go,' he told her. 'I'll follow on my bike. Tell them I sent you.'

'And your name is…?'

'Sebastian Becker?' He said it like a question as he slid the lock shut at the back of the cart.

Her blue eyes grew wide in shock. 'Dr… Becker?'

Finally. He opened his mouth to say something about the coincidence of another encounter all these years later. But he couldn't exactly admit to her that he'd forgotten her name.

It was only after she'd disappeared in a cloud of dust that he finally remembered it.

Annabel.

CHAPTER TWO

'SHE NEEDS ANTI-VENOM,' Mila called out, hurrying through the doors of the Blue Ray Clinic.

She flashed her security card at a man in the small, busy lobby. The bearded Indonesian man in his mid to late fifties sprang into action. The name badge on his white coat read *Agung*.

In a white room off the hallway, the tiled floor squeaked under her flip-flops. 'Sea snake,' she told Agung. He was already observing the bandage. 'She needs anti-venom. Dr Becker will be here any second. I'm Dr Mila Ricci—I'm new at the MAC. I just met him at the harbour.'

That scuba diving poster model in a wetsuit—that *doctor*—was the surgeon she'd soon be working with.

She was still in shock.

She closed the door behind them, noting the fresh paint on the cream walls and the Indonesian art hanging by the window. A palm leaf tapped at the glass from outside.

They helped the still dripping girl to a bed and onto fading sheets. Her breathing was laboured—probably due to her writhing around, not to the venom spreading too much. But then, she hadn't stayed very still in the jostling cart, even with Mila's assistance.

A rush of air-conditioning blasted her face as the door swung open to admit Dr Becker. 'Agung, how's she doing?'

He was pulling on a white coat, arm by long, bulked-up arm, and striding towards the bed in black sports sandals. He was every bit as striking in the white coat as he was in a wetsuit.

He made to pass her, then stopped, placed a hand on her shoulder. 'Thank you for what you just did.'

'You're welcome.'

The words came out smoothly, calmly, as she'd intended, but she didn't feel calm. The look he was giving her now had suspicion all over it.

'Put this on,' he told her, throwing her a white coat from a hook on the wall. 'Nurse Viv is with another patient, so I hope you won't mind staying a bit longer. I need you to cut the suit,' he said, motioning to the pair of scissors on the tray.

Mila snipped carefully at the girl's wetsuit and discarded the flimsy material. She was following commands when she'd usually be giving them, but that was OK. She wasn't a hundred miles away from base in Ghazni. No one had been blasted by shrapnel from a rocket-propelled grenade, There were no wounded soldiers crying out for attention. There was only this one girl…right here, right now.

She put a gentle hand to Gabby's leg and soothed her as Dr Becker administered the anti-venom and the meds kicked in.

Agung's pager made a sound. 'Excuse me, Dr Becker… Dr Mila,' he said.

He left the room and instantly the air grew thicker. Sebastian was appraising her again.

'Mila?' he said in a surprised voice, as soon as it was only the two of them. He stepped towards her.

'She looks much better,' she told him, looking up to see his eyes narrow. 'I think we got to the bite just in time. She just needs to rest now.'

He folded his arms, towering over her. He must be at least six foot two inches to her five foot three.

'Why Mila? I thought your name was Annabel?'

All the breath left her body.

'I couldn't remember at first…back there. It was at least six or seven years ago, right? Before this clinic or the MAC existed,' he said. 'You were late to our snorkelling party—you'd had too much to drink, remember?'

He grinned, laughing at a memory that wasn't hers.

Tears stung her eyes. She could have wrestled him to the ground when he reached for her wrists, but his long, tanned fingers ran gently over her scars and she felt bolted to the floor.

He was turning her arms in the harsh overhead light, studying the faint silvery lines as if they were clues to a mystery game. 'You didn't have these before,' he said, frowning. 'What happened to you?'

She bit her cheeks as the tears threatened to spill over. *He'd met Annabel.* This must be the guy her sister had come back talking about all those years ago. Bas. Sebastian. It made sense now. Dr Sebastian Becker was Bas. And she had to work with him?

She had to set him straight. This was unbearable.

'I'm not…not who you think I am,' she managed. The room felt suddenly way too small. She took a step back, pulling her arms away. 'Dr Becker, I'm Dr Mila Ricci. I've come to work at the MAC for a while and learn your techniques. I would have met you earlier, but I missed my transfer. I apologise for the confusion.'

She watched him rake a hand through his hair as she struggled for composure.

He paced the room, then stopped. 'Am I going crazy here? I did meet you before, didn't I? Did you change your name?'

'I'm not Annabel,' she said through a tight throat. 'Annabel was my twin sister. She's dead, Dr Becker. She died three years ago. It was her you met—not me.'

The cat padded her way across the bar towards them, its black shiny fur glowing pink under the LED lights. Sebastian ran a hand along her soft back. 'I'm so sorry about the mix-up this morning,' he said to the woman in front of him, his newest albeit temporary employee.

He'd been thinking about her all day. He'd sent Mila to her hotel to get some sleep and had somehow kept things on schedule back at the MAC, even though his mind had been whirring. He'd even checked in quickly on Gabby, back at the Blue Ray, who was fine. She'd found the strength to ask for his number, but he had no intention of entertaining her now. He just wanted to clear things up with Mila.

'It's not your fault. It's a coincidence and a surprise, that's all. Annabel talked about meeting a guy called Bas—I just didn't put the pieces together.'

Mila's legs were crossed in his direction on the swing seat beside him.

'What's her name?' she asked, watching his fingers stroke the length of the cat's tail.

'This is Kucing. I found her when she was a kitten. Someone dumped her in the garbage can down by the bottle store. Nice, huh? She was in a real sorry state—weren't you, girl?'

Kucing rubbed her nose against his fingers and promptly sat down to lick her tail.

'She likes it here. The guys give her tuna from the can on Wednesdays.'

He watched Mila reached out a hand to rub the cat's ears. The scars across her wrists glinted in the light of the candle in a coconut shell.

'Why is she called Kucing?'

'It's Indonesian for cat.' He shrugged. 'We like to keep things simple around here.'

Reggae drifted in from the speakers outside on the palm trees. Ketut's wife, Wayan, slid two empty glasses across the bar towards him, followed by a jug of ice water. It wasn't a fancy bar, more a rustic boho shack, but it was usually quiet—which was why he liked it. He hoped Mila was OK. It was hard to gauge how his new recruit was really feeling about this mix-up.

'It was brief. Meeting your sister, I mean,' he said.

She nodded, her eyes still on the cat. It was surreal. She looked absolutely identical to Annabel. He still couldn't believe it. He didn't recall Annabel ever telling him she was a twin—not that they'd really spent much time together.

'How did she die? Is it OK if I ask?'

'She went out one night to a party,' Mila said slowly, without looking at him. 'She was driving our mum's car...'

'You mean she died in a car crash? I'm so sorry. Was she alone in the car?'

Mila stiffened, picked up her drink. 'I don't really want to talk about this now, if that's all right with you. I'm here to work, Dr Becker, to focus on what's here and now—not on what happened in the past. What's the deal with the Blue Ray Clinic, by the way? Do you work there too?'

'I drop by if I'm needed. And I've done some work on the place. It was more of a shack when I got here,' he said, admonishing himself for prying. 'Look, we don't have to talk about the accident if you don't want to.'

'Thank you.'

Mila had changed from the red dress into a long, pleated pale blue skirt and a low-cut white top. He assumed her slender frame would look good in most things—including an Army uniform. She had an air of sophistication about her, he mused. And a bluntness, too. It was unequivocally British—like her accent.

He'd only met her twin a few times when she was here, but Annabel had been very different. She had danced in a skin-tight dress and drunk tequila shot after shot, hogging the microphone on karaoke night. He couldn't picture *this* woman doing that, somehow.

He felt a slight awkwardness between them as she petted Kucing. 'You don't have to call me "Dr Becker", by the way, Sebastian is just fine,' he said, to break the silence.

'OK—Sebastian.' She smiled slightly, tucking her hair behind her ear. 'So, you also teach scuba diving? Sounds like you have a lot on your plate.'

'That's what happens, I guess, on an island. You kind of end up taking on a little bit of everything.'

He ordered them both a smoothie—the house speciality. He didn't think of his efforts at Blue Ray as anything different from his work at the MAC any more. He was just living his life, doing what was necessary to keep things moving.

He still harboured some small hope that one day Jared would leave Chicago and join him here, but that would mean the rest of his family giving up the show and all the fame that came with it.

His brother was a little different from him where that was concerned. Jared and his wife Laura hadn't come under half as much scrutiny as he and Klara had. He assumed that because they'd already been married a while they weren't as exciting. They had never been splashed on magazine covers or stopped for trick photos outside jewellery stores.

'From what I know about your background, I could probably learn some things from *you*, Dr Ricci,' he said now, shoving away the thought of the time he'd been stopped by someone pretending to be homeless just so that someone else could get a photo of him reportedly shopping for an engagement ring. Up to that point he hadn't even considered proposing to Klara, but the pressure from the public had been on after that.

'Call me Mila, please,' she said, scanning his eyes now with her vivid blue ones. 'What do you know about my background, exactly?'

'I know from your résumé that you risked your life in Afghanistan,' he said.

She looked vaguely amused. 'I was safe most of the time.'

'And I know you know your way out of an awkward situation.'

She paused, a half-smile still playing on her lips. 'Well, I'll let you think you know about me for now. So we don't make things even more awkward.'

Were they *flirting*? For a second it felt as if she was flirting with him. With any other woman it would already feel like a date.

'So, why did you sign up for the Army?' He poured ice water into her glass, watched Kucing nuzzle her chin and then snake around the coconut shell candle. 'Did you always want to end up out there in a combat zone?'

'I joined the Army reserve for money, plain and simple.'

She twirled the ice cubes in her glass. He noticed her nails—plain, neat, unpainted. Her earrings—tiny silver studs.

'I thought it would help me to pay for medical school. I was only twenty-four and my plans were rock-solid—you know what it's like when you're young.'

'Did you have any choice when you found out where you were going?' he asked curiously. He hadn't met too many women who'd spent so long in military service.

'I didn't question it. I knew what I'd signed up for. We trained for four months before we left for Afghanistan and I was sent to two forward-operating bases as part of a mobile surgical team. Straight in at the deep end.'

'You only trained for four months?'

She nodded. 'Four long months of saying goodbyes and firing hand grenades…'

Sebastian felt his eyes widen.

'You think I couldn't still fire a hand grenade if I really needed to?' she teased.

He found the idea vaguely arousing, somehow. He cleared his throat, took a sip of the smoothie Wayan had presented him with.

'Annabel was out of her mind when I told her they were placing me close to the frontline,' Mila continued. 'We all thought I'd be on the base in Bagram—not some tiny outpost. On the plane it kind of hit me like a bomb—no pun intended… That's the only time I thought I might die out there.'

'How do you even train for something like that?' he asked, watching her lips close around the bamboo straw in her smoothie. She looked at him over the rim of her glass.

'We had to kick down doors, do escape and evasion stuff, urban combat manoeuvres—a lot of things that were probably unnecessary, now that I think about it.'

'Like the hand grenade lessons?'

She shrugged. 'Those actually came in handy. I just wanted to be the toughest soldier and the best trauma surgeon I could be—and it didn't feel like more than I could handle to be both those things. I enjoyed the training. I wanted to be the face of resilience and strength, you know? I wanted to be the one who could keep her cool in the middle of all that…' she paused. 'All that horror…all those soldiers with devastating wounds. So devastating, Sebastian. So pointless.'

'I can't imagine,' he said.

Her lips were pursed, as if she was trying not to let any more emotion than necessary escape with her words.

'Every patient that came to us was critical,' she said. 'I do miss that type of patient care sometimes. The team-work out there is like nothing else I've ever experienced. The things you go through you're not going to go through anywhere else.'

He found he was listening intently, as if she was taking him on a journey. He almost forgot where he was.

'It's an adrenaline rush, you know? But you're still human at the end of the day. I exercised it out—all the excess trauma that felt like it was spreading from them straight into me. I ran miles on the treadmill every day to get it all out, but I still cried every night in the shower.'

Sebastian was silent. What the hell could he say?

'You never really stop seeing it,' she told him. 'I'm not going to lie to you: it took a lot to get over that stuff. But not as much as it took to get over my sister's death. I was home on leave when the accident happened, and after that I got out as soon as I could.'

Mila ran her hands through her hair, revealing those scars again. He didn't dare ask again how she'd got those; she'd recoiled from him in horror when he'd examined them before.

'Like I said, I'm here now to be *here*—present. I don't see why the past should affect what I'm doing,' she said, sitting up straighter.

He wondered if she really believed that.

'So, tell me something about *your* life, Dr Becker. Why did you move your skills so far away from Chicago and from the States in general?'

He sat back. He hadn't been expecting such directness. 'You don't read the news?'

'News always finds me eventually, if it's important.'

'Interesting perspective on communication,' he said dryly. She was fascinating. 'But, seriously, you never even looked me up on the internet after I hired you? You don't know about the infamous, record-breaking, highly rated— or should I say *overrated*—TV show *Faces of Chicago*? Or how the "scorned Becker brother" left town after only one season, all alone…?'

She slowly spun her glass on the bar, with one finger on the rim. 'I don't follow celebrity news or social media.'

'I don't have social media accounts any more,' he told her, wondering what it was, exactly, that was making him feel the need to earn her respect before he left this bar stool.

She met his eyes. 'I know about your work. I know you've spent three years revolutionising your facial scarring reduction procedure out here—mostly alone. I know your skills had brought unprecedented fortune to The Becker Institute in Chicago even before the TV show brought you fame. Was it your father's practice?'

'Late father,' he said. 'He passed away.'

'I'm sorry.'

'Thank you.'

She didn't ask how, or when it had happened, but she looked for a moment as if she wanted to.

'If I'm honest,' she said, and sighed, 'a friend filled me in on some things about your personal life which may or may not be true… I always prefer to ask people about this sort of thing to their face, if I need to. I wasn't anywhere near a television when your show was on.'

'I'm sure you had better things to do than watch me and my brother performing tummy tucks on spoilt pop stars anyway.'

'I'm not sure that's true…' she said thoughtfully.

Kucing leapt back on the bar and padded straight towards Mila, almost knocking over her smoothie glass. She caught it deftly, avoiding any spillage.

'It would have been nice to switch off and see what else was happening out there in the world. Some nights the silence was worse than the sound of the guns firing.'

Not for the first time in her company, Sebastian found himself speechless.

'Sorry,' she said, shaking her head in bewilderment. 'Talking about this is a bit of a Pandora's box. I don't want you to think I'm always like this. I'm just tired. Back to you?'

He was stumped. There was a lot he wanted to say, but he didn't know where to start. So he just said, 'I very much look forward to working with you, Mila. I just hope the island and the MAC live up to your expectations.'

'I try not to have any preconceived expectations,' she told him. 'So… I'm guessing you really didn't like being on that show?'

Sebastian tipped the ice cubes in his glass to one side and back again. She had a lot of questions. 'It wasn't so much the show I didn't like—more the way the media ate us up. They're vicious out there…hiding in the shadows, waiting to pounce.' He made his hands like a cat's paws and she smiled.

'I know a bit about people like that,' she said.

He hoped she wouldn't talk about Klara, but even if she knew anything about her she didn't ask.

'So you still take the high-paying clients if they seek you out here? The celebrities?' she asked.

'Yes. They like the luxury of the island. But I do also have plans for a place over in Bali—a wellness centre for trauma patients in recovery. Something a little less… expensive. We have to start reaching more people.'

'You seem to have things under control,' she said. 'Your brother Jared—is he involved here too?'

'He's still busy being a television star,' he said, hoping he didn't sound as if he begrudged his older brother the life he'd chosen in the spotlight. 'We should get a snack—I'm hungry.'

He ordered them chips, then moved the topic to a patient who was heading in for a routine penis enlargement. Anything seemed better than bringing up his family issues. They were small fry compared to what this woman had been through.

So she talked, and he listened, and Sebastian couldn't even remember when he'd met a woman quite like Mila. She was definitely going to keep him on his toes.

CHAPTER THREE

'I'M OPEN TO SUGGESTIONS, Dr Becker. What do you think might improve…this?'

The woman in the plush leather chair opposite them stretched out the skin on her cheeks with her fingers. Mila watched Sebastian push his glasses further up the bridge of his nose.

'Turn to the left, please,' he said. 'Now the right.'

Incense swirled from the polished window ledge of the cosy, bamboo-panelled consultation room. It floated about his thick dark hair as he studied their patient's face. Mila fought not to look too long at his handsome profile in the sunlight.

It was already a week since she'd first stepped through the high-arching, intricately hand-crafted doors of the Medical Arts Centre, and she'd been transfixed by everything in it ever since.

This facility was a world away from the Blue Ray Clinic, which she'd noticed still looked a little rough around the edges in places. Everything about the polished marble floors, the potted palms and golden vases spoke of peace and control. It was the least traumatic place for a trauma victim she'd ever seen. It was as if she'd fallen asleep in the back seat of a convoy truck, been pelted with an AK-47, and then woken up here.

Rachel, their bubbly radiology technician, who had a penchant for wearing pink sandals around the place, had told her they hadn't remodelled the entire Blue Ray Clinic yet because Sebastian was funding everything himself.

'Rumour has it there are problems in the Becker family, and it all started with the show. Did you know his brother Jared has never even been out to visit the island?'

Mila had remained quiet—she wasn't about to join in gossip. But she had found something else the other woman had said rather intriguing:

'I heard that Dr Becker was so devastated about his ex-girlfriend after she left him that he used to fly out of here every weekend to go and try to find her.'

There was a lot of gossip going around this island about everything, she'd noticed. And she couldn't help wondering what was true about Sebastian and what wasn't. She'd enjoyed their chats so far—he was interested and interesting... certainly not the flashy ex TV star she'd imagined.

Sebastian was absently tapping a pen against the side of his black-rimmed glasses...clearly thinking. 'Have you considered a general lift instead of going under more knives?'

Their patient was a fifty-seven-year-old California-based criminal lawyer called Tilda Holt. She'd lost over one hundred pounds and needed some help smoothing things over. Tilda didn't like what she called her 'bingo wings', and even though she was already booked for a brachioplasty she was intrigued by the work other people were having done on the premises and had come to find out more.

'Can he give me a face that reflects my young soul, do you think, Dr Ricci? Or is that too much work?' Tilda was looking directly at Mila now.

'Dr Becker's work is some of the best I've seen,' she said tactfully. 'I think you can count yourself lucky you found your way here. How did you hear about Dr Becker's work, can I ask?'

Tilda was back to looking at him in admiration. 'I saw him on the television. I said to my husband, That's the guy for me. He can help me.' She took Sebastian's hand in hers across the table. 'You always had a way of really *seeing* people, Dr Becker, that's why people loved you on that show.'

Mila caught the flicker of embarrassment in Sebastian's eyes as he looked at her over his glasses. She smiled at him. She couldn't help a flutter of affection.

She'd noticed how he gave every consultation himself—in person or via video call. He went to the mainland a lot, too, for people who couldn't travel this far. He wanted to know everyone who walked through his door.

He must know his personality still counted for a lot, she thought, no matter how he appeared to dislike his own celebrity label. And he allowed these patients in, along with their money, because it was helping the island.

Sebastian was leafing through a brochure with Tilda. 'No filters necessary on your photos after this particular procedure. At least, I don't think so. How it works is we fire ultrasound energy into the muscles you'd usually get tightened in a face lift…here, here, here…so no knives and no needles.'

'No knives?'

'Absolutely zero. We get new collagen forming under smoother, brighter skin. Sometimes the cheekbones look more sculpted and defined. I had a patient last month email me to say she hadn't enjoyed wearing make-up for twenty years until she had this procedure.'

Tilda let out a groan. 'I used to love make-up.'

It amused Mila, the way Sebastian could turn these procedures into scenarios that sounded almost exciting. He knew just how to keep a patient's attention—maybe he'd honed that skill on television.

She'd been expecting to find this man a bit spoilt—arrogant, maybe, even flashy. She'd thought maybe he'd come with all the trimmings of a reality TV star. But he was none of those things, from what she'd seen so far. She thought of Annabel and wondered if her sister had felt this same attraction to him when they'd shared their brief encounter.

At the bar she hadn't asked him about what had happened between them. It had been too much even to think about it at the time, reminding her of Annabel and the accident.

There hadn't been time to talk privately since then either. Too many meetings, introductory briefings and shadowing surgical procedures. And in between all that calming breaks spent sipping green tea out in the sun with the staff.

It was beautiful here, and the patients were appreciative and relaxed after their treatments. It was everything she'd hoped for when she'd boarded that plane at a blustery Gatwick Airport. But it was a little unnerving that she was thinking so much about Dr Becker when he wasn't there—especially as he'd only been completely professional with her.

'So, these muscles come up here, and the brow comes up here, and the whole face and neck treatment takes about thirty minutes. It'll cost you less than surgery—a lot less.' Sebastian was back in his swivel chair. He was wearing blue sneakers with jeans under his white coat: trademark Chicago boy.

'Would *you* do it?' Ms Holt asked Mila.

'Only you can decide if you want this procedure, Ms Holt,' she said, blinking herself back to the moment, 'But I can assure you if you choose to do so you'll be in good hands.

'What happened to your arms, Dr Ricci?'

Tilda's question came out of the blue. The woman was studying her scars over the frangipani flowers and candles. Mila felt obliged to leave her wrists facing up on the desk, so Ms Holt could see them. It wasn't the first time she'd been asked about her scars.

'It was an accident,' she said simply. 'I don't really notice them now.'

OK, so that last part was a lie.

Tilda looked sympathetically at Mila. 'Can't you fix them? Someone like you? Can't *you* fix them, Dr Becker?'

Sebastian coughed and stepped in quickly, before Mila could even answer. 'I'm afraid our appointment's almost over, Ms Holt. I'd just like to add that with the ultrasound treatment there's no downtime at all—not like with surgery. You'll just look a little suntanned for an hour or so. But that's nothing new around here. We'll let you think about it.'

He stood and ushered her politely towards the door, talking about seeing her on the MAC's private beach in a few days' time for the sea turtle sanctuary fundraiser.

Why did he have to step in? Mila thought in annoyance. He wasn't her protector. She didn't need one.

She'd earned her high position in combat support hospitals, where she'd trained medics on the military camp in spite of her age. She'd even taught a fresh medical team to handle trauma victims her first time in command. In fact, she had excelled at everything she'd ever done—without any guy stepping in on her behalf.

Maybe she was being unfair... He probably assumed she was embarrassed whenever someone mentioned her scars because she hadn't elaborated on how she'd got them. Men often thought they had to protect her because of what she'd been through.

'So...'

Sebastian turned to her when Tilda Holt had gone. Sunlight was streaming from the window across the polished floor onto his sneakers. She was still a little annoyed with him…but he looked really, really good in those glasses.

For a second she thought he was going to come right out and ask her again how she'd got her scars. He must have been wondering ever since he'd first seen them, back when he'd thought she was Annabel. He probably thought she'd got them out on deployment—most people did. Would he ever imagine she'd got them trying to pull her twin sister through a smashed-in car windscreen?

She felt sick even thinking about it. She didn't want him to imagine that. He had his own clear picture of Annabel, whatever that entailed. She wouldn't ruin a nice image of her beautiful sister for anyone.

'Will we see *you* at Friday's fundraiser, Mila? We've got some pretty fun live music lined up. And the turtles could do with your help.'

She caught herself. 'Friday?'

'Yes—you didn't forget about it, did you?'

She wasn't about to tell him, but she *had* totally forgotten.

Sebastian's phone was buzzing on the desk. His brother's name flashed on the screen before he swiped up. 'If you'll excuse me?'

'Jared? Your brother?' she said, remembering how he'd never been to visit—if indeed that rumour was true.

'More like my nephew Charlie on Jared's phone.' He touched his hand lightly to her shoulder. 'I really do have to take this. It's his birthday and he needs to tell me all about his presents—you know how it is.'

He left the room, chatting to his nephew in an excited voice she knew he probably reserved only for him, and Mila felt her unfortunate soft spot for her current employer soften just a bit more.

* * *

'When he gives you that look you can see in that moment *exactly* what millions of viewers saw, watching Dr Sebastian Becker on television,' Rachel sighed. 'Do you know the look I mean? You've seen it, haven't you?'

Sebastian stopped in the shadows at the sound of his name. He couldn't see their faces, and they couldn't see him. But Rachel was what he would call *swooning*. Mila was saying nothing.

'Watch out, Dr Ricci! The Becker boys can change your face and steal your heart,' Rachel enthused, gesturing to Mila's heart with a glass of wine.

They were at the turtle fundraiser, standing on the MAC's beach in the light of a flaming torch stuck in the sand.

'What did I steal?' Sebastian knew his voice would make them both turn around.

'Oh, God.' Rachel covered her face with her hands. 'I'm sorry,' she mumbled through her fingers.

Mila was biting back a smile.

'It's OK, I promise not to steal your heart, Rachel,' he teased, but he couldn't help his eyes lingering on Mila and her curves in a blue dress which swooped at the back in a low V.

'I should go and check on the turtle cake,' Rachel muttered, gathering up her skirt to walk hurriedly in the direction he'd come from.

In the next moment it was just Mila in that dress, and him, and the buzz of the fundraising crowd behind them.

'Catching up on the island gossip, are you?' he asked pointedly. 'I thought you weren't into that.'

'I think Rachel likes to talk.' Mila shot him a sideways glance. 'I was put in an involuntary listening position.'

He swiped up a seashell and led them both down the

beach, turning to look over his shoulder and see Rachel watching them from the buffet table.

'She told me she watched every single episode of *Faces of Chicago* before applying to the MAC—all in the name of research,' he disclosed.

'Of *course* for research,' Mila replied, a smile playing on her lips.

She waded out a foot away from him into the shallows, bunching up her dress. He watched the breeze playing with her hair and the silky blue fabric as she inhaled long and deep with her face to the sky. She looked as if she was breathing in life from the water. He wondered if she'd ever been diving.

'So, I heard your big speech earlier,' she said, when she had taken her moment. 'You've been raising tiny turtles till they're big enough to thrive around the coral which you are regenerating with electromagnetic technology? Is that right?'

Her accent was so great when she said, *'Is that right?'* He liked a British accent. Annabel's had been the same, but again it struck him how Annabel had been so very different from Mila.

'That's correct. We're hoping for seventy per cent regeneration in the areas where we've invested. It's early days yet, but we'll keep on monitoring it.'

'Is there *anything* on this island you're not involved in?' she teased, wading with him towards a wooden swing.

'Maybe a couple things,' he consented. 'There's always something to do.'

He held the swing so she could sit on the polished driftwood—and so he'd be able to admire the slope of her shoulders and the backless cut of her dress from behind when he pushed her. He had the swing put here—had even done most of the work himself, with a little help from Ketut. He wouldn't tell

Mila how he'd sat here most nights before the MAC had even been built, from sunset into dusk, trying to count the reasons not to jump on a plane, to go and look for Klara.

'Most things are a team effort in a place like this,' he told her, pushing her out on the swing and watching her toes skim the surface. 'And it has to start with ocean conservation—that's what keeps us all afloat on this island.'

'No pun intended?'

'None whatsoever.'

He let the waves lap his calves as she dug her feet into the sand again. The wind picked up strands of her hair and they tickled his face as he tightened his fists around the swing's ropes.

'Have you ever been diving, Dr Ricci?' he asked over her shoulder. Her hair smelled good…like the incense that swirled on the MAC's reception desk.

'No,' she answered on a breath. 'Not in the ocean. Describe it. The feeling—not the technique.'

He considered this. 'It's like a cranial cleanse,' he said, loosening his fists around the ropes. 'When you're down there it's possible to completely switch your mind off. You have no internal chatter—nothing pressing, at least. It's just you and the sound of your own breath in your ears.'

'It sounds magical. Like the very best kind of meditation.'

'It is. Close your eyes.'

One strap of her dress tumbled down over her shoulder in the breeze. She left it there and obeyed him.

You're drifting with the current,' he told her. 'Like you're breathing with the earth itself. In. Out. In. Out. You don't need your hands much, just your eyes, and it's all about controlling your breathing.'

'You're really selling this to me,' she said after a moment.

Her eyes were still closed and her head was tilted back slightly, almost against him, not quite touching.

'Maybe I'll try it...'

'I'll take you,' he told her. It surprised him how much he wanted to show Mila Ricci all the things he loved most about the ocean. 'I can't believe in all your Army training, you never went scuba diving.'

'I did dive a couple of times in a lake, but I was always too busy up on the surface throwing hand grenades to put it into practice in the ocean.'

She was smiling as she turned the swing around to face him, making the ropes twist tightly above her. Her bare legs were locked between his for a second, or maybe he pulled her there...he wasn't sure...

'Hello? Dr Becker! Hello!'

A man with blue hair was waving a coconut at them from the shoreline.

Sebastian released the swing's ropes and Mila was almost thankful for the interruption. Sebastian had placed her under some kind of spell and she'd been momentarily transfixed by what he was saying and his presence in general.

She was supposed to be shaking off this attraction to him—they had to work together. Not to mention his previous... whatever it had been...with Annabel. But it was pretty hard to stay away when he had that...*thing*... Rachel had been talking about. Magnetic appeal.

The man with blue hair greeted Sebastian with what she could only describe as reverence and seemed not even to notice her presence. She recognised him from the patient files: Hugo O'Shea. He must have just arrived for his treatment. She believed it was a routine penis enlargement.

According to Rachel, the man was a renowned internet

gossip queen. 'He loves gossip more than I do,' she'd told Mila, which Mila found hard to believe.

Hugo's board shorts were a patchwork of colourful bananas. 'Beautiful evening! I'm sure the turtles are as grateful for your work as I am, Dr Becker.' He raised an eyebrow at Mila.

'Apologies, Hugo, this is Dr Mila Ricci,' Sebastian said smoothly. 'She'll be with you during your surgery.'

Hugo swivelled his entire body towards her, extending a hand with a flourish. 'I don't mind a woman's touch,' he said as she shook it. 'But I think we both prefer Dr Becker's—am I right?'

He winked and leaned into her, fanning his face.

Mila smiled politely.

'Can I get a photo of you both? Just the one? The moon behind you is perfect.'

'No, not tonight,' Sebastian said curtly, before she could reply, and turned to leave. 'Enjoy your night, Hugo.'

Mila considered letting Sebastian go alone, and ending their conversation entirely, but she realised she wasn't done yet. She shouldn't let a pushy patient come between them—that much she knew—but it was something else that spurred her legs into action and made her follow him away from the crowd, up the rocks to the viewpoint.

This side of the island was quieter. The waves lapped at the rocks with big, loud sloshes and ahead the black night sea was like a blanket rolled out by the mountains in the distance.

'You really don't like anyone taking your photo, do you?' she said cautiously, lowering herself to the sandy rocks beside him. Up here, they were safe from prying eyes on the beach. She knew that was what he was most afraid of.

'O'Shea signed an NDA,' Sebastian said. 'He knows we don't let cameras in the MAC.'

Mila pulled her knees to her chest. 'Is this about what happened in Chicago?' she probed gently. 'I know you were stalked by the paparazzi. But I don't know the exact details…'

'They followed me and Klara everywhere—relentlessly,' he told her. His jaw was clenched now, his shoulders stiff and tense, as if even the memory was painful to contain. 'They caught her getting out of the car once, outside the Valentine's Gala on Lakeshore Drive. It was windy, and Klara's dress was—unfortunately—blown into a highly compromising position. The paps were all over it: zooming in, pointing out all the things you wouldn't want anyone pointing out. You haven't heard all this from anyone else?'

Mila put a hand to her mouth, shaking her head. The humiliation. She couldn't bear it. The poor woman…

'It was the worst possible outcome for a kindergarten teacher,' he continued.

'She was a teacher?'

'We were different,' he admitted. '*Very* different. I guess I liked it that she wasn't part of my world. I met her through my nephew Charlie. I went to collect him from school one day. Klara was there, stacking all these tiny plastic chairs…'

He trailed off, as though he realised he was telling her too much.

'Some of the kids' parents got together…made a huge deal out of the photo,' he said. 'They made out she was unfit to be around their kids. She *loved* those kids,' he stressed. 'They were her whole world. She was devastated. Then one publication…' he paused to sit up and make quotation marks with his fingers '*"…revealed"* that she was seeing another guy, which made it worse. He was a colleague— the principal of the kindergarten—but they printed photos of them talking outside the school. His wife got all suspicious, and then she was dragged into it…'

'This is horrifying!' said Mila.

He nodded slowly, his eyes on a night dive boat chugging out into the blackness.

'The principal offered her a sabbatical, to get away from it all. I quit the show. I thought maybe I'd go away with her, but she wanted to go alone. She got a volunteer position at some school in Thailand, deleted all her social media accounts, changed her number... She wouldn't even see me before she left.'

Mila pulled her eyes away from his biceps as he leaned back on his elbows with his face to the sky. 'Not at all?'

'Not even to say goodbye. I guess she thought I might show up with a bunch of photographers behind me. I couldn't really blame her.'

'But you had no closure?'

She realised this was probably getting far too personal now, but she couldn't help wanting to know. She would rather hear the truth from him than some rehashed version of the story on the rumour mill.

Mila remembered now how Rachel had told her he'd used to fly from Bali every weekend to try and find Klara. She didn't ask if it was true, and Sebastian didn't mention it, but the look on his face told her that he must have really loved this woman.

She felt a flicker of envy strike unannounced at the thought. She hadn't ever loved anyone like that—she might not *ever* love anyone like that.

'I guess I found closure here,' he said. 'I brought a skeleton team out with me and we worked bit by bit on renovations at the Blue Ray while the MAC was being built. I signed up to teach people to dive, set up the turtle foundation with Neesha and her husband—you'll meet them later—and spent a lot of time just getting to know the locals. That's important in a place like this. We had to ease our way in slowly on the island…build the trust. Then we opened the doors to the MAC and it's been non-stop since then, pretty much.'

'And what about the show? What happened when you quit?'

Sebastian bristled, once again examining the distant fishing boats. 'I half expected Jared to call it quits too, and follow me out here. He saw what I went through with Klara, and he knew they could have done the same to him and Laura—that's his wife.'

'Why didn't they?'

He shrugged. 'They were married, they were stable—influencers for the perfect family life. Laura has a cooking blog and she does a podcast for mums. Maybe that's not so titillating for readers? I don't know. You can't tell who they'll make their next target, or what lies they'll choose to spread, but I guess they chose me and Klara because we were younger, we went out more—we gave them more chances to pair their headline-grabbing stories with photos. They took *so many* photos!'

Mila was shaking her head, still hugging her knees. This was all news to her, and she wondered what it must have been like for him and Klara, living in the eye of a media storm. She supposed it wasn't dissimilar to being in Afghanistan in some ways—living in fear, priming herself for things that might not even happen.

'The network wanted to try another season,' he continued. 'They found a replacement surgeon, so Jared wouldn't have to, and threw more money at us. They basically made it impossible for him to leave. The show took off again without me, and Chicago's media found something else to do instead of ramming their camera lenses into my business. Life goes on.'

He tossed a pebble over the rocks, dragged a hand through his hair and shot her a sheepish smile.

'I don't know why I'm boring you with all this, Mila. It's not exactly a life-threatening issue.'

'You're not boring me. It's nice to get to know you,' she said truthfully. 'The man behind the surgical mask.'

She watched the way his shoulders relaxed suddenly, as if in relief.

'What does the future hold for you, then?' she pressed. 'Do you want to stay here for ever? Don't you want a family of your own?'

He turned to her. 'Why can't I do that here?'

Mila paused. For some reason she hadn't expected that. 'I can imagine there would be a lot to inspire kids growing up here...' she told him carefully, and realised she was picturing it herself now.

A future here, teaching kids how to love the ocean, seeing them running around the island barefoot, taking reading classes on the sand... That all seemed pretty good to her, even though she'd decided a long time ago that she was never having children.

'There would be worse places to raise a family, don't you think?' he asked.

'I don't know... I don't really think about raising a family anywhere.'

He studied her with interest for a moment. She was ashamed to admit it, but she was afraid to have a child herself. What if she lost it or something happened to it...? Or what if something happened to the father? She couldn't bear the thought of enduring that kind of emotional loss a second time round.

'Well, I'd rather do it here than in Chicago,' he told her. 'I'm not saying I never go back there to visit—in fact I'm heading back soon for my mother's birthday. But, between you and me, I never wanted to do that show in the first place. The further I am away from all that now, the better.'

Sebastian's shirt was open...four, maybe five buttons. It was the most she'd seen of him outside his scrubs since the last time they'd talked properly, like this. The breeze was teasing his thick brown hair and she wondered momentarily what it might be like to touch it.

'Why did you do the show then?' she asked.

'Mom wanted it—she thought it was something that our father would have done if he'd still been here. Jared wasn't sure, but he saw the potential for attracting new clients. It was closer to home than my idea anyway...which was to set up this place here.'

He gestured around them.

'This place was always my passion—not theirs. It was on hold for a long time while the show was taking up all my time. I wanted to quit as soon as they started sensationalising everything. We all knew Dad wouldn't have wanted *that* kind of attention on the institute—all those cameras that never turned off, the ones that started following me and Klara home. But it took that photo getting out for me to quit for good. Maybe Klara thought I'd quit too late.'

He picked up a stone and smoothed it between his fingers.

'She wouldn't have wanted to stay here anyway. She was always a city girl, really. And I guess this place was always going to steal me away, sooner or later. I mean—look at it.'

He gestured at the sweeping ocean ahead of him, then turned to offer her his full attention.

'When are we going to find the time to take you on your first ocean dive, huh?'

Mila took the opportunity he was giving her to change the topic, and soon they'd both lost track of time talking about manta rays and shipwrecks, and Charlie's school projects, and their very different school days, their very different preferences in clothing back in the nineties, when they'd taken their boards for Surgical Critical Care certification…and how they'd both somehow grown up having never seen *Star Wars*.

Sometimes Mila saw Annabel in her mind's eye, sitting there with them on the lookout, daring her to ask Sebastian what had happened between them when she was here.

Why couldn't she do it?

Mila knew why. She just found it hard to admit. It was the same reason something prickled inside her when he spoke about his past with Klara.

She was starting to really like this man. And it frightened her.

CHAPTER FOUR

'YOUNG GIRL, EIGHT years old.' Dr Fatema Halabi looked harried. 'We're vaccinating for rabies, but she's going to need more than a few stitches. We brought her straight here from the Blue Ray.'

Dr Halabi was a new recruit on the MAC's medical residency training programme. She'd done three years of general surgery in a practice in Charlotte, North Carolina, and now she was filling in with general duties around her plastic surgery training under Dr Becker's guidance.

She'd wheeled this patient into the light, airy, jasmine-scented treatment room before Mila had even pulled on her gloves. The unfortunate dog-bite victim was a French tourist—Francoise Marchand. Her mother was close behind.

Mila peeled back the huge bandage that was struggling to soak up the blood and surveyed the damage. She saw immediately the lacerations to the child's nose and lips. It looked pretty bad, but not as bad as she'd anticipated… considering the last dog bite she'd had to treat.

'How big was the dog that bit you?' she asked the little girl.

'It was some kind of Alsatian—big, very huge!' her mother cut in, in broken English. Her chin wobbled, as if she was struggling not to cry as Fatema applied fresh cloths to the wound. 'The crazy dog! It was lunging at her!

It should have been tied up! What is wrong with this place? It's just not safe for children here…'

'Mrs Marchand, I can assure you the island *is* safe,' Mila informed her, wondering if the statement was indeed correct. 'The dog *should* have been tied up, I agree, but we're here now. We're going to help Francoise, OK?'

Francoise sniffled, watching Fatema, who was the picture of calm. Mila knew she had to stay the same—as much for this mother as for her child, who was still conscious and in pain. Francoise's long blonde hair was matted with blood. So was her watermelon-patterned T-shirt. She was being braver than her mother, though.

'Francoise didn't m-mean to upset the d-dog,' Mrs Marchand stammered, clutching the side of the bed. 'She was just trying to get to the puppies. The mother dog must have thought she was too close… She just went for her… There was nothing I could do… This island is *not* safe!'

Mila put a hand to her shoulder and led her to the leather chair in a corner of the spacious room. It all made sense now, she thought with a frown. Approaching a mother dog and her new puppies without the owner's consent was never a good idea. This might have happened anywhere.

'This is not your fault, OK?' she said, although it wasn't true. 'I need you to stay calm, for Francoise's sake.'

The frazzled-looking woman swiped at her watery blue eyes. Mila knew it was imperative she stay calm. Her daughter was absorbing her panic like a sponge and amplifying it.

'Maybe you'd like to wait outside? We'll come and get you when we're done.'

Mila walked Mrs Marchand to the door. She needed to focus. The periorbital oedema was obvious around the girl's left eye—severe bruising that must have come from her struggles. She'd noticed lacerations to the soft tissue around her upper lip too, and to the skin across the lower left jaw-bone. Hopefully there wouldn't be any nerve damage.

Fatema excused herself and Rachel ran the X-rays.

Mila found she was waiting for Sebastian. His trademark treatment would be needed here. The new revolutionary thread dissolved faster in the skin, meaning there was no need for removal and less visible scarring on the lips, face, or mouth. Francoise and her mother likely didn't know how lucky they were that this had happened here. Not that she should be using the word *lucky*, really.

'You're being so brave,' she soothed Francoise, and the kid almost smiled—before wincing again in pain. She was handling the injections and the clean-up well, thank goodness.

Mila knew that dog bites accounted for thousands of facial injuries every year, and that over half the victims were children. She'd seen a few dogs around the island. She'd never thought to fear them.

She studied the X-rays on the computer monitor, but she couldn't help the flashbacks. Last time she'd dealt with a dog-bite it had been even worse than this. The German Shepherd had been terrified when they'd found it. It had been chained to a fence at a tiny military outpost. His paw had been a bloody mess, slit by razor wire.

He'd lunged as they'd approached the body of his owner—an Afghan officer who'd been shot in the back. She could still see his face, and the dog, too. The poor thing must have been there a while, listening to the blasts and seeing the shrapnel raining down, watching his owner lose his fight for life just feet away. No wonder it had launched itself at them and almost torn her colleague Neil's face off.

'Are you OK?'

Mila looked up from the screen with a start. Sebastian was looking at her strangely. She hadn't heard him come in. He was clean-shaven, wearing a red shirt and jeans with black sneakers.

'I'm fine,' she answered, though she knew her heart had sped up.

He pulled on a white coat and she caught a whiff of sunscreen and a new cologne she'd never smelled on him before. She briefed him quickly on the situation, noting how her palms were clammier than they had been before he'd walked in.

She resented this sudden rush of nerves at performing the revolutionary treatment Dr Becker had perfected. This would be her first time using the lasers, but it was him more than the notion of performing that unsettled her.

'I have it under control,' she told him, looking him square in the eyes.

Of course Mila was in full control. But Sebastian kept throwing her speculative looks, as if he was monitoring her mood as well as her capabilities.

An ER doctor over at the Blue Ray could stitch up a wound, maybe even conceal it pretty well, but it took a surgeon's work to stop a person living with noticeable scars for the rest of their life. She had to block him out—or at least pretend she wasn't so damn attracted to the man that she physically felt his eyes on her wherever she moved in the room.

Mila woke with a jump. 'No, no, no...' she muttered to herself, reaching for her phone. It was only midnight, but she'd had the dream again. She knew she wouldn't be able to get back to sleep now.

Flustered, she lay back down under the fan, trying to let the cooling air work its magic, but images were coursing through her brain at a million miles an hour, as usual.

She squeezed her eyes shut. No, she couldn't bear it any longer.

Wearily she threw back the cotton sheets, splashed some cool water on her face in the bathroom. Looking at herself in the mirror, she let out a long sigh. *Why* was she still having the dream?

She pulled on a dress over her underwear and stepped out onto the porch. The moon and the stars were bright above the waving palm trees. She considered lying in the hammock there, trying to go back to sleep out there in the safe confines of the MAC's staff quarters. But maybe a short walk would clear her head.

She slipped into her sandals and set off into the warm, muggy night, taking the path around the MAC's grounds.

The dream played on in her head, no matter how she tried to block it by appreciating the island scenery. It never got boring to her—the mountains glowing in the moonlight, the twinkling lights on the bobbing boats, the gentle lap of the waves on the shore. But the dream was a nightmare every time. It threw her right back to the night of the accident. There was Annabel, slumped over the steering wheel.

Mila stopped at the swing in the water, settled on the heart-shaped seat. She couldn't even stop the dream invading her memories now that she was awake.

In reality, on the night it had happened, Mila had known she was going to be too late to help her twin the second she'd seen her—maybe even before that. She'd sensed it somehow…the lack, the loss. Maybe that was why all her years of training had flown out the window and she'd frozen.

But in her dream Annabel's car was in Afghanistan, not rural England. Mila was heaving her out through the windscreen on her own, just as she had in real life. Rocket-propelled grenades blasted all around them. Fire blazed and flames lapped the blown-out windows of a tall building. Women were screaming in the dust from the fallout, staggering over to her with their wounded children, begging for help.

Mila couldn't save Annabel and she couldn't save anyone else either. It was stress, grief, guilt—all of it tangled up in one dream. She'd had it over and over again since she'd arrived here on the island.

The ocean helped a little, she thought, letting the ripples wash over her ankles. Maybe going on a dive with Sebastian would help even more. He seemed to think diving was like switching your brain off for a while. She could do with some of that. They hadn't managed to squeeze it in yet, though—they'd just been too busy.

Mila was walking back towards her room, thinking of Sebastian, when the sound of the dog barking close by made her jump. She was probably on edge, after what had happened to Francoise, but she hurried on, back towards the staff quarters, hoping it wasn't the same dog that had bitten the child.

Hadn't Sebastian said that someone had removed the animal and her pups and put them somewhere safe?

It couldn't be the same one, she thought. But it didn't stop a spike of adrenaline flooding her veins anyway.

The barking tore up the night again. At first she couldn't see a dog. Then it appeared on the sandy path, right in front of her. Mila stopped in her tracks. There was no one else around. The dog was big and stocky, speckled with black and white spots. It was staring straight at her, not barking any more, just looking at her inquisitively.

She took a tentative step towards it, taking a calm approach. 'Are you lost, buddy?' she asked softly. His tail was the longest she had ever seen. This was a real Bali Dog, she observed, wondering if it was friendly or not.

'Bruno!'

Mila spun around at the voice.

Sebastian was sprinting towards them. The dog met him in the middle of the path, jumping up at the Chicago Cubs sports shirt he was wearing, pressing his big paws against his chest. Sebastian was wearing board shorts and flip-flops too, looking the most casual she had seen him since the day they'd met. She couldn't help running her eyes up and down his body.

'Hey, Mila… Sorry, did he scare you? He got out through the gates—someone must have left them open by mistake.'

Someone?

'This is your dog?'

Mila smoothed down her dress, embarrassed suddenly by her un-brushed hair and just-out-of-bed look. She hadn't even cleaned her teeth. She watched Sebastian crouch to the ground and ruffle the big dog's fur lovingly. The dog repaid him by licking his cheek, arms and neck…everywhere he could reach.

'He's only with me till we find him a new home,' he disclosed, laughing at the dog's enthusiasm. 'Mila, meet Bruno. Bruno is…a handful. He wouldn't hurt anyone, though, if you were worried…?'

'I wasn't,' she said, maybe too quickly. 'What are you doing up so late?'

He stood up straight, fixed her with a piercing gaze. Damn him for looking so good—even at midnight.

'I could ask you the same thing,' he said.

'I couldn't sleep,' she confessed.

'Something on your mind?'

She nodded, and walked with him along the path, past the swaying palms. The sea was still swooshing behind them. His private home was only metres away, but she realised she had never seen beyond the tall wooden gates before. He kept them locked, as if his house was like some kind of ivory tower. Knowing a little about his past with the paps, she could understand why.

They stopped when they got to the now open gates. Bruno charged back inside and Mila caught a glimpse of Sebastian's place for the first time. Modest. Small. One level. No swimming pool. Nothing like what she'd been expecting. She'd thought it would be something more extravagant, reflective of his fortune, maybe.

He put his hand to her arm gently, looking at her in concern. 'You looked like you had something on your mind today, when that kid with the dog bite came in. Are you OK? We're not overworking you, are we?'

'No, Sebastian, I'm used to hard work.'

'Well, I *know* that.'

She looked down at his hand on her bare arm. The warmth of it flooded through her, and with it came a surge of emotion that threatened to turn into tears. She swallowed it back, looking away.

'It's just…sometimes I dream about her, you know… Annabel. It's the anniversary of her death, soon. I guess she's just been on my mind more often than usual. Don't worry, it won't affect my work. I hope it hasn't—'

'Hey.'

He caught her chin for a second, guiding her eyes to his. His features wore a look of pure concern now. She felt her lungs tighten and her breath catch.

'Mila, your work is not what I'm worried about.'

She fought not to let those tears spring from her eyes. She shouldn't have told him about the anniversary—it was way too personal. But it had just slipped out. She was so exhausted and his kindness was killing her.

'I want you to be happy here,' he added.

He looked as though her happiness was genuinely important to him. Mila's heart swelled just a little bit more.

'I love it here,' she told him honestly, pulling her eyes away. 'It's everything Annabel said it was. Better.'

For a moment she considered asking him what had happened between her sister and him. She should just ask him, so she could let it go either way. But it made her feel like a paranoid teenager, which was certainly not the impression she wanted to give him. Whenever she plucked up the courage to ask whether he and her twin had been intimate or not, the thought of the ensuing conversation, focused on Annabel and the way she'd died…because *she'd* been too frozen to help her…was just too much. She couldn't do it—not yet.

Behind him she could just make out the living room of his place. The decidedly non-ostentatious, cosy-looking room was lit up softly and the door was open, as if he'd left in a hurry to chase the dog. The huge window revealed some gym equipment, a black sofa, and a coffee table with a bottle of wine on it.

She could see two wine glasses, both empty. Her stomach started churning.

Had he been drinking with the same 'someone' who'd left the gates open?

'Do you want to come in? I have some tea…' Sebastian paused, looked a little sheepish, as if maybe he knew it wasn't very professional to be asking her that.

But now she just couldn't help wondering who'd been drinking wine with him so close to midnight. She felt him watching her, seeing her looking at his lit-up living room and the wine glasses. Embarrassment flushed her cheeks.

Why did she care if he'd had a guest over?

'I should probably be getting back,' she told him, hoping he wouldn't see how this was affecting her. 'See you at the MAC. Goodnight, Sebastian.'

CHAPTER FIVE

'HE WAS ADVISED against XXL, so he's going for extra-large,' Dr Halabi confirmed out loud, reading from the notes on the monitor.

Sebastian winked at his resident trainee. 'Extra-large is enough for this guy. If he had XXL he'd fall over,' he said, and Fatema giggled.

Hugo O'Shea was almost under. His eyelids were fluttering. His blue hair seemed even bluer in the surgery lights. The long, slick piece of silicone they'd insert into Hugo's currently not so prized manhood floated promisingly in a beaker of antibiotic solution next to them.

Sebastian had done this procedure hundreds of times—on and off camera, he thought wryly. He'd done it so much he could probably do it with his eyes closed, but he still loved teaching others these skills. Fatema was a keen student. Soon she'd be doing the routine procedures herself, while he got back to scar repairs with Mila…and the million other things that demanded his attention.

There was a knock on the door. Mila stepped in.

'Sorry to interrupt, Doctor,' she said. 'Is it OK if I grab that light?' She motioned to the mobile surgery light in the corner.

'Of course, Dr Ricci.'

He let his eyes linger on her bare ankles as she crossed

the floor in her white sneakers. She was wearing her brown hair in a bun, pinned to the top of her head. It reminded him of Annabel for a second. Annabel had worn her hair like that…he was sure of it. Sometimes it still blew his mind that he'd met Mila's twin first, but the two were completely different women in his mind. They looked alike, but that was all.

Mila was an entirely new species.

He still couldn't figure her out.

He hadn't seen her outside of the MAC for the last few days. The last time they'd spoken without other people around had been outside his house in the middle of the night, after she'd come across Bruno. He'd asked her inside, but she'd hurried off. He assumed he'd made her feel a little awkward. They were colleagues after all—and he never invited colleagues from the MAC home, nor patients.

He'd realised when he'd gone back inside and seen the wine glasses on the table that she'd probably seen them too, and had maybe thought he'd been entertaining a woman.

Not this time. It had been just Neesha and her husband Dan—his friends from the turtle sanctuary. They'd been adding up the profits from the fundraiser and planning where the money should go, along with a little extra donation from his own private funds for some new tanks for the baby turtles. Neesha had poured wine for herself and Dan. He'd had a herbal tea himself.

In one way he liked it that seeing those wine glasses might have evoked a stab of jealousy in Mila; it wasn't as if he hadn't been admiring her work…and her eyes…and her body…but in another way he couldn't deny that he was concerned for her.

She clearly thought about Annabel a lot more than he did, and more often than she was letting on. Coming here was reminding her of her twin—especially because he'd met her here, too. He knew how grief could flare up when you least wanted it to. He'd been through it after his father died.

Mila went to leave the room with the light she'd come in for, without looking his way.

'See you later?' he asked her as she reached for the door.

She turned back to him and he saw Fatema glance up at them over Hugo.

He cleared his throat, hoping Mila hadn't forgotten. 'The dive centre this afternoon?'

It had taken ages to get a slot when both of them were free.

Mila blinked. Her phone buzzed in her pocket. Distracted, she fished it out as she said, 'Yes, Doctor... Sorry for disturbing you—excuse me.' And she left the room.

When she'd left, Fatema couldn't get her words out fast enough. 'Diving? You and Dr Ricci? Better not tell Rachel about that. She likes to pair people up, and I think you're both on her hit list. Young, single, beautiful, tortured... It's like you belong together. Sorry, Doctor, am I speaking out of line?'

Fatema flushed a little at the realisation that she had just called him beautiful and tortured. Sebastian fought to stop the amusement from showing on his face; he'd been called worse things in his time on the show.

'Shall we begin?' he suggested.

His afternoon off couldn't get here fast enough.

'How's it going over there? It's been a while since I've spoken to you...'

'Sorry, Mum,' Mila said, sinking down onto the low stone wall outside the MAC and observing the patients lying around, reading or chattering in the grounds. 'The time difference here is crazy—plus we've been so busy.'

She heard her mum let out a sigh down the phone. 'I figured as much. I won't keep you.'

'No, no, it's OK. I have a few minutes. Dr Becker is training someone at the moment, and then we're in for a scar repair. It really is non-stop around here, but I'm sorry I haven't called you as much I should.'

'I don't expect you to, darling. I'm fine over here.'

Mila wasn't so sure. Her mother had a way of putting on a brave face. 'Are you really fine? What have you been doing?'

Her mum paused. 'This and that. I watched a couple of episodes of that show your famous doctor used to be in. *Faces of Chicago.* Is he married?'

Mila shook her head at the sandy ground. Trust her mum to ask that. 'No, he's not married.'

She pictured Sebastian a few nights ago, outside his house, all smiles and moonlit muscles and charm. She was still so embarrassed at having shown her weaknesses around him. She knew she'd appeared overly emotional, telling him about her dreams and then hurrying off after seeing those wine glasses. The man was entitled to entertain whoever he wanted. He must think she was crazy.

She'd been so mortified about it she'd been keeping away from him whenever possible. She wasn't used to men stirring up her emotions. It made her feel far too vulnerable for her own liking. Besides, she wasn't here for *him*, technically speaking.

'Well, I was just calling to say I've posted you a letter,' her mum said.

'A letter? That's delightfully old-school of you, Mum. What's in it?'

'It's just a few photos. I found them in Annabel's drawer. I thought you might like to have them over there with you as keepsakes.'

Mila's throat felt tight. 'You were looking through Annabel's drawers?'

'I…I was missing her. And you. I think I needed to do it.'

'Oh, Mum.'

Mila could picture her mother at home, curled up with her legs under her at her usual end of the sofa, a book on the arm. Maybe a cup of her favourite tea. They had both cried together on that sofa for days after Annabel had—

No. She couldn't think about it again. She felt guilty for being so far away. And now her mother had started going through Annabel's things without her.

'I saw someone else wearing her clothes the other day,' her mother continued. 'That yellow dress with the black spots—remember it? The one she ordered from the Japanese warehouse?'

Mila swallowed. 'I remember.'

'Annabel loved that dress.'

'I know, Mum.'

She and her mother had made the mistake of taking some of Annabel's clothes and shoes to the local charity shop a few months after the accident. Their good deed—intended as a method of coping with their grief—had backfired badly when they'd started seeing women around the town wearing the donated clothes. Her mother had come home in tears several times, thinking she'd just seen Annabel.

After that neither of them had been able to bear to go back to her things. There were boxes and drawers of her personal items that hadn't been touched since.

'Let me know when the letter arrives,' her mum said. 'I don't know how long it will take to reach you out there, but I thought you might appreciate something on the anniversary…you know. You will call me, won't you?'

Mila's heart ached. She fixed her eyes on the ocean.

Someone was swinging on the sea swing where Sebastian had first offered to take her diving. 'Of course I'll call you.'

Her mother sounded concerned. 'You won't be alone on the day, will you?'

Mila bit her lip. 'I won't be alone, I promise. *You* won't be alone, will you?'

'I might have company. Either way, I'll keep busy. Maybe your famous doctor can distract you, Is he as good looking as he is on the television?'

She rolled her eyes, smiling now. 'He's an inspiration, Mum. He's even taking me scuba diving.'

'Really? He dives, too?'

'He pretty much does everything on this island.'

'Did he take Annabel diving? You said before that he met her. I still can't get over that—what a coincidence!'

Mila felt the usual stab of envy, confusion and nausea. She felt it whenever she thought about Sebastian and Annabel together—which was often.

'I don't know, Mum. I haven't asked what they did when Annabel was here. It's none of my business, is it? I have to go. Thank you for sending me the photos. I love you.'

She was determined not to let her emotions overwhelm her with people around, but her mother was still talking.

'When you finish your stint out there and come home we'll go through the rest of her things together, OK? It's time, Mila.'

The coral reefs surrounding the islands were home to some of the planet's most diverse marine life. Sebastian watched Mila admiring the brown and white stripes of a solo lion fish with a look of total awe as he floated beside her.

She'd said she'd done some diving training before, in her Army days, but she'd never been in the ocean. Looking at her now, he couldn't believe it. She exuded confidence—

more than many of his other students on their first dives. She'd followed Big Al, one of their rescue turtles for a good ten minutes, and he'd got a little kick out of the way her eyes had lit up just at drifting along, observing his barnacle-speckled shell, his scars and his wise hooded eyes.

Damn, she was beautiful with her hair down...and up.

He usually couldn't remember his thoughts after a dive, but when they finally climbed back onto the boat he realised he'd spent most of the dive both admiring her and worrying about what she might be thinking.

'So, did you switch off completely down there?' he asked, watching her shake out her hair.

He'd reserved the boat just for them, but his buddy and driver Ketut was watching them intently, just like Fatema and Rachel were clearly doing behind their backs. Maybe next time he'd take her out alone.

'I don't actually remember.' Mila looked pensive as he placed her heavy tank back in its holder and signalled to Ketut to start the engine. 'But it's true what you said. It's so peaceful down there. I really needed it. Thank you, Sebastian.'

He stepped closer, softly brushed a strand of damp hair back behind her ear. 'You're welcome.'

Ketut cleared his throat at the steering wheel and Mila looked uncomfortable for a second, then broke contact by stepping back.

'That turtle...' she started. 'The big one...'

'Big Al? Yeah, he's a pretty special guy.'

'What happened to him? I saw his fins, with all those scars.'

'He got into a fight with a boat propeller. That's what we think happened anyway.'

'He does look sad,' she mused, following his eyes to

the jagged slashes across her left inner forearm. 'But he's so beautiful.'

Sebastian tossed their fins into a box along with the masks and snorkels. 'So are you, in case you ever doubt that. Turn around,' he instructed.

He lifted her wet hair and released the zip of her wet-suit slowly, noting the shape of her shoulders, the contours of her body as he helped to pull it down to her waist. Mila was tense, though.

'I should tell you…that dive was so much more enjoyable than the lake dives we did in training, pulling all those…' She grimaced as she turned around in his arms.

'All those what?' he asked curiously.

'Fake bodies,' she replied. 'They had us helping rescue divers treat the bodies so we'd know how to handle it if it really happened. I don't need to tell you this was a thousand times better.'

He motioned for her to follow him up to the roof of the boat—his favourite place. Her bare midriff was taut and toned. He caught her appraising him too as they stood there on the roof of the bobbing boat.

His hours in the home gym had paid off, he knew that, but Mila had probably always been this way. She'd worked her brain and her body equally in the Army—he had probably only heard about a fraction of the things she'd done and seen. It was eternally fascinating to him. Her scars were beautiful to him. She was beautiful inside and out.

'Maybe next time we'll go to Shark Reef,' he told her, taking a seat on the hot wooden roof and rolling his own wetsuit down to his waist. 'It's a little further out…off the next island. The current has to be just right.'

'I thought you said there aren't any sharks any more?'

He dangled his legs over the side and folded his arms over

the railing. Mila's wet hair caught the afternoon sun as she sat beside him. Their bare arms brushed on the hot metal.

'Not many, and it's a gift if you actually get to see one. We donate to the shark nursery off Lombok, so the numbers are rising slowly.'

'Sharks, turtles, dogs, humans…is there anything you're not saving on this island, Dr Becker?'

For the first time in days Mila offered him a real, genuine smile and he felt a weight lift from his shoulders.

'Talking of dogs, thank you for walking Bruno home with me the other night. My friends Neesha and Dan came over—they must have forgotten to shut the gates. They did have a little wine while they were at my place.'

Mila looked indifferent, but he swore he saw her cheeks flush just a little. He didn't have to explain himself—he knew that. He could have anyone he liked over to his house. He could have a woman over if he wanted. But he didn't. Not any more. It surprised him, this need for Mila to know he wasn't playing around.

'You know,' she said, letting out a sigh, 'this is where I first saw you—up here on this roof, the day I arrived. I'd be lying if I told you that you didn't get my attention, looking all…like that.'

She pulled a face and motioned to his bare chest and wet hair, and he laughed.

'Is that so Dr Ricci? Well, I'd be lying if I told you I didn't see you then, too.'

'But you thought I was Annabel.'

Mila rested her head on her arms as he floundered for words.

'It's OK. I wonder what she'd say if she could see us now, working together…diving together.'

'She would probably think it was a pretty funny coincidence. Wouldn't anyone think that?' he asked, slightly annoyed with himself for his initial mistake over her identity. It still bothered him, the way he'd confused the two of them and been so vocal about her changing her name.

'I don't know. I can't speak for my twin. She's not here. I wish she was.'

'When is the anniversary, exactly?' he asked cautiously.

He'd sensed her tense up the second he'd said he thought Annabel would find it amusing, knowing Mila was with him there. He shouldn't have put words in her mouth. It had clearly bothered Mila.

'You mentioned it was coming up to three years since she died?'

She closed her eyes to the sun. 'It's in a few weeks. I might take a day off, if that's OK—do something nice for her. I don't know yet. I haven't had a chance to really think about what I'll do besides call my mother. It's a tough day for her, too.'

'I'm sure. Is she alone over there?'

'You mean, does she have a man? I don't think so. There hasn't really been anyone since she divorced my father. She has a lot of friends, though.'

'I can help you think of something to do here, if you want…to take your mind off it.'

She seemed to contemplate his offer for a moment. 'Thank you. I don't know if *anything* will take my mind off it, but I appreciate that, Sebastian.'

Colleagues or not, the urge to touch her, to reassure her that he was here for her, was overpowering. He couldn't help it. He reached his hand to the back of her head and drew her gently against his shoulder, keeping his hand in her soft damp hair.

They rode back to shore like that, in silence.

Thank goodness it was only a short boat ride back to the beach. Mila could practically feel the sparks flying between them on the roof. It was getting more difficult to ignore their obvious chemistry. Even resting her head on his comforting shoulder felt as if he was rolling out the red carpet, inviting her further in.

What had possessed her to admit she had noticed him on day one, before she'd even got off the boat? She didn't know. But something about his presence was comforting, and real, and he'd seemed to want her to know he hadn't been entertaining anyone in his house lately except friends.

No. She couldn't go there.

Would Annabel really think their meeting was a funny coincidence?

She had asked that very question out loud and sent it off on the wind, many times, longing for an answer. All she'd got in return were more bad dreams that woke her up in a cold sweat.

Sebastian had taken care of returning the dive equipment. It was after four p.m. now, and the afternoon sun cast a flattering light on his biceps as he ordered them both takeaway smoothies at the dive shop bar.

She was trying and failing to find an excuse not to spend the rest of her afternoon with him when a child in blue denim shorts tugged at her shirt from behind. It was Francoise, the French girl who'd come in with the dog bite.

'Hey, you!'

Her mother was hovering at the entrance to the dive shop, waiting for her daughter. They raised their hands at each other from afar.

'I was on my way to find you,' the child said, in excellent English for her age. Her big round eyes observed Mila's wet hair, the beach towel sticking out of her bag. 'Have you been snorkelling?'

'I was scuba diving...with Dr Becker.'

Sebastian appeared with the smoothies. His tall frame threw the young girl into shadow.

'Well, if it isn't our brave canine-fighting superhero. I see you found us.'

'Hello, Dr Becker!' Francoise beamed from beneath her red sun hat. 'My *maman* saw you here. We go home today—back to Bordeaux.'

'Your wounds look much better already, Miss March-and,' he told her, crouching down to her level to inspect Mila's handiwork on her jaw. 'You'll only have a small scar there, if anyone can even see it at all.'

'I'll be more like a stripe, for braving your ordeal,' Mila followed up.

'Like *your* stripes.' Francoise placed a finger softly to the scars on Mila's left wrist.

'A bit like mine,' she mused aloud.

She didn't pull away. She didn't mind Sebastian looking either. It wasn't like he hadn't been looking at them ever since they'd met. He had called her beautiful on the dive boat earlier on. The memory caused a stir in her heart, but she certainly wasn't about to relive how she'd got her scars in front of strangers.

She couldn't imagine telling Sebastian about her failure to save Annabel. She wouldn't be able to do it, knowing he had met her twin. She couldn't stand the pity on people's faces when she told them how she'd tried to drag her out, too late, just as the car went up in flames. She'd scarred herself for life, trying and failing to get her out through the windscreen, even though Annabel had already been dead when she'd done it.

Francoise took Mila's hand and dropped a tiny wooden dog onto her palm.

'What's this?' Touched, Mila turned it over in her hand and showed it to Sebastian.

'I wanted to say thank you for helping me. It is to protect you from bad dogs.'

'It's a lucky charm,' Sebastian told her, admiring it in her palm. 'You'll see carvings like this all over Indonesia. This one is exceptionally crafted. That's so nice of you, Francoise.'

'It's beautiful,' Mila agreed. 'Thank you, honey, I'll keep it for ever. It will remind me to be brave in the future, like you were.'

Francesca rocked on her flip-flops, looking shy. 'Is Dr Becker your boyfriend?' she asked Mila innocently.

'No, he's not,' she shot back, trying to laugh.

Sebastian gasped in faux shock to make the kid giggle.

'I think he *should* be your boyfriend,' Francoise volunteered. She gave them both a quick hug, reaching her tiny arms around of them, drawing them together. 'You can help people like me together. You can stop all the bad dogs biting other children. I am going to tell everyone about you.'

Sebastian almost dropped the smoothies as their sides were crushed together. For a little kid, she was strong. They watched her skip her way happily up the dust track with her mother.

'Wow.' Sebastian was laughing, resting on one elbow on the bar, even though the tension was a tangible object between them, even bigger than before. 'Looks like you're gathering fans wherever you go.'

'Says *you*. You were really good with her.'

'So were you. Do you really never think about having a family?'

His question caught her off guard and she reacted evasively. 'Me? I'm pretty sure I'd prefer a dog.'

His eyebrows shot up. 'A dog? In that case, maybe you can have Bruno.'

'Bruno needs a permanent home. I'm not here for ever.'

'Shame…' he murmured, and his eyes lingered on her lips just long enough to start a slow simmering burn in her for more of his attention as he sipped his smoothie.

His phone rang then, and saved her having to respond to his obvious flirtation. 'It's Ketut. He'll only just have got home, so something must be wrong. One sec?'

He wandered out to the forecourt with his phone. A couple of twenty-somethings in bikinis looked up at him from the pool, admiring his physique as she did way too often.

His posture quickly told her something bad had happened. She hoped it wasn't serious.

Ketut was a local guy, who worked at the dive shop and drove the boat amongst other things, and she knew Sebastian and Ketut had been good friends since Sebastian had first arrived on the island. He talked about him and Ketut's wife Wayan a lot.

When Sebastian hung up, his mood had done a one-eighty.

'Mila, I have to go,' he said apologetically, slipping into the sandy sandals he'd left by the bar.

He tossed his empty cup expertly into the nearby trash can and hooked his backpack over his shoulder.

'Unless you want to come with me?'

CHAPTER SIX

KETUT FLUNG OPEN the door before they'd even made it up the path. Wayan stood with her arms held out to Sebastian, her belly swollen with their baby, in the doorway of their modest bamboo shack. It was surrounded by terra-cotta pots and jungle plants, and a moss-covered statue of a Balinese goddess stood to one side. It looked as if it doubled as a bird perch.

'Sebastian! Thank you so much for coming.'

Wayan's voice wobbled and Mila's heart ached as she watched him walk straight into her embrace. It was a real hug, tender and heartfelt, the kind you might give to a family member.

The kind he'd given her on the boat when she'd talked about Annabel's anniversary, she thought, feeling her stomach clench. He must trust her to bring her here. This was personal.

'You know Dr Ricci... Mila? I explained to her a little about the situation on the way over here. Wayan, you should have called me sooner—I would have come.'

Sebastian guided Mila ahead of him across the threshold, kicking off his sandals on the inside mat. She did the same.

'Wayan didn't want to ruin your dive, so she didn't tell me either,' Ketut explained as he closed the door behind them.

The smell of burning scented candles hit Mila's nostrils as they were ushered into a small, cosy living area. Three dozing cats occupied a tattered pink couch in one corner. Books were stacked haphazardly on chairs, shelves, and even the floor, and soon Ketut was pouring herbal tea from a silver teapot under a whirring fan.

It was simple, but homely. Only the mood was tense.

On the boat on their way over to their house, on a neighbouring island, Sebastian had explained how he spent a lot of time here, so it was almost a second home, and that these two were like his island brother and sister.

Short, fatigued-looking Wayan was likely in her mid-thirties, dressed in a colourful patterned skirt and a white blouse that revealed the lower part of her pregnant belly as she dropped heavily into a tattered armchair. She started biting her nails. On instinct Mila sat beside her just as Sebastian took the wicker chair next to Ketut.

He took the tea cup he was offered. 'So, tell me what's going on, man. What are we dealing with here?'

'I'm hoping you can tell *me*.' Ketut handed Mila a cup too, then pushed a set of ultrasound pictures forward on the coffee table. 'Wayan was given these at Blue Ray. She was too upset to call me, so she came back here and told the cats before she told me.'

'They say the baby will need surgery...' Wayan sniffled.

Her quivering lip turned into a sob and Ketut was beside her in a second, both arms around her shoulders. He was trying to be strong for her, but Mila could tell he was heartbroken. Mila reached for Wayan's hand.

Sebastian pulled his glasses from his backpack, put them on and studied the black and white prints intently.

'Cleft lip and cleft palate,' he confirmed out loud, handing her the X-rays with a deep sigh. 'I'm so sorry, guys, they're right. This is going to have to be fixed in surgery. Usually the procedure's done after about three months…'

'We will love him anyway, of course, Sebastian… Mila. You know we would, no matter what. Even if you can't help us.'

Wayan's sad eyes broke Mila's heart. She had seen a thousand women broken over babies deformed, wounded, stillborn or killed. Again, she put herself in a mother's shoes. The thought of anything happening to a child of her own made her go icy cold… She just wouldn't know what to do if it was her. She'd already proved that in the worst way.

'Why wouldn't he help you?' Mila asked now, looking from Wayan to Sebastian.

'We don't have medical insurance.'

Sebastian stood up, knelt in front of her, and put a hand reassuringly on her knee, over her bright skirt. 'I told you before, you guys did the right thing calling me. I can help you.'

'*We* can help you,' Mila added.

He had brought her here for a reason. She could see the future of this baby meant the world to him, just as his nephew Charlie did, back in Chicago. And he knew she had a way of injecting a certain calm into a situation… Unless that situation involved saving her twin sister from a burning car, in which case she froze like a useless snowman.

Sebastian thought she was stronger than she was. He would never know how the flashbacks and her guilt over Annabel's death still consumed her.

'What can you do, Sebastian? Mila? Will our baby be deformed for ever?' Wayan was pale now, in spite of Sebastian's comforting words.

'Not if we can help it,' Sebastian said defiantly, taking his seat again.

He was looking at Mila from across the room, dragging

his hands through his hair. Behind him, through the window, she saw the daylight fading into twilight.

'The surgery is relatively simple, though it sounds quite complex when you try to explain it,' Mila said, finding her voice. 'Once your child is born we'll do another assessment, and there might be a few operations over time, but as for scarring...'

'Minimal,' Sebastian finished for her, meeting her eyes.

They were on the same page. One of the cats leapt from the chair and started curling around her legs. It purred softly in the silence until Ketut spoke.

'By the time the baby is born you might be gone. Sebastian says you're not with us on the island for very long.'

All eyes were on her now—even the cat's. Mila's throat felt dry in spite of her tea. 'I don't know what to say about that...honestly,' she admitted, putting a hand down to pet the purring animal. 'I'm here for a while yet. I don't have an exact departure date. I gave in my notice in London, so I'm pretty flexible, I guess.'

Suddenly she didn't want to leave the island—at least not until this baby was mended and declared healthy. But what could she do? She might have agreed to an undetermined date for the MAC personnel department to arrange her flight out, but still, her life wasn't here. This wasn't her family—as much as she wanted to help them.

Sebastian was biting the inside of his cheek hard, as if he didn't know what to say either...

'Jared, hey, what's up?'

Sebastian kicked the refrigerator door shut, balancing the phone on his shoulder as he carried a bowl of oats and a carton of milk to the countertop.

He was on the verge of running late for a consultation, followed by a scar revision on a car crash victim who was currently on his way from the mainland. But he needed to eat first. Surgery on an empty stomach was never a good idea. He needed all the brain capacity he could muster—especially now.

'Sorry, bro,' Jared said. 'I know it's early over there, but I really need your confirmation for Mom's birthday thing. I need numbers. Does the world's most exclusive surgeon have a plus one in mind this year, or will you be flying solo like last year?'

'I don't know yet,' he told his brother, pulling a spoon from the cutlery drawer.

He noticed a frangipani flower in the drawer—a gift from his cleaner. She hid them everywhere. He slipped it into his pocket idly. He would re-gift it, like he always did, to one of the women in Recovery at the MAC.

'Hi, Uncle Bas!' Charlie's voice was loud on the end of the line, as if he'd stolen the phone for a second.

Sebastian grinned. 'Hello, trouble. Why aren't you in bed?'

It was a time difference of thirteen hours between Chicago and Indonesia, so he rarely got to speak to Charlie.

He saw his reflection in the glass of the window. He looked tired. He hadn't slept much, worrying about Ketut and Wayan and the not so distant departure of Mila Ricci. She might have a while left on Gili Indah, but he'd been realising lately that he wasn't much looking forward to island life without her.

'He's been on a school trip today—haven't you, bud?' Jared said, taking the phone back. 'He's pretty fired up still…'

'We saw dinosaurs!' Charlie enthused in the background, and proceeded to roar like a T-Rex. 'Listen, Uncle Bas!'

Sebastian sniggered. 'Sounds like fun.'

'Sounds like they gave him E-numbers. We'll get him to bed eventually.'

Sebastian smiled. 'How is everyone else?'

'Good, good…same, same. Wrapping up the season. Mom thinks it should be the last one—did she tell you? I think she's finally getting tired of the show.'

Sebastian sat at the breakfast bar, watching Bruno chasing a bird around the yard outside. Jared had said this before, at the end of the last season. And the one before that, too. He didn't want to tell him he'd believe it when he saw it. The network always came back with a better offer.

'I fully support any decision to make this season the last one, but you already know that,' he said instead.

'I know… I know.' Jared let out a sigh. He knew better than to start that conversation again. 'So, back to the party,' he diverted—predictably. 'I think Mom would like it if you brought someone. Laura's rented the Opal Marquee at the Langford—the one in the orchid garden? It's a surprise for Mom. We've invited all her friends from the badminton club. Actually…if you can't think of anyone to bring from your string of island vixens I can ask Theresa. Remember her? That cute blonde dentist from Smile Right in Lincoln Park…'

Sebastian spooned the oats into his mouth as his brother went on, naming women he couldn't care less about getting to know.

'Jared, I'm not going to take some woman to a party if I'm never going to see her again. And I can only stay three days, remember? I have a lot to do here.'

Jared make a clicking sound with his tongue. 'I get it, bro—your life is there. Can't you think of *anyone* to bring, though? You've come on your own for the last three years.'

'You know why that is.' Sebastian felt his jaw start to tick.

'Yes, I *do* know why. You're paranoid that some pap will catch you doing something shady and make your idyllic island life a misery, But I told you—we don't invite the media to family events, Bas. Any new woman of yours is perfectly safe from prying eyes. None of us wants a repeat of what happened with Klara.'

Sebastian scraped the stool back and dropped his bowl and spoon into the sink—heavily.

Jared's voice softened. 'Sorry to bring it up. I just want to see you happy again, man. You work so hard out there on your own. I hope you're finding time for some fun, too?'

'Actually, there is someone,' he said, before he could stop himself.

'Oh, yeah?'

'I'm not sure she can come with me to Chicago, however. Technically, she's only here on a short-term placement.' He grabbed his backpack and sunglasses, locked the door behind him and patted Bruno in the garden on his way out. 'She's new at the MAC,' he said reluctantly, making sure to close the gates properly.

'Wow. OK…'

Jared drew a breath through his teeth and Sebastian could picture the look on his brother's face.

'You know how I feel about mixing business with pleasure, but I guess that's up to you. Why can't you bring her?'

'For a start we're colleagues—even if it's temporary,' he said, lowering his voice as he walked towards the main MAC building. 'And we're friends too… I think. God, we haven't even been on a date, or anything. I just…'

'You just want to get in her pants before she leaves for good?'

'No, Jared.' He rolled his eyes to the blue sky. 'It's more than that. She's…she's different. Anyway, we have too much to do here, so we can't both be getting on a plane…'

'Stop making excuses, Bas. You deserve a vacation,

don't you? And you deserve a decent woman at your side. It's been a long time, bro, since you and Klara broke up.'

'I know.'

'Tell me about this woman! Where's she from?'

Encouraged by his brother's rare enthusiasm for anything that didn't involve the show, Sebastian told Jared a few minor details as he walked—but nothing that would enable him to search for her online. He trusted Jared, of course, but he wouldn't put Mila's privacy in jeopardy for anything.

He spotted Tilda Holt, basking in the sun on a lounger by the swimming pool already. She was recovering from her non-invasive face lift with a cheeky Bloody Mary. He hoped it was a virgin Bloody Mary. He returned her cheery wave and then, remembering the flower in his pocket, turned back and presented it to her with a flourish, his phone still pressed to his ear.

For you, he mouthed in silence.

Her new crease-free eyes shone with delight. She thanked him profusely and proudly placed the tiny white and yellow flower in her hair.

Hugo O'Shea waved enthusiastically from his seat at a table on the sand, looking up from his laptop. He was still hanging around after his enlargement procedure—'working remotely in Recovery,' or so he'd said.

Something about him made Sebastian bristle as he chatted on with Jared. He didn't trust the guy.

But Sebastian's mind was half in the moment, in the MAC's grounds with his patients, and half on the penthouse balcony back home, on showing Mila the views of Belmont Harbour and the lakefront. She'd get a kick out of Charlie, too… He could tell she liked kids a lot, even if she maintained she would prefer a dog herself.

'*Ask* her, bro,' Jared demanded, when he told him he really had to run.

Sebastian swung into the air-conditioned reception area. Mila looked up from the desk, where she and Rachel were studying some papers.

'Hey,' they said at the same time.

Mila was wearing lipstick. He didn't notice anything about Rachel.

God he really wanted to be alone with Mila right now. They'd both been so busy he hadn't seen her much in the last week. But tonight they'd be alone for some of the time. Maybe he should ask her to accompany him to Chicago then.

He pushed the thought aside instantly. He should absolutely *not* do that. They were professional colleagues. Besides, Jared might think the media would leave Sebastian alone in Chicago, and Jared might think he was being exceptionally paranoid, but there were plusses to being paranoid. Being paranoid meant he would never mess up again. Being paranoid meant he would never hurt another woman to the point of her refusing ever to speak to him or see him again.

Sebastian had never said it, and he barely acknowledged it even to himself, but what had happened with Klara had affected him deeply. He would never subject another woman—especially Mila, who clearly had her own vulnerable past to protect—to anything like that again.

'Wayan can really cook,' Mila groaned, putting a hand to her full stomach. 'That veggie *rendang* was probably the best thing I've ever eaten. How do you say delicious again?'

'In Indonesian? *Lezat*.' Sebastian smiled.

He held out an arm to help her step back into the tiny boat and Mila felt the butterflies instantly overpowering her satiated stomach. The water was warm and inviting under her feet, swishing up her legs, almost to the hem of her skirt. The stars were out in force.

With their busy schedules it had taken over a week to arrange another trip for her and Sebastian to see Wayan and Ketut at the same time.

Wayan had made them a *lezat* Indonesian feast that defied all logic, coming from her tiny kitchen, and the conversation had flowed easily—from the cleft palate surgery and scar repair to general pregnancy issues and the brand-new project Sebastian was developing in Bali—a retreat for recovering patients on the mainland.

Mila had also heard countless stories of Sebastian and Ketut's island endeavours, and had been charmed by the way he conducted himself around his adopted family. She'd been about to cancel tonight, out of sheer exhaustion and nightmares three nights running—but, while she needed rest, the thought of being around Sebastian again outside of the MAC was like a comfort blanket somehow.

She admired him and she respected him. Which only served to fuel her growing attraction to him.

She sat on the wooden slats of the tiny fishing boat's seat, watching his muscles flex as he pushed it out from the beach and hopped in. The butterflies swooped in again as he sat down and started the motor. His knee in khaki shorts brushed hers so lightly she might not have felt it if she hadn't been so acutely aware of his closeness.

'Beautiful night,' he said, gesturing up to the stars.

She murmured agreement and looked to the sky. She could feel him watching her. Their mutual attraction was undeniable. She'd seen the looks Ketut had given him, too, and the not so secret smiles between Ketut and Wayan at the dinner table. She knew she lit up in his presence, and that whenever that happened her worries drifted off. But all too often they sprang back unannounced.

Annabel had met him first. Annabel was the one he'd liked first. She had no business entertaining this attraction. Twins did not ever go after the same guy, and those rules hadn't changed just because Annabel was dead.

She shifted slightly, so they were no longer touching. If he noticed her futile attempt at creating distance he said nothing. The boat was skimming the ocean, heading back to the island.

'Did you know the oldest map of the night sky is a map of the Orion constellation?' Mila said, to fill the excruciating silence. 'They found it carved on a mammoth tusk.'

'A mammoth tusk? Really?'

'They think it was carved over thirty-two thousand years ago,' she continued.

Sebastian was looking at her in admiration. She liked it when she taught him things he didn't know.

'So, you're interested in the stars, Doctor?'

'The ones in the sky, yes—not so much the ones on television.'

She was teasing him, and she knew he knew it.

Sebastian grinned at the horizon, one hand steering the boat. 'Are you calling me a star, Dr Ricci?'

'Maybe…'

'A fallen star?'

'Maybe.' She smiled in spite of herself. 'You know how to turn your shine on, though, don't you? Tilda Holt showed me the flower you gave her. She said she was going to press it and put it in a frame.'

Sebastian chuckled. The night was calm and still around the chugging boat. The moon was a thumbnail in the sky. Mila pulled her loose hair over one shoulder to hold it. The wind was tugging it in all directions, along with her white knee-length dress.

'Seriously, we used to study the stars…me and Annabel. But not so much as I did on my own, when I was deployed in the Middle East.'

'Really? You had time to stargaze out there?'

'The quiet nights were the scariest sometimes,' she confessed.

She wondered again why she found it so easy to talk to him about some things, and other things felt impossible to address…like what he might or might not have done with Annabel.

'We never knew what was coming next,' she continued, fighting a vision of Annabel as she pictured her suddenly, right there in the boat with them. 'There wasn't much else you could do on those nights but wish on the stars that the worst would never happen. That's Scorpius—see the long, curving tail?'

She pointed to a constellation above them. Sebastian slowed the boat. It made her heart speed up.

'I see it,' he told her, cutting the engine and shifting on the seat. 'And just to the east…that's what the Balinese call Danau—*danau* means lake. If you want to learn more there's an app. You just point your phone up and it tells you—'

'Stop.' She cut him off.

'What?' He looked alarmed. His knee was back against hers.

'There's an app that you can point at the stars and it tells you what they are? *All* these stars? How is that even possible?'

Sebastian laughed out loud again. The sound was so unexpected it shocked her into laughing herself.

'You're amazing—do you know that?' he said, with genuine affection.

Mila's heart kept on thudding. The way he was looking at her… The engine was still off. They were facing each other now on the seat, so close she could see the lights from the surrounding boats reflected in his eyes.

'I'm not kidding about the app,' he informed her. 'Wait till you see the Zodiacal light.'

'What's that?' she croaked, searching his warm eyes for reasons to back off, to stop this thing before it started. She could feel it coming.

'That's a free show from the skies here that you won't want to miss. It hovers like a cloud over those mountains at sunrise or sunset. It's basically sunlight, reflecting off dust grains that are left over from whatever created our solar system over four and a half billion years ago. They just go round and round, circling the sun in the inner solar system. All these grains…'

Her heart was beating wildly now. The air felt thick and hot, and the back of her neck was damp.

'Sounds like a lot of grains.'

He shifted even closer to her. 'A *whole* lot of grains.'

Sebastian reached a hand to her face and cupped her chin, stroked a thumb softly across her lips. It felt as if time stood still. Her mind went blank.

'You know something?' he said after a pause. His eyes seemed to be clouded over with longing. 'It's not just the fact that I shouldn't have you that makes me want you.'

Mila swallowed. All the hairs on her body stood to attention as he trailed his thumb across her cheek. He made a sound like a strangled groan that spoke straight to her churning insides.

'I know this could be complicated, but…do you even know how hard it is, Mila, keeping away from you…?'

His fingers made tangles in her hair, drawing her face even closer to his with each knot.

'Tell me to stay away and I will,' he whispered, but his lips were so close, and his fingers weren't leaving her hair.

'Don't stay away.'

It was Mila who caved in first and kissed him.

Sebastian's tongue was like his hands—soft at first, then harder, more possessive. His slight stubble razored her chin as her own hands found his hair, felt the delicious softness of it in her fingers. He was urging her closer, as close as they could get on the seat of the bobbing boat. He drew her legs around him, his kisses firing up parts of her that had been dormant way too long.

Mila was so caught up in the thrill of this new connection that she almost forgot who or where she was. So the sound of the swinging boom from an approaching boat and several panicked cries came completely as a surprise.

CHAPTER SEVEN

THE MAN IN the yellow shirt didn't see his boat's boom lunging violently towards him, but Sebastian heard the crack as it hit him in the face and chest.

'Oh, my God…' Mila fists dropped from his hair to the sides of the rocking boat as they were forced apart in a flash. 'What's happened?'

There was blood on the deck of the other boat already. Sebastian saw it glimmering in the floodlights as he re-started the engine and inched closer, standing to see over the side. It was a sailing catamaran, three times the size of theirs, but there looked to be hardly anyone on it.

Mila's knuckles were as white as her dress as she gripped the boat's edge. 'I can't see anyone injured…'

'He's on the floor.'

Sebastian steered the boat as close as he could get. A woman in a long pink dress was shrieking uncontrollably, hunched over the motionless body of her friend, or maybe he was her lover. Three more men and a woman were doing their best to swing the boom back into place and secure it.

'Don't move him!' Mila shouted from their boat.

He watched as she lifted the boat seat and grabbed two medical kits. He made sure all of the MAC's boats had them on board, and he always brought his own.

Unsurprisingly to Sebastian, Mila needed no help climbing over the side of the boat, and in less than three seconds flat she was barefoot on the catamaran, crouched at the man's side.

'Help me, please—he's out cold!' The woman in the pink dress was beside herself.

Sebastian threw a rope onto the other boat's deck, jumped across himself and hurriedly tied the boats together, impressed by Mila's quick action. The medical bag was already open and she was supporting their victim's head on her own lap, instructing someone to get a cushion.

'What's his name?' Mila checked the man's pupils and pulse.

'John—he's John Griffiths, my husband. I'm Janet. Something must have got loose on the boom. Oh, my God... the blood.'

'Get me some clean towels,' Mila ordered the others on deck.

She had sprung into doctor mode so fast it was almost as if the woman Sebastian had just kissed so passionately was another person entirely.

'Where did this glass come from?' she asked next, indicating the broken shards all around them on the hardwood decking.

He had only just noticed them himself.

'We were drinking champagne,' the woman explained, raking a hand through her thick bleached blonde hair. She looked guiltily to Sebastian. Then she lowered her head over her husband, weeping and clutching his lifeless hand.

Sebastian tried not to pass judgement as he prepared for evacuation. They were fairly close to shore. The island's nightlife was still pumping on the tourist side—he could smell the beachfront barbecue dinners from here. Maybe they'd been sailing drunk...maybe they hadn't. But it wouldn't be the first time someone had come to a 'party 'island' and got a little too complacent about the way the ocean worked.

He pulled out his phone and dialled the Blue Ray, telling Agung where they were.

'Agung's sending help to the harbour—let's get him back quickly,' he told Mila, hurrying to her side.

Mila was strapping an oxygen mask to their patient's head, being careful not to move him any more than was necessary. He was still out cold.

The water was deep out here, rocking the boat as if it was nothing but a fragile toy. With both engines off it was enough to make anyone feel seasick. Maybe that was why Mila looked so ghostly pale.

'Tell him we have a suspected pulmonary contusion, broken nose, and I'm pretty sure a shattered left eye socket,' she said.

He relayed the message, then hung up. He fought the urge to ask if she was OK. Of course she was OK. She was being her usual professional self. But he knew she probably hadn't been involved in an emergency at sea before—she'd been stationed in the desert, after all.

Sebastian had seen a couple of deaths at sea caused by booms. If they didn't sweep people overboard, their lines were trip hazards. In this case he could already agree with Mila. The boom's swinging power had broken this man's nose…at least.

Mila's heart didn't stop its mad pounding the whole time they were transporting their patient to shore.

John's wife, Janet, continued to grip her arm as John was loaded onto a stretcher bound for the clinic. She was seemingly in shock and unable to speak. The petite blonde in her mid-forties wore more dramatic jewellery than Mila had ever seen: bangles, beaded necklaces, earrings shaped like mermaids holding coconuts.

And her wedding ring was just as flashy, Mila noted—a huge sparkling jewel on a silver band. She focused on that as she took her hand in reassurance.

In spite of her being aware of her bare feet sinking into the wet sand, and all the stars and flashlights and equipment beeping around John, Mila felt only half there. First the kiss. Then all that blood on the deck. The swerving of the boat…the way it had all happened so suddenly. Despite her training, it had totally thrown her.

'X-rays show his nose is broken,' Agung confirmed ruefully, soon after they'd arrived at Blue Ray and were all standing in the critical care unit, observing the monitor. Mr Griffiths was on breathing support, but the monitor kept blinking on and off. It was only when Sebastian slammed a hand to the side that the screen stayed lit.

'Damn thing… Don't worry—the new one's been ordered.'

'He's also fractured several bones in his left eye socket,' Agung said. 'Good spot, Dr Ricci.'

Mila caught Sebastian's look of admiration and approval. No doubt they were all impressed with her keen eye, but she wasn't here for compliments. She'd seen worse—much worse. She was trained to see the detail in the fall-out.

If anything, she was embarrassed and annoyed that Sebastian had spotted her ashen face and the way she'd stalled back there, after seeing all that blood. He hadn't asked if she was OK in front of those people, but he'd been about to—she'd seen it in his eyes.

Maybe they should have tried to call out a warning. Maybe this could have been prevented if they hadn't been so lost in kissing each other like that.

She dug her fingernails fiercely into her palms, internalising her self-loathing. Janet Griffiths was looking to her to be strong, and John would need her soon.

'I'm scheduling him for surgery right after the physician's done with the realignment.' Sebastian cut into her thoughts. 'Emergency reconstruction. We'll get him over to the MAC when he's stable. I'll go now.'

'What can I do?' she asked.

Sebastian ushered her into the corner behind the door. His brown eyes were flecked with concern. 'Stay with Mrs Griffiths till her daughter arrives, if you don't mind. Or Nurse Viv starts her shift soon...'

'Yes, of course. I'll stay here till then.'

A volunteer was helping the distraught Janet Griffiths, now wearing a borrowed jacket, over to a seat in the waiting area.

Sebastian lowered his voice, leaning in to Mila. His breath on her ear made her want to reach for him, but she crossed her arms over her chest instead.

'Mila, I'm so sorry.'

'Don't say it, Sebastian.'

He urged her further behind the door, so no one would see or hear. 'Did that freak you out back there?'

'Sebastian, I kissed you too...'

'I meant the boat, the accident—not our kiss...'

'This is my job. I'm used to it.'

His brow furrowed. 'You turned completely white, Mila.'

She looked at her feet, still sandy in her shoes. Guilt raged through her like a fire. It was Annabel's accident all over again. She hadn't been paying attention to her surroundings and she'd been caught totally off-guard. She'd promised herself that would never happen again, and it just had. She'd also promised herself that she wouldn't let her attraction to Sebastian get the better of her.

'It's not me you should be worried about,' she managed.

'John Griffiths will be fine, Mila. You probably saved his life.'

She folded her arms tighter, building a wall, but she knew it was too late for that. She'd kissed him first. The resulting guilt and tension were unbearable, but she wasn't having this conversation here.

'We'll talk later,' Sebastian told her, as Agung called him away.

And it took every ounce of her strength to resume normality for poor Janet Griffiths.

CHAPTER EIGHT

IT WAS FIVE days since their kiss. Sebastian had been trying to get her alone outside of the MAC for dinner, a drink, a dive…but Mila had apparently been trying even harder to ensure they were surrounded by people at all times. She was avoiding him—he knew it. He had crossed a line with that kiss—they both had—and Mila probably felt that being intimate with him…her employer…had been some kind of immoral move.

Or was it something else?

He couldn't think why else she would be acting this way. Maybe it *was* less than ideal to be making out with his employee on a fishing boat after dining with his friends, but so what? He couldn't get her out of his mind.

Today, though, she couldn't avoid him.

'Morning,' he said, as she approached him on the outside terrace of the MAC.

'Morning, Dr Becker.'

She looked around her, pulling her sunglasses down over her eyes. Several patients were looking their way from the breakfast tables and pretending not to. One of them was Hugo O'Shea.

'Ready to set sail to the mainland?' he asked, starting down the steps.

She followed him, light on her feet in brown sandals and a blue striped dress. 'This won't take all day, will it?'

'Not all day, no. I do believe the staff have transported John and Janet Griffiths to the harbour already, with their luggage. They'll meet us at the boat.'

Sebastian had been in the reception area last night when Mila had promised Mrs Griffiths that she would accompany the couple back to the mainland. It was time for them to leave the island, after their ill-fated vacation, and fly home from Bali, but the couple were understandably a little apprehensive about making the crossing after what had happened on the catamaran. Mila had offered to go with them, for company.

He knew Mila probably wanted some time off the island without him. But he'd offered to go with them. In fact he'd told them, he'd do better than that. He would take them all on the MAC's private boat. He had two new monitors to collect from Bali, anyway, along with a few other chores to get done.

Mila had gone quiet when he'd offered, as if she was annoyed. But *he* was annoyed by her refusal to be alone with him—that was what Klara had done before she'd left him. She'd just flat-out refused to talk. Nothing put him more on edge than when people refused to discuss their problems like adults.

It wasn't all his fault, though, this thing with Mila. He'd told her on the boat that he would stay away from her if she wanted him to, but she had kissed him first. Whatever might have changed between them since then, they definitely needed to talk about it.

'Can I ask you a quick question, Dr Becker?'

Hugo O'Shea appeared in front of them suddenly, blocking their exit at the gates. His hair and beard were dyed bright blue again, bluer than ever before. Where on earth had he got that hair dye on an island this size? Sebastian thought, half amused. He must have brought it with him.

'Is everything OK?' Sebastian asked, trying to inch around him.

'You mean with this?' Hugo gestured to his newly enhanced groin area and grinned. 'Couldn't be better, This is about something else. I have a commission, Dr Becker, to write an exclusive story on you and your work here on the island. What drove you from Chicago? What brought you here?' His eyes fell on Mila. 'What keeps you here?'

Mila crossed her arms. Sebastian couldn't read her eyes behind her sunglasses, but her body language suggested she would rather be anywhere than here, with them.

'I have the agreement right here for you to read and sign.' Hugo pulled a piece of paper from the pocket of his shorts and thrust it at Sebastian. 'It's time we got moving. It's great publicity for the MAC. We can do the interview wherever you like. On a boat at sunset, maybe—it doesn't matter. This is your side of the story for *USA World*. It's a big magazine, Dr Becker…think about it. Your chance to explain all about Klara, your ex…'

'I know who Klara is, thank you,' he snapped. 'And my answer is no.' Sebastian folded the paper in one hand against his thigh, then squeezed his fist around it, scrunching it up. 'Now, if you'll excuse us, we have to go.'

'Are you sure you won't just—?'

'No. And I'd like to remind you about the NDA you signed before coming here, Mr O'Shea.'

He gave Hugo the mangled piece of paper, ignoring his look of shock and horror, then put a hand to Mila's back and walked them quickly up the path, to where a horse and cart were waiting to take them to the harbour.

* * *

Bali was crazy, loud, and a shock to her senses after weeks on the much quieter Gili Indah. Mila wasn't used to seeing cars or motorbikes any more. Hordes of tourists were crowding the jetty or sitting with their bags on the beach, drinking beers, waiting for their transfers. Catamarans and boats bobbed everywhere, but Sebastian's yacht was catching the most attention.

Bright white and gleaming, with three bedrooms and an indoor lounge bigger than her last apartment, it was clearly the prize of a very rich man. She hadn't said so on the journey over here—she'd chatted to Janet most of the way, and besides he'd seemed distant, probably because of Hugo O'Shea—but she'd felt like a VIP the whole time, reclining in a leather couch while the ocean sped by through the windows.

Everything Sebastian surrounded himself with on the island was modest, and gave no hint of the billionaire lifestyle he probably enjoyed everywhere else. This was like seeing a new side of him—a taster of his old life, maybe. She couldn't help wonder what his place in Chicago was like.

'Do you think we'll make it to the hospital before the rain starts?' Janet asked now, casting her eyes to the heavy, grey sky.

Mila had only just noticed the change. The port was heaving and John was being wheeled towards the waiting ambulance, Sebastian and a paramedic at his side.

'You'll be fine,' Mila told her. 'You're in good hands, and John is making a great recovery. The hospital will arrange for your hotel and airport transfers once they've given him the final go-ahead to fly tomorrow.'

'I can't thank you enough for everything you've done.' Janet took her hands in hers and her bangles jingled on her arms as she squeezed them. 'I know I've said this a hundred times, Dr Ricci. But we might have lost him if it wasn't for you.'

Mila extended a warm smile. 'Well, I'm happy we were there,' she replied.

What else could she say? She was more than happy to have been able to help John Griffiths, of course, in spite of the resulting situation she had put herself in with Sebastian.

Her dreams had changed since then. Annabel was in them all—sometimes alive and dancing, sometimes exactly as she had been when Mila had found her in the car—and sometimes it was herself in the car, Annabel and Sebastian were trying to get *her* out.

It had sent her spiralling into a world of confusion. She'd been hoping for a day to herself over here, to hire a driver and see some of Bali, do some much-needed thinking, but Sebastian had encroached on her plans by coming, too.

'So, forgive me…but I can't not ask you before we go. You and Dr Becker *are* an item, am I right?'

Janet's green eyes flooded with mischief suddenly and Mila realised she'd been gazing absently in Sebastian's direction. He was talking on his phone now, an umbrella tucked under one arm.

She shifted her bag awkwardly onto the other shoulder. 'Not exactly.'

Janet obviously didn't believe her. What the hell?, Mila thought. They were leaving anyway.

She scrunched up her nose. 'There is…something there,' she admitted. 'But it's complicated. And I'm not here for long.'

'Then you'd better get a move on! I met my John at work, by the way. He was a new, arrogant theatre director—I was a new, pushy production manager. We argued like crazy— Shakespearean proportions—till we realised it was actually love and not hate we felt for each other. He proposed on the stage in front of our audience. Over a thousand people saw me cry.'

She held up her big sparkly ring and Mila felt a rush of longing—not for the ring, but for the deep, mutual love Janet had found. It was the kind of love Sebastian had once felt for Klara, she thought, surprising herself with her envy of a woman she had never met.

Janet put a hand to her arm. 'I saw you two out on that dive boat, before the accident. And I've seen the way he looks at you.' Her seashell earrings swung like pendulums and jingled along with her bangles as she leaned in to speak in her ear. 'Everyone adored him on that show—his brother Jared, too. Quite the handsome partnership. They wrote some terrible things about him when he left…something about his ex-girlfriend…'

'I never watched it.'

Janet looked shocked. 'OK. Well, it was years ago, anyway,' she said flippantly. 'And who knows? Maybe all that had to happen just so he could find his way to *you*.' She flattened a hand to her heart dramatically, then shook her head, smiling. 'Sorry…ever the romantic, me!'

Sebastian was heading towards them through the crowds, head down, baseball hat on, still talking on his phone. A couple of people were trying to take photos without him knowing. Women in particular were staring at him.

Mila realised she had probably underestimated the impact his presence on the show had made, despite him leaving more than three years ago, and how popular it had really been and still was. No one paid him this much attention on the island.

'You're all set Mrs Griffiths.' Sebastian slid the phone into his top pocket, then adjusted his hat on his head. 'We're going to leave you in the ambulance crew's capable hands. Dr Ricci and I have an appointment.'

'Limitations live only in our minds—don't forget that,' Janet quoted conspiratorially in her ear, before she gave Mila a huge hug and left.

Instantly the busy harbour seemed to close in. It was just Mila and Sebastian and the thunder starting to rumble on the horizon.

'Are you ready?'

Mila was still distracted by Janet's words. 'What for? Isn't someone delivering a patient monitor for us to take back later?'

'The plan just changed—that was them on the phone. They can't deliver it for a couple more hours. Bali traffic—you know the deal. There's something I need to do. If you decide to come with me it'll give you a chance to see some of Bali with a driver I trust.' He paused. 'Unless you'd prefer to go your own way and meet up later? It's up to you.'

She deserved the disparaging tone in his voice—she knew she did. She also knew they probably needed to talk about what had happened. And Annabel. She couldn't avoid discussing *that* with him any longer.

Sebastian was inching towards the road, where a shiny chauffeur-driven car with blacked-out windows was pulling up in the dust. He looked as though he was exiting the scene whether she went with him or not.

CHAPTER NINE

SEBASTIAN PULLED ON the crisp white shirt, sleeve by sleeve, and buttoned it up in front of the mirror. He studied his jawline in the light, frowning at his reflection. He should have shaved, but it would have to do. He could use a haircut, too.

'How do I look?' he asked, sweeping the curtain aside dramatically and squaring his shoulders in the tailor-made suit. 'Do you think anyone would guess I spend half my life in scrubs and the other half in a wetsuit?'

Mila stood up from the plush white seat. She put the book of designs down on the table, next to a dish of frangipanis. Her eyes appraised the navy blue pinstripe jacket and he realised, feeling some small element of doubt over his own sanity, that even though he knew he looked good he was still seeking her approval.

She trailed her gaze up his body, from shoes to shirt collar, not giving anything away. 'What's the occasion?' she asked.

'My mother's seventieth birthday party. I have to go back to Chicago.'

He hadn't asked her to accompany him, of course. Maybe he would have done if she hadn't spent most of the last week trying to avoid him.

She raised her eyebrows. 'I recall you mentioning

something about that. When is that? Before or after I leave the island?'

'I don't think we've talked about your exact leaving dates yet, have we?' he said evasively.

Mila seemed closed off—distracted, even—so now was clearly not the time to discuss it. She was glancing at the rain outside, and the palms lashing at the tailor's windows. There was a storm on the way, all right. It was only supposed to be a quick downpour, but...

'This is definitely getting worse,' she announced, right as his cell phone buzzed again.

It was the delivery guy, delaying the monitor's arrival yet again.

'They might not get it to us till the morning now,' he told her with a frown.

Mila looked like a deer who wanted nothing more than to run away from his headlights. 'What will we do till then?'

'You stay here. I make something for you,' the tailor cut in. 'Something beautiful. I think blue is your colour!'

Mila turned, holding up her hand. 'Oh, no, that's OK. I don't have anything to...'

'It not take long.'

Sebastian watched Mila in the mirror as Anya, his favourite tailor, bustled off to the storeroom. She came back three seconds later with armfuls of fabric. Before Mila could dissuade her, the tailor was pulling out a tape measure, holding her arms out one by one, whirring around her in her patterned sarong. Then Anya got to her knees and measured each leg, then her hips, waist and bust—quickly, efficiently, enthusiastically.

'You look at designs. I get you samples!'

'Get something made. We can have someone bring it over to the island later,' he told Mila.

He'd been coming here for years, but he'd never brought a woman with him. No wonder they were treating her like royalty.

She shook her head though, resolute. 'No, really… I don't need anything, Sebastian.'

He cocked an eyebrow at her, pulling the shirt off and reaching for another one. This was pale pink. He pulled it on with the curtain still open. He wasn't afraid to wear pink.

He caught Mila in the mirror, biting her lip, watching him dress. 'Have I met the one woman in the world who *doesn't* want a dress made for her?'

'I've never had a dress made for me before, if I'm honest.'

The tailor seemed to notice the way she was covering her arms. 'This one?' She jabbed a finger to a long-sleeved floaty dress in the design book.

Mila let out a defeated sigh. 'OK, fine…yes. I like the ones with long sleeves, actually.'

'Please make whatever dress she wants, Anya. She will find an occasion to wear it.'

Mila looked perplexed. 'Why are you being so nice to me after…?'

'I have no idea,' he grunted. 'Maybe because you're driving me crazy.'

He swiped the curtain closed before she could respond. Anya shuffled quietly into the back room, and he heard Mila stepping closer to his curtain.

She exhaled deeply. 'Look, Sebastian, I'm sorry, OK?'

His irritation faded when he heard the anguish in her voice.

'I'm sorry I've been shutting you out after what happened. You have every right to be annoyed with me. And I know it must be driving you crazy, because you did nothing wrong. I kissed *you* first. It's just…we have to work together, so…'

He stayed quiet. He sat down on the stool in the changing room, put his head in his hands for a moment. This was what he'd wanted to hear—kind of. But he still needed answers she hadn't yet supplied him with.

He couldn't talk with her here. The tailor was tottering in again already.

'I think we should go my place—it's not so far from here,' he said eventually. 'We can ride this storm out there.' He started unbuttoning the pink shirt and pulling off the dress trousers. 'It's not safe on the yacht right now.'

'You have a place close by?' Mila was standing just behind the curtain. Her silhouette looked stock-still through the fabric.

'He has many house,' the store manager whispered. 'Dr Becker very rich. You very lucky lady. You want dress? I send to island when ready.'

'Yes, she wants the dress—thank you, Anya. And please keep her measurements on file.' He stepped from the changing room, holding his new garments. 'Who knows? We might be needing you again.' He took out his wallet.

'What are you doing? Sebastian, really, I don't need…'

'Just let me do this for you, Mila. You deserve it. We'll take all these, please, Anya—excellent fit as usual. You really do have skills like no other.'

He went about paying for everything and then, holding the store door open for Mila, reached for the umbrella he'd left in the corner and led them back outside into the storm.

'Which is your place?'

Mila was flummoxed. The rain was coming down in thick, hard slashes, turning the hem of her blue-striped dress an even darker blue and whipping up the ocean of palm trees around them. They had hardly seen anything of Bali, even though he'd promised—not that it was Sebastian's fault. The rain had concealed everything through the car windows.

'We need to take the funicular railway up to the top.'

He held the umbrella over her, to protect her as far as possible from the ever-imposing rain, and snaked an arm around her waist so they could both take shelter. The gesture had her tensing slightly, even though she liked it.

'Of *course* you would have the villa on top of the mountain,' she said out loud.

He smiled, walking them towards the small red carriage on a track. It looked like the start of a rollercoaster, and promised a rickety journey up through the steep green terrain. They were right at the bottom level of some kind of terraced valley. Each level seemed to house a different villa.

'Is it safe?' Mila had travelled in scarier conditions in her time, but she wasn't too thrilled about taking a wobbly funicular in a storm.

'It's perfectly safe. I would never take you anywhere that wasn't safe.'

Sebastian tightened his arm around her protectively and at the waiting carriage flipped the latch, urging her inside ahead of him. Leaves thrashed the Perspex windows, jostling them along with the wind as he slammed the door behind them and dropped to the seat beside her. He pushed a hand through his wet hair. Droplets landed on her arm.

'Maybe someone called the witch doctor,' he said.

'Witch doctor?'

'Practitioners of the dark arts, if you believe in that kind of thing. They're called *dukuns* in Indonesia, and they can control the weather. Amongst other things.'

Mila felt far away from everything and everyone as Sebastian pressed a big red button and the carriage shuddered into motion. They'd already headed past smoky mountains, mystic grey temples covered in carvings, and endless green pastures to get here. He'd told her all about it, even though she hadn't really been able to see any of it though the rain.

They weren't far from the yacht, but now, with the jungle all around them, it felt remote and exclusive.

They were sitting so close on the tiny seat she could make out each of the thick black hairs along his jawline, dotted with grey. She liked it when he didn't shave for a while.

'People hire the *dukuns* to make it rain. And to stop it raining,' he said.

His shoulder brushed hers near the strap of her dress, giving her goosebumps.

'But I hope they don't make it stop just yet,' he went on. 'I think we need to talk about what happened, don't you?'

'I know,' she relented.

His left arm was stretched across the back of the seat behind her. He smelled like a mixture of surgery, incense, musky soap and rain.

A gust of wind rocked the carriage and her hand found his knee. Behind his head the lush green valley stretched for miles under a blackened sky. The thought of the carriage tumbling down into the valley with both of them in it at the whim of a Balinese witch doctor flashed briefly through her mind.

Annabel was there too, suddenly, in the carriage with them—just like she'd been on the boat before Mila had given in to their overwhelming chemistry and kissed him. It felt too small.

'I bet Hugo O'Shea would love a photo of us right now, in here together,' she tested, trying to fill the silence.

Sebastian shook his head, releasing her fingers. A bolt

of lightning lit the sky, followed by more thunder. 'Can you believe that guy?' he asked.

'Why is he still on the island?'

'He says he's been working remotely while he recovers, but now I know he really wants a damn story. He's just been hanging about, waiting for the right time to ask.'

'Why don't you just talk to him? Tell him what you want him to print? You can have the final say over it, surely?'

'I don't talk to the media,' he said bluntly. 'Neither should you.'

'I'm not Klara,' she reminded him, before she could think about it. Janet had clearly got to her, talking about Sebastian's ex.

The carriage had stopped on the top level. Sebastian was quiet.

'Sorry,' she said. 'I know you despise the media because of what happened to Klara. But publicity is not *all* bad, is it? You're doing good things for the island, and people should know about it.'

'Maybe it's none of their business.'

He flung open the door and stepped purposefully from the carriage, opening the umbrella over her as she followed. The subject was clearly closed.

Through the rain she made out the villa. It was smaller than she'd pictured, but undeniably exclusive. A Balinese statue of a lion guarded the carved wooden door. An infinity pool appeared to melt into the jungle all around them.

She was just about to say she'd bet it was beautiful in the sunshine when a dog started to bark uncontrollably. She jumped and her bag fell into a puddle with a thud. The important envelope she'd put in it just that morning drifted straight into the swimming pool...

CHAPTER TEN

'No, no, no!' Mila leaned over and fished the envelope out. She looked visibly upset.

'Stay still.'

Sebastian stepped in front of her, making his body a shield between Mila and the growling black dog. It was nothing like Bruno, his docile rescue animal. He suspected it was more like the one who had bitten poor little Françoise. It was flattened to the floor on its belly now, baring its teeth just inches from the poolside.

Mila started shaking the water off the envelope in distress.

'Get on the porch!' he ordered as the dog started snarling again, louder than before.

Mila froze.

'We won't hurt you,' he soothed, holding his hand up to the dog and risking getting closer for a better look.

It was a bitch. She had scruffy pointed ears, thick, coarse fur in tortoiseshell swirls, and what looked like a cut on one paw.

He kept his voice low and his movements slight, crouching down in the rain under the umbrella to retrieve Mila's fallen handbag. 'I know you're just scared.'

He threw the bag towards Mil on the porch. The dog kept on snarling but didn't move.

'She might have been hit by a car on the road at the top and got lost trying to get down. She might have been attacked by another dog. We should take her inside,' he said.

Mila had pulled something from her bag. She was holding it in the palm of her hand, clenching and unclenching her fist over it.

He tossed her the key. 'Open the door. There'll be treats on the table—bring me something to give her.'

He watched her shake off her shoes, slide the glass door open and enter the apartment barefoot as he braved putting his fingers closer to the dog's nose.

'We won't hurt you,' he said softly.

Mila reappeared with some of the tiny ginger biscuits the housekeeper always left him. 'These?'

'Those will do.'

He unwrapped one quickly and held it out on his palm. The dog sniffed his hand tentatively before taking the biscuit. Her temperament softened instantly. She seemed to have decided to trust them, thankfully.

'Are you hungry, girl? No collar…no obvious owner.'

Sebastian shook his head. It broke his heart that so many animals were abandoned and ignored. He gave her another treat and was rewarded with a lick from her wet pink tongue.

'We should get you cleaned up. Want to come in with me?'

'Is she OK?' Mila flattened her back to the wall, holding the wet envelope to her chest as he carried the dog past her on the way to the bathroom.

'It's not as bad as I thought—just a flesh wound, I think.'

The white marble floor would be good enough for now. He pulled towels from the top drawer of the wicker bathroom storage unit and the first aid kit from the bottom one.

'Help me lay these down. We can clean up the cut, give

her a couple of stitches. If it's not looking better by morning we'll take her to a vet.'

Her threw her some towels and she crouched beside him. 'Morning? We'll be here till morning, now?'

'We definitely can't take the yacht back in this weather.'

'I know, but...'

'If you want to stay in another villa I'll give you the keys.'

'That's not what I meant...' She paused. 'How many of the villas do you *own*?'

'All of them. But this is the only one that's furnished beyond the basics right now.'

Mila looked stunned.

'What is that you've got there?' He gestured to the other object she was holding in her hand.

She unclenched her palm reluctantly and he felt his eyebrows shoot to his damp hairline.

'You carried that in your bag this whole time?' It was the wooden dog charm that Francoise had given her at the dive shop.

Mila shrugged. 'She did say it was for protection. It didn't help my bag, though, did it?'

'Sorry... I guess it still worked a little, though. The dog seems OK now.'

The dog's paw must be sore, and she'd likely been scared outside in the storm, but otherwise she really did seem OK. She wasn't barking or growling any more, and she seemed to be appreciative of their help. The licks were now coming thick and fast.

It took them about twenty minutes to stitch and bandage her paw. Then they showered in different bathrooms and changed their clothes. Luckily they'd brought more, in case they wound up swimming somewhere.

The rain was still hammering the pool when Mila met

him in the open-plan kitchen. He could see it through the floor-to-ceiling windows. He pulled out cold soda and glasses.

'This place is beautiful,' she told him in genuine admiration. 'I love the walls.'

'Thank you. I had an Indonesian designer do those.' He pointed to his favourite mandala feature wall, and then the carved timber hanging plaques. 'And that rug happens to be the softest rug on earth. Try it.'

Mila walked onto the plush cream rug in her bare feet and moaned in pleasure. He chuckled under his breath.

Much like his other place, he had filled the place with trinkets to make it feel more like a home: wooden and bamboo bowls and baskets, brass and gold utensils, textiles in fabulous colours, gorgeous cushions, glass pineapples…

'What will you do with the other villas?' she asked. 'I'm guessing this is the place you talked about over dinner that night with Wayan and Ketut?'

He nodded, then handed her a glass fizzing with soda. 'I'm hoping Jared will get over here at some point soon. Like I said, this extension of the institute will be more like a health and wellness centre for convalescing trauma patients and people who can't afford the luxury of the MAC. There's a huge building down at the base of the mountain, before you get to the funicular. You wouldn't really have seen it in the rain, I guess. These villas will be the guest quarters. If this really is the last season of the show Jared should have more time, so…'

'They're wrapping up the show for good?'

Mila looked at him in surprise. He hadn't told her this, or anyone for that matter, because he didn't really believe it himself.

'He has said it before and it hasn't happened,' he explained. 'I guess I'll find out more in person when I go home.'

'You didn't say when you were going back to Chicago?'

'I think it's around the time your official term ends at the MAC,' he replied, evading the question again.

Truthfully, he knew it was exactly the same time as her leaving date. He'd tell her soon, but he couldn't bring himself to think about her leaving yet… Or going to Chicago alone and coming back to find her gone.

He poured some dried fruit snacks into a bowl. The housekeeper always kept provisions here.

Their canine patient barked in the bathroom and Mila flinched. 'Is she OK in there?'

'She's just reminding us she's there. You really don't spend much time around dogs, huh?'

'Not as much as you,' she admitted. 'I don't mind them, but I don't particularly trust them as a species. We found a crazy dog once at a military outpost—bit half of my colleague's face off. We were only trying to help it. Annabel got bitten by a dog once, too. When we were kids in Ibiza.' She paused, then added, 'I felt her pain when happened.'

'Physically?'

Mila followed him to the couch, putting her wet envelope down on the table to dry. 'Yes. On my ankle. It felt like I'd got bitten myself. So strange… Personally I try not to have a thing against dogs. We must treat the insurgents, too, am I right?' She gave a wry smile.

Sebastian couldn't help laughing. 'Insurgents?'

'One time a bomb went off, northeast of our base in Helmand. We found two dead—a British soldier and an Afghan interpreter—and two injured soldiers—a Brit and an Afghan. We treated them both, side by side. If local nationals and insurgents were injured as a result of our conflict they were always entitled to a medevac.'

'That must have been…' He blew a sound out through his lips and shrugged apologetically.

'It was the biggest source of conflict out there for some people. But in my eyes if someone is wounded I have to help them—regardless of who they are. There's no first-come-first-served. If someone's dying and I can help stop that happening I'm going to do it. Wouldn't you?'

He stared at her. What else had she seen out there? 'Yes, I would. Of course.'

'I know you would—actually, you're putting Ketut and Wayan first, whenever they need you, even if they're not paying customers.' She paused. 'I wish I was going to be here to see the baby.'

'We don't know for certain that you won't be—babies have a habit of coming when they want to, don't forget.'

Mila shifted awkwardly against the frangipani-printed cushions, sipping on her soda. It was strange having her here in this villa. She hadn't even stepped foot inside his place on the island, and he suddenly regretted never asking her there. He'd been concerned someone might see—someone like Hugo O'Shea—but people were always going to talk anyway. And he was always going to be slightly paranoid. It was just the residual effects of his past life in the spotlight.

He wanted to ask if she really had to leave at the end of her term, but he knew people like Mila didn't stick around in one place too long. She had done too much, seen too much of the world, to want to be cooped up on an island for ever…hiding away with him.

'Is that a twin thing?' he ventured now. 'Feeling each other's pain?'

She curled her legs up on the couch. 'It *was* a twin thing—with us, anyway. I always felt it. Whenever she had a headache, I'd always get one, too. It was the strangest thing…that connection. Sometimes when I get headaches now I still think it might be hers I'm feeling, but then I remember it can't be. The pain is all mine.'

'Talk to me about her,' he said, drawing his legs up on the leather couch opposite hers.

'I'll do one better—I'll show you,' she said. 'If it's not ruined.'

'If what isn't ruined?'

Mila reached for the wet envelope, pulling out a photograph that was damp around the edges. She handed it to him.

'You and Annabel,' he stated.

It shouldn't have surprised him, seeing them both together in the photo, but he found himself staring at it, battling a sudden surge of emotion. He couldn't have told them apart, side by side.

'That was the Christmas we got each other the exact same silly scarf without knowing,' she explained.

The twins were grinning in front of an orange sofa in a cosy living room, both wearing a yellow scarf with the words *Crime Scene* knitted into it. Seeing this image now of them both together made her plight and her grief all the more real.

'You brought this with you?' he asked.

'My mother sent me a package from home recently, and this was in it. We shared a bedroom till we were eighteen, and there are still lots of old photos there in boxes. Mum keeps hinting that I should go home and sort it all out with her…throw some things away. I know I have to do it eventually.'

'I can't even imagine how tough that would be…to have to do that for your twin,' he said, as she took the photo back. 'But have you considered that it also might help?'

She stared at the photo, eyes narrowed. 'Maybe. I still see her everywhere. I dream about her all the time.' She paused then, and took a deep breath. 'Sebastian…what happened when Annabel was here? The two of you…what did you do?'

Mila's words took him completely by surprise. Her eyes were closed now, as if she couldn't even face what he might say.

'I need to know, Sebastian. I should have asked you sooner, but I like you, so I couldn't—no, I didn't *want* to hear it. But I really need to know. Did you kiss her, like we…?' She scrunched up her face, as though the very thought caused her physical pain. 'Did you sleep together?'

'No!'

He put his drink down, took hers away, too. Shuffling up close, he reached a hand to her face. She turned into his palm, exhaling in relief.

'Mila, I thought you already knew that nothing happened with me and Annabel?'

'Nothing at all?'

'No—nothing! Maybe a little mild flirting, but it didn't mean anything to either of us. She was just a typical tourist here—to me anyway. She was drinking and dancing and killing it at karaoke. "Total Eclipse of the Heart" never sounded so adorably terrible as she made it sound. She even missed a snorkelling trip because she couldn't get out of bed one morning. Is that what you wanted to know? Mila, she was just like you—but actually nothing like you at all.'

Mila swiped at her eyes, let out a laugh. 'That sounds like Annabel.'

He put his forehead to hers, both hands to her face. His mind was reeling now. Was this why she'd been distant ever since they'd kissed? Not because she was afraid of putting their working relationship in jeopardy, but because she thought he'd already been intimate with her sister?

'God, Mila, I wish you hadn't carried all this around inside you. You should have talked to me sooner.'

Mila reached for him at the same time as he gathered her into his arms. Their mouths collided, and then all he could do was kiss her till they were stumbling their way together to the bedroom.

Mila let him worship her body and revelled in worshipping his. How could she *not* want to be with this man when he treated her as if she was the only woman he'd ever wanted? It was easy to forget everything, even the horrors she'd seen that kept her up most nights, when they were buried in each other.

They found their way together so easily, so perfectly, time after time on the soft satin sheets of his carved wooden bed—and, when sleep finally came for her, for the first time in a long time Mila had no dreams about Annabel, or the accident, or Afghanistan. None at all.

CHAPTER ELEVEN

THE WOMAN HAVING the mastopexy had a small tattoo of a star on her left shoulder. It seemed to shine under the OR lights as Mila guided her to the wall, where she put her into position on her feet.

'We need you standing up for the markings,' she said. 'I hope you're not feeling too nervous, Mrs Pilkington-Blythe?'

Their patient, a well-to-do forty-four-year-old interior decorator and perfume designer from the UK, didn't look as if she was nervous at all. In fact she looked excited.

'Thank you, Dr Ricci, but it's not exactly a nerve-racking thing to get your boobs out once you've had kids, is it?'

Mila took the marker from Sebastian. 'I suppose not.'

'Mine used to be pert—really up here.' Madison Pilkington-Blythe heaved her breasts upwards for a moment towards her chin, creating a cleavage. 'I miss that,' she moaned.

Sebastian's face was the picture of professionalism as he tapped away at the new touchscreen monitor. It was two weeks now since they'd brought two new monitors back on the yacht—one for the MAC and one for the Blue Ray Clinic. They had almost forgotten to pick them up. They had been more than a little preoccupied the morning after the storm...

It still felt like yesterday that they'd spent hours making

love in every corner of that bedroom in Bali…right up until the dog had jumped on the bed the next morning, wondering what all the noise was about.

The rain had finally stopped and they'd been late to the harbour. There had probably been a thousand more responsibilities she'd ignored, but something big had changed between them. A new lightness had surrounded her. She'd let this new level of intimacy with a man sweep her away with its depth and passion.

Madison Pilkington-Blythe didn't know any of this, of course. Their patient had just been flown in to the island on a private helicopter. But Mila had made love to Sebastian that very morning in the shower at the dive school, and again back at his house before coming in to do this procedure. Making love to him took her to a different place.

'You'll know what breastfeeding does to your nipples too?' Mrs Pilkington-Blythe was still talking. 'Unless you were one of the lucky ones.'

'I wouldn't know about breastfeeding myself—only from what I see in my patients,' Mila returned absently, starting the marking.

'You don't have children?'

'Not me.'

'I suppose it must be hard meeting someone when you live all the way out here…' Mrs Pilkington-Blythe sounded almost sympathetic. 'But don't you worry, Doctor, you've got time. Don't take too long, though—the later you leave it, the harder it is to get your figure back. Trust me—I know. That's why I'm here.'

'Can I interest you in any particular kind of music?' Sebastian cut in—probably to save her.

On this occasion Mila was grateful. She knew he was listening and the topic put her slightly on edge, because she knew Sebastian wanted kids while she…she couldn't think of anything more terrifying.

'What do you two usually like to listen to?' Mrs Pilkington-Blythe asked.

'We play all kinds of different things in here,' he answered, turning to the old gramophone she knew he'd kept from his father's surgery. 'Dr Ricci has some pretty good moves.' His eyes flicked to hers mischievously and Mila turned her back before her glowing cheeks gave her away.

They worked to the sound of Beethoven, raising their patient's breasts and leaving no hint of the children they'd helped to feed and nourish.

What would it be like, being responsible for someone? A tiny, helpless human? A child who looked a little like her and a little like Sebastian… A child who needed her for food and advice and survival.

It would be…*beautiful*, she thought.

Then Annabel flashed into her head again. Annabel who'd also needed her for survival and who'd died because she hadn't got to her in time.

She had no right even imagining herself with Sebastian's baby, she scolded herself. Not only was she getting too far ahead of herself, but she wasn't fit to be a mother—she hadn't even been able to take care of her sister.

'What's on your mind?' Sebastian asked her, looking at her in mild concern.

'Nothing,' she lied.

'Sebastian? It's me.'

'I know it's you, Jared. I have your number saved in my phone. How's it going?'

He and Mila were on a rare two-hour break from work, and were spending it at his place. He was inside, mixing jasmine tea with ice in a blender, and Mila was outside wearing a red bikini under a see-through sarong. He hadn't anticipated being interrupted.

'I'm calling to find out how you're doing with this photo.'

'Photo? What do you mean?'

Outside, Mila was running the length of the yard with Bruno and the dog they'd rescued on her heels. She'd named her Stormy.

He lowered his voice and crossed to the dish rack for glasses. 'What photo?'

'Social media, bro. Don't you even follow your own hashtags?'

'I try not to.'

'Well, I hate to be the one to break it to you, but some so-called journalist—Hugo O'Shea—has posted a photo of you and some lady. Interesting caption… And you look pretty damn cosy on board your yacht with this… Mila Ricci. Is she the woman you were telling me about before?'

Sebastian saw red. If he hadn't just given Hugo O'Shea a new penis, he'd be very inclined to chop it off…not that he'd say that out loud.

'Yes, that's her,' he said through gritted teeth. 'How the hell did he get photos of us on the boat? He was at the MAC—he can't have known where we were…'

He trailed off and ran the order of events through his head. Hugo had stopped him on the way to the harbour to ask for that interview. He could have asked around, found out where they were going, when they were due back with the new monitors. He could easily have lined up a photographer.

'I can't believe that guy!'

Jared let out a snort. 'Hey, chill… I was going to say you look cute together. You told me she was "different", and you said you liked her. She doesn't exactly look like she hates *you*, standing behind her with your arms out like you're acting out a scene from *Titanic* either. And is that a…a dog with you in the photos? What were you *doing*?'

Sebastian clenched his jaw. He hadn't exactly been mimicking the *Titanic* movie. When the dog had jumped up behind them on the bow of the yacht he'd been trying to maintain balance on a particularly bumpy wave at the request of their skipper.

He closed his eyes, with his back to the countertop. 'What was the caption?'

'Billionaire Doc Re-enacts Titanic with Mystery Brunette.'

'Great. That's just great.'

Jared was laughing.

Outside Mila was calling to Stormy. She loved that dog already.

'Jared, you know I can't stand this kind of thing. You know what happened before…'

'Listen, forget it—it's just one photo. It doesn't matter. Mila's leaving soon anyway, isn't she?'

Sebastian bit his tongue. 'That's not the point.'

He almost felt Jared's sigh in his ear before his brother said, 'I'm sorry about Klara, bro, you know I am. But this is one photo in over *three* years. No one cares about what happened before. You're doing great work out there. But still you refuse to talk to anyone so the media is feeding off scraps. What do you expect? You're an icon.'

Sebastian's heart was thudding at his ribs. He couldn't process it all.

'Just bring her to the party with you, will you?' Jared said.

Sebastian drummed his fingers angrily against the countertop. He had tried his best to avoid this kind of situation— he'd even put up *'No Photography'* signs around the MAC just in case anyone had ideas. But still… Was nowhere safe?

He could see Klara in his mind's eye, slumped distraught on the kitchen floor after reading that email from the parents of the kids at her school. They'd all turned against her. They'd told her she was unfit to be a teacher—when she'd loved those kids more than anything. And now Mila was about to see first-hand what it was *really* like attempting to date a world-famous surgeon.

'Sebastian? Are you bringing her?'

'I haven't asked her yet,' he snapped. 'How can I ask her *now*? The cameras will be waiting for us at the airport.'

'I think you're being way too paranoid. I went ahead and put you down for a plus-one anyway. Mom's excited to see you. I've sent you tickets for the jet—one's blank, so you can fill in her name if you decide to bring her. I'm looking forward to seeing you too, bro, it's been too long.'

Sebastian was fuming. He stood by the kitchen sink under the air-conditioning, watching Mila and Stormy through the window as Jared changed the topic.

From now on he'd have to be even more careful.

CHAPTER TWELVE

'NEARLY A MILLION likes already,' she said as she turned towards the sink and pulled at the strings of her bikini. 'That's impressive.'

'It's not impressive.'

Sebastian's jaw ticked from left to right as if he was grinding his teeth. He was half scrolling through the comments on his phone, half watching her reflection in the mirror from the bathroom doorway.

The sun was streaming in on her body through the trees overhead. At first Mila had felt self-conscious in this outdoor bathroom at Sebastian's place, but the way he worshipped her body in it had shifted her perspective somewhat.

'Those comments, though…' She was determined to lighten the situation. He had a face like a thunderstorm and they didn't have long before they had to get back to the MAC. 'They're not bad. People are just interested in what you're doing out here.'

'I could do without their interest, Mila. So could you. We shouldn't be seen together.'

She pulled the bikini top off completely, dropped it to the floor beside her. He was behind her in a second, folding his arms around her. Her body seemed to attach itself to his like a magnet, and she was shocked for a second by their reflection in the mirror. He looked for a moment as if he never wanted to let her go. Adrenaline flooded her veins.

'Sebastian. Whatever people think or say about me, I can handle myself,' she told him.

The familiar tingle of anticipation had started in her toes. The more she told herself this was just a temporary fling, that they were entirely incompatible on so many levels, the more she craved being with him.

'I don't doubt that you believe that, soldier,' he rasped in her ear.

She shuddered at his intoxicating closeness. 'I don't need you to protect me.'

'What if I need you to protect *me?*'

He was urging her bikini bottoms down now. She stepped out of them, found the button on his shorts, snapped it open, reached into the shower and flipped the lever.

Warm water gushed onto their heads as he sat her on the seat and lowered himself to his knees between her legs. It was moments like this that Mila lived for lately. She hadn't experienced this level of sexual spontaneity till now. Maybe she had just never let herself really trust anyone this much.

A dog barked.

Sebastian pulled away from her in a second, snatching up a towel. 'What was that?'

He stopped the shower, moved to wrap the towel around her shoulders, but she stood up and grabbed his wrist, taking it from his hands.

'Bruno or Stormy must have seen someone go past the gates, that's all. The gates are locked, so nobody can come in,' she said calmly, and dropped the towel again.

He was so on edge after that social media post. She couldn't appear to be affected; he would just get even more jumpy.

'It was nothing,' she promised.

Sebastian looked as if he wanted to leap over the wall, brandishing a baseball bat, but she urged him back into the shower till he stuck his hands up in surrender, groaning under her mouth and her lips.

She knew the gates were locked. And no one could get over them—he'd told her he'd made sure of that himself a long time ago.

'It's only us,' she assured him. 'No one can see us here. Trust me, Dr Becker… I'm a soldier.'

The girl was out cold. Blood had formed dark splotches on her yellow cotton T-shirt and on the hem of her bleached white shorts.

'Female patient, Zuri Lerato, twelve years old. Looks like she's fallen somehow. She was unconscious when her father found her in the hotel bathroom. There was blood on the floor and walls.'

The glucose machine beeped between Mila and Nurse Viv.

'Forty-three,' Viv reported. 'Blood pressure one-six-seven over ninety-three. Pulse one-twenty-three. O2 sat ninety-two…'

Mila put a hand to the girl's chest. This time she stirred and her eyes fluttered open. She blinked up at the ceiling fan, tried to sit up, but Mila encouraged her back down. 'Don't move,' she told her.

The girl looked as if she was lost for words—as if nothing was familiar and it scared her.

'It's OK, sweetie, you're safe,' Mila soothed, stroking her arm softly. We're all here to help you. Do you remember what happened?'

Zuri just groaned and shook her head. She still looked confused. It was worrying, to say the least. She had clearly fallen, and Mila suspected from the girl's father's account that she had hit her head on the bathroom sink and passed out. She was likely to be in shock, but Mila wanted to get this girl a bedside brain scan.

'Another blood pressure reading, please!'

By now Mila was used to having to be in ten places at once on the island, but today of all days she was finding it almost impossible to keep her mind off Annabel. And as her team took care of a dazed young Zuri she couldn't wait to give herself the all-clear and be alone.

It was the day of the anniversary. She had considered taking the day off, as she'd planned, but things were just too crazy.

Sebastian had a facial scarring consultation over on Bali for a guy who was too fragile to be moved to the island yet. He had stayed in his villa on the mainland last night, and although she'd insisted that she would rather they both continue their duties and stay busy, rather than take time off and dwell on what the day meant for her, she was itching to see him later.

They were going to his favourite diving spot off the island: a night dive just for the two of them.

He'd suggested it himself.

'I know you switch off down there too, like I do. Maybe it will help you finally feel at peace with what happened.'

Mila wasn't sure it would be possible not to think of Annabel constantly on a day like this, but she had agreed to the night dive, grateful for his compassion.

When she was finally able to discharge herself, with Zuri stable in Recovery and Nurse Viv on night watch, she realised just how much tension she had been holding in all day. Walking back to her cosy little villa in the MAC grounds she couldn't wait to be under the water. First, however, she had to call her mother.

She reclined in the hammock on her porch with a cup

of hot tea. The moon was rising beyond the palms as she dialled the familiar number.

'How are you, Mum?'

'Oh, my darling, I was hoping you would call. I'm as OK as can be expected.'

'I said I would call. I know today is hard, Mum, and I wish I was there with you.'

Mila closed her eyes to the emotions as tears blurred the trees ahead, feeling the knots start to tighten in her stomach. She'd been doing so well, keeping her cool all day around other people, but her mother's caring voice had the ability to knock the wind from her sails in a heartbeat.

'I'm just about to head out, actually,' her mother informed her.

She swiped at her eyes. 'Where are you going?'

'Just out with a...friend.'

Her mother had paused before the word 'friend' and Mila felt her eyebrows knit together. She stopped swinging the hammock, put her tea on the floor.

'He's taking me to a gallery. There's an exhibition on Tudor England and the reign of King Henry VIII—he knows I'm into that kind of thing.'

'He?' Her mother had never mentioned a male friend—at least not a man who took her to things like art exhibitions. 'Who is "he"?'

'I told you—just a friend. He's good for me, Mila. Today especially.'

Mila decided to store this new information for another day, when they could talk about it without the shadow of Annabel's death hanging over them.

'I'm glad you have company today, Mum.'

'Have you been keeping busy yourself?' her mother asked. 'With your Dr Becker?'

'He is taking me out soon, yes.'

'Does he know what happened? I mean, does he know what day it is?' Her mother's voice faltered suddenly. 'Oh, my… Sorry, Mila, I thought I had this under control.'

Mila swallowed the urge to cry, too. They'd both done well till now, trying to sound strong for each other, like they usually did.

'He knows today is the day Annabel died,' she told her mother apprehensively. 'But he still doesn't really know exactly what happened.'

'What do you mean, "exactly"?'

'He doesn't know that I failed to help her…help her get out of the car in time.'

'Oh, Mila…'

Her mother's voice was faltering now, and Mila cursed herself. She swung her legs from the hammock and paced the porch, taking in a deep lungful of sea air. She was trying to think of something happy to tell her mother, willing the calm to come back.

'We have been over this before, Mila—so many times. I won't let you blame yourself.'

'I know, but I can't help it, Mum.'

She swallowed back her tears. Sebastian was picking her up soon—she couldn't look as if she'd been crying. He was kind, and understanding, and tolerant of her intermittent bouts of PTSD, but he didn't even know how she'd got the scars on her arms. He probably assumed she'd got them in Afghanistan. Maybe he felt asking her about them might upset her—which was true.

She didn't want him to think any less of her for her failure to save Annabel—especially not now she was falling for him.

It hit her like a brick.

She was absolutely falling for him. It was much more

than a brief, casual fling to her now—she'd been missing him badly all day.

'When are you coming home, baby?' her mother asked eventually, just as Mila had known she would.

'Soon, Mum. I haven't forgotten about clearing out our old room…the rest of Annabel's stuff. It's the first thing we'll do together when I get back, I promise.'

'You're putting it off as much as I am.' Her mother sighed. 'Or maybe you have another reason not to want to come home now?'

Mila couldn't argue with that. 'You know me too well…' she muttered, casting her wet eyes to the clock through the bedroom window.

It was past eight p.m. Sebastian was supposed to have been here twenty minutes ago.

A small, fuzzy torpedo of love hurtled at her the second she was through the gates. Sebastian had given her a spare key, so she could always get in without ringing the buzzer. Usually it felt like breaking the rules, but tonight she didn't care. He wasn't answering his phone and she was starting to get worried.

'Did you miss me, huh? Did you…?'

Stormy and Bruno barked and nuzzled at her ankles as Mila took the steps up to the front porch. She put her home-made paper lantern down on the table by the hammock, careful not to let the dogs damage it in any way.

'That's for Annabel,' she told the nosy animals, ringing the doorbell. 'We're going to set it off on the water from the dive boat, in her memory. You didn't know Annabel, but you would have liked her.'

Stormy cocked her head with her tongue hanging out and Mila patted her affectionately. Sometimes it was nice not to be answered or buried in questions, just acknowledged by a living creature whose sole responsibility was to give and receive unconditional love.

The house was quiet. It seemed to be all locked up.

Frowning to herself, she peeked through the bottom window into the sitting room. The dogs jumped up at the window too, paws to the glass alongside her, probably anticipating a feed.

'Where is he? He was supposed to be back from Bali by now.'

Stormy let out three barks in quick succession. 'I wish I could understand your language.' Mila sighed, then let herself into the house. 'Sebastian!'

Nothing. There were no sounds coming from his bathroom either.

The couch looked so appealing… She was beyond tired and could almost have napped on it. Maybe he was just late coming back. She was more than ready for her night dive. She didn't want to be alone with her thoughts. She didn't want to sleep in case the dreams came back. She needed distraction.

'Did he have an emergency that I don't know about?' she asked the dogs, pouring them some kibble from the giant bag under the sink. They wolfed it down hungrily from their bowls.

She picked up the brochure on the coffee table. It was for the Becker Institute. She sank into the couch and flicked through it absently, lingering on a photo of Jared Becker in a white coat. He was handsome, like Sebastian, smiling in a trustworthy fashion with a full set of whiter-than-white American teeth.

She considered whether he was as handsome as Sebastian. Absolutely not, she decided. Sebastian had rougher edges; he looked like he lived on an island in the sun and he looked like he loved it, too.

Where was he?

Two thin pieces of paper fell from the pages of the brochure onto the hardwood floor. Stormy made a run for them.

'Don't eat those!' Mila snatched them up as the dog went to sniff them with her wet nose. 'Tickets to Chicago on a private jet,' she told the dog aloud, realising what they were with a start. 'Sent from Jared for their mother's seventieth birthday, I suppose. One for Dr Sebastian Becker, and one for...'

She trailed off, turning the ticket over and over again, as if it might start to reveal her own name. The spare ticket was blank.

Her hands shook like jelly as she stuffed the tickets back inside the brochure and dropped it onto the table. Jared had sent him a spare open ticket. Was this plane ticket for someone else entirely? If not, why hadn't Sebastian even broached the subject of her accompanying him?

She tried his phone again. Then she tried calling the dive shop, but no one had seen or heard from him.

Panic started setting in. Annabel had left for a party on this day three years ago and never come back. They'd been having dinner when Annabel had announced she had to leave early. Some guy was waiting for her at a party.

Mila tried to fight the creeping paranoia and despair as she walked to the beach. How could he forget her, today of all days? She wasn't even particularly angry about the plane tickets, she realised. She trusted that he was hers for now at least. She just wanted to see him...to know he was safe.

A horse and cart shuttled past on the street behind her as she found a private nook behind some trees and dropped to the sand. The sound of distant music and clanging dishes mingled with the smell of barbecues and incense in the muggy air. The island was alive and the moon was bright for their planned night dive, but there was still no sign of Sebastian.

She drew her knees up, feeling anxiety form around her like a cloak.

She was back in the driveway of her mother's house now, yanking the chain off her bicycle five minutes after Annabel had left for the party. She'd been talking to her sister on the phone when the line had suddenly gone dead.

'Where are you going?' her mother had called from the driveway.

'Me and Annabel got cut off. Wait here!' she'd yelled back to her mother.

She had pedalled so hard down that road. The night had been black, the trees a frenzied mass of bare branches in the wind, and the rain had been threatening to turn from spit and drizzle into a full-blown downpour that would drench her.

But Mila had hardly felt the cold. Not from the weather anyway. She'd had a feeling. It had seeped through to this earthly plain from somewhere else and chilled her bones. *Something wasn't right with her twin sister.*

Then she'd seen the car, wrapped around a tree. She'd seen the smoke pouring from the back and from under the bonnet. She'd seen the motorbike rider, sitting in a crumpled sobbing heap at the roadside. His bike had been a twisted wreck, but the car... It hadn't even looked like a car.

And Annabel... She hadn't even looked like Annabel by the time Mila had came to her senses and tried to heave her out through the broken glass.

Mila's eyes sprang open. She couldn't go there—not again. She could have helped if only she'd been fast enough. She would never forgive herself for freezing up and wasting those precious seconds.

Mila watched the dogs sniffing around the beach for

sand crabs, chasing them as if it was the greatest game in the world. If only life were so simple for humans, she thought, wading into the shallows with her lantern.

Both dogs ran over to watch as she pulled matches from her shorts pocket and lit the tiny candle at the centre of her paper lantern.

'I'm so sorry, Annabel,' she whispered as it drifted out to sea on the pull of the tide. 'I miss you so much. Please, if you're out there, send me a sign that you forgive me.'

CHAPTER THIRTEEN

MILA SLATHERED THE jasmine-scented shower gel every-where, from her fingertips to her toes. Standing in the shower at her place, she scrubbed at her body as if she could scrub away the memories, too.

Annabel wasn't leaving her head now. The night of the accident…all that blood. And that was interspersed with her confusion and frustration over Sebastian, as if one of her nightmares had turned into the real world.

Why hadn't he called?

She was just getting started on the shampoo when the lights flickered out above her.

'Great,' she mumbled. As if the evening wasn't bad enough already, now she had to shower in the dark?

She slid down the wall to the tiled floor. Exhaustion made her bones feel heavy as she watched a yellow butter-fly flit against the window outside. All those long nights of delicious sex, losing herself in Sebastian when she should have been sleeping, were taking their toll.

She let the water wash over her, trying to clear her head. They never spent time together outside, where anyone could see them. He was so concerned about her being pictured with him that they were limited to rooms with four walls and total privacy.

At first it had been kind of exciting…even though she

knew it wasn't exactly sustainable. Now it was making her think that maybe he'd 'forgotten' tonight for the same reason. Maybe he didn't want to risk being seen out on another boat with her.

Mila blinked back water from her eyelashes as the lights flickered on again.

Those damn island generators.

Something strange caught her eye. The yellow butterfly was still and silent on the glass now—odd—but that wasn't it. She peered closer at the tiny red dots appearing on her bare arms. They were small and strange, blending in with the shower gel...

Wait a second. They were wriggling!

'Oh, my God!'

Mila shrieked and almost slipped as she tried to jump clear of the water. More of the tiny red creatures were landing on her shoulders, trickling down her stomach with the shampoo trails.

Scrambling out of the shower, she grabbed up a towel and broke into a fit of sobs. She reached for the door handle just as a heavy knock on the other side made her jump out of her skin.

'Who's there?'

'Mila, it's me. Are you OK?'

She froze, trying to swallow back tears, but it was impossible.

'Mila? Let me in!'

Her body was heaving with sobs and writhing with shock and disgust—and now with utter embarrassment—but Sebastian was right there on the other side when she finally pulled the door open. He caught her in his arms as she tumbled forward in the towel. Stormy was close behind him, jumping at the doorframe.

'Mila, what's going on?'

She stayed flat against his chest in nothing but the towel, too emotional to move. Sebastian was short of breath, as if he'd run all the way here or something. His arms folded around her instantly and for a moment he just held her while she cried with the force of someone fighting to live through suffocation.

'The front door was open,' he said into her hair. 'I was looking for the dogs and for you. Mila, I'm so sorry I wasn't here for you earlier. I know what today is...'

'I'm not crying because of *you*,' she said, gathering herself together. It was partly true, at least. She forced her body to detach itself from his and pressed a palm to the bathroom door. It swung open in a cloud of hot steam. 'There are *worms* coming out of my shower!'

His brown eyes widened in horror. 'Worms?'

'Go and look,' she told him, running a shaky hand over her eyes.

She wasn't sure what had just happened, but him holding like that, just saying nothing, was making her cry even harder. He hadn't forgotten the anniversary. He'd come to look for her.

Sebastian strode purposefully into the bathroom. She heard the water still running in the shower. Then she heard him curse and turn it off. He strode back into the room, wiping his wet hands on his open blue shirt. She wanted to be touching him again.

'That's not good. It's mosquito larvae...'

'What? That wriggling red stuff is *larvae*?' Mila was repulsed. 'Are you serious?'

His broad frame dominated the room as he walked around the bed towards the door. 'It must be in the water tank. I'll get someone over here...'

'Where *were* you, Sebastian?'

She was still shaking. There was probably still soap in her hair. But Sebastian was in her bedroom after all this time. Usually they went to his place—which probably explained the larvae in her shower. She hadn't used it for a few days.

'There was an emergency,' he told her, taking her hands now, reaching one hand to her face in concern. 'I left without my phone. I meant to call…'

'I was so worried, Sebastian. I went over all the reasons why you hadn't come. You can't just tell someone you'll be somewhere and then not show up. You can't just leave… That's what Annabel did to me—three years ago on this day!'

As soon as her words were out he seemed to realise the severity of his mistake. 'Baby, I'm so sorry…'

He pulled her to the edge of the bed with him and sat her down. She folded against him in the towel.

'It's my fault Annabel died,' she blurted. 'It's all my fault, Sebastian.'

Silence.

She sobbed into his shoulder till his shirt was wet—but she didn't care and he didn't seem to care either. His arms were still wrapped tightly around her. She had to get it all out now.

'We were on the phone while she was in the car. She was asking me about a guy. I was telling her what to do—or what *not* to do. I don't know… I can't remember. We always did that. We talked on the phone while we drove—hands-free, of course. We always had so much to say… we couldn't stop. She'd only just left the house. Then the phone went dead…'

'It's OK.' He pressed a kiss to the side of her head.

'I just had this *feeling*, like I always did.'

Her voice was as shaky as she felt, even as she tried to pull herself together for his benefit.

'I knew something was wrong. I took my bike and I found the car. There was so much blood…all coming from her…from my *sister*. I couldn't think straight. I completely froze, Sebastian. After all my training, all my combat experience, all the times I'd rescued soldiers from burning convoys and tanks… As soon as I saw my twin sister I couldn't think of anything… Then I tried to pull her out though the windscreen. I couldn't get her through the glass, but I tried anyway. I had to do *something*. But by then I was too late. Those seconds were critical…'

'You did everything you could.'

Sebastian's gentle eyes were making her heart hurt even more.

He reached for her hands and turned her wrists over. 'Your scars,' he stated, running his thumbs along the tell-tale lines. 'They're not from Afghanistan.'

'They're from trying to pull her out of the car. But I was too late. I was just too late…'

'It wasn't your fault Annabel died, Mila.' He held her at arm's length. 'You of all people should know that. Listen to me—I cannot be the only one ever to have said this to you, but I'm going to say it again. This was *not* your fault. You need to let this go.'

He kissed her nose, her eyes and lips, then looked at her incredulously.

'That's why you didn't get plastic surgery on your arms, isn't it? You felt like you should live with those scars because you deserved them?'

Mila couldn't even answer. He stood up from the bed. For a second she assumed he was so repulsed by her that he was leaving, but he'd picked up the long green dress from the hanger she'd hooked on the wardrobe door.

'What are you doing?' she asked him. 'We've missed the dive. And I already sent my lantern out, too.'

'Get dressed,' he commanded, holding the dress out to her. 'Come with me.'

'Agung? Can we see them?'

'Sure thing, Dr Becker. They're doing really well, in spite of... Well, you know.'

It was midnight now, but Sebastian had known Ketut and Wayan would be awake after what they had been through. The Blue Ray Clinic was quiet, but the sound of a gurgling baby made its way down the hallway as they squeaked along in their shoes.

Mila's eyes grew wide in surprise.

He hadn't told her yet.

'Is that...?'

'Come see.'

After what had happened he wanted to give Mila a surprise and make this awful night a little better—to show her exactly why he'd lost track of time and forgotten his phone.

Later he would give her the other surprise—an offer of a trip to Chicago. He'd been over the pros and cons of asking her so many times, and he'd concluded finally that he would always regret not asking her if he didn't. So he'd been saving it for tonight.

He had the plane tickets on the table...a boxed gift behind the couch... A stomach full of knots.

Agung led them through to the little recovery room which the staff had filled with balloons already.

Mila's hand flew up over her mouth. She stepped to the edge of the bed with him. 'Wayan! You had the baby!'

Wayan was beaming. 'Dr Ricci, it's so good to see you.'

'Meet baby Jack,' Sebastian said, stroking a finger across the tiny boy's cheek.

He had fallen in love with this kid already—all swathes of jet-black hair and crinkled feet and fingers…and a mouth he thought was pretty cute, even if the rest of the world might deem him in need of fixing.

'Oh, Wayan, he's beautiful.'

'Sebastian really helped us tonight,' Ketut told her, adjusting the fluffy white pillows behind Wayan. 'I called him when the contractions got too much and he brought the boat over himself…brought us back here.'

'I left my phone at the MAC when it happened,' Sebastian added.

'It's OK,' Mila told him, touching her fingers to his arm.

He put a hand on top of hers. They were supposed to have been out diving by now at Shark Reef. He was supposed to have given her the plane ticket and the gift. He'd planned it all for late evening, because he still wouldn't risk them being seen out together where anyone could take a photo of them.

Jared had laughed when he'd told him this earlier.

'You can't keep her all locked up just because of what happened with Klara, bro.'

'I'm not keeping her locked up. It's called being careful—for her protection.'

'Didn't you say she was in the Army? Does she really need your protection?'

Sure, let them all think he was paranoid…

But they hadn't seen the look on Klara's face when she'd read that letter from the parents. They hadn't seen her when her whole world fell apart. If anything like that happened to Mila—especially now she'd opened up to him about Annabel and shown she trusted him—he wouldn't forgive himself.

He knew they would have to be extremely careful in Chicago, but he considered it worth the risk to have this woman there at his side.

'I'm so happy for you,' Mila was telling Wayan and Ketut now, extending her finger to stroke the back of little Jack's hand.

The baby only went and took her finger between his tiny ones. Sebastian looked on and felt something strange... a mixture of pride for Ketut and Wayan and envy.

'You decided to join us a few weeks early, huh?' Mila whispered to Jack.

'Maybe he wanted to spend more time with Auntie Mila before she leaves the MAC?' Ketut chimed in.

'Auntie Mila... I kind of like that.' Mila smiled at Sebastian.

Sebastian reached for the cluster of balloons that had floated between them in the draught from the fan.

'Cleft lip and cleft palate, exactly as shown on the scan,' he confirmed, seeing the way Mila was studying the baby's mouth. 'Two birth defects: a right unilateral cleft lip and palate with complete deformity.'

'You'll help him, Sebastian, when the time comes,' she said conclusively.

'Of course. My team will take care of everything this little guy needs—no question,' he replied, breaking eye contact and moving the balloons to the corner of the room. His stomach had just twisted at the idea of working on Jack without her.

The trip to Chicago was to be around the same time as her flight to the UK was due. The date of her return had now been confirmed, and it remained an unspoken certainty between them. He was aware that she had things to get home to—her mother included—and asking her to meet his family was a huge decision that could change everything for them.

The media was one monster to slay, but he realised that maybe he hadn't asked her about Chicago yet because he was afraid she might say no. He was already concerned that nothing he could do would keep her in his life...that she would leave him anyway, just as Klara had.

He was totally paranoid, he concluded ruefully.

Wayan was talking again now, looking between them. Holding the baby close against her chest, she looked tired, but elated.

'No matter how many ultrasounds we saw, we couldn't really know what we would see when he arrived. I knew he would be beautiful, though, no matter what. Nothing can prepare you for the love you feel for your unborn child, Dr Ricci. And it's only intensified when it's born.'

'I can't even imagine,' Mila replied with a smile, as Ketut dropped a kiss to his wife's head.

'It's the kind of love you know you've been waiting for your whole life,' she told them, and Sebastian didn't miss the look of awe and wonder in Mila's eyes.

Was that a flicker of sadness he saw too?

CHAPTER FOURTEEN

'OPEN IT,' SEBASTIAN told her, presenting her with the long, rectangular box he'd just pulled from behind the couch.

'You're giving me gifts now?' Mila released Stormy, who had demanded a hug the second they'd walked through the villa door. 'What's this?' she asked as the dog hopped to the floor and sniffed around the couch looking for more surprises.

'Open it!'

She did as she was told, pulling the golden wrapping from the flat box, intrigued. Sebastian threw the paper to the floor, along with the huge red ribbon. Stormy pounced on it straight away, and Bruno soon joined in.

'The dress!' she exclaimed, pulling the soft, floaty light fabric from the box. 'The one from the book at the tailor's in Bali?'

It felt incredible in her hands. She was stunned, and embarrassed because it must have cost so much. But then she remembered he was rich. It was easy to forget, with the way he seemed to treat everyone and everything as an equal.

'I had Anya expedite it and bring it over for you.'

He took her hand and helped her off the couch and out of her wrap. She raised her arms above her head, then slowly he helped slide the dress on, until the soft blue fabric was cinched flatteringly at her waist and floating about her calves. She ran a hand along one almost transparent sleeve. Adrenaline spiked in her veins as he caught her wrist where the fabric hovered over her scars and brought it to his lips.

'It's beautiful on you,' he said, and kissed her.

He'd remembered that she liked long sleeves, to cover her scars, and even as she kissed him back Mila was mortified by the way she'd broken down in front of him earlier. It was almost two a.m. now, but her eyes were still red from crying. Bless Wayan and Ketut for not saying a word. It had been a rough day for all of them...

'Thank you,' she sighed, putting her arms around his broad shoulders. 'I love it.'

'I want to you wear it in Chicago,' he said.

Mila's heart skipped a beat as he reached down for the brochure on the coffee table—the one she had picked up earlier.

'You're asking me to meet your family?'

'I'm asking you to accompany me to what will undoubtedly be the most lavish, over the top celebration in honour of a seventy-year-old woman you'll have ever seen. My brother and his wife Laura know how to throw a party. They've invited the entire badminton club.'

She didn't smile as she was clearly supposed to. She felt queasy. She hadn't told him she'd already seen the tickets, and she felt a little bad for jumping to conclusions about him not wanting her there.

She turned to him, still in the dress. 'I appreciate you asking me, Sebastian, but I don't think it's a good idea, do you?'

It was the honest truth. How could she go to his home with him, involve herself in his life to that extent, when they were fundamentally different at the core? She'd seen him with baby Jack. At the end of the day he wanted a family of his own here, on the island. If she went with him she would fall for him even harder. And it would only hurt her even more to lose him.

'It's just a few days in Chicago. We'll take the helicopter to Denpasar, then it's a direct flight on the private jet. We'll have our own bedroom on board.' He kissed her passionately, ran his hands through her hair, and his words against her lips gave her tingles. 'Imagine the fun we'll have on the way…'

Mila broke away from him, imagining exactly that—the mile high club…high on each other.

The dress swished heavily around her ankles as she crossed to the doors to the garden. 'I don't know if I should be meeting your family at this point, Sebastian. I mean, I appreciate the offer, but…'

'But what? I know you need to go home and see your mother, Mila, but you can go *after* the party, can't you? And then you can come back here?'

'You mean, extend my contract at the MAC?'

'If you want.'

Her heart raced wildly. He made it all sound so simple. He was sitting there on the couch, holding the brochure and the plane tickets. The night was quiet and still, apart from the dogs, who padded past outside. Stormy was still gripping the red ribbon in her teeth.

Sebastian's jaw started to tic when he realised she wasn't as excited as she should be, but she didn't know what to say. She was so torn.

'I want you in my life,' he said seriously. 'We're good together, Mila.'

'You won't even be seen with me in daylight!'

He wrinkled his nose. 'I wouldn't want to take you home if I didn't think you could handle what might happen there. Jared won't invite the media, so no one will take any photos we don't want them to…'

'I can't live like that, and neither should you. I'm not afraid of what people think or say about me. But that's not the point, Sebastian. I can't give you what you want—not in the long run.'

'What are you talking about?'

'A family, Sebastian. I saw the way you looked at Jack, and I see how you look when you talk about Charlie, too. I *know* that's what you want.'

Sebastian fell silent again and her cheeks flamed. She had pretty much just divulged that she'd both considered and rejected the possibility of having his children—all without him even knowing.

'This thing we have…it's complicated,' he said.

He stood up and crossed to her, and she felt his soft breath on her cheek as his strong hands found her waist from behind, urging her back against him gently.

'And I'm not asking you for anything more than your company right now,' he told her, sweeping her hair aside and dropping kisses along the nape of her neck. 'Just some time off this island together, while we figure out what's going to happen next. What do you say, Dr Ricci? You wouldn't make me listen to the badminton club gossip all alone, would you?'

CHAPTER FIFTEEN

RACHEL CAME FLYING through the MAC reception doors so fast, Mila almost mistook her for the crew bringing an emergency patient in.

'Where's Dr Becker?' Rachel asked excitedly.

Her face was beetroot-red, as if she'd run here from her villa in spite of the blazing heat. She pushed her sunglasses up to the top of her head.

'He's on the mainland again, for consultations,' Mila explained, moving out from behind the desk and closing the window on the computer screen.

She didn't want Rachel to see she'd been looking up the Beckers on the internet, in anticipation of meeting them, as well as double-checking the schedule for the day.

'He'll be back tomorrow. What's happened?'

'*This* has happened.'

Rachel fished an iPad out of her bright pink beach bag. The cover on it matched.

She stepped to Mila's side and showed her the screen. 'It's in French, but you can see what it is,' she enthused. 'I think it's super-exciting! I know Dr Becker doesn't like photos and stuff, especially of you two...'

Mila didn't respond.

'But I think this is something different, right? I mean, it's a *kid*!'

Mila took the tablet in her hands, frowning to herself. What was she talking about? French? A kid?

She was trying not to let on, but she felt sick to the core suddenly. Was it the smell of the detergent they'd just used on the floors? Or maybe it was the eggs she'd had for breakfast? She fought to focus on the tablet. Rachel crossed her arms proudly.

Fatema walked in, and peered over Mila's shoulder. 'What are you looking at?'

'I don't even know,' Mila said, putting a hand to her stomach. 'It's in French.'

Rachel tutted and took the tablet back. 'It translates as "Breakthrough scar surgery saved my face!" It's that French kid…you know, Francoise Marchand? She got bitten by a dog. Dr Becker and Dr Ricci saved her from serious scars with his new laser treatment and now she's written this. She's only eight—can you believe it? Her story's got published in the newspaper—probably because she's so young. Kids who do cool stuff like this always get famous. I wish I was eight years old again… I would do things differently.'

She said it a little wearily, even with a hint of envy, but Mila was only half listening now. She put her hand to the back of a chair and sank slowly onto the seat—just as her next patient glided in through the doors in a full purple sarong.

'Are you OK, sweetie?'

Amita Ahluwalia's perfectly symmetrical eyebrows met in the middle as she crouched in front of her. Mila noticed the smell of the beautiful Indian model's perfume instantly.

'You've gone very pale.'

'I'm OK…don't worry,' she reassured her, swallowing back a slight gag reflex.

This was embarrassing.

'We were just showing her an exciting piece of press coverage,' Rachel explained. 'Anyone would be over-whelmed. This eight-year-old kid has written a story about her dog bite and how our new revolutionary treatment helped her heal. It's a great testament to Dr Becker's work here. We'll get even more appointments after this. No one can resist a kid with a story… Are you OK, Dr Ricci? Do you feel sick?'

They all turned to look at her.

Mila couldn't take it any more. 'Excuse me,' she mum-bled, clutching her stomach and bolting from the seat. She couldn't throw up in front of her patient, and the bathroom was just down the hall.

She heard Amita Ahluwalia's voice calling out to her to eat some charcoal as she made her dash down the hall-way. Embarrassment coursed through her veins along with the nausea. She almost knocked over a vase of flowers in her hurry.

'Doctor?' Rachel was hot on her heels. 'I'm sorry if I upset you. But the article is *good*! I think Dr Becker will be OK with it. There aren't any photos of you, and it's not like you're in the same boat as his ex…'

'I don't care about that, Rachel.'

Why did everyone think she should care about that? There were far bigger things to be concerned about—like the fact that she was about to be sick at work.

Mila pushed through the door to the ladies' room and half ran, half stumbled to the toilet. With her hands on the porcelain bowl she threw up as quietly as she could—which, she realised in dismay, wasn't particularly quiet.

Rachel was in the bathroom, too. 'Dr Ricci…?'

Mila reached for the lock on the cubicle door and pulled it across. 'Please, Rachel, I'm OK—really. Nothing I can't handle. Can you just go and apologise to Miss Ahluwalia?'

She wiped at her sweaty face with her white coat sleeve,

slumping back against the wall. The tiles were cold. And the lights were too bright—they were giving her a headache.

Rachel's sandals shifted beneath the door. Her voice was laced with concern now. 'Is this the first time this has happened to you?'

Mila covered her face with her hands. It was the first time she'd thrown up, but she'd been nauseous before this on a few occasions over the past few days, now that she thought about it.

'I'm… I'm sure it's nothing,' she managed.

'Go home, Dr Ricci, lie down. We'll make sure you're covered here.'

'Thank you.'

'Are you going to tell Dr Becker about this?'

'About the article?'

'No, about you being sick?'

A cold sweat prickled on her back against the tiles. 'No need to tell him anything, Rachel. Like I said, I'm OK.'

Rachel said nothing as she left the bathroom, but Mila knew what she was thinking. Her romance with Sebastian was hardly a secret around here any more. If it wasn't the floor cleaner, or the eggs… She could barely even entertain the notion of what might be causing her nausea.

'Thank you so much for agreeing to do this, Mila!'

Wayan handed over baby Jack, who was gurgling sweetly to himself. He was the epitome of cute, dressed in a little blue onesie. Then promptly put a giant padded bag laden with nappies and toys and bottles of formula over Mila's shoulder. The weight of it threatened to send her toppling sideways onto Sebastian's porch.

'Are you sure you don't mind?'

'Wayan, I told you—I love babysitting,' she enthused, straightening up with the giant bag.

She had never babysat in her life. She'd simply overheard Ketut asking Sebastian if he knew of a good baby-sitter, and figured it would be a chance to do something nice for the couple while Sebastian was away on the mainland. She also hoped spending some time with little Jack would help her relax, and think things through.

She eyed the paper bag on the dining table, feeling her throat dry up. There was something else she had to do, too...

'You guys just go and enjoy your dinner,' she said to Wayan, plastering a smile onto her face as the dressed-up woman gave her son an extra kiss on his chubby cheek.

Stormy and Bruno bounded ahead of her into the house and, carrying baby Jack under her arm, Mila made herself some tea. It wasn't the easiest thing, holding a baby... But she was doing fine, she told herself, nothing to worry about here.

The paper bag on the table seemed to be calling her.

Take the test! You know it's going to be negative! Just put your mind at rest!

She would do it later. Maybe even tomorrow.

Right now she would continue her research on the Beckers. She might even watch an episode of *Faces of Chicago* and see what all the fuss was about.

She would do anything, she realised quickly, other than take the damn test.

Jack snoozed on the couch next to her as she scrolled through Francoise's article on Sebastian's spare iPad. The kid had written some really sweet things about the MAC and her time on the island, and how she was proud to have been brave like Dr Mila Ricci.

Mila couldn't deny that she was proud to be part of the story. She hoped Sebastian would be proud, too. It wasn't anything close to the kind of 'publicity' that vultures like Hugo O'Shea liked to print. This was only drawing attention to the positive impact his work was having on the island and their patients.

The sharp, shrill ringtone of her phone woke the sleeping baby. He coughed and then started screaming like a banshee. She had never heard a sound quite like it. She bundled him onto her lap and held him close, rocking him.

'No, no, no…it's OK, Jack. I'm sorry.'

Jack's shrieks of discomfort burrowed under her skin, filling her with dread, as a yellow butterfly flitted in through the open door and came to a stop on the arm of the couch. It sat there even as she reached past it for her phone, to decline the call.

Sebastian. She would have to call him back. She couldn't talk to him when Jack was crying like this.

Something maternal seemed to take control of her body as she rocked and whispered and cooed. 'There you go… you're doing fine, little man.'

But Jack cried and cried, and Mila contemplated singing to him.

What did babies *want*?

She had no clue, but the way he smelled was heavenly. Did all babies smell this nice? His skin was so clear and bright around his little misshapen mouth, and she loved the way his all-seeing eyes shone when he wasn't screaming. He'd have an idyllic life here…seeing the ocean every day, diving in it with his godfather, Sebastian. It must be an incredible privilege to watch a little person grow, to know you'd influenced their life decisions.

She felt a familiar dread creep in again, even as Jack fell silent in her arms. She liked the idea of it…but then she remembered why she wasn't cut out for motherhood—that she'd be terrible at it.

It was all her friends at home who wanted to be mothers, and her mum would've loved to be a grandma, and Sebastian… They all wanted the babies—not her.

Speaking of Sebastian, she should call him back.

Anything to put off taking the test.

CHAPTER SIXTEEN

SEBASTIAN WAS SEATED at a chequered-cloth-covered table between two potential investors who were keen to know more about his plans for the villa complex in the valley. Their waiter was already delivering plates of seafood pasta to their Italian-themed place mats.

'Dr Ricci?' He answered the voice call when the vibration in his pocket didn't stop. 'I have to be fast—I'm in a restaurant. Is everything OK over there?'

Her face flashed onto the screen just as one of his investors peered at it over his spaghetti.

'So this is Dr Ricci? The little French girl painted a wonderful picture of you in her article, but look at you— you're even more delightful in person. Whose baby do you have there?'

'Baby?' Sebastian realised that baby Jack was there, swaddled in a fluffy grey blanket next to Mila. His own *Chicago* shirt was still draped across the cushions on the couch behind her, where he'd left it.

'You're babysitting?' he said in surprise.

The investors were taking in Jack's cleft lip, witnessing Mila with the baby at the same time as him.

'It's my godson,' he explained. He probably shouldn't have picked up her video call—this wasn't looking too professional right now. But he'd thought she would be at the MAC. Mixing business with pleasure was risky...

'What's wrong with his face?' one of them asked.

'He has a cleft lip and palate. I'll be operating in a couple months or so—'

'He's so good, though,' Mila cut in. 'It's almost like he knows Dr Becker is going to help him—so he's being very brave, aren't you, sweetie?'

They all watched as she cuddled him close. Sebastian had never seen her like this. The investors looked truly touched for a moment, and a sudden rush of pride swept over him for both Mila and for Jack.

'Seems you're very close with your staff and your patients,' one of the investors observed. 'Do you open your home to them all like this?'

'Not at all.' Sebastian cleared his throat. 'But things are certainly different on the island. Excuse me just a second...?'

He inched his way past the chairs and tables and the harried waiters, through a waft of parmesan cheese to the door. Outside the air was thick and muggy, reminding him that he was actually still in Bali—not Italy.

'Sorry about that,' he said to Mila. 'I called you earlier to say I should be back by tomorrow, but I need to stay here another night with these investors. I can't get into the base facility till morning and I want to show them around.'

'So the investors have read the article by Francoise?'

He told her he'd been forced to read young Francoise's story that morning, and while he could hardly be angry at the kid for singing his praises, it was a little irritating, putting it in some French newspaper without his consent. More than irritating. Sure, there were no photos of him with Mila, and it wasn't a 'celebrity scandal' angle at all, but the publicity still drew attention where attention wasn't needed.

'Not all press is bad press,' Mila reminded him. 'Sebastian, you have to be OK with people writing things about you if it's done with good intentions. You're doing great work—you deserve to be recognised.'

'Thank you,' he told her sincerely. 'It's sexy when you put me in my place.'

She laughed.

Mila hadn't experienced the extent of the media's wrath enough to appreciate why he despised any hint of attention on him, but he was grateful for her indifference about such things—it was refreshing. It kind of calmed him down.

He told her how these investors from Jakarta were interested in his project there on the mainland. They loved the outside space, the funicular and the villas. They saw incredible potential *and* they were excited.

'I'd prefer Jared to get on board too,' he added quietly. 'He had some great ideas when we talked about it… But I have no choice except to move forward now. There are too many people who can't afford the MAC—we need facilities in both places. So the sooner we can get things moving the better.'

'You love creating more work for yourself, don't you?' she teased him.

He grinned. 'It's how I thrive.'

He turned back to the restaurant, saw the two investors toasting each other through the window. He knew they were likely congratulating themselves on getting involved, even if they hadn't signed anything yet. It was a good sign, he supposed. And he had Mila to thank for this. She had made a lasting impression on Francoise. And vice versa.

'Is everything else OK?' he asked her. 'I should really get back to them.'

Mila looked torn for a moment. She opened her mouth to speak, but then seemed to think better of it. 'Nothing that can't wait,' she said finally.

'You sure?'

'Quite sure.'

He took in the sight of her with baby Jack just for a moment longer before hanging up. She might only want a dog in her family in the future, but it hadn't escaped his attention that she looked pretty hot with a baby.

The clear blue line seemed to darken ominously as Mila studied it from the toilet seat. She was trembling ferociously and her head reeled in the candlelit outdoor bathroom. The crickets seemed to be singing into the night, taunting her from behind the stone wall.

How was this possible? *It couldn't be possible.* She'd been taking her pill the whole time—at the right time.

She would do another test.

Panic strangled her heart as she made her way back to Jack. He was still snoozing soundly, swaddled in his blanket. It seemed so telling, somehow, that the test should come up positive while she was babysitting.

Annabel flashed into her mind. She dropped to the floor beside the couch. She had asked for a sign on the night of the anniversary. Maybe this was Annabel's sign that she'd forgiven her for the accident and was encouraging her to start a family. Stranger things had happened, right?

Mila scowled at the floor, dragging her hands through her hair. She was being ridiculous. This wasn't some divine message from the other side—this was her own fault. She had probably forgotten to take her pill one night, or taken it too late.

You love him. This is the right thing for you.

The voice was in her head, but somehow it came from somewhere else. Mila spun around to Jack. His eyes were open and he was gazing up at the ceiling from the cushions.

Getting to her feet, she put her finger to his little hand,

but he didn't stop looking at the ceiling, as if he was seeing something that wasn't there.

'What are you doing, little man?' she whispered, trying not to feel spooked.

Tears prickled her eyes. She wouldn't speak to her twin sister. She wasn't in this room. Annabel was gone and Sebastian had made her feel it was OK to let her go, to forgive herself for not being able to help when she'd still had time.

She rarely had nightmares about Annabel any more—in fact, she'd only had a few since she'd started sleeping in Sebastian's bed—but of course she was still in her every thought. She was part of her.

'We always said we'd have babies at the same time,' she said aloud. What was the harm in talking to her just for a bit…just in case? 'But by no means was an accidental pregnancy ever on the cards—especially one that's the result of a fling with an ex-celebrity doctor from Chicago. You would tell me off, if you were here, Annabel.'

You love him. This is the right thing for you.

She heard it again, loud and clear.

Mila shook her head at herself, petting Stormy when she padded over for some attention.

'Good girl,' she said softly when the dog pressed her nose to Jack's little foot.

She sat there in silence as Jack drifted off to sleep again.

What to do?

She couldn't ask anyone at the clinic to test her for pregnancy—it would have to be another kit. It had been tough enough getting the first one from the storeroom without anyone seeing her.

If anyone even suspected she was pregnant they would know without a doubt that Sebastian was the father. It wasn't ideal, showing up as his employee and leaving pregnant with his baby. Besides, he hated attention—and people would surely fix their attention on *this* juicy piece of scandal.

What would he say when she told him, if the second test came back positive too? Would he want this baby with her? And if he did…what if something happened to it?

This was everything she'd been afraid of and all of it was unbearable to contemplate.

'Help me through this, Annabel,' she begged out loud, in spite of herself. 'I don't think I can do this on my own.'

CHAPTER SEVENTEEN

Two weeks later

'WHERE'S THAT NICE female surgeon who was here for the initial consultation?'

The fifty-six-year-old British woman blinking up at Sebastian was nervous without Mila there for her blepharoplasty.

'She had to leave unexpectedly this morning,' he explained, reaching behind him to the gramophone to lay the needle on the vinyl. Beethoven filled the room and he thought of Mila. He hoped she was all right.

'Nothing serious, I hope?'

His patient's eyes were full of genuine concern and so were Fatema's. Mila had clearly touched their patient on some deeper level, in the brief time they'd been in contact, just as she had Francoise.

'Dr Ricci was truly encouraging,' his patient was saying to them now, taking Fatema's arm. 'She said I didn't need this. She said that lines around our eyes are proof of all the times we've smiled, and the more we smile the more beautiful we are to everyone who sees us. Isn't that a nice thing to say? She could have just tried to sell me more plastic surgery.'

'That's not really our policy here,' Sebastian told her, fighting a smile.

It sounded as if Mila had made an even bigger impression that he'd thought. This was the sort of thing he'd been hearing ever since Mila had arrived at the MAC: *'Mila is so wonderful...' 'Mila is so caring...' 'Mila is so good for you...we mean, good for the MAC.'*

Shame she'd left the MAC earlier on today, saying she felt sick.

He was used to the gossip about them by now, of course, and he didn't care about that as long as their photos weren't splashed about the internet. It still gave him chills to think about how it had ended with Klara, and with Mila still set to come to Chicago with him for his mother's birthday party there was always the chance that someone would stick a lens where it wasn't wanted and make things difficult.

He was praying it would all go smoothly. She was well aware he wanted her to stay on at the MAC for various reasons, but they'd agreed that spending some time away from the island to talk about things would be the best course of action before putting it officially on paper.

It was the right thing to do. She had come on board as a temporary employee after all. Neither of them had expected this, and they couldn't exactly keep it a secret with the island itself more like a gossip factory than his last surgery in Chicago, just with more sand and fewer cameras.

Fatema cornered him when he went for the anti-bac. 'Is Mila still sick, then?' she asked him.

'Dr Ricci? I guess so... Maybe she ate something bad.'

'Like before?' Fatema seemed concerned. 'She needs to watch her diet.'

'Before? What do you mean?' He shook the anti-bac from the bottle, then handed it to her.

Fatema looked sheepish. She turned her back to their

patient and lowered her voice. A couple of weeks ago—she was sick then, too. I think you were away in Bali. She didn't tell you?'

'Why would she tell me?'

Fatema cocked an eyebrow. 'We *all* know why she would tell you, Dr Becker.'

He grunted. 'Fine. But, no, she didn't tell me.'

The information nagged at his brain even as he forced himself to return to the task at hand. He should be focusing on the fact that he oversaw the most capable and qualified team in Indonesia, instead of wondering if Mila's strange moods and impromptu sick leave were something he should worry about.

She had been sick before today and not told him...?

Fatema was talking to their patient about the procedure. 'So, just to recap, Dr Ricci must have told you to avoid taking any medication that might thin your blood and prevent it from clotting normally prior to this surgery?'

'Yes, Dr Halabi, she explained all that.'

'That includes pain relievers, aspirin and ibuprofen. I trust you stopped those too? And you've only eaten very lightly today, if at all?'

'Dr Ricci told me not to have breakfast or drink anything after midnight the night before my procedure. So I had no margaritas last night—which was such a shame because they were buy-one-get-one-free.'

'You can make up for that later,' Sebastian interjected.

'She also said not to wear make-up—hence this mess you see here before you.'

His patient gestured to her plain face and mascara-free eyes, but he left the make-up chat to Fatema. She was more than capable of handling this.

He couldn't help replaying in his mind an episode from

earlier in the week, when he'd taken Mila out on the dive boat. She'd gone for the ride, but she hadn't wanted to dive.

'You don't want to go down?' he'd asked her. 'I was kidding about the sharks. There won't be any sharks, but the manta rays around here—they're something else!'

'I think I'm just liking the feeling of the sun on my skin right now,' she'd told him distractedly.

He'd gone down with the group without her, but he hadn't been able to fully switch off as he usually did.

Mila was being quieter than usual, less involved. Just as she'd been after they'd first kissed, back when she'd pushed him away because she'd thought he'd hooked up with Annabel. She was supposed to be diving with the group tonight, but she'd already told him she couldn't go. He hadn't questioned it because he'd seen she clearly wasn't feeling one hundred percent.

He frowned as Fatema talked details to their patient with exemplary confidence. Mila always went quiet when she had something on her mind. Maybe she was just a little nervous about meeting his family, he mused. They were set to leave tomorrow, so he could understand that. His family could be difficult to handle.

Or maybe she was nervous about finishing her placement at the MAC with nothing set in stone for the future. He couldn't help mulling over that one himself. He hadn't and wouldn't put any extra pressure on her, but the thought of being here without Mila weighed heavy on his heart.

Mila woke from the dream with a jump. She flung her legs over the side of the bed, grabbed the cool pillow beside her and pressed her hot face to the cotton. Thank goodness Sebastian wasn't there—although his comforting arms would be a relief to sink into right now.

In the dream she'd been holding a baby on her lap in a

car, but there hadn't been any seatbelts. She'd been forced to travel anyway, as the base camp wasn't safe. They'd been in convoy, cruising by night across the desert plains, taking bumpy secret routes that didn't even exist in reality, dodging insurgents like characters in a video game.

Then the car had been hit—attacked from behind by Afghan soldiers with larger than life AK-47s. The bullets had rained down through the roof and the windscreen and when she'd cried out, begging for the baby's life, the baby had been gone. Vanished.

She'd woken up hotter than fire, still shaking.

Somehow she made it to the bathroom, ran the cold tap and splashed her face. Thank goodness someone had been in to clear the mosquito larvae from the tank, but there were other things wriggling under her skin now: the second test had come back positive and her dreams had returned with a vengeance. They even had a new twist to torture her with.

She studied her face in the mirror as shame washed over her. Would Sebastian comfort her if he knew what she was hiding? It had taken her several days to build up the courage to take the second test, and she still hadn't told Sebastian she was pregnant.

She hadn't told anyone.

The time difference might be a blessing in one way. It would be a good time to talk to her mother in the UK. Surely she could tell her mother?

No. She couldn't tell her—not on the phone anyway.

Every time she so much as thought about telling her mother it became more real in her head. And the more real the baby was for her, the harder it would be to lose it. And she would lose it, surely—because she wasn't a suitable mother. She couldn't care for a baby as a baby needed to be cared for. She just...*couldn't.*

Mila pulled on a T-shirt and shorts. She slipped into her

flip-flops and left the room, heart pounding. It was almost five a.m. She realised she was holding her belly protectively as she walked, looking out for dogs that might attack, and when she caught herself doing it she forced her hands away.

She was already looking out for this baby when she didn't even know if she could keep it.

She hadn't been diving, even though she'd wanted to, but Sebastian had gone diving again last night. She'd made another excuse, which she'd felt terrible about. He was worried about her, she could tell. She'd simply told him she would see him the next day. It had bought her more time, but it had brought her nightmares, too.

She had no clue how he'd react to her news, but she had to tell him. The secret was killing her.

It was only the gardener out at this hour, raking leaves from the pathways, and she squared her shoulders at Sebastian's gates and psyched herself up to let herself in. Her legs felt like jelly.

As usual, the dogs greeted her as if she'd just come home from war.

'Hey, Stormy. Hey, Bruno. Oh, it's good to see you, too.'

Sebastian's suitcase was still on the porch—the one he'd half packed for Chicago. He'd spilled milk on it, thanks to Stormy, and left it by the hammock to dry. Just the sight of it made her feel sicker. She'd put this off for so long that they were due to leave tonight and she still hadn't told him.

Was she crazy? She wasn't usually the kind of person who had difficulty speaking up; in fact, the strength to do that had defined her entire career. Why was this any different? You just said it and then it was out…just like the way she'd told him about the car crash that had killed Annabel. Eventually.

But it was so hard.

Maybe she should tell him once they'd left the island.

When they'd have more space and time to talk things through privately. That was what they were due to be doing anyway—he wanted her to come back here with him, didn't he, after Chicago? He had told her as much.

He just wasn't anticipating an unplanned baby with the package, Mila!

She stepped up to the porch, but she could tell Sebastian wasn't home. Her instincts kicked in.

There must have been an emergency.

CHAPTER EIGHTEEN

'Is she going to be OK?'

Pedro's eyes were tired and full of panic, and he'd bitten his fingernails almost down to the cuticles. The twenty-eight-year-old from Brazil hadn't left the Blue Ray Clinic or the decompression chamber room all night. He was still wearing his wetsuit. So was Sebastian, under his white coat.

'The team will keep an eye on her, but we've done everything we can up to this point,' Sebastian said, taking the coffee an intern had handed him and peering through the circular window at Pedro's girlfriend, Rose. 'We'll know more when the tests come back.'

What a crazy night. He was utterly exhausted, but he felt it was his duty to stay with the guy; he'd been down there on the dive with him when it had happened. He was glad Mila hadn't gone with them in the end—things hadn't exactly gone to plan.

Pedro's girlfriend, twenty-seven-year-old Rose, had panicked over something under the water at fifteen metres down. He still wasn't sure what it had been, but there had been nothing the team could do to stop her as she'd pushed her way up to the surface without a safety stop. They always did a safety stop at five meters…

'Sebastian?'

Mila's voice made him spin around—Pedro, too. She

looked as dazed as he felt. For a moment, in his deep fatigue, he almost went to wrap his arms around her, but he stopped himself. 'Dr Ricci, good morning.'

'Can I see you outside?'

He excused himself and took her out of the room into the hallway, shutting the door behind him. Agung and the resident intern threw them a look, but he signalled with his coffee as if it was perfectly normal to be standing with Mila in his wetsuit at six a.m. in the Blue Ray Clinic's hallway.

'Good *morning*?' she said, lowering her voice to a whisper. She looked him up and down. 'You haven't been to bed, Sebastian.'

'That girl has been in the decompression chamber since we brought her in from the dive.'

Mila looked horrified. 'The dive you were on last night?'

He nodded, noting her pink toenails in her flip-flops. 'We had to call the air ambulance from Lombok to get her back—she might not have made it on the boat. She's still out with decompression sickness... What are you doing here so early?'

Mila's face was pale, he noticed. She was watching the cleaner with her mop and bucket at the other end of the hall, and covering her mouth with her hand.

'Are you feeling sick again?' he asked, resisting the urge to put a hand to her cheek.

She averted her eyes. 'I'm not feeling sick. This is just awful, Sebastian—are *you* OK?'

Sebastian hadn't realised till she'd said it that he probably *wasn't* entirely OK. It was really rare for something like this to happen. It was shocking, to say the least, and he'd been running on adrenaline all night.

'I wasn't her dive buddy—that was Pedro, her boyfriend,' he told her, resting a foot against the wall behind him and tapping the bottom of his coffee cup. 'But we were all there. There were six of us. I guess that's one good thing—we managed to help her pretty fast after she came up.'

'I'm so sorry this happened.'

Mila was studying his face as if she was looking for signs that he might crack. Of course he wouldn't crack, but her eyes were so full of concern. He couldn't remember the last time any woman had cared this deeply about his well-being.

'You must be so tired. We can talk later. I'll let you get back to Pedro.'

She made to turn around, but he caught her arm. 'Wait. What did you want to talk to me about so early in the morning?'

She paused, half with her back to him. She was still looking at the cleaner's mop and bucket as if it was causing her physical pain.

'Mila?'

'Dr Becker?' The obstetrician, Dr Raya, had exited the room opposite. 'Rose's tests are back. Do you have a moment?'

He looked at Mila. 'You can talk to us both,' he said quickly, following Dr Raya back into the room.

Mila had crossed her arms beside him as they waited. Dawn was breaking outside and he could hear the ocean close by through the open window. It didn't calm him down. He was on high alert now—he could tell something was wrong.

Dr Raya looked him right in the eyes and took a long, deep breath. 'Dr Becker, Dr Ricci… The tests show your patient Rose was pregnant. I don't think she knew, as neither she nor her boyfriend mentioned it, I believe?'

Sebastian shook his head gravely as Mila walked over to the window, wrapping her arms around herself. This was not what he'd hoped to hear. 'Pedro didn't mention it, no. Poor guy.'

'Poor Rose,' Mila croaked, metres away now.

'It was four to five weeks, but I'm afraid with the decompression...'

'There's no chance of a pregnancy surviving,' he finished, tossing his coffee cup into the rubbish bin under the desk, hard. 'Damn—could this night get any worse?'

He shoved his hands into his white coat pockets, fists clenched. 'We should tell Pedro, so he can prepare himself before Rose wakes up. We don't want to distress her any more than necessary. She might need a few more sessions in the decompression chamber, so he'll have to decide when to let her know.'

Mila was shifting on her feet now, holding a hand to her mouth again. Before he or Dr Raya could say anything she raced from the window right past them, yanked open the door and stepped into the hallway.

He followed her halfway to the reception area her before she threw up—right into the cleaner's bucket.

Mila was mortified. It was that smell again. If it hadn't been for the smell she might have avoided throwing up—but she couldn't think about it again, she was far too humiliated.

'You should go back inside to Pedro,' she heard herself say as the sea breeze outside caught her hair, cooling her down.

Sebastian had ushered her out, past the stunned cleaner and several patients already in Reception.

'You were the one diving with him—he should hear this news from you.'

'I know,' he said, darkly.

She sat down on the wall outside the Blue Ray Clinic in the shade of a palm tree. It was getting lighter by the second and she felt even more exposed now he was standing in front of her, arms folded.

'You want to tell me what's going on?'

She considered her regrettable timing. This was not the time or place—especially with poor Rose in there in the decompression chamber and her poor boyfriend Pedro about to learn she'd lost a baby he hadn't even know she was expecting.

It was the worst time to tell him she was carrying a baby of her own, and she felt guilty. Why should *she* be pregnant when Rose...?

'Mila, Fatema told me you were sick before...when I was in Bali. Now this?'

Sebastian crouched down to her level. He still had his wetsuit on under his white coat, she realised. He hadn't slept all night and now he was here, trying to take care of her.

It was all too much. Above everything else she despised feeling so trapped and vulnerable; this wasn't who she was.

'And you wouldn't come diving. I mean, I'm happy you didn't come last night—don't get me wrong. Accidents happen, but you never expect a dive student to dismiss every single thing she's learnt in the face of panic...'

He trailed off when he realised what he'd said. His face said it all, though. He blamed Rose for what had happened—just as she still blamed herself for Annabel.

She needed to get away. She needed to be alone.

But Sebastian was holding her hand tight to her own lap. 'Talk to me.'

'I don't know what to say, Sebastian. It's the worst possible time.'

He stood up again. 'You're pregnant, aren't you?'

The world seemed to go white around her. How did he know...? *He's a doctor—that's how*, she told herself wearily.

'Mila? Are you pregnant?'

She still couldn't speak. Instead she just nodded and covered her face for a moment, taking deep breaths. She felt as if she might pass out.

'My God. You are.'

Sebastian sounded devastated and it made her heart ache. If she hadn't already thrown up, she might have done it again.

He turned towards the mountains and watched an early-morning horse trot past with a cart-load of boxes full of beer. This was surreal. She felt as she was looking at herself from outside her own body, hearing someone else saying these things about another person.

'I'm so sorry... I didn't know how to tell you before. It's not exactly something I planned—it's not even what I want...'

'How long have you known?'

'Two weeks.'

'Two *weeks*?' He kicked up the sand at his feet in frustration, then appeared to regret it, but he looked less than happy when he turned back to her. 'You've known for a whole fortnight and you didn't tell me? Mila, we're about to go and see my family—when exactly were you planning to tell me this? This involves me too, doesn't it?' He narrowed his eyes. 'It *is* mine, right?'

'Of course it's yours!' she exclaimed hotly.

'Then when were you going to let me in on this?'

'Today. Now.'

The disappointment on his face at her secrecy brought a lump to her throat. She knew she deserved it, but she felt cold as she struggled for composure. 'I thought we could talk about it when we'd left the island. I realise in retrospect that wasn't the best decision on my part—'

'I have to go deal with Pedro,' he said, cutting her off.

'OK.'

She watched helplessly as he rubbed his tired eyes, a foot away from her. 'We'll talk about this when I'm done. Will you be OK getting back to the house?'

She nodded mutely. Of course she would.

But her heart sank to the pit of her stomach as he strode purposefully back inside without another word. He was furious with her. He would probably end things between them now, seeing as she had basically just taken a firearm to his trust.

Her mind was a running commentary of self-loathing as she hurried back to his house. She needed to cuddle the dogs or something.

She should have told him sooner. She should *not* have told him today, when he'd had no sleep and had something pressing to deal with. Now she'd have to sit on a plane with him, meet his family, with this hanging over them… If he even still wanted her to go with him.

This was all too much. She had to get off this island— think about things rationally and logically somewhere no one could influence her decisions. Not even him.

Mila turned around and made for her consulting room instead. She'd forgotten to tell Personnel to cancel her transfer to the UK because Jared had organised the Chicago trip—she still had her ticket back to Gatwick.

CHAPTER NINETEEN

'WE DIDN'T EVEN know she was pregnant, otherwise we wouldn't have gone diving.' Pedro was slumped over on the leather couch under the ceiling fan with his head between his knees.

'I'm so sorry to have to tell you,' Sebastian said, wringing his hands together on the chair opposite.

He was too exhausted to process anything properly—too sleep-deprived to think about anything beyond the answers to Pedro's questions: *'What happened to the baby? How many more sessions will she need in there? Should we even tell her she was pregnant? Does she need to know? Won't that upset her more?'*

It was almost inconceivable that he was breaking this tragic news to Pedro, hearing him contemplate such a personal dilemma, when he'd just found out about Mila's pregnancy.

What would he do in Pedro's shoes?

He would tell his partner—he knew he would.

But Mila hadn't spoken to him about anything. She'd left it *two weeks* before telling him. And she'd been reluctant even then.

Pedro's phone rang.

'I think I can take over here,' Dr Raya said kindly, taking Sebastian aside. 'You were up all night, Dr Becker, and

I'm sure this has been pretty shocking for you, too. And poor Dr Ricci... I hope she gets better soon.'

Dr Raya had offered to help Pedro break the news to Rose about her pregnancy—because of course Rose should know. It was important information. Wasn't it? Someone being pregnant? All parties involved deserved to know.

Instead of going straight back to the house, he went to the rocks off the bay where he'd sat with Mila the night of the fundraiser. He was feeling emotional after last night and because of Pedro's situation. He didn't want to take that out on Mila any more than he already had. He was furious that she'd kept such a secret—he wouldn't deny that—but maybe he was more angry at himself for not noticing the signs.

He should have picked up on her pregnancy. He should have known what was happening right in front of him. He was a doctor, for crying out loud. How could he have been so blind?

He'd been too caught up in their relationship... He hadn't felt this way about anyone before—not even Klara, he realised with a jolt—and now this.

Guilt crept its way in with the sea breeze as he made his way back from the rocks barefoot, relishing the occasional stab of coral to wake him up.

When he'd snapped at Mila before he'd been in total shock. It had been pure self-defence on his part, a grappling for control. He hadn't had the capacity to process everything that was going on and he'd freaked out.

It wasn't as if either of them had been expecting this. This was an accident...

He fixed his stare on the shadows drifting across the mountains. He still couldn't wrap his head around the fact she hadn't told him.

Was it because she really didn't want a baby?

They'd joked about how she would rather have a dog, but he liked to think he knew her better now. Mila was always going to be cut up about Annabel, which meant she was always going to be scared about losing anyone close to her.

She didn't think he knew her at all, but he did.

'Mila?'

Sebastian took the porch steps in one jump with the dogs at his heels. The house was still locked up. It didn't even look as if she'd been inside.

'Damn,' he cursed as he almost fell over his suitcase, right where he'd left it himself.

He wheeled it inside with him, sweat sticking his wetsuit to his back. He was so tired... He hadn't finished packing for Chicago...he hadn't even had time to get changed.

'Don't make me spill anything else on this—I need it,' he said sternly to Stormy, who was sniffing the case as if it was loaded with ice-cream.

The dog wagged her tail and cocked her head. He wondered what it must be like to think only thoughts of food and love all day—certainly a hell of a lot less complicated than being a human.

'Mila!' he called again, dumping the suitcase on the bed.

She wasn't in the upstairs bathroom. She wasn't anywhere.

He pulled out his phone. No missed calls. He kicked off his shoes and heaved himself out of the wetsuit. He needed a shower badly, but he barely even registered being under the water when he stepped into it.

He was mad at himself for the way he'd acted earlier. Why *would* she call him?

He would check her place next...

'Mila!'

He went to knock on her door, then caught himself. He

checked in every single direction for anyone who might have followed him with a camera, then pounded it with a fist. His hair was still wet from the shower. A woman passed by and eyed him up and down.

'I know her,' he explained. 'Mila, come out—we need to talk.'

He shot to the window and peered inside. 'No, no, no, no.... Are you kidding me?'

Her bedroom was practically empty. There were barely any clothes left on the hangers she always kept on the wardrobe doors instead of inside it. He loved it that she did that. The dresser was empty, too. Nothing but the hair dryer that had been there before she'd moved in.

When he called her it went straight to voicemail.

He set off at a jog, in the direction of the dive shop. She might have moved to a hotel—somewhere more private, he thought, trying to think of some logical explanation. She might have gone to another part of the island, where she wouldn't have to be around the MAC.

But why would she do that?

They were supposed to be leaving for Chicago in a matter of hours.

He was starting to get a very bad feeling. She had packed all her bags...she hadn't said goodbye...

His phone buzzed, hot in his pocket.

'Mila?' he answered, without checking.

He stopped at the beach shack, sank to a stool in the shade. Someone he knew offered him a coconut and he accepted it gratefully.

'Dr Becker? It's Ava in Personnel—is everything all right?'

His human resources manager and all-round star player. 'Ava? What's going on?'

'Maybe you can tell me...' Ava sounded confused. 'I

just had a check-in announcement come through on my email. Dr Ricci has checked in at the airport in Denpasar. Something didn't strike me as right, though. I thought I'd heard her say a while ago that she was going to void the ticket and go to Chicago first.'

Sebastian dug his straw hard into the coconut flesh and swivelled the stool away from the bar. No one should see his face right now.

'I'll deal with this—thank you, Ava,' he said.

Amelia Ricci's face was a picture of confusion as she flung the front door open seconds after Mila had stepped wearily from a taxi. It was so cold in Rye…the hedges round the lawn were bald. She wasn't used to it.

'Mila, what are you doing here? My God, you must be freezing.'

Mila felt numb inside and out as she was bundled into her mother's soft cardigan-clad arms. She couldn't cry… she'd run out of tears—or at least she'd thought so, until she smelled the scent of her childhood.

'I've missed you, Mum.'

Mila crumpled into the familiar warmth. She had missed this. Even though she had felt this sense of home in Sebastian's arms until she'd messed it all up.

'I think I've done something really stupid, Mum.'

'What's happened?'

Her mother ushered them both inside, wrapped a green woollen blanket around Mila's shoulders and placed her on the sofa. She sank back against the cushions with the elephant covers on—the ones Annabel had brought back from India one time.

'Mila, are you hurt?'

She'd only just realised she was crying again. 'No, I'm not hurt, Mum. I'm pregnant. It's Sebastian's.'

Her mother's hand found hers and grasped it tight. Then she wrapped her arms around her again and held her for a long time.

'It's OK…that's not the end of the world. Here, take your jacket off…'

'I told him—or rather he guessed—and then he freaked out because I'd kept it a secret. I don't want to lose him because of this, but I can't do it.'

'What can't you do?'

Her mother helped her remove her leather jacket, sleeve by sleeve, she was too weak at this point.

'My goodness, look how tanned you are!'

'I can't have a baby, Mum.'

Her mother tutted, shook her head. 'Mila, you *can* have a baby. You're already pregnant.'

Mila took a cushion and pushed a strangled noise out into an elephant. 'It was an accident.'

'But you do you want this baby with him?'

'I don't know… Yes… I shouldn't have left without talking to him properly…it's absolutely the worst way to hurt him. I tried to call him when I got off the plane but his phone's turned off. He's probably halfway to Chicago by now.'

'Chicago?' Her mother placed a hand to her knee.

'I was supposed to go there with him to meet his family.'

'So this is serious? With Sebastian?'

Mila offered a non-committal shrug, but the depth of what she'd done and how she felt was really sinking in now. She might have just run away from the best thing ever to have happened to her.

'Listen, I'm going to make us some tea and then we can talk about this.'

Mila watched her mother fuss around the kitchen through bleary eyes. She must look such a mess—she hadn't slept at all on the plane. She'd sat there listening idly to meditation podcasts, feeling terrible after her snap decision, which she'd made when she'd been in fight-or-flight mode. She hadn't expected the regret to start as soon as the plane took off.

She grimaced into the cushion. She had gone without talking to him first. Just like his ex, Klara, had done. They'd barely ever talked about her—it was a moot point for the most part, because Mila had been able to see he'd moved on…with *her*.

But she knew him well enough by now. She'd been trained to read his body language. His moods had used to darken whenever Klara's name had come up. Her departure and subsequent refusal to talk to him had devastated him, and now *she* had done exactly the same thing.

CHAPTER TWENTY

THE TOURISTS AT the gift shops, the queue for business class… It would usually have been torture. But Sebastian had somehow succeeded in zoning out the drone of chatter and the beeps of loud speakers. If people took photos of him he didn't notice, but he waited till he was checked in and standing by the window in the departure lounge to call Jared.

'I can't come to Chicago. Something's come up.'

He explained the situation as best he could, told him Mila was pregnant and that it wasn't planned, that he had to go and make things right.

He wanted to. He'd booked the next flight out to London. He figured if he could get to her maybe she would listen to him before she decided on anything too rash.

'This is crazy, brother!' Jared was confounded. 'Do you love this woman? I mean, *really* love her enough to have a kid with her?'

'I do—absolutely.'

Jared let out the longest sigh down the phone. 'Then we'll miss you at the party. So will Mom. We have some news for you that would've been better given in person. But I support you.'

Sebastian didn't need his support on this—not that he would tell his brother that.

He'd asked for Jared's opinion once before, when Klara had left him. Brother to brother, Jared had advised him not to go after her—not to fly over to Thailand, or Kathmandu, or any of the other places she'd gone to teach after humiliation had forced her to abort all form of contact with him. So Sebastian had let her go…until he'd missed her too much.

Then he'd flown to all those places, searching for her—of course he had. He'd just never told anyone. It had been a regrettable set of moves, on reflection. Klara had refused to see him in any of those places either.

Luckily he'd fallen in love with Gili Indah while he'd been flying out from Bali every weekend to try and find her, until eventually he'd never left the island at all—not to look for her, anyway. He'd made a life there at the MAC, he was needed and respected on the island, and there was so much more for him to do.

He wouldn't leave the island now for anyone.

Except Mila.

He was a zombie by the time the flight landed. His phone was dead, but it was probably best not to announce his arrival to Mila; he'd keep it a surprise in case she tried to escape him. He'd been through that before…never again.

Even his bones were cold by the time he was watching the English scenery float past from a car. And it was raining.

He'd found her mother's address on the system at the MAC, told his team where he was going, left the dogs with Ketut and Wayan…

But he still couldn't quite believe it when he found himself standing on the doorstep of the small redbrick house in Rye.

Amelia Ricci stood up from the bed at the familiar *ding-dong* sound and smoothed down her red-striped skirt. Mila hadn't even noticed before that her mother was all dressed up. She'd been too distracted by her perfume. At first it had smelled so good, but now it was abhorrent to her insides.

'That will be Julian.' Her mother glanced at her in the mirror on the dresser and bouffed up her hair.

Mila fought a smile and placed a hand to her belly. She'd been wondering when this would come up.

'Who's Julian?'

'I wasn't sure things would become serious, so I didn't say anything much to you about him before now, but I think that maybe he's a keeper. He's a doctor, like you— a paediatrician down at St Germaine. Come and meet him.'

Her mother hovered in the doorway.

'On second thoughts, meet him later,' she said.

Mila was grateful. She was happy her mother seemed to have acquired a boyfriend in the time since she'd been gone, but she didn't want to meet him right now.

She had slept for a few hours and showered, and booked an appointment with the family obstetrician, but now it was evening in the UK and her jet lag was playing with her mind as much as the thought of Sebastian, whose phone still appeared to be dead or switched off.

'Will you carry on with this while I'm gone?'

Her mother gestured to the open drawers and boxes, shooting her a look of apprehension. They'd been going through Annabel's stuff. Photos, books, rosettes, love letters still in their envelopes.

'I'm OK with it, Mum,' she said. And she was, she realised.

She heard her mother make a strange sound as she opened the front door downstairs. Mila smiled to herself. Her mother deserved someone who treated her like a goddess. She'd been through so much.

She was studying a photo of herself and Annabel on

either side of a man dressed as a giant strawberry when the stairs outside the room creaked again.

'Um… Mila?' Her mother looked quite sheepish, peering around the doorway. 'It wasn't Julian.'

The door opened wide.

Mila stood up in her socks and leggings and her heart started crashing against her ribs even before she saw him.

She dropped the photo.

Sebastian stepped into her old bedroom and the familiar scent of him took her hyperactive nostrils by surprise. It did something strange to her insides, where their baby was—something good—and her eyes clouded over with tears. In a second she was falling against his chest as he stood there in the middle of the floor, on the rug where she'd used to play dolls and cars with Annabel.

'You're here…'

'You gave me no choice.'

'I'm so sorry I left you…' She breathed into his jacket, clutching the lapels and kissing his lips. He was cold; she'd never felt his lips so cold. 'Sebastian, I know it was terrible of me, but I totally freaked out.'

'I know,' he said, putting equally cold hands to her face.

She leaned her cheek against one palm; she had missed him.

'And I know why you're scared of this, Mila, but you can't ever do this to me again. This is something we will deal with together from now on, OK?'

Mila had almost forgotten her mother was there until the doorbell rang again.

'That *will* be Julian. It was nice to meet you, Dr Becker,' she said. 'I'll leave you two to talk.'

Before she left she shot a look of approval at Mila, for Sebastian.

'You were meant to be in Chicago by now,' Mila whispered, stepping back and keeping hold of his hands. She never wanted to let him go.

He looked exhausted and unshaven but utterly perfect—even out of context in the house she'd grown up in. He was wearing jeans and a designer sweater, and a brown leather jacket. Her hands found her belly again. He'd brought a ray of hope with him from the island.

'A strawberry man?' he said now, half smiling as he bent to pick up the photo.

'It was a pick-your-own-strawberries day and he was the mascot,' she explained, running a finger over Annabel's face in the photo.

Her twin was here in this room—she could feel her right now...just as she had sometimes felt her on the island, too. Was this what Annabel wanted? To see her happy with a guy she'd unknowingly approved for Mila years ago?

She would have shivered at the thought before, but maybe she just hadn't wanted to allow herself happiness, she realised. She'd been wrapped up in her guilt over the accident for so long... She had someone else to think about now, though. She was going to need to be strong.

Sebastian scanned the items on the floor, taking in the trophies and trinkets, the weird-looking carved camel Annabel had got from Dubai.

'This was the room we shared till we were eighteen,' said Mila. 'And this is me finally moving on.' She sighed, motioning to the half-empty drawer she'd already sorted through. She smiled tentatively at him. 'Can you ever forgive me?'

'Mila...' he said, shaking his head.

He shut his eyes, dragged a hand across his face, and for a second she thought that maybe he had come here to break things off. That she'd damaged something that couldn't be fixed.

'I was angry with you for keeping the news about our baby from me,' he admitted, chewing his cheek.

Her stomach sank.

'I'm not going to pretend you didn't rip me to shreds. You must know how much I love you. You must also know how much raising a kid with you would be...' He trailed off, as if he couldn't find the words.

She covered her mouth with her hand. She had never heard him tell her he loved her until now. She was utterly shocked at how the words thrilled her.

'It would be the kind of challenge I'm ready for.'

He shook his head again, almost as if he couldn't believe the words coming out of his mouth either. It made her heart soar again.

'I mean, this kid's going to be feral...running about the island with two dogs, all sandy...'

'Let it be feral. I love you, too. Sebastian. I *do* love you. And I know I haven't been the easiest person to deal with, but I'm willing to try and make things work. On the island.'

There was no question in her mind that she'd go back to the island. She missed it already—and the MAC, and little Jack.

'We can do this together if you're really sure it's what you want?'

'*You* are what I want, Mila, and this baby.'

His words were like a confetti bomb going off in her chest and she moved to sit astride him on the edge of the bed, arms and legs wrapped around him.

'I'm so sorry I made you miss your mother's birthday,' she said, kissing him everywhere she could reach, as though he might suddenly disappear in a flash.

She had been through worse, but he was her safe place now. She could feel it—warmth, security and...*home*, she thought. She was home with him.

He let out a sigh into her hair. 'Technically we were supposed to be on that plane to Chicago,' he said, wrapping his hands in her hair, the way he always did. 'But the party's not till Friday, so there's still time for us to get there.'

He kissed her, and the scent of his jacket was driving her hormones crazy.

'You could take me round some of the English countryside, show me off to your friends...'

'Stop talking,' she told him.

She was already sliding his leather jacket off and unbuttoning his shirt.

CHAPTER TWENTY-ONE

SEBASTIAN POPPED THE olive from his virgin martini into his mouth, appreciating Mila from a distance. Her hair was up in a bun again, with soft tendrils framing her face. And she was wearing the fitted blue dress from Bali he'd brought with him—just in case. She looked incredible; she was clearly the best-dressed, most eye-catching woman at the party. But maybe he was biased—she was carrying his baby, after all.

'She seems to have made a good impression on them already,' Jared observed next to him, sipping his own martini. 'Shame you had to move all the way to that island to find her. but still...'

He grinned, slapped his shoulder, and Sebastian shifted on his feet as the box in his jacket pocket dug into his skin.

'I guess this is your way of giving me final brotherly approval,' he said.

'You did the right thing, going to get her,' Jared said seriously.

'I know.'

The party was in full swing. Mila was standing by the buffet table now, chatting happily to Jared's wife Laura and little Charlie, and Sebastian's mother, too. His mother seemed to adore her already.

It hadn't been that tough to convince her to come once

he'd shown her a photo of the double bed on the private jet. They'd slept there, eaten caviar, indulged in some other bed-based activities and even watched *Star Wars*—which he'd remembered neither of them had ever seen.

They'd spent part of yesterday quietly breaking the news of her pregnancy to his family. His mother was so excited about being a grandma again she had already asked her assistant to book her a flight to Bali. She had never even been to visit him on the island before, Sebastian realised, but this was not the moment to feel offended.

The crowds seemed to part as he made his way over to Mila.

'Mila Ricci, do I need to tell you how much I love you in that dress?'

She sighed contentedly and leaned against him as he ran a hand gently across her stomach. He still got a kick out of imagining their baby. Boy or girl, he wasn't bothered which—he knew it would be the love of his life…after Mila.

'I'd better wear it some more, before I get too big for it to fit,' she replied, turning in his arms.

'I'll just get you a bigger one made.'

'I'll wear it every day in surgery.'

'You can wear whatever you like under your white coat…or nothing at all.'

She laughed.

He knew his family and the entire badminton club were watching surreptitiously from their various spread-out social circles around the flower-decorated marquee.

Jared had spared no expense, as usual. There were flowers, multiple musical performers—including a six-piece band— a lavish feast to put an eighteenth-century king to shame, and later there would be fireworks in the gardens by the Japanese koi lake to close the monumental evening.

He could tell Mila had been a little surprised by the

extravagance, but there was one more thing to do. It was now or never.

His heart sped up as he lowered himself to one knee in front of her.

'Sebastian, what are you...?'

A crowd started gathering and on the orchid-covered stage the band's jovial tune quivered into quiet.

'Sebastian...' Mila had gone red.

Jared handed him a microphone. He'd considered waiting till they were alone, but there were five hundred people gathered here—he had to give them something worth gossiping about.

Slowly he opened the lid of the little black velvet box.

He heard her gasp, watched her eyes pool with tears as she took in the stunning diamond ring set in platinum. He'd had ten diamonds studded around the main one, so it sparkled the way he knew all women dreamed their engagement ring would sparkle. He'd had to wait till Mila had been whisked off by his mother for an anti-jet-lag massage to go and collect it.

'I can't believe this...'

'Mila,' he said, focusing on her face.

She met his eyes and he knew he'd made the right decision. He wanted to cement this *now*.

'I know this has been crazy, and quick, and God knows neither of us expected any of it, but you are the best thing ever to have walked off the boat onto that island and I want you there with me for the rest of our lives.' He took a deep breath. 'Will you do me the immense honour of becoming my wife? Will you marry me?'

Mila looked as if she couldn't speak. For a second he thought maybe he'd gone too far. Someone pulled out a camera, but he saw Jared put a hand across the lens to stop them.

'Mila?'

'Yes, Sebastian—yes! Sorry, I'm in shock. *Yes!* Of course I will marry you.'

They were kissing now, and she was laughing, crying, hugging him. All before he'd even slid the ring on her finger.

'She said yes!' he yelled needlessly to the crowd, pulling her into him again. Relief flooded through him. 'God, I love you when you're blushing,' he growled into her ear.

'Can I get a photo of the happy couple?' someone asked. And suddenly there were cameras everywhere.

Mila stepped in front of him. 'No, thank you, we don't want any photos.'

'It's OK,' he said, taking her hand.

She squinted up at him. 'What do you mean? You hate all this!'

'This is a moment I'm proud of,' he replied decisively, and they happily posed for the crowd, with Mila's ring the centrepiece.

'You've changed,' she teased him.

He rolled his eyes, smiling. He knew people would always gossip, but he'd learned to let it go a little more since Mila had arrived. If she didn't care about the media, why should he care any more? And that little kid's newspaper article had thrown a positive light on his mounting new reputation as an island entrepreneur.

He knew the negative press—if it ever came again—wouldn't affect his work, or the people he loved. That was all that mattered. He had new priorities now.

Jared was at the microphone suddenly, tapping it. Charlie was gripping his father's pocket, holding a toy dinosaur in his other hand.

'Congratulations to my brother and his fiancée Dr Mila Ricci, everybody!'

The crowd went crazy. His mother was wiping tears from her eyes.

'And, seeing as this is a night for announcements, I have one myself,' Jared continued, clearing his throat. 'I am delighted to say happy seventieth birthday to our wonderful, long-suffering mother!'

The applause was rapturous and their mother performed a curtsey, but Jared wasn't done.

'I would also like to say that that this will be the final season of *Faces of Chicago*.'

The gasps around the marquee were audible.

'From early next year I'll be spending more time in Indonesia, concentrating on getting a new Becker Institute facility for wellness and healing up and running. My brother and I...*and* his fiancée...will let you know more as soon as we can. For now, however, I'm sure he'll be busy with wedding plans.'

Sebastian shot Mila a secret smile. Jared had discussed this with them last night, of course, but it still felt strange to know it was actually happening, after all this time.

He'd turned those investors down already, telling them he was keeping this one in the family, and Jared was coming over for three months initially, to partner him on planning, recruitment and development. He and Laura would also look for schools on Bali for Charlie.

'I have a feeling things will be different around the island pretty soon,' Mila said, admiring her ring again.

'I have a feeling you're right,' he said, drawing her closer for a photo with Charlie and his dinosaur.

One year later

Baby Hope Annabel Becker was watching the tiny turtles on the sand with keen interest as Mila sat with her near the surf.

'Do you want to release one?' she whispered, revelling in the baby-soft curls of Hope's hair against her cheek.

They were sitting at the shoreline, barefoot. The moon was high in the sky. The annual sea turtle fundraiser was the perfect opportunity to introduce Hope to the baby turtles who'd grown from eggs in the sanctuary and were now ready to explore their new ocean home around the reef.

'We've released a hundred so far—thanks to Jack, here.' Sebastian grinned as his sandy feet appeared alongside little Jack's in the water. 'He wants to show you this one.'

Little Jack was learning to walk and talk. Wayan looked on from a seat nearby as her son shoved a baby turtle in Mila's face enthusiastically, and she laughed as Wayan rushed over and swept him up, handing the turtle back.

'Was that ice-cream on his face?' Mila asked Sebastian.

Wayan was wiping some kind of smear from Jack's cheek behind them and Sebastian grimaced.

'What can I say? I'm a bad godfather. Good thing I'm so great at everything else.'

Mila laughed and handed him Hope as he sat down beside her. A wave washed up and soaked them fully to their waists. Hope giggled, the way she always did. She loved the ocean.

'Uncy! Uncy!' Jack's vocabulary was improving. He was calling his Uncle Sebastian back already.

'Just taking a moment with my wife, buddy,' he called back. 'And maybe your future girlfriend?'

He glanced down at Hope, put a finger to her tiny hand and winked.

Mila nudged him playfully. 'Are you setting our daughter up already? We're not the only survivors on this island, you know. She'll be free to make her own choice, just like you were.'

'I wasn't free. You trapped me the moment I met you.'

Mila leaned in to kiss him. She didn't care who saw. No one bothered them, and there was no gossip anyway. They were happy together—just a regular couple with a baby—and to everyone else that was probably boring.

They had worked on Jack's cleft lip and palate, reduced his scarring to a minimum, and now he looked like any other rambunctious one-year-old. He was growing as fast as baby Hope.

Everyone on the island seemed to be charting Hope's progress. And luckily for them there was no shortage of willing babysitters, or people to read bedtime stories in the MAC grounds.

When her mother and Julian had visited, they'd started a children's circle—five p.m. on Wednesdays—and Mila had kept it up when they'd left. She still averaged about twenty kids each time.

Sebastian had teased her. 'For someone who said she'd rather have a dog than a family, you now have two dogs and twenty kids!'

'I'm calling this one Sergeant Major,' Sebastian said now, taking Hope's tiny hand and placing it on the turtle's smooth shell.

Mila watched as he dropped a kiss on their baby's head. *If Annabel was here now she'd be so happy to be an auntie*, she mused, just as a yellow butterfly fluttered down and perched on Hope's nose.

Sebastian looked at her. He didn't say it, and neither did she, but butterflies had a habit of landing on Hope. It was mostly whenever Mila thought about her sister...

* * * * *

FALLING AGAIN
FOR THE
SINGLE DAD

JULIETTE HYLAND

MILLS & BOON

For Sarah,
who lovingly read my early works and cheered me on.

PROLOGUE

ELI COLLINS PULLED at the collar of his tux and tried to relax as he walked toward his dad's study. The Collins Research Group Fundraiser was always a stressful event. At least this time, he'd finally brought Amara with him. For the first time in forever, he didn't feel like he was completely living in his dad's long shadow.

Despite the hectic schedules of his last year in medical school, and Amara finishing her nursing degree, they'd been almost inseparable. Amara made Eli believe he could be Dr. Eli Collins, not just the son of Dr. Marshall Collins. He could be as good as his dad. *Better!*

Eli had even spent last weekend looking at engagement rings. He'd agonized over the rings, waffling between two, unable to pick which one was best. After Eli spent an inordinate amount of time staring at each, the polite salesman had finally suggested he consider his options a bit longer. His younger brother, Sam, had goaded him all afternoon, enjoying Eli's indecision—something he couldn't quite seem to kick these days.

Though it wasn't Amara or marriage Eli was questioning. His professional goals had changed. *No*, altered. He was still going to be a doctor. Just not a surgeon—like his dad.

Eli pushed away the prick of anxiety at the base of his

spine. He'd made his choice…he had. But Eli still hadn't found the right words to tell his dad.

His main objective hadn't changed: *be the best doctor.* But he doubted his dad would understand his choice of emergency room medicine when Eli had been groomed to join his dad in surgery. He wasn't questioning his decision—*he wasn't.*

And now his waffling was spilling over into other things. Eli wanted to marry Amara, wanted her to stand beside him and wanted to wake up with her in his arms each morning. Picking out an engagement ring and planning a proposal were supposed to be the easy part.

He'd never considered marriage before he'd met Amara Patel. His parents hadn't set the best example. Marshall was rarely present, and Eli's mother never seemed content. But that wouldn't happen to him and Amara. They loved each other too much. She knew his hopes and dreams, and Amara would cheer him on as he became the best emergency doctor in the city. And he'd never treat her as an afterthought.

The door to his dad's study flew open, and his mother wiped a tear from her cheek before offering her son a watery smile. "He's busy, Eli."

Dr. Marshall Collins was *always* busy. His dad was one of the top heart surgeons in the US *and* a genius inventor of medical devices.

The Collins Valve had drastically decreased the mortality rate of transplant patients waiting for a heart. Dr. Marshall Collins had one of the highest success rates of any transplant surgeon in the country. His dad's reputation was ridiculously impressive, and living up to it seemed almost impossible.

"What's wrong with Mom?" Eli asked as he entered the study. He made sure to get the question out before his dad could tell him what he wanted. Once Marshall started a conversation, he rarely let anyone get a word in.

Marshall's brows knit as he looked up. "Your mother?"

Eli sighed. "She was crying when she left."

How could he not notice that?

If Amara had been crying, Eli would be chasing after her—not sitting behind his desk casually reading emails.

Rubbing his chin, his dad shrugged. "Your mother wanted to go on vacation at the end of the month. Greece, or maybe Jamaica?"

"Those are two very different locations." Marshall really didn't know where his mom wanted to go.

His dad's eyes narrowed slightly at the small criticism. "I wasn't involved in the planning, and the location is irrelevant anyway. I can't go. I have four patients that could get a heart at any time. I told her to take one of her girlfriends."

His dad always had patients that might get a lifesaving gift at any moment. It was his excuse for missed track meets, choir concerts and all of the other activities Eli and his brother Sam were involved in. Though he'd made sure to be at Eli's senior awards ceremony when he was honored as the class valedictorian. He'd even slapped Eli on the shoulder and told everyone that Eli might be better than him one day. That memory had carried Eli through the long stretches where his dad barely seemed to notice him.

But his mother mattered too. And she deserved a vacation with her husband. "Couldn't your partner handle it?" If Eli could unask the question, he would.

The patient came first. That was a rule every Collins family member understood.

"Your mother knows I love her."

"You love her?" The question slipped into the room, and Eli was surprised by the tenderness that hovered in his dad's eyes. But it disappeared almost immediately.

"Of course." His dad's gaze slipped to the picture of his wife on the corner of his desk. "You can be a great doctor, Eli, or a wonderful spouse. Not both. Something always suffers." His father's eyes met Eli's. "And *you* will be extraordinary one day."

The rare compliment tripped along Eli's skin. He and Sam craved these moments. The smallest acknowledgments that their dad saw them—really saw them and their potential.

Eli stood just a hair taller as he asked, "What did you want?"

"Ms. Patel and I had a disagreement. She stormed off, very unbecoming." Marshall shook his head as he typed something on his computer screen. "You know how important what I do is. Make her understand."

Eli listened as his dad dictated the rest of his instructions. The Collins Research Group Fundraiser was a black-tie event designed to highlight the company's research and raise obscene amounts of money for a good cause. It was also his dad's evening to shine. The family always acquiesced to Marshall's demands for the night.

Always...

He'd tried to prepare Amara for what to expect, as the Collins family could be overwhelming—even for those raised in it. But tonight's festivities needed to be perfect—then he'd be able to tell his dad about his change of medical specialty. Surely Amara would be able to put aside any arguments for one night—to make Eli's life easier.

As he opened the door to her suite, Eli saw Amara brush a tear away before she looked at him. Her small bag was sitting on the bed, and he tried to silence the alarm clanging in his brain. "Amara—"

"Did you tell your dad that you plan to go into emergency medicine?" she interrupted.

"What?" Eli blinked. He'd prepped his response for a complaint about his dad. His tongue was thick, and no other words materialized as she raised a delicate eyebrow.

"Did you tell Marshall your plans?" Amara repeated.

"Not yet. It will be easier after the fundraiser," Eli muttered. Tear-filled eyes met his, and Eli hated the reminder of his mother.

"Will it? Because he got you into the surgical residency program at Chicago Memorial Hospital." Amara raised her chin, but he saw her lip wobble.

"That's not possible. I didn't apply for any surgical residencies." Eli shook his head. Chicago Memorial was one of the top surgical residency programs in the country.

"I suspect most anything is possible for Dr. Marshall Collins," Amara countered.

"Maybe." Eli rubbed the back of his head.

"Are you going to take it?" Amara's question was barely audible.

His throat tightened. Chicago Memorial was the chance of a lifetime. "Maybe." The whispered word floated between them, and Eli's stomach dropped as Amara's lip trembled—again. "Chicago Memorial…"

Her dark eyes held his, and a touch of cold swept across him at the despair he saw. Holding out his hands, Eli stepped toward her. She pulled back, and his feet faltered.

What was going on?

"Eli, you have to live *your* life, not his. You don't have to follow the script Marshall has planned for you." Amara hugged herself as her eyes pleaded with him. "Emergency medicine…"

"Is not surgery," Eli bit out, hating the defensive tone in his voice. "I'm the son of Dr. Marshall Collins. I have to live up to that."

"How?" Amara challenged.

Eli shrugged, trying to ignore the tightening in his stomach. Why was she asking this?

And why was her bag sitting on the bed?

"By making the *US News & Reports* annual Best Hospitals and Physicians list, like Dad." His dad had made the list for the last five years, and given Eli and Sam framed copies for inspiration.

"Your dad sleeps at the hospital a few times a week, even when he's not on shift," Amara argued. "He snapped at me for asking if he might be free to have lunch!"

"It's the week of the fundraiser," Eli told her. He knew Marshall slept only a few hours in the lead-up to the event and often ate in his office.

"And the last time I checked, he is still human, Eli. So, he must consume food," Amara bit out. "Are you going to work like that? Be that consumed by the hospital?"

"If that's what it takes."

And then his dad would accept him.

Eli's heart burned as that thought tore through him.

"At what cost?" Amara's teeth bit her bottom lip.

Eli felt like he was failing a test. "Meaning?"

"Are you willing to give up your dreams of working in the ER to be the best surgeon? Are you willing to give up my dreams?"

He watched another tear slip down Amara's cheek, but she didn't wipe this one away. That terrified him more than the lone bag on the bed, but Eli wasn't sure why. "You can come to Chicago with me. I want you to come."

Need you to...

"My father chases success too, and my mother stands by him through every crazy business venture, exciting opportunity and each new goal."

"Because she loves him." Eli stated.

Like you love me.

"That's what love is. Supporting each other."

Amara scoffed. "Really, Eli? I've listened to her cry herself to sleep. Where is her support? Or your mother's support? She's spent a year planning a vacation with your father. It's their thirty-fifth wedding anniversary, and she believes he won't come. Our mothers are part of the perfect picture of our fathers' accomplishments. They're both loving wives, but behind the perfection, they're sleeping in lonely beds."

"My dad saves so many lives." Eli hated his mother's distress, but his dad was right. Their calling had to come first. Amara would understand that. He'd held her after good and bad days during her clinicals. She knew what they did was important—*the most important thing.* "You're going to be a nurse—" His voice cut off as she reached for her bag.

Eli's mouth was dry as he asked, "What are you doing?"

"Going home." Her voice cracked as she laid a hand on his chest. "I'm not what you need."

"You are." He wanted to say more, but the words were trapped in his throat. His breath was ragged as he ran a finger along her cheek. "Stay, please."

"I love you, and I know you see medicine as your calling. But I won't play the role our mothers play for our fathers, showing up to fundraisers or supporting the next big move, the next prestigious business or hospital. I won't pretend everything is fine while inside I'm dying of loneliness. Eli, you want to be the best doctor…" Amara paused, shrugged and added, "Or surgeon, I guess."

"And I will be, but that doesn't mean that we don't belong together," Eli pleaded. His soul was shaking as he tried to think of the right words to make her understand.

"I know what I want, Eli, and it has nothing to do with accolades and ratings. I want to be a nurse, but also a partner, a wife, a mother. And I want a man who will sleep beside me each night, raise our children, plan vacations *and take them—with me*. The patients are important, but so is family. Are you willing to put your family first, even if that means I may be the only one who calls you the best?"

He wanted to say yes. Eli's heart was begging him to scream it, get down on one knee, promise her all those things. But his brain refused to utter the word. Amara was right. He wasn't sure he could promise her that life, not if he wanted to be great—just like his dad. Her lips touched his, and the fire they always brought ripped through him. His soul cried out for her, but he let her walk past him.

Eli loved Amara, but his dad loved his mother too. Love wasn't enough to stop the hurt, and Eli refused to spend a lifetime hurting Amara. "I love you," Eli uttered the words, wishing they were enough.

He heard a soft sob as Amara pulled open the door, and he barely managed to keep his knees from hitting the floor.

"Goodbye, Eli."

Amara's last words tore through him, but Eli didn't let himself break. There was the fundraiser to get through, then he could spend the rest of the night mourning what he'd lost.

Spend the rest of his life trying to put the pieces back together.

CHAPTER ONE

DR. ELI COLLINS's breath caught as he stared at the gaggle of new employees. The first night was always a bit disorienting for the new hires, and they tended to arrive in packs for the first week or so. A petite woman, with long dark hair, lagged behind the rest.

The graceful way she moved sent a pulse of need through him. *Amara?* He hadn't seen her in years.

And he wasn't seeing her now.

Still, Eli's heart pounded as he tried, and failed, to control his reaction to the miniscule possibility she was here. Hope, need, love, all wrapped around him before pain dismissed the fantasy.

Amara Patel was the best part of his past—and the worst. Any time he saw someone who bore a vague resemblance to her, Eli would stare for just a moment. It was never Amara, but after nearly a decade of trying, he still couldn't break the habit.

"The new crop of nurses and doctors start tonight." Dr. Griffin Stanfred slapped Eli's shoulder as he slid in front of him.

"I know." Eli shifted, trying to catch another glimpse of the woman. But she'd disappeared with the rest of the group. He wanted to run after them, force his mind and heart to realize that the mystery hire was just another look-alike. A beautiful, graceful, jet-haired woman, a talented nurse or doctor, sure, but it wasn't his Amara.

His—that was a ridiculous thought. Amara hadn't been his for nearly a decade. It was just a symptom of Eli's loneliness.

He had let his desire to be the perfect son of the great Dr. Marshall Collins cost him his happiness. At least he'd come to his senses before taking on a surgical residency he didn't want. That decision had been the right one, but Marshall had refused to speak to Eli during the entire duration of his residency and subspecialty training or the years that came after.

Only after Eli had given a keynote address at the second-largest emergency medicine conference in the country, eight months ago, had his father reached out to him. Their relationship was still more professional than personal, but Eli couldn't stop the hope that one day Marshall might finally soften toward him. If Eli just achieved enough…

He let his eyes linger on the staff lounge door for a moment longer. Eli took a deep breath. Amara wasn't at his hospital—*she couldn't be.*

She'd landed a job at a prestigious university research hospital a week before graduating with her nursing degree. And two weeks after they'd broken up. Eli had watched from the corner of the room as she celebrated with their friends.

He'd wanted to reach out to her, to tell her how proud he was, celebrate with her. But he'd worried that if he said anything, he would beg her to take him back. Instead, Eli had made his excuses and left the party. It was one of the many moments in his past he wished he could change.

But life didn't have a rewind button.

Eli hadn't gone into surgery, but every activity he did was weighed against what it could do for his career. How it would improve Boston General. Make the institution great. Get it noticed.

Get him noticed.

Because no matter Eli's achievements, he couldn't stop the questions about his father. Even when he was surrounded by emergency professionals, someone always asked if he was related to Dr. Marshall Collins. Their eyes inevitably widened when Eli admitted he was his son. And part of him evaporated as they peppered him with questions about his father's legacy.

You're enough...

Eli's soul lifted a bit. Even after all these years, Amara's voice still floated through his memories just when he needed it. That constant kept him sane and yet sometimes drove him mad.

Eli had considered calling Amara so many times. Just to check in, say hello. See if she'd like to catch up; if she'd gotten the life she wanted; if she'd moved on. But he couldn't, because if she had, then the tiny ball of hope Eli had never managed to extinguish would die. His heart didn't want to accept that final loss.

It was easier to imagine Amara in the ER than at home with a husband and family who loved her. *Safer...* They'd both believed emergency medicine was their calling. Even if he'd doubted it for a brief period.

"Gina quit. Took a job in Baltimore." Susan Gradeson, the ER's head nurse, sighed as she laid her laptop on the charging pad at the nurses' station. "Luckily, one of the new hires agreed to take her shift." Before Eli could ask any questions, Susan hustled away.

Boston General's emergency room had one of the highest trauma rates in the nation. It was used by physicians and nurses as a launching pad to one of the nationally ranked academic hospitals that dotted the city. If only they were recognized on that list, then maybe the other hospitals wouldn't have such an easy time siphoning away Boston Gen.'s talent.

Eli had been offered a position at several of those academic hospitals too. But he loved the chaotic nature of Boston Gen. He thrived on the constant challenges, and even took pleasure in turning down the jobs. He'd bring in the offer letter and let the staff help him draft a blistering no-thank-you note. Eli never sent those, but it was an excellent way to let his friends and colleagues blow off steam.

His cell dinged with an image of his niece, Lizzy. She was waving at the camera; her cheeks covered in chocolate pudding. Eli darted around the corner and video called his mother. She'd taken to the role of grandma the minute Lizzy was born. And she'd refused to allow him to hire a nanny when Lizzy came to live with Eli eight months ago. He didn't know how he would have survived without his mom's calming presence.

He'd never expected to be a father. Marshall hadn't set a great example, but Eli was doing his best. Which mostly meant Googling everything and hoping the mistakes he made were minor. His insides relaxed a bit as Lizzy waved again. Lizzy looked a lot like her father—a man she'd never remember.

Eli pushed his grief away. The months since his brother's passing had dulled the pain, but there were still moments where Eli had to remind himself that he couldn't call Sam after a hard day. Or text him a celebratory note after an unexpected success.

At least he had Lizzy.

"Hi, cutie!" Eli cooed as his niece played with the chocolate pudding on her high chair tray. Lizzy needed a happy parent, not a concerned, uncomfortable uncle who was still terrified that he was going to screw everything up.

He smiled and laughed at her silly antics as worries niggled at the back of his brain. Eli never wanted Lizzy to see how terrified he was to be a father. He may not have planned to be a dad, but he couldn't fail Lizzy now that he was.

"Did she eat any of that?" Eli shook his head as he stared at the messy, almost two-year-old.

"A bit." His mother laughed. "I was just getting ready to put her in the bathtub. Figured she might as well have some fun. Every kid loves to play with pudding at this age. I've got pictures of you and—" she paused for just a moment "—and Sam covered in the sweet stuff."

A nurse with dark hair passed by in Eli's peripheral vision. *Amara?* She'd already slipped into a patient's room by the time he turned to get a better look.

Why was his mind playing tricks on him tonight?

"Look!" Lizzy giggled as the pudding dripped off her fingers.

Focus, he reminded himself. Smiling at Lizzy, Eli shook his head. "You really are a mess—a cute mess."

"Daddy!" Lizzy stuck her tongue out at the camera.

Eli's stomach clenched. That title still felt off. Like he was robbing Sam somehow. "It's Uncle Eli, sweetheart."

"Daddy," Lizzy repeated.

"Well, I'm going to get her cleaned up." His mom offered a soft smile, though he could see her blink away a few tears. "It's okay to be daddy, Eli. Maybe it's what she needs. Sam would understand—even give you a hard time about it."

"Probably." Eli agreed, then waved one last time before his mother shut off the video connection. Eli wasn't Lizzy's father. Sam was…always would be.

But he was gone.

He'd been killed in a plane crash along with his wife,

Yolanda, heading to a surgical conference, just as Lizzy was starting to say her first words.

Like *Daddy*.

Daddy... It held so much meaning. Eli still felt lost, but Lizzy was his responsibility. *No*, she was his daughter. When she was older, he would make sure that Lizzy knew as much about her parents as possible.

Sam was the good son, after all. The one who'd followed in his father's footsteps, though he'd refused to take on any roles at his father's research facility after Yolanda announced she was pregnant. It was unfair that Eli was now the one putting Sam's daughter to bed, getting to watch silly pudding videos, planning her future.

And hearing the word Daddy.

When Sam and Yolanda had asked him to be Lizzy's guardian less than a week after her birth, Eli had agreed without thinking about it. But he'd never expected to take custody of Lizzy. He loved Sam, though watching him with his wife and daughter had always sent a wave of jealousy through him. But Eli's goals didn't include a family.

Hadn't included a family.

In the horrid days after the accident, Eli had held their sleeping child feeling devastated. But he'd sworn to raise her with all the love Sam had shown for her. Somehow, Eli was going to be both an amazing father and a top emergency room doctor. The patients *and* Lizzy came first. He could do this—*he had to*.

Turning, he stared at the room where the dark-haired nurse had disappeared a few minutes ago. Eli didn't think she'd exited yet. If a patient was being difficult, she might need help. That was why he was moving toward the room. Not because he needed to prove to himself that it wasn't Amara.

Just before he got to the door, Susan grabbed his arm.

"I've got a kid in room 7 that needs stitches and an elderly man in 4 that probably needs to be admitted for pneumonia. Any chance you can clear either of them out of *my* ER?"

"*Your* ER?" Eli echoed. "Last time I checked, I was the senior doctor on staff this evening."

"That supposed to mean something?" Susan quipped as she marched toward another room.

That was Eli's running joke with Susan. The head nurse had worked at Boston General longer than anyone, and she ran a tight ship. Everyone fell in line when Susan Gradeson ordered it.

Eli looked over his shoulder one last time. But the nurse, or more likely, the figment of his imagination, still hadn't materialized.

He tried to convince himself that it wasn't Amara. *It wasn't.*

Eli had a few hours left on his shift. He'd see the dark-haired woman before he went home. Then his brain could stop hoping that a miracle had occurred. He had never stopped loving Amara, but that was a feeling he'd learned to live with.

Amara held her breath as Dr. Eli Collins finally walked away from the room where she was hiding. Her pulse rate was elevated, and she could feel the heat in her cheeks. Eli was here…*here.*

She'd already double-checked on the patient, a young woman waiting on her release papers following a minor fender bender. Amara had gone over the concussion protocol with her and made sure she knew the indicators for internal bleeding. Now Amara was hovering. Her stomach twisted as she tried to work out what to do.

She'd left Massachusetts Research after her relationship with Dr. Joe Miller had crashed and burned in full view of all her colleagues. No matter how high she'd held her head, there'd been whispers when Joe immediately started dating her ER colleague Kathleen Hale. Louder whispers when they'd eloped a few weeks later.

Amara had been considering a change for years. If Joe's affair was the catalyst for it, so what? But now she was facing working with another ex—and she'd never fully recovered from their breakup…

Amara was independent. That was the word she used to describe herself. *Independent*…that word sounded so much better than afraid of commitment. Terrified of losing your dreams to someone else's goals. Of disappearing in the one relationship where you were supposed to stand out.

That was the fear that had driven her to walk away from Eli. It had been the right choice. But it didn't stop the regret that sometimes seeped deep into her bones as she lay awake at night. They wouldn't have worked. It was the mantra she'd repeated for years. He wanted to chase glory, like her father. Eventually, that need destroyed everything it touched.

She'd watched her mother give all of herself to her father. All her dreams, her goals had been sacrificed to support him. And she'd gotten almost nothing in return.

Even after her mother was diagnosed with breast cancer, Amara's father hadn't put away his bid to secure funding for his newest start-up. Her mother had fought for her life without her husband by her side. And it had been Amara holding her hand at the end, not the man she'd stood beside for nearly forty years.

The patient coughed, and Amara's cheeks heated again. The young woman hadn't commented on her extended presence—*yet*, but she was watching Amara count the supplies in the cabinet. Amara made a note to restock the extra-small gloves, and wanted to shake herself.

Coward! her brain screamed. She should march out of the room and pretend that Eli was just any other doctor on the ER floor.

Boston General was supposed to be her fresh start. Her new place.

And Eli was here.

Did he still have to look so handsome?

Amara hated the selfish thought. Eli had been gorgeous in college, and the last decade had been very kind to the man. No beer belly or receding hairline for him. No, he was still the tall, broad-shouldered, dark-haired medical student that had been every woman's dream date. Except now, he was an ER doctor. *Not a surgeon.*

Joy tapped across Amara's skin. Eli had evidently followed his own path. That didn't make it any easier to walk out the door and say hello, but she was surprised by how much it warmed her heart.

Amara once believed they'd grow old together. That they'd work in the same ER and go home to a small house with a couple of kids. It had been a good fantasy, and for a short period, she thought those dreams were enough for Eli too. But what was a happy home life compared to medical glory?

Amara's heart clenched as she forced the past away.

What was Eli doing at Boston General?

She'd assumed he'd gone to Chicago. It was ridiculous, but every year she checked the online annual hospital report to see if he was listed with the other top surgeons. He'd wanted to be like his father so much, but working at Boston Gen. wasn't likely to land Eli on that list.

In a city full of prestigious academic hospitals, Boston Gen.'s administration wasn't interested in attracting investors that would make demands that took resources away from the hospital's patients. Which meant it was chronically underfunded in its quest to provide quality care. Eventually, many of its talented physicians and nurses sought out the hospitals with research dollars, beautiful new buildings and better hours.

The low retention rate for employees at Boston Gen. was well-known. It was one of the reasons why, when Amara figured she needed a change to jump-start her life, she'd applied here.

If she'd known Eli was working at this hospital… She forced that thought away. It didn't matter. Amara was not going to be another retention statistic on Boston Gen.'s ledger.

Squaring her shoulders, she marched from the room and ran directly into the head nurse, Susan.

"Sorry!" Amara grabbed her to keep them from tumbling to the floor. She instinctively looked over Susan's shoulder. Eli was gone—at least he hadn't witnessed her bout of clumsiness.

What would he say when they finally crossed paths?

Amara ignored that thought. She didn't want to think about Eli, now. Or ever, though there was little hope of that.

"No harm done…?" Wrinkles ran along Susan's forehead as she stared at her.

"Amara," she said helpfully. She'd stepped in at the end of their orientation yesterday when Susan had announced that the ER was short-staffed for this evening's shift. Amara doubted the head nurse had even bothered to write her name down before rushing back to her post.

She looked around Susan one more time and then mentally chastised herself. Amara needed to get Eli out of her head.

"Looking for someone?" Susan raised an eyebrow.

"A doctor… I…no," she stuttered.

Amara suspected Susan knew she was lying, but at least

she didn't press her. "While we have a lull, I wanted to see if you'd help with the health fair in a few weeks. All the hospital's departments have a few booths. Several of the ER doctors always run their own. There is a competition—the winner gets two extra vacation days."

Eli would love that. He'd thrived in competitive environments in college—always pushing himself to come out on top. But Amara hadn't been the right prize. She knew that wasn't fair, but a decade later, she still woke up from dreams where he was holding her. Her subconscious refused to give up the whisper of hope Amara was too scared to voice while awake.

Pain rippled up her spine, but she ignored it. Amara was starting a new chapter, and it did not include Dr. Eli Collins. Straightening her shoulders, she gave Susan her full attention. "Put me down for whichever booth needs help." Her voice didn't sound as strong as she wanted, but at least it was a start.

A man walked behind Susan, and Amara made sure to keep her gaze focused on the head nurse. She was not going to look for Eli again—*she wasn't*.

"You might want to get to know the doctors who are participating first. Like I said, this helps the community, but the competition…"

Amara waved away Susan's concerns. "It's fine. I don't need extra vacation time." Her father and his new wife lived in California now, and she had no desire to visit.

Not that she'd been invited.

Jovan Patel had barely waited until her mother was gone to set a wedding date. No long mourning period for him.

"We've got a four-car pileup coming in!" one of the nurses cried as she ran past Amara and Susan.

Susan turned and yelled, "Dr. Collins was talking to his

daughter over by room 3, but he might be in room 7, putting in a few stitches now, and Dr. Stanford is in room 6."

Amara's insides chilled. Eli had a daughter. Perhaps even a wife. Her heart raced as she headed for the ambulance bay doors. It was her body prepping for the incoming wounded, not because of Eli.

How simple would life be if she could believe that?

Amara joined Eli as he raced along by the gurney carrying a child. There wasn't time for her to unpack any feelings. She had spent a year in her mother's sick room. She'd been her mother's rock, providing comfort and never letting her emotions show. Never breaking. She drew on all those reserves now.

If Eli was surprised to see her, he didn't show it. "Do you know how old he is, Javier?" Amara asked.

The paramedic shook his head. "Sorry, Amara, no."

"Tell me what we know so far," Eli stated as he guided them into an exam room.

Javier was already passing the child's paperwork to the admissions assistant. "He was in the backseat. Car crushed the driver's side door. He was behind his mother."

"The mother?" Amara asked quietly as she grabbed a pair of gloves. Her insides curled as the paramedic looked over her shoulder at the small boy.

Javier lowered his voice. "Meredith and Landon were bringing her in. She'll go straight to the operating room."

The paramedic's eyes hovered over the child again, and Amara saw him shudder.

"I don't know if he can give you any information, but you might…" Javier's eyes were downcast as he headed for the door. "I've got to get going, two more people were trapped in another car."

The boy's mother might not make it. That was the truth

Javier couldn't bring himself to voice. The child couldn't be more than five. Amara's heart tore. She'd been an adult when her mother passed, and her life had altered completely.

What would happen if...?

"Amara?" Eli asked, his dark eyes moved between their patient and her.

"Nice to see you again, Dr. Collins." She could see the piles of questions buried in his stare. Or maybe she just hoped there were questions to match the dozens clamoring in her brain. This wasn't the time or the place for a reunion, though.

She offered him and their patient a smile as she sat on the bed and started wiping dried blood from a cut above the child's eye. There was no reason to think of her mom now. It was ridiculous. If it wasn't for Eli's shocking presence, she was sure her nerves wouldn't feel so raw.

"I'm just going to look at your eyes." Eli raised his penlight.

"Momma!" The little boy screamed as he pulled at the collar stabilizing his neck.

The yell echoed in the small room, and Amara saw Eli's head pop back. He seemed as surprised by the previously silent child's outburst as she was. Amara slowly ran her gloved fingers along the boy's chin. The motion seemed to calm small kids. She wasn't sure why, but when you found something that worked in the ER, you used it.

"Dr. Collins and I are going to help you while some of the other doctors look after your mom." Amara nodded to the child. "Can you tell me your name?" She patted his hand as she carefully turned it over. There were a few scrapes on his palm, but they were no longer bleeding.

"Momma!" he cried again as his eyes moved between Amara and Eli.

Eli bent over. "Hi, buddy." He waved and stuck his tongue out too.

The action was ridiculous, and Amara had to force her mouth closed.

What was Eli doing?

The little one blinked and then stuck out his own tongue. The child let out a laugh as Eli made another ridiculous face.

Amara barely caught the surprised giggle from escaping her lips. Eli was apparently a pro at calming kids.

He's a father, her brain reminded her.

"Your tongue looks very healthy," Eli cooed. "Now, can you tell me your name?"

The little boy sniffed before pursing his lips and trying to shake his head no. When the child couldn't move his head much, he let out another wail.

"His eyes look normal, and besides the cuts on his forehead and chin, there doesn't appear to be any head injuries," Eli stated quietly. "Can you tell me your name?" he repeated. "We really need to know it, little man."

The child's bottom lip stuck out, but he didn't utter a single word. His small free hand pulled at the neck brace again. Then his eyes darted to the door.

Amara knew he was terrified, and she offered him a bright smile as she got his attention. "You can't move your head until E…" Amara caught herself, but she could feel the heat in her cheeks. They were at work; she couldn't call him Eli.

"Dr. Collins and I need to make sure you are okay. Then we can take this big brace off."

When the boy still didn't say anything, Amara shifted tactics. "Let's play a little game. I want you to squeeze my hand once if the answer is yes, two times if it's no. Understand?"

One light squeeze pressed against Amara's palm. Eli—

Dr. Collins nodded to Amara as she briefly glanced at him before refocusing on the little boy.

"I bet your mom tells you not to talk to strangers, right?" Another soft squeeze pushed against Amara's palm. "That's really smart of your mom," she stated.

Amara wiped more blood away from the cut above the child's eye. It was going to need several stitches. "Did she ever tell you that it was okay to talk to police officers or firefighters if you got lost?"

Another light squeeze and the little boy's eyes started to water. Amara wished there was a way she could put him at ease. If he would just give them his name…

Pushing a bit of his hair off his forehead, Amara patted his cheek to get him to look at her. "Well, we are helpers just like firefighters and police officers. I'm Amara, and I'm a nurse. This is Dr. Collins."

"Eli," he interjected.

His soothing tone washed over the room. Amara's heart beat a little faster. She'd always reacted to Eli. That hadn't changed, but she didn't appreciate it right now. "Can you tell me your name now that you know both of ours?"

"Ricky." The whispered response was barely audible, but it was enough.

"How old are you, Ricky?" Amara leaned closer.

"Five and a half." His lip trembled.

Eli grinned at Amara. The dimple in his left cheek sent a small wave of happiness through her. They'd been a great team years ago. At least that hadn't changed. "Ricky, I need you to tell us if anything hurts."

His blue eyes floated with tears. "My belly."

Standing, Amara squeezed Ricky's hand. "I'm going to lift your shirt, so Dr. Eli can see your stomach."

Deep bruises were already appearing along his chest, where the five-pointed safety belt had held him in place.

It looked painful but had likely saved the boy's life. As Eli slowly felt along Ricky's stomach, the child laughed, and Amara let out a breath she didn't realize she'd been holding.

"Ricky, I think your belly is okay, but I am going to order some pictures to look and make sure. Now I need to check the rest of you." Eli's gaze shot to Amara.

Was he happy she was here? Annoyed? Confused? There were dozens of reasons for her not to care. Dozens...

If only her brain could manage to produce a few on command.

Amara distracted Ricky while Eli finished his examination. She talked about her cat knocking her cup of milk off the counter and was rewarded with a tiny smile. These were the moments she lived for as a nurse. Making a patient's horrid day just a little bit better.

As Eli ran a pen up Ricky's foot, Ricky's toes curled, and the boy giggled. The little guy was probably going to be all right. *At least physically.* If his mom... Amara forced those thoughts away. Boston General was a good trauma center. Ricky's mom was in excellent hands.

"I have a dog named Ketchup." Ricky leaned toward Amara. "What's your cat's name?"

"Pepper," Amara answered without hesitation. Her cat had passed away a few months ago, but Amara still regaled people with his stories. After all, Pepper had been distracting patients for years. His antics had always made Amara laugh, and his snuggles had gotten her through some of her darkest days. Amara still sometimes looked for him when she entered her apartment.

"I think we can take the neck brace off," Eli said.

Amara kept rattling on about Pepper as she removed the brace, enjoying each of Ricky's giggles.

Susan rushed into the room. "The ambulance just radioed in. They managed to free the people in the car behind this little guy and his mom. What's the situation here?"

"Stitches needed, and I want an X-ray and an ultrasound of his belly, but Nurse Patel and I can see to that after."

Nurse Patel...

Eli hadn't almost called her Amara. Clearly, he didn't have any problem thinking of her as a colleague. But then, why would he? She'd ended it, but not because she didn't love him.

But he'd let her walk away.

"Ricky is only five." Amara voiced her concern. "I should stay with him."

"No!"

Eli's forceful command stunned her. Squaring her shoulders, Amara held his gaze. "Eli, we can't leave him alone. His mother..." She puckered her lips. Amara was not going to discuss the fact that Ricky's mother might not make it in front of him.

"This is Boston Gen." Eli crossed his arms. "We don't have medical personnel to spare. *If* you're going to work here, you need to get used to that."

If? How dare he? She wasn't trying to shirk any duties. They couldn't leave an injured child in the ER alone. What would happen if he left his room, or got bored and started exploring the room he was in?

Ricky could get hurt. Eli was a father. Surely, he understood her concern.

The head nurse stared at Eli for a moment before turning her focus back to Amara. "We need all of the medical staff focused on the incoming injured, Amara. I've called one of our volunteers, Stephen. He has four children and six grandchildren. He often sits with our little ones until social services or their parents get here."

An older gentleman bearing a remarkable similarity to

Santa Claus stepped into the room with a backpack full of toys and a stuffed elephant. "Hi, little man."

"Ricky," Amara stated.

"Well, I'm going to hang out with you for a little while, Ricky." Stephen dumped a few toys on the bed, and Ricky's eyes widened.

Eli didn't wait for Amara to follow him. That shouldn't hurt. This was just a job, and, if they were on opposite shifts, they could probably go weeks without seeing each other. Except this was Boston Gen., she reminded herself. If she stayed, Amara was going to be seeing a lot of Eli.

She could do this—*she had to.*

Amara took a deep breath and then marched from the room. If he didn't like her presence here, then Eli could seek new employment. Amara was not going to run.

CHAPTER TWO

SHE WAS HERE. Eli's brain tried to focus as his soul screamed with joy. He wanted to believe his heart was racing from the adrenaline of the emergency, but he knew that wasn't the reason.

Amara was here.

He needed to find a way to keep his emotions in check.

Why had he shouted at her?

Eli wanted to kick himself, but there wasn't time. He hadn't been lying; they didn't have the medical staff to spare with two more critical patients arriving. But he'd demanded Amara come with him because Eli was terrified that if he blinked, she might disappear.

He had no idea why Amara had chosen Boston Gen., but for however long she stayed, she'd be an asset. And he'd see her almost every day. Eli clamped down on the excitement that brought. Amara was kind, intelligent and gorgeous. She was probably happily married with a couple of kids. Which meant working with her was going to be a dream.

And a nightmare.

He'd been impressed with how she'd calmed Ricky, quiet, authoritative and comforting. Eli's interactions with children still felt a bit stilted to him. Like he was an actor pretending. Even with Lizzy, Eli worried that he wasn't showing her enough affection. He never wanted Lizzy to think that she had to earn his love.

Like he'd had to with his own father.

Dr. Griffin Stanfred was already paired with Renee, another nurse, as the first patient rolled through the door. The elderly woman was covered in blood but conscious as Griffin took her into a trauma room.

Javier, the paramedic who delivered Ricky earlier, raced through the glass doors with the other patient. "Crushed legs, head trauma. He's coded once already."

Amara grabbed the other side of the gurney as they headed for trauma room 2. Her face tightened as she listened to Javier describe the injuries. Her dark eyes met his, and Eli knew what she was thinking. Their odds of saving this patient were slim.

Some nights he hated his job.

Susan and two other nurses were waiting for them in trauma room 2. Before they could get him transferred to the hospital gurney, the patient started coding again. Eli initiated CPR.

Amara fit seamlessly into the hectic room. It took over an hour, but they managed to stabilize the patient enough to get him up to surgery. Eli leaned against the door of the trauma room as he watched the surgery nurses rush him off. The man had a collapsed lung and internal bleeding, wounds that on a healthy man might be fatal, but given his age…

Eli sighed. Some nights the ER was filled with infected scratches, burns and coughs. Things that, if people had the resources, they could get treated at their family physician before it needed emergency care. Those nights were horribly dull. He'd take a million of them over the chaos of treating patients he knew were unlikely to survive.

"You okay?" Amara's soft question hung in the quiet trauma room as she put away the last of the supplies.

For just a moment, Eli wanted to tell her the truth. Wanted to shout, *No!*

His life had been crazy—was still crazy. In the last year, he'd gone from being a single professional who spent so much time at the hospital that he'd killed half a dozen easy-to-raise house plants, to a single father.

The transition was terrifying, and as Eli stared into Amara's large brown eyes, his soul begged him to unload a bit of its burden. Explain all the new fears that had materialized when fatherhood was thrust upon him.

Amara had been his safe space once. The keeper of his secrets. The person who listened to all his dreams and never questioned why he wanted a different path from that of his father. Who saw him as Eli, not the son of Dr. Marshall Collins. It would be so easy to pretend that she was asking more than a simple question after a difficult patient. But she was his colleague now, nothing more.

His heart shuddered, but Eli forced himself to nod. "I'm fine." He wanted to say how much he'd missed her; how he wished he'd kept her close all those years ago. His chest seized as he stared at her. She was really here, less than three feet from him.

Amara raised an eyebrow and shook her head. "Not sure I believe you." Her eyes searched his face, but she didn't push him further.

Before she could walk away, Eli added, "Thanks for checking. But I *am* fine. Just stunned to find myself coming down from an adrenaline rush next to you. Sorry I yelled earlier. That was unprofessional and uncalled for."

Amara nodded. "Thank you."

Eli crossed his arms and tried to think of something other than kissing her. "I still can't believe you're actually at Boston Gen." Amara's dark eyes met his, and for just a moment, Eli felt like he was home again. But Amara wasn't home anymore. He'd given that up when he let her go.

"I'm the one that should be surprised!" Amara let out a soft chuckle. "What is Dr. Eli Collins doing at Boston Gen.? And in the ER!" She winked as she leaned against the other side of the door.

Was she intentionally putting distance between them?

"I told my father I wasn't going to be a surgeon the day after you left…" Eli felt his cheeks heat as Amara's lips slipped open.

Did she wish Eli had called her after that?

He'd thought about it, so many times… "He…uh…didn't take it well." An uncomfortable laugh escaped Eli's lips. Marshall's response still made him wince after all these years.

Amara's hand reached for him, but she pulled it back. "I'm sorry, Eli."

"Don't be. This is where I belong," he said. It had hurt, still hurt, to realize that his father might never see his successes as worthy. But the ER was Eli's second home.

"Yes, it is." Her smile was radiant in the small space between them.

For the millionth time, he wished he could have figured where he belonged before Amara had walked away. But that hadn't been the only issue to come between them. All the women he'd dated since Amara had complained that he was married to his job. And he was—or had been before Lizzy came to live with him.

Now he was trying to figure out his plans to advance the reputation of Boston General's ER and be a present dad for Lizzy. *Balance* was his new mantra; he could manage that even if Marshall had failed. What would Amara think if she knew he was committed to being home as much as possible?

He pushed away the hope pressing against his heart. "Why are you here, Amara? Why Boston Gen.?"

"I needed a change." Her eyes rotated from his to the floor, and she wrapped her arms tightly across her chest.

What had happened?

He managed to keep the question buried. She didn't look like she'd appreciate it. "Well, Boston Gen. will definitely be that. The pace here is often chaotic. We're understaffed and serve a higher proportion of the uninsured than any of the other hospitals. Some nights it's downright crazy. But with a few changes, we could be the top place in the city, Amara."

As her name slipped from his lips, his heart begged him to tell her how much he'd enjoyed this little interlude, ask her if she'd like to grab a cup of coffee. Or if she still preferred tea. But Eli locked those words away.

"Thanks for the warning." Sliding away from the wall, she said, "I can handle it, Eli."

"I have no doubt about that."

Amara nodded before she walked away.

Her shoulder almost brushed his as she headed to the nurses' station. Eli wished she'd touched him, even a brief accidental touch.

God, he'd missed her.

It had taken him nearly a year to feel like himself again after she'd ended things. No, Eli amended; he'd never felt quite whole again. Instead, he'd learned to deal with a missing part of his heart. But Eli still felt the hospital and the patients were his ultimate priority.

He was learning to balance things with Lizzy, but he was a doctor first—*always*. And one day, he was going to be in that annual report of the best physicians. But reminding himself of that did nothing to stop the yearning for Amara.

Eli just needed to get through this shift.

But she'd be here tomorrow too and the day after that.

Amara's soft scent spun through him, and Eli told himself to stop being ridiculous. It was the memory of how she'd smelled, how she felt, how she made him feel, that was chasing him now.

Nothing more.

Could he work with her? Eli shook the question away. Of course, he could. Amara was an excellent nurse, and she'd be an asset to the hospital, that was all that mattered.

His gaze wandered to the nurses' station. She was here. As a colleague, his brain ruthlessly reminded his heart. But it didn't care.

Amara yawned as she signed off on a few case reports. The rest of her shift had been blessedly quiet, and she and Eli had managed to avoid each other for most of the night. That should make her happy, or at least it should be a neutral feeling. But Amara had found herself looking for him countless times.

Even with Eli's unexpected presence, Amara had had a good night. Here at Boston Gen. she'd just been Amara. No one had asked how she was doing. No one questioned if she was feeling lonely or offered to set her up with someone. No one commented on how Joe wasn't good enough for her, while also asking if she'd heard about his impending parenthood.

She'd tried to be grateful to everyone in her last hospital for their concern, but she'd felt like a fool there. Here the only hiccup was Eli.

Amara's chest hurt as she remembered their brief conversation. She'd almost confided how much she'd missed him. How glad she was that he hadn't taken the surgical residency his father had sought for him. She hadn't lied; Eli did belong in the ER. But his comment that Boston Gen. could be the best in the city with only a few changes had sent a chill down her spine.

Eli was clearly still worried about that annual report— the recognition he thought he needed. Still measuring success by a metric his father had laid out.

Boston General didn't need fixing. Part of what made this hospital so special was that it focused only on its patients, not fundraising, recognition, or awards. It just served the community—and it was a shame that it didn't earn the respect it should. At least that was Amara's opinion.

She looked around one more time but then shook herself. She shouldn't be searching for him, hoping they would work on the same shift, shouldn't be focused on him at all. Still, after they'd worked on their last patient, Eli had seemed a little lost. Her palms had itched to reach for him. At least she'd managed to avoid that urge. It wasn't professional. But for all the confidence he exuded, Amara still saw the insecurity in him. And maybe loneliness too.

Or maybe she was just exhausted. Eli had a daughter, a family. There was no reason for him to be lonely. Amara was starting over, and that meant looking forward—not back.

It had hurt to walk away when she'd loved him so much. But she'd wanted a partner, a true partner. Someone who didn't chase business deals or national rankings while skipping dinner, vacations and recitals with their family.

She couldn't live in her partner's shadow. Joe had claimed she hadn't really needed him. That she'd made decisions without considering him. That he'd had to cheat on her. *Had to.* But if you needed someone, they could destroy you.

Amara flinched at the intrusive thought. She hated that she'd believed that was one way to protect herself from feeling like her mother had.

Like Amara had when she'd ended things with Eli.

She'd needed Eli, though she hadn't realized how much before she walked away. For months, years, her heart had felt like it had evaporated. Leaving him was the right choice back then; she'd loved Eli so much that she'd have lost herself eventually. At least that was the story she always told herself when the memory of what they'd shared chased her.

And she hadn't let herself fall that hard for anyone since.

"Amara?" Eli's hand pushed lightly against her shoulder.

"Eli?"

Her heart sang, then cried as he broke the connection. How was she supposed to work with him if she still responded to the simplest touch? Blinking, she covered a yawn.

"Sorry, did you need something?"

"You looked lost in thought." His eyes dipped to her lips. Eli opened his mouth to say something else, then closed it and shook his head.

Amara nodded and shrugged "Nightshift does cause the mind to wander if you aren't too busy with patients."

"Did it wander anywhere good?" he teased.

"Nope." Amara's cheeks felt hot, and she kept her gaze focused elsewhere, away from his dark chocolate eyes. Years ago, he'd have challenged the lie, but now Eli just raised an eyebrow. "Did you need something, Dr. Collins?" she asked again.

His lips turned down, but his voice was steady as he nodded toward the door. "Our shift is over. I wanted to make sure you didn't stay past quitting time." Eli waved to an incoming doctor as he started for the elevators.

After grabbing her purse, she stepped beside him. "It was nice to see you again, Eli."

Before he could respond, his phone dinged and lit up with a picture of a sleeping little girl sucking her thumb. Amara's stomach clenched at the thought of Eli's family. She hated to think of someone else claiming him. It had been years; her heart shouldn't bleed because he'd moved on. Amara's emotions were simply too close to the surface from the long night.

That was all.

Eli stepped into an elevator. "It was good to see you too. How long do you think it will be before it doesn't feel a little weird?"

Never.

Amara let out a soft chuckle to cover the nerves spinning through her stomach. "Did it feel weird?"

Eli raised an eyebrow and laughed with her. "Maybe just a bit."

"Yes," Amara agreed, enjoying the sound of Eli's laugh. The rich sound reverberated in the enclosed space, and she felt her shoulders relax. They could do this, work together and be friendly.

The spell broke as the elevator doors opened on the parking level. How was she supposed to do this? Amara forced a casual smile as Eli offered her a small wave before heading in the opposite direction.

"Goodbye," Amara whispered before pulling her keys from her purse. Tomorrow would be better. She'd be prepared to see him, and the raw emotions scorching her now would be dulled. She could do this—*she could.*

"Damn it!" Eli's curse echoed in the parking garage as she reached her car.

Her key was in her door; Amara could pretend she hadn't heard anything, but she hated the unkind thought. Her body was wired from being near him all night, but Amara blew out a breath. It shouldn't matter that Eli was her ex; he was a colleague who'd had a long night and wanted to get home to his family. If anyone else had sounded distressed, she wouldn't hesitate to see what was wrong.

Tossing her purse in the front seat, Amara locked her car and followed the sounds of Eli's rant to the other side of the parking garage. Her eyes widened as she watched him kick at the wheel clamp that had been placed on his left back tire. "Did you break any of your toes?"

"No!" Eli huffed as he leaned against the driver's side door. "I forgot to renew my parking pass."

"Parking security at Boston Gen. seems pretty serious. Don't most places just slap a ticket on your window?"

Eli glared at the bright yellow wheel clamp. "Our parking attendant takes her job very seriously." Eli pulled out his phone. "Fiona, I'm sorry about the pass. It slipped my mind with everything. Call me back, please." He blew out an exasperated breath as Amara leaned beside him. "She'll call back eventually. Guess if I want to go home sooner I need to order an Uber."

She jiggled her keys. "Want a lift?" Amara made the offer without thinking—but she couldn't withdraw it now. Forcing herself to sound cheery, she joked, "You have to promise not to kick my tires, though."

Eli's eyes wandered across her, and Amara held her breath. He used to be able to read her so easily. Did he realize how uneasy he made her? How part of her wished she'd just gotten in her car and gone home? *And* that an even larger part of Amara yearned to lean into Eli and pretend that a decade hadn't passed?

For almost three years, he'd been her sanctuary. The person she told her secrets and fears to. The world had disappeared when she was in Eli's arms. No other partner had ever managed to make her feel so loved and cherished.

Except their love hadn't been enough to make him put her first once the residency searches had begun. And his desire to be the best had colored every choice. Amara was a nurse. Of course she cared about her patients, but you had only one family. Once they were gone...

Water under the bridge, she reminded herself.

They'd been young and still expected the world to be kind when they'd found each other. The universe didn't operate on kindness or fairness. If it did, Boston Gen. wouldn't have such a hard time balancing its accounting books while serving its community. The sick would be able to get care regardless of their ability to pay, and her mother would have found a man to truly stand beside her in sickness and in health.

The air seemed to evaporate as she stared at Eli. He still hadn't answered her. Amara shrugged. Fine. She wasn't going to beg him to let her drive him home. "Have a good day, Eli."

She hadn't taken three steps before he was striding next to her. "What if one of your tires looks at me weird?"

"What?" Amara stared at his brilliant grin.

"Am I allowed to kick one of your tires if it looks at me weird?" Eli winked. "Usually my jokes are funny, but I'm tired. I'll do better next time."

"Oh, my gosh, Eli Collins tells dad jokes, now." His grin sent a small thrill through her.

"I guess I do."

Just for a moment, Amara thought he might reach for her.

But of course he didn't.

Placing his hands in his pockets, Eli matched each of her strides. He'd done that years ago too. Slowing his gait to make sure they stayed together. Pressing her keys into her palms, Amara wanted to shake herself. She was looking for small things to hold on to, and that wasn't going to make working beside Eli any easier.

Eli sent a quick text to his mom, thanking her for the picture of Lizzy as he gave Amara directions to his home. His mom had told him to let her know if she sent too many pictures, but Eli couldn't get enough.

That still shocked him. Sam had always loved kids. He'd volunteered as a Big Brother to elementary school kids while in college and med school, and had developed a repertoire of dad jokes before he'd even met his wife. His brother had also gone into pediatric surgery.

But Eli hadn't felt drawn to kids, not like Sam. He'd done his pediatric rotations but never considered its specialties. The adrenaline of the ER was too great. He'd been so focused on his goals that he'd never thought of being a parent.

No, his mind ruthlessly reminded him. He'd thought about it. Specifically, how Amara would be a wonderful mother...

"Your daughter is adorable." Amara glanced at another image on his phone.

"Lizzy is my niece," Eli stated. He needed Amara to know that. It seemed ridiculous after all their time apart, but Eli wanted her to know he hadn't found someone else. She'd been right. Family was important. A lesson he hadn't fully learned until he'd taken Lizzy in. At least he hadn't ever seen the despair his mother had finally learned to hide hovering on his own partner's face.

Like it had clung to Amara so long ago.

"Sam and his wife died in a plane crash about eight months ago, and Lizzy came to live with me." His voice caught just a bit, as it always did when he talked about Sam.

"I'm so sorry, Eli." Amara's hand reached for his. She squeezed it once but then let go.

Clearing his throat, Eli clenched his fist to keep from reaching for her hand. That simple touch sent fire up his arm. He'd spent years dreaming of her, and now she was here, so close, and there was no reason for him to hold her hand. Or push the lock of hair away from her cheek, ask what she was thinking, kiss her... All those things he'd taken for granted until she'd walked away.

Leaning back against the headrest, he drummed his fingers against his knees. "I have no experience with kids. Sam met Yolanda at a pediatric surgical conference. The two were natural parents. I'm not really sure what I'm doing."

"I think most parents feel that way." Amara shot him a quick wink. "For every parent that rarely has doubts, I suspect there are hundreds that question every minor decision."

"Do you have children?" She'd wanted to be a mother, a wife... Was her husband waiting for her at home? Was she going to send her kids off to school before climbing into bed?

"No." Amara's tone was light, but he saw her lip tremble. His eyes flashed to her bare ring finger, and she shook her head. "Not married."

He stared out the window. "I'm not married either." The words sounded so stilted, and Eli wanted to slap himself. Luckily, Amara seemed willing to let the statement go.

For years he'd been jealous of a man who didn't exist. The thought reverberated around his skull as the traffic inched forward. Eli had always figured Amara would find someone. A man to have a life with, to love. It hurt to think of her with someone else, but the slight wobble in her lip hurt more. She was alone, and there was more to the story, but he couldn't ask—*shouldn't*.

The car was silent as Amara stopped at a red light.

They'd hit downtown at morning rush hour, and the grid-lock stretched before them. It didn't matter that they were trying to go only a few miles, the red parking brakes high-lighted the extended time they were going to spend together.

"How old is Lizzy?" Amara's question broke the uncomfortable silence.

"Almost two. I have to figure out how to throw a birthday party in a few months." Eli shook his head. What did you do for a two-year-old's birthday?

"Now, that is definitely one of those minor issues that you *don't* need to worry about." She let out a soft chuckle. "You just get a cake and a few presents. Parties aren't hard. I seem to remember throwing you a very cheap one my senior year."

"It wasn't cheap!" Eli protested. Amara had thrown him a surprise party in college. They'd played loud music, danced with friends and had a blast. It had been perfect—she'd been perfect.

"I hung streamers that I got seventy-five percent off because they'd lost half their dye sitting in the store's sunny window. I handed out chintzy dollar store hats. I only splurged on the magic relighting candles."

"I loved everything about that party." Eli smiled as she grinned at him. "Except for the relighting candles. We could have burned down the apartment with the way those things were sparking."

Amara shook her head. A few strands of her dark hair had come loose from her braided bun, and she pushed them behind her ear and said, "No, we could not have!"

Eli laughed. "So, what kind of cake do you think I should get for Lizzy?" It wasn't one of the hundreds of questions he wanted to ask, but birthday parties seemed like a safe topic right now.

Much safer than *Have you thought about us for the last ten years too?*

"A pretty one. I bet the grocery store has a book you can pick from. Lizzy's so little that she won't remember the specifics. She'll just feel loved. That's what matters most, Eli," Amara said.

He shrugged. That sounded simple, but how did you convey love to a toddler? "I want her party to be special. To be the best!"

"No pressure." Amara playfully rolled her eyes. "It's a toddler's party. Does she like princesses? Or flowers or superheroes?"

"She enjoys *The Princess and the Frog* story. We read it at least ten times a week," Eli replied. Right after she'd come to live with him, he had painted her room bright yellow and hung pink flower carvings across it. It looked almost exactly like the room she'd had at her home. It was a small thing, but Lizzy had climbed into his lap for the first time that night and dropped *The Princess and the Frog* in his hand. That was the moment when Eli had felt like he might be able to handle fatherhood.

The weird feeling of parental pride and grief warred inside him. Sam should be the one planning the party, but he wasn't here. Shaking the thought away, Eli continued, "She likes dolls too. She carries around one that Mom got her. It's named Baby."

"Nothing like the creativity of young children." Amara's face lit up. "You could get her a doll cake. I always wanted one of those. One of the grocery stores had a display. The cake was the doll's dress, and she looked so pretty. I used to beg Mom to get me one, but she always made my cakes. That's another option. You could bake Lizzy's cake!" Amara's eyes sparkled with the dare.

He was a better cook now than he had been, but not by

much. Before he took custody of Lizzy, most of his meals had come from the hospital vending machine or the frozen food aisle at the grocery store. Eli threw a hand over his heart. "I feel like you might be mocking my fear of birthday party planning."

Amara shook her head, but her lips twitched. "Maybe a little." She met his gaze and shrugged. "Or a lot."

The traffic finally started to clear, and Eli almost hated to see it move. He needed to get home, but the last thirty minutes had almost felt like old times. As he gave Amara directions to his place, part of him didn't want it to end.

A large part.

A car was sitting in Eli's short driveway. He frowned as Amara pulled in next to it. Any other morning he might have been excited that his father had finally stopped by. But Marshall's timing was terrible. He'd agreed to look at some of The Collins Research Group medical studies. Eli hoped reviewing the papers might help overcome the distance between them. Maybe then his father would see him as an equal. That would be almost as good as landing in the *US News & Reports* rankings.

Maybe better.

Still, it was too early to deal with his father. Amara was here. Marshall Collins could wait for a few minutes.

"Remember to pay for your parking pass, Dr. Collins."

Amara's grin chased away the worry pooling in Eli's stomach. "What if I want to use the excuse of not having a pass in order to see the new nurse at Boston Gen. after our shifts at the ER?" The question left his lips, and Eli's chest seized as he waited for her reaction.

Amara sucked in a breath, but she didn't tell him to knock it off. That was enough for him to take a risk. Eli wasn't ready to say goodbye. *Not again.*

"Want to meet Lizzy?" That was safer than asking if she might want to grab dinner or a drink.

Amara looked toward his town house before she shook her head. "I don't think that's a good idea."

"Why not?" The question was out before he had time to think. He wasn't sure he wanted whatever answer Amara was going to give.

She offered Eli a tired smile. "We…it's been a long time…" Amara shrugged.

It had been a long time. Too long.

A sharp knock interrupted them, and Amara jumped.

Marshall Collins motioned for Amara to roll down her window. Before Eli could stop her, she did. Why hadn't his father waited for Eli to come inside? Better yet, why hadn't he called or texted, like he usually did?

"The Collins Research Group made some headway on the study you recommended. There are some papers I want you to look over." Marshall looked past Amara. He hadn't bothered to say hello to his son either, but the slight against Amara annoyed Eli more.

"Good morning, Marshall." He'd stopped referring to his father by anything else after their argument over Eli's refusal to go into surgery. Not that it seemed to bother Marshall. "You remember Amara Patel."

"Good morning." Amara yawned.

"I need you to look over this research, Eli," Marshall repeated, handing him a stack of papers through the window and then heading toward his car.

"Still not big on small talk, huh?" Amara remarked as Marshall got into his vehicle and drove away. Gesturing to the stack of papers, Amara asked, "You help at The Collins Research Group?"

"I work for the company part-time and serve on the board." Eli flipped through the documents.

"When do you sleep?" Amara stared at him, but the playful exchange they'd had a moment before had evaporated with Marshall's appearance.

Eli shrugged. "I get by. Want to come inside? I have tea."

Amara's nose scrunched up as she stared at him. "I seem to remember you saying that tea was the worst caffeine infusion there was." Her eyes dipped to the papers in his lap, and her small smile disappeared again.

"I don't drink the stuff." Eli rubbed his forehead, trying to determine how much to say. She was so close, and he didn't want her to leave or to scare her away. "The cupboard never looked right without a can of tea next to the coffee." So much hadn't looked right, felt right, without the little touches Amara added to his life.

"Eli." Amara's fingers grazed his leg, and she bit her lip as she yanked them back. "We can't do this."

Heat traveled across his body where Amara's fingers had touched him. His heart beat faster as her eyes held his.

Stay with me.

Eli kept those words buried deep inside as she leaned back. "It's just tea."

"Is it?" Her eyes once more darted to the stack of papers in his lap.

No!

Before he could find any words, Amara continued, "I need to get going. Get some rest, Eli." She started the car. "See you at the hospital."

"Thank you for the ride." He got out and watched her drive away before heading into the house. His body was heavy with exhaustion, but the light of hope was burning in his heart. Amara was at Boston Gen.

CHAPTER THREE

AMARA'S STOMACH RUMBLED as she headed to room 4. She made sure to keep her head down as she passed Eli. During the last two shifts, she'd kept her distance. When they were working on a patient, Amara made sure to leave as soon as the job was done. No more personal conversations in the doorway after difficult cases. No time alone. She was at Boston General to work, not to reconnect with Eli.

She wasn't the same person anymore. *Inside or out.* Life had scarred her in more ways than she'd thought possible as the happy nursing student who'd dated Eli.

He was a different person too. And for a moment—a long moment—she'd wanted to go into his home, meet Lizzy and enjoy that cup of tea. Find out if the connection between them had survived both time and distance. But then she'd stared at the stack of papers in Eli's lap and pushed that desire aside.

Even if she was interested, which she wasn't, where would she fit into his life now? Eli was working part-time for Marshall, on the board at The Collins Research Group, and maintaining a full schedule at Boston Gen. And he was raising Lizzy.

A smile touched her lips as she thought about Eli as a father. He'd be a great dad, *was* a great dad. Bad fathers didn't worry about birthday cakes. Amara wasn't sure her father could recite her date of birth without checking his calendar. Any extra time Eli managed to carve out of his intense calendar would go to Lizzy.

As it should.

The sob echoing from room 4 surprised Amara. The triage nurse had stated the patient likely needed a few stitches, but it was marked as a minor issue. As she opened the door, another racking sob traveled down the hall, and she saw Eli start toward the room.

Why couldn't one of the other doctors have been close by?

Amara shook herself at the selfish thought. Eli was one of the finest emergency room doctors she'd worked with. If this patient was experiencing something more than what the triage nurse had identified, then he was the best one to see to it. The patient mattered more than her fragile heart.

A young woman with a bandage on her cheek was bawling on the bed. She didn't look up as Amara and Eli stepped into the room.

Quickly washing her hands and donning gloves, Amara sat carefully on the edge of the bed. "I'm Amara. What's your name?" she asked, her voice soft but firm.

"Han... Ha... Hannah," she sobbed.

"I'm Dr. Collins," Eli stated as he put on a pair of gloves. "What's going on?"

"I cut my cheek!" Hannah cried as she stared at them.

Amara nodded and raised her hands. "Can I take a look?" Blood coated Hannah's cheek, but the wound wasn't bleeding through the bandage. Amara gently pulled aside the dressing, revealing a long cut from the side of Hannah's nose to just under the edge of her right eye.

The wound was going to need several stitches, but Amara was surprised by Hannah's reaction. Some patients didn't handle pain well, but Amara didn't think that was the issue. Scars were frightening, *life-changing* sometimes, and there would always be a hint of one on Hannah's cheek. Taking a guess, she stated, "The scar won't be that bad."

"Yes, it will." The girl's watery stare met hers. "I tripped over the bathroom mat, hit the counter, and now I'll have this large ugly scar forever." Hannah's wail echoed in the small room. "And then Brandon will break up with me."

Amara's heart broke at the sad statement. She wanted to reassure Hannah that her fear was impossible. *But...*

"You are a lovely young woman." Eli's voice was calm and so sure as he tilted Hannah's head to get a better look at the wound. "No one is going to dump you for a scar, which will soon be barely noticeable. Right, Amara?"

Her throat seized as she looked between Hannah and Eli, but she managed to nod before heading to grab the suture supplies Eli would need. That hadn't been her own experience. But the scars on her body were much more significant than a cut across the cheek.

Joe had said her independence, her refusal to rely on him for everything—anything—had caused their breakup. But he hadn't looked at her the same way after her surgery. Joe was never able to see past the ragged scars on her chest.

So it was a good thing she hadn't relied on him.

She'd hoped it was just Joe. But the few men she'd dated since had ghosted her after she'd told them what she'd been through, despite telling her it wasn't an issue.

Get it together, Amara mentally chastised herself.

She threaded the needle as Eli numbed Hannah's cheek.

"And *if* someone can't see past a scar, then that means there's a problem with them, not you," Eli stated. His voice was low and comforting, and Amara saw Hannah take a deep breath.

Eli was an excellent doctor, and Amara was glad that

he'd been the one to follow her into Hannah's room. Amara handed him the needle and saw him look to her.

"A problem with them," Eli repeated, holding her gaze for just a moment.

Her breath caught, but she nodded before returning her focus to Hannah. Eli's statement was so sure, so confident. He wouldn't see a minor scar as an issue, but Amara's weren't minor...

She patted Hannah's hand. "You are beautiful. Imperfections are what make us special." Her tone was upbeat, peppy, but uncertainty pressed against her spine.

"Your belly is rumbling," Hannah stated as she wiped away a tear from her uninjured cheek.

Amara winked, glad that their patient was focusing on something other than the row of stitches Eli was putting in her cheek. "Yes, well, nurses don't always get lunch breaks."

"Don't you worry about Amara," Eli told his patient as he tied a final stitch. "I'll make sure she gets a break as soon as we're done here."

The small bursts of excitement popping through her body when she was near Eli shouldn't be happening. Amara knew that, but for a moment she didn't care. He'd been so sincere when he told Hannah her scar wouldn't matter—and it wouldn't. But he'd managed to take away just a bit of the pain Amara carried with her, as well. What would he think if he knew that her scars wouldn't disappear, would always make her body look different?

Not that it mattered, because Amara wasn't going to mention them.

She wasn't.

Amara had avoided him over their last few shifts. Eli tried to ignore the pain that pierced him each time she averted her eyes. They were colleagues now. That knowledge did nothing to stop the ache in his heart.

"Your stomach isn't rumbling, it's growling. And mine is turning over on itself," Eli said as they exited Hannah's room. "The ER is..." Eli looked around and pursed his lips. Saying an ER was quiet was almost guaranteed to result in a wave of patients.

"You almost jinxed us." Amara's lips tipped up into a smile, and his heart untwisted just a bit.

"But I didn't!" Eli nodded toward the staff lounge. "Let's take our break. Eat when you can—right?"

Amara's eyes shifted to the door, and he could see her hesitate.

Her belly growled again, and Amara glared at it before laughing. "Sounds like my stomach is answering in the affirmative."

She pulled a small lunch box from her locker and sat at the small table in the corner while Eli headed for the vending machine.

He wouldn't push, but something about Hannah's scar had affected Amara. She hadn't had any significant scars when he'd known her, but she had them now. He was almost certain. And someone had made her think they made her less than perfect.

"Hannah's scar won't be that bad," Eli stated as he fed a dollar into the machine. "Scars fade over time." Amara didn't say anything, but he saw her frown as she poured some dressing on her salad.

Her eyebrows rose as he tossed a chocolate bar, bag of chips and a granola bar on the table. "That is not a meal."

Eli shrugged. "My mother says the same thing, but it's easy."

Amara looked at her wilted salad and glared at it. "Mine is almost as sad, but at least there are nutrients in it."

Her knee bumped his under the table, and he saw her bite her lip. Was being close to him making her think about them too?

"How is your mother?" Amara asked as she pulled her knees to the side.

Eli swallowed as heat ran along his neck. He was craving tiny touches, bumped shoulders, knees, any contact as long as it was from Amara. If Eli was smart, he'd avoid her. He still wanted to be the best doctor, still thought the hospital and the patients were the most important thing. But he was balancing family life now, and doing it well, in his opinion.

But could he tell Amara she came first? *No*, his brain counseled as his heart cried *yes*. Still, the thought of not spending any time with her hurt more than the moments where she pulled away.

"Mom is doing well. She loves being a grandma. Lizzy calls her Oma. I have a room set up for her at the town house where she stays when I'm on night shift. Mom started taking watercolor classes a few years ago. Her studio puts on an art show each session. I always make sure to request the night off so Lizzy and I can cheer her on."

"You take nights off for an art show?" Amara's eyes were wide, and she shook her head. "That is sweet. I bet your mother loves it." Her voice died away as she pushed her salad around with her fork.

She was surprised he'd take a night off work. "Of course." Eli kept his voice level, but defensiveness flooded him.

Letting out a deep breath, Eli pointed to a flyer on the corkboard. "Her next show is at the end of next week at the community center on Ridge Avenue. Since I'm on day shift then, I can go after work. Susan stops by sometimes. Mom loves showing off."

"I'm on day shift next week too." Amara dabbed her lips with a napkin. "I'd…"

The door to the lounge opened, interrupting whatever Amara planned to say. Dr. Griffin Stanfred's eyes hovered on them for a moment. "There you two are." Griffin called as he walked toward them.

Eli saw Amara's shoulders tense, and she started packing up her food without looking at him. They were just eating. Why was she acting like they'd been caught doing something wrong?

"I need to get back to the nurses' station," Amara stated as she pushed back from the table.

"Bye, Amara," Eli called as she headed for the door.

Griffin raised an eyebrow as he sat in Amara's recently vacated seat. "Did you two fight?"

"Why would you say that?" Eli shook his head. Long hours in the hospital often resulted in hospital staff dating, and he'd seen a few epic arguments after bad breakups. But they'd been eating in the lounge not…

I needed a change…

Amara's words from the other night cascaded across Eli's memory.

Was that why she was here?

Griffin's playful joke hadn't meant anything, but rumors had been started on less. Eli sighed as Griffin launched into a recital of plans for Boston Gen. It was usually Eli's favorite topic, but he couldn't seem to focus on the conversation tonight.

Amara grinned as sunshine hit her cheeks. After a week of night shifts, she was enjoying seeing the sun instead of the moon. She'd decided to try the food truck parked outside the hospital. Anything was better than the salad she'd eaten the other night with Eli.

She was glad Griffin had interrupted them. Amara had been about to say that she'd love to see his mother's art show. That was too close to asking Eli on a date. And she did not want to admit to herself how much she might want that.

Might...

Spending time with Eli felt good. That was a dangerous thought, but Amara couldn't push it away. The brief snatches of time they'd had sitting in her car, talking in the hall, had sent her heart racing. It was terrifying, but Amara was finding it harder to come up with reasons to keep her distance. Or maybe she just didn't care to look for reasons...

"The tacos are the best thing they make." Eli stated as Amara looked up from the food truck's menu. "Honestly, you will not be sorry if you get two of them and then come sit in the courtyard with me."

Amara returned Eli's smile and tried to ignore the energy that danced along her skin anytime he was nearby. After she'd fled the other night, he hadn't pushed her for reasons why. Eli had just kept smiling and asked how she was over their next few shifts. It was such a small thing, but Amara couldn't stop herself from looking forward to seeing him each day.

"Two tacos, please." Amara handed over her money before looking at Eli again. "I'm trusting you."

But only with tacos, Amara reminded herself. If she got close to him again, and it didn't work out... Amara's throat felt tight as fear wrapped around her. She never wanted to feel that much heartache again.

Eli placed a hand over his heart and took a playful bow. "They're great; I promise." Lifting the lid of his own container, he continued, "See, tacos."

Amara laughed as she stared at the foil-wrapped food.

"You realize right now they just look like tinfoil. You could have anything in there."

"But they're tacos," he said. *"Promise."* Amara thanked the worker as the tacos were handed to her. The food did smell almost divine. She started to walk back toward the hospital but stopped. Eli had invited her to sit with him. Could she just walk over and sit down?

Should she?

Taking a deep breath, Amara stood in the warm sun, fighting her indecision. It was just a friendly lunch between colleagues. Except they weren't just colleagues. They were exes, and she'd left Massachusetts Research after a breakup. Most hospital romances didn't work out.

Most romances anywhere.

She knew that, but her feet seemed to move of their own accord.

Eli grinned as she took the seat across from him. If he'd noticed her hesitation, he didn't say so. Instead, he just handed her a few paper napkins. "I forgot to mention that the tacos get messy."

"Thanks for the warning." His fingers brushed hers, and Amara forced herself to keep breathing as heat and desire raced along her body. She knew Eli had an effect on most women. The man was the definition of temptation. He was absolutely gorgeous, intelligent and charming. But Amara felt like their connection had been unique. Stronger, almost ordained by the universe. It was a ridiculous notion, but Amara had never been able to fully shake it. And she'd never felt it with anyone else.

"How is Lizzy?" The little girl was a safe topic. Plus she loved seeing Eli talk about his niece. He glowed—it was adorable.

"Ornery, but all the books I've read say that's normal for toddlers." Eli pulled up his phone and opened his camera. It was full of images of Lizzy, and Amara's heart wanted to explode at the cuteness. "She was getting into everything last night. I think I waited too long to babyproof the place."

Amara laughed at a picture of her wearing a pot on her head. "Did you give Lizzy the pot to play with? Or did she pull it out of the cupboard?"

Eli sighed and pulled up another picture. "It was a mutual decision that she would play with the pots while I ensured she was unable to get to the cleaning products or open the fridge."

His eyes softened as he showed her another photo. "She was still toddling around when she came to live with me eight months ago. I swear she learned to run overnight."

Amara laughed, "My mother always liked to say *It was just yesterday that you were two.* I hated it as a teenager and thought she was crazy. How could sixteen years just fly by? I get it now. Time seems to speed up the older we get."

Eli nodded. "I know. I blinked, and a decade went by."

Amara looked at him.

Was he talking about them?

Did it matter?

Amara had spent more time thinking about Eli over the last week than her brain wanted to admit. Her heart wanted Amara to remember all the fun times they'd shared. And there had been so many good moments. She swallowed the last bite of her taco and pushed back from the table. "Thanks for the recommendation. I need to get back inside."

"If I'm free and the weather is nice, this is my standard break spot. You're welcome anytime."

Amara nodded and started to get up. She wasn't running…she wasn't.

"Oh, one more thing." Eli tapped her shoulder.

Her heart leaped.

Was Eli going to ask her out?

She'd say no. Of course, she'd say no. "What?" Amara was stunned by how level her voice was.

"Their tacos are amazing." Eli closed his own box and dumped them both in the trash. Leaning over, he whispered, "But their club sandwich is the worst. Seriously, you will regret spending six dollars on it—it's terrible."

He was so close, if she turned her head at all, her lips would graze his cheek. That thought sent desire racing through her. "Good to know." Amara breathed out.

Then he winked and walked away.

Amara's heart skipped several beats as she watched Eli head into the hospital. He hadn't even waited to walk in with her. She'd completely misread the situation.

Which was good, she thought, trying to rationalize away the little bit of hurt she felt. That way, she didn't have to tell him no. Because she would have.

Shaking her head, Amara headed back into the hospital. She did not want to examine the discomfort in her stomach or the tightness in her chest. She was fine.

She was.

Amara waved as she stepped up to the food truck, and Eli felt his insides dance. He still hadn't managed to work up the courage to ask her out. In fact, he'd practically run away the first time they'd eaten together. Afraid his question would bubble out before he was ready. But he looked forward to meeting her at the truck. She'd joined him each day for lunch. That had to mean something, right?

That she wants to be friends? his mind ruthlessly asked. Even though his brain raced with thoughts of what if, that didn't mean hers did. Eli forced those thoughts away.

"They were out of tacos!" Amara complained as she opened her container displaying, a sad-looking sandwich.

"Tell me you didn't order the club sandwich after I warned you." Eli gripped her hand and then immediately let it go. It was so easy to be around Amara, and yet so hard. Reaching for her had been unintentional, but he wanted to do it again. Pull her close and just hold her.

Amara's eyes shifted to his hand, and Eli swallowed the nervousness crawling through him. He forced himself to look at the sorry bread lying in Amara's container. "It's the club, isn't it?"

"No!" Amara's hand tapped his arm, and then she placed both her hands on the table. Was she afraid touching him would lead to wanting more too?

"It's a BLT. It does look rather sad, doesn't it?" She sighed.

"Switch with me." Eli offered his tacos. "I only took one bite. They're still perfectly good."

"I can't take your tacos." Amara stared at them, eyeing the unopened tinfoil. "At least not the one you already took a bite of."

He laughed as she traded him half her sandwich.

How had he ever let her walk away?

"Want to get dinner somewhere better than this?" The question hovered between them, and Eli's insides tossed as she looked away. He wanted her to say yes, *needed it*.

"I—I—I'm not sure," Amara stuttered.

Eli held up his hand. "No problem, Amara. I can wait."

"You can?" Her brown eyes glittered as she looked at him. "I don't know if…" Amara broke off and shook her head. "I'm not the same person."

"I'm not either." Eli shrugged. "Maybe that means…" He blew out a breath. "I like spending time with you." That was the truth, all of it. For the last week, he'd gone to bed each night thinking of her, woken each morning thinking of her. She'd wormed her way into his heart years ago, and he'd never gotten over her.

Never even tried…

Eli pushed the thought away and held up the awful looking sandwich. It looked remarkably unappetizing. Leaning forward, he whispered, "If they're out of tacos, order the chicken salad."

Amara rolled her eyes "Now you tell me."

Amara pulled at the edge of her skirt and tried to work up the courage to open her car door. Or turn the ignition back on and head home. She wasn't even sure why she'd decided to come to Eli's mother's art show. Sitting at home alone watching television hadn't held much appeal, even though it was her standard Friday evening routine.

So she'd come here… Eli had said Susan usually came, and the head nurse had told Amara she might stop by. It *was* just an art show, and she wanted to support Martha. That was all.

Sucking in a deep breath, Amara counted to three and then forced herself to open the door. She'd driven all the way here, and Martha had been kind to her in the past. Amara could do this.

Besides, Eli would be busy with his mother and Lizzy. He wouldn't have time to spend with her. She was just here to see the watercolors. The argument sounded so weak her heart laughed at her.

"Amara?"

Eli's voice caught her off guard, and she gripped the side of the car to keep from tumbling over.

"I didn't mean to startle you," Eli stated as he stepped closer. "I was just leaving and—"

"Is the show over?" Amara interrupted. She'd thought

the flyer said it went until nine, and she hadn't been in her car that long.

Eli smiled and shook his head. "No, it's just getting going. But Mom isn't feeling well. I came to let her instructor know she wouldn't be able to make it."

"Oh." What was she supposed to say? "Well…" Amara brain fumbled for something to say as she stared at Eli. He was dressed in dark gray pants and a light blue button-up that accented his dark eyes. He looked delectable and dangerous and like all the things she wanted.

Why had she thought coming here was a good idea?

"I didn't get a chance to walk around, and I already hired a babysitter. Want to take a gander?" Eli's eyes never left hers as he offered his arm. How was it fair for any man to look this good?

She *was* already here. "Sure." Her heart shuddered as she slipped her arm through his. This was a mistake; she knew it, but Amara suddenly didn't care. It was one art show, one night, nothing more. "Make sure you point out which ones are your mom's."

Eli opened the door to the community center. "Just try to stop me."

If there had been a slow-motion camera on him when Eli saw Amara get out of her car, he knew it would have showed him picking his jaw up off the ground.

He'd blinked a few times before he'd believed it was really her. The black skirt she wore hugged her hips perfectly, and the flowy pink top she had on made his mouth water. Amara's dark hair was wrapped in an intricate bun, and Eli could barely keep his mind from wandering past the thoughts of what it might look like down, and remembering how it felt as he ran his fingers through it.

"Isn't this lovely?" Amara stared at the picture of a bowl of fruit sitting right in front of the door.

"That's the image many of the novice students worked from," Eli whispered. "You'll see it recreated a lot in here." He had helped his mother hang her work last night and had already seen all the paintings currently on display. But if Amara was here, nothing was going to drag him away.

"Oh." Amara's fingers brushed her lips. "So where are your mom's paintings, then?"

Amara had dropped her hold on Eli's arm as soon as they stepped through the front door. His arm felt painfully bare without it.

Gesturing toward the back, he guided her through the crowded facility. Eli was grateful for the small excuses to touch her. The moments were fleeting, but they were all he had.

"This is Mom's bowl of fruit." Eli couldn't stop himself from sounding proud. He knew his mother's work was amateur, but she'd come so far over the last few years. "You can see that she uses light more, and her strokes are finer."

Amara smiled at him and shook her head. "Sorry, Eli. I have no idea what I'm looking at. I mean, I know it's a bowl of fruit. A very nice bowl of fruit, and it looks so…" Amara's eyes widened as she caught herself.

She looked at the people passing them and leaned toward him. "Hers look better than the ones at the front, but I don't see the brushstrokes."

Her lips were centimeters from his cheek, and he was thrilled she'd wanted to quietly mention how much better his mom's paintings were. It was silly and kind and exactly the sort of thing Eli expected from Amara. The fact that it also meant she was so close to him was a delightful bonus.

Closing the distance slightly, Eli whispered, "I'm happy to show you whatever you like."

Her smile sent a shiver of longing through him. Eli forced himself to turn toward the paintings before he gave in to the urge to kiss her. He'd promised her time, and Eli could be patient.

He could.

Eli's throat felt dry, but he managed to outline what his mother had told him about the paintings. Somehow, forcing words past the desire clouding his mind.

It was lovely watching Eli gush over his mother's paintings. They were good, not gallery quality, but his mother had skill. And Eli's pride in her accomplishments sent such a wave of emotion through her that Amara didn't think she'd stopped smiling since she got here. Thank goodness she'd gotten out of her car.

"Thanks for staying with me, Eli." Amara's skin was hot despite stepping into the cool night air after the show. This hadn't been a date, but she'd enjoyed spending time with him.

"Thank you for coming. Mom will be so glad you made it." His deep voice carried in the empty parking lot.

Where had the time gone?

"Tell Martha her paintings were beautiful." Amara held her car door to keep from touching Eli, again. If she did, she'd kiss him. And he'd kiss her back. That knowledge made her grip the door even harder.

"I will. She'll be sorry to have missed you." Eli's gaze held hers, but he didn't lean toward her.

Her decision would be so much easier if he did. But Eli stood still, just staring at Amara. Making her want all the things she was trying to convince herself she didn't need.

"I should get going." The words were breathless. Should she hug him? No, that would lead to kisses too. And Amara would lose the final bit of control she was clinging onto.

Eli placed his hands in his pockets and tipped his head. "Good night, Amara." The bubble of tension between them burst as he walked away.

She ran her fingers along her unkissed lips as her body trembled with emotion. She'd made the right choice. She had... Kisses would lead to her wanting more, and Amara already wanted more than was good for her.

CHAPTER FOUR

"HERBAL TEA." ELI smiled as he handed it over.

The deep dimple in his cheek sent a thrill through Amara as she took the cup from his hand. His thumb brushed her pinky, and she couldn't ignore the butterflies that floated through her belly. Eli had delivered a cup of herbal tea to her during her last three shifts.

"Thanks." Amara put the warm cup between her fingers. *Do you wish I'd kissed you the other night?* She bit back the question.

He hadn't asked her out again, and there weren't any more art shows that she could crash anytime soon. That should make her happy, but it didn't.

He was different now, her heart argued. Eli took off shifts for art shows, went home on time. He video-called Lizzy at bedtime if the hospital wasn't swamped. And Amara could fall for him again. If she let herself…

She looked for him when she was on shift. The last two days, she'd even arrived a few minutes early just to be able to catch him in the staff lounge before their work started. If she wanted to protect her heart, Amara needed to stop.

But Eli made her laugh. Something she hadn't done much after her mother died. And even less since Joe left her. Eli made her happy, and that felt dangerous. The walls she'd put around her heart a decade ago had protected her when other men walked away. But were they strong enough to protect her from Eli?

Nick, a radiology tech, rushed to the desk and laid a few images on the counter. "Can you see to the woman in room 10? Broken scaphoid." Then he was gone.

"Shall we go plaster a wrist?" Eli asked as she stood up and followed him into room 10 where an older woman was on her phone.

"Gotta go, Marie. A hot doctor and a smoking nurse just walked in to patch my busted hand. Should be able to make it to hang gliding next week."

"No, you won't." Eli shook his head. "You broke your wrist, ma'am."

"I know that, *young man*." The patient was wearing a jumpsuit and looked to be in good spirits as she winked at Amara. "Is he always this serious?"

"No." Amara bent her head, trying to keep the giggles at bay as she stepped beside the woman who had to be at least seventy. "How did you injure yourself?" Amara asked as she prepped the plaster for the cast.

"Call me, Dot, please." Their patient leaned on her uninjured hand as she studied Amara. "I broke it after skydiving."

"After?" Eli raised an eyebrow as he began to splint Dot's wrist.

"Yes, *after*." Pushing a wisp of white hair behind her ear, Dot sighed. "I tripped over the step on the way to the car and tried to catch myself. Gone my whole life and never broken a bone. Seems like a shame to break the streak at seventy-five." Dot glared at the offending wrist. "It's not going to slow me down, though!"

Amara saw Eli look at her, but she didn't meet his gaze. If she looked at him, she was going to laugh. And Dot didn't need any encouragement!

"I'm sorry, but a broken wrist is going to slow you— at least a bit. You can't hang glide with a cast." Eli kept his tone firm, but Amara saw his lip twitch. He was impressed by Dot's spirit too.

"You sweet man, they strap you in with a partner. He'll be doing all the work—as he should." Dot's eyes twinkled as she smiled at Amara.

Eli didn't comment on Dot's joke, but Amara knew it took all his control. No doubt, he'd spend the rest of their shift regaling people with the story. "I'm impressed you're so active."

"Because I'm old?" Dot laughed as crimson stained Eli's cheeks. "No shame in admitting the truth. I spent the first sixty years of my life being careful. Do you know what it got me?" Her bottom lip quivered just a bit as she looked over Eli's shoulder.

"Nothing." Her large green eyes met Amara's. "It got me nothing. I never risked my heart or did anything that would result in broken bones. I hit retirement and realized I was alone with little to show for my sixty-plus years on this planet." Dot sighed.

An older gentleman stepped into the room, carrying two bottles of water. "They said no frozen margaritas in the ER, Dot."

"You tried bringing frozen margaritas into a hospital?" Eli said as he stared at the visitor.

"Of course not," he replied with such exaggerated vowels that Amara didn't know if he was kidding.

"This is Richard. My fiancé." Dot grinned as she gestured to her cast. "We're getting married in three weeks, and I'm going to have a purple cast."

"I'll just wear a purple tie to match." Richard laughed. "Does this mean we aren't skydiving on the honeymoon?"

"No!"

"Yes!"

Amara laughed as Dot and Eli answered at the same time. Then realization struck her. She wasn't risking anything either.

She wanted to scream as a chill raced down her back. She was letting fear rule her. Worrying that if she loved anyone too much, she'd get hurt, just like her mother. But fear hadn't gotten her anything either.

"We'll just have to find other ways to occupy our time." Dot laughed as Eli's face heated again. "Nice work, Doc." The woman twisted her wrist, admiring her cast. "It makes a real statement."

Amara stared at Eli. What if she let go of fear? Her heart wanted Eli, but what if… She shook her head. She'd lived a life of what-ifs, and she was still alone.

As Eli explained cast care to Dot, Amara slipped from the room and tried to gather her thoughts. Unfortunately, they were all over the place.

"Amara?" She turned as Eli spoke from behind her.

"Amara, Eli." Susan stated as she stepped between them.

Amara was grateful for the interruption and made sure to keep her gaze focused on Susan. But she could feel Eli's eyes on her.

"I wanted to let you know that you're partners for the health fair." Susan looked at Amara quickly before addressing Eli. "As last year's winner, you have the first pick of the booths, Dr. Collins."

"You won last year?"

Eli's eyes studied her, but he let the change of conversation happen. "I've won the last five years. And I'll win this year too. We'll win—I mean."

It took all her control not to sigh at the intensity in his eyes. "Seriously, Eli? It's only a community health fair."

"That helps Boston Gen. as well as the community. It

makes people think of us. Community involvement should help us if we can figure out how to get on the survey for the national rankings. This year I'm even trying to get the press to show up. Our booth needs to be spectacular."

The national rankings...

Amara did sigh then. What was so important about a magazine that most people never read? She knew the list hit the major news sites, but it was splashed across the front page for only a few hours before dropping into the void of the internet for another year.

The nerve at the base of Eli's jaw twitched, and Amara took his hand. Under the sheen of self-assuredness, Eli doubted himself.

He was a remarkable doctor at a respected hospital—no matter what any piece of paper said. She squeezed his hand before dropping it quickly as she remembered herself. They were at work *and not together*, she reminded herself.

"Whatever we do will be great. I'm sure."

Eli nodded and looked across at Dot's room. "What happened in there? You suddenly looked..."

Another nurse passed Amara a chart, and she looked it over rather than meet Eli's gaze. "Just a busy night, Eli. I'm fine."

"Not sure I believe that. I'm here if you want to talk." He blew out a breath.

Her mind flashed to the long conversations they used to share. And to the intimacy that had so often followed when their talking turned to touches and kisses. Her body heated, and she bit her lip. She needed to focus. Gripping the file, she offered him a polite smile. "I need to see to the patient in room 6. Thanks for the tea, Eli."

Glancing at the chart again, Amara frowned. The admitting nurse had only written *low-grade fever*. The patient had been sitting in the waiting room for a good part of the day. Most people would have gone home to wait out the infection, but Amara had treated many nonemergency issues during her years in the ER. Some people just worried.

As she walked into room 6, Amara nodded to the man sitting in the bed and he lowered his novel. He wore a paper mask over his face, and exhaustion coated his eyes. A bag of books and puzzle magazines sat on the end of the bed. He'd come prepared for a long wait.

"Good evening, Mr. Dyer. I'm Amara."

"Please call me Seth." His voice was hoarse. "Sorry for not shaking your hand, but my immune system is still compromised. Germs and chemo don't mix, I guess."

Amara almost lost her grip on the paper in front of her. "You're a cancer patient?"

Seth nodded. "Leukemia. Finished my second round of chemo last month."

She felt her stomach drop. Cancer had changed everything in Amara's life. Her grandmother had died when she was five, and her mother had lost her own battle with the disease three years ago. Neither woman had lived to see their fifty-fifth birthday. Then Amara lost part of herself in a quest to keep the dreaded disease from claiming her too.

When her mother's oncologist recommended Amara take the genetic test due to her grandmother's and mother's early-life diagnoses, she'd done it. And it had confirmed her fears. Amara's genes carried the BRAC1 marker, raising her risk for breast cancer to over 70 percent.

Amara had scheduled a preventative mastectomy the week after she'd received her results. But she'd been surprised how much she'd mourned the loss of her breasts. She was a nurse. She understood her risks, what the procedure entailed. Amara thought she'd prepared herself enough.

It had been a shock to realize that part of her was really gone forever. It was the right choice—she was certain of that. But it had taken Amara months to be able to fully examine her own scars. She still kept her eyes away from the mirror when she toweled off after a shower.

Joe hadn't touched her chest after the procedure, not even once. Everyone Amara had dated after looked at her differently when they found out. Then they stopped calling or texting. At least she knew why she was being ghosted. But that only encouraged the fear that never seemed to stop worming its way through her.

"You sat in the emergency room waiting area all day?" Amara wanted to scream at the admitting officials. Boston Gen. saw more trauma than most area hospitals, but a fever wasn't just a minor thing when you had a compromised immune system. He *should* have been back here hours ago and either treated and released or admitted.

"A car accident arrived right before I did. The triage nurse was understandably busy. I wore my mask and isolated myself."

She'd seen other patients like this. People who didn't want to burden others with their condition and didn't want to admit they'd slipped from healthy to sick.

Rather than give Seth a lecture, she plastered on a smile. "Who's your oncologist, Seth?"

He fidgeted with the edge of his book. "My wife, kids and I are here from Florida visiting her parents. My oncologist, Dr. Peppertree, cleared the travel. But I think maybe I overdid it." Seth closed his eyes. "Still not used to treating my body with kid gloves."

She heard the frustration in his voice. Her mother had hated taking it easy too. She'd fought for every normal moment she could get.

Grabbing a thermometer, Amara ran it over Seth's forehead and behind his ear. His fever had risen, but only slightly. "You still have a fever. How are you feeling otherwise? I need all the symptoms, no matter how minor you think they might be."

"Tired, but I'm always tired. My throat is sore. Other than that, I just feel weak, like I have for the last six months. My boys are six and eleven. I used to play outside with them all the time. They walked the Freedom Trail today. My wife sent pictures, but…" Seth's voice cracked. "Sorry."

"You don't need to apologize." Grief warred within Amara, but Seth wasn't her mother. His cancer had a high survivability rate. If she let her emotions control her, she wouldn't be able to do her job. "Can you please write down the number for your oncologist? I am going to get a doctor and see if we can expedite your stay." She handed him a pen and a pad of paper.

Amara hustled down the hall and collided with Eli. His fingers gripped her shoulders for just a moment too long. The connection between them had always been electric, but now it burned. "I need you to see my patient in room 6," she told him.

"Can't. Four kids got into a knife fight on Salem Avenue. Multiple victims are arriving in the bay. You're with me," Eli stated as he moved down the hall.

"Eli!" Amara held her ground. "Seth's a cancer patient from out of town. He's got a fever, *and* he's been sitting in our waiting room all day!"

Eli shook his head, and she thought she heard a curse slip from his lips. "We need to focus on the critical patient."

"I know, but…" Amara looked at the closed door where Seth had waited nearly all day to be seen.

Eli's eyes softened. His voice was low as he stared at her. "You know how triage works. I've got to see the kid that might bleed out *now*."

He was right, but that didn't stop Amara's feelings of

failure as she followed him down the hall. Seth wasn't her mother—*he wasn't*. As soon as this crisis was over, she'd make sure he was taken care of. That was all she could do.

Seth had strep throat. Amara had delivered the lab work herself and then promptly taken off. Eli couldn't blame her. Today's shift had been terrible. They'd lost two of the stab wound patients. But Amara's reaction to the cancer patient had surprised Eli—something else was going on there, but he didn't know what.

Glancing at the clock, he sighed. They'd been off duty for twenty minutes. Eli had stayed to deliver the bad news to Seth that he'd have to be admitted until his infection cleared. Amara had already gone home. He needed to do the same.

As the elevator doors opened to the parking garage, Eli paused. Amara's car was still parked two cars away from his. He'd noticed where she'd parked ever since she'd given him a lift that first day. Eli wanted to pretend that the lot wasn't that big, so it was easy to notice her car. But it was a lie. He'd worked with Susan since his residency ended and couldn't pick out her vehicle. It was just Amara.

A soft sob echoed from her car as Eli passed by. If you worked in the ER, you left exhausted, tired and sad more days than most wanted to admit. No one should cry alone in a parking garage.

Eli stepped beside the passenger door and knocked. "Want some company?" Amara shrugged but didn't order him away. Climbing into the car, he reached for her hand. At least she wasn't alone now.

"Today sucked," Eli stated.

"Two young men lost to senseless violence and a cancer patient that had to be admitted. I think sucked is an understatement," Amara countered. "Sometimes, life is just unfair."

"Dot was a hoot though, wasn't she?" Eli murmured as he let go of her hand and wrapped his arm around her shoulders. "A patient who genuinely makes you laugh is a treasure. And we saved two of the stabbing victims. That's not nothing."

She leaned her head against his, and Eli's soul sang as the soft scent of raspberry shampoo hit his senses. It was weird how the little things about her were still the same.

Amara turned slightly and her eyes met his. Then she closed the distance between their lips. The kiss was light, but it sent a thrill through him as her hands rested on his cheek. It was over far too soon, and Amara eyes were wide and panicked as she leaned away. There had never been anyone else who made him feel the way she did. And once you'd found a person that made you feel whole, it was hard to accept less.

"Sorry, Eli. I—,"

Running a finger along her cheek, Eli interrupted. "Please don't apologize. I've wanted to kiss you since the moment you walked into the ER."

A sigh escaped her lips. "It seems wrong to kiss after such a terrible day." Amara smiled, but he could see the uncertainty that enveloped her.

Eli knew what she meant, but he would never be sorry for that kiss. For any kiss with Amara. "Life is too short not to reach for every good opportunity. Working in an ER, we know that better than most."

"Life *is* so short." Amara's voice was tight.

There was more to that statement than a bad night on the job, but the parking garage at Boston Gen. wasn't the ideal place to explore it. "I need to get home." Eli squeezed her hand. "Come with me. I have a bad frozen lasagna that I don't mind sharing."

Hesitation hovered in her dark eyes, and Eli told her, "We can swing by your place if you need to feed your cat." He didn't want her to say no.

"I don't have a cat." Amara wiped a final tear from her cheek. "Nothing is waiting for me at home—not even a wilted bag of salad or a bad frozen meal. But I'm tired, and I *should* go home."

Why was she making up a cat when talking to patients?

That was something he was going to find out too.

"Well, I don't know that my well-stocked fridge is my finest asset, but how about we do lunch at my place tomorrow. We can discuss the health fair."

And he could find out exactly what had happened today.

A bit of color flooded her cheeks. What was she thinking? He didn't want her to turn down the offer, and they did need to go over their health care booth. Even if it wasn't his top priority.

"Okay," Amara whispered. "Tomorrow. So, we can discuss the health fair, and I can get some bad lasagna. Or do you want me to bring some decent food."

"I'll handle lunch." Eli winked as he squeezed her hand again. They could talk about the health fair, but Eli was going to find out what had sent her over the edge tonight. If it was something he could fix, he'd do it. Amara belonged at Boston Gen.

With him.

After hesitating a moment, Eli dropped a light kiss against her cheek and then exited from her car.

CHAPTER FIVE

ELI SMILED AS he saw Amara pull into his driveway behind his garage. She'd kissed him last night. It had been amazing and far too short. But the hope the brief kiss had given him was still blazing inside him today.

Having lunch together at his home to talk about the health fair wasn't a date, but his heart pounded as she walked up his driveway. She was really here.

Amara was here.

As he opened the door, Eli nearly tripped as Lizzy rushed at his legs to wave at Amara. It still amazed him how such a tiny child could expend so much force. "Daddy!" She squealed as he lifted her into the air.

His heart sped up as she waved at Lizzy. The toddler stuck her tongue out, and Amara did too. His heart warmed at the simple exchange. Amara had always been good with children; she'd even considered specializing in pediatrics before deciding she loved the ER as much as he did. She'd make a wonderful mother...

Eli shook the thought from his mind. It was true. But it was also way too soon.

"She's very swift for someone with such tiny legs." His mom rounded the corner. She grinned as she saw Amara. His mother had always loved her, but Martha had understood better than anyone else why she'd walked away. She'd told him this morning to be very careful. His mother loved Marshall, but she'd finally divorced him.

Tired of living alone in her marriage.

Those words had sent a chill through Eli when Martha had told him and Sam of her decision five years ago. Amara had worried that she'd be lonely if she stayed with him too, so she'd left. But he wouldn't make the same mistake his father had. He'd find a way to balance his professional goals and family responsibilities, so nothing suffered.

"It's nice to see you again," Martha said. "Thank you for coming to my art show. That was incredibly sweet."

"I enjoyed it. You're very talented." Amara stated as his mom pulled her into an unexpected hug.

Martha turned to Lizzy. "Come to Oma." She laughed as Lizzy launched into her arms. "We're going to the park now."

Eli dropped a light kiss on the top of Lizzy's head before hugging his mom. Then he turned to Amara. "Hope you're hungry. I ordered some roasted tomato pasta." Eli nodded toward the kitchen.

"That sounds much better than a frozen lasagna," Amara teased.

"Or wilted salad." Eli winked as he pulled a few plates from a cupboard.

"Bagged salad is easy. My kitchen is tiny and cooking for one…" Amara cleared her throat as she stared out the small window, "I always end up with more leftovers than I can eat."

Before he could comment, Amara rushed on. "Besides, bagged salad is better than vending machine snacks." Her nose scrunched up.

He hated that she didn't cook much anymore. Amara had loved cooking. More than one person had stopped by to ask for a recipe as delicious scents floated from their windows. "You're free to use this kitchen anytime." The words slipped from Eli's lips, and he was rewarded with a brilliant smile.

"You shouldn't offer that up so lightly! I'll have this place smelling like lemon rice in no time." She laughed, her eyes holding his.

"I love lemon rice." Eli couldn't stop the grin from spreading across his face too. Amara had always been able to make him happy. Whether he was buried in med school homework, stressed about his family, or dealing with a bad night at the ER, Amara simply made things better.

Amara stood against the kitchen counter as Eli piled tomatoes and pasta onto large blue plates. He was dressed casually, in jeans that hugged his backside perfectly and a green T-shirt. Stubble covered his jaw, and she sighed. Eli looked delicious.

She hadn't meant to kiss him last night, but she was surprised that she didn't regret it. She'd almost agreed to follow him home last night too, but she'd managed to catch herself. Lunch to talk about the health fair had felt safer... but it wasn't.

Not really.

Her stomach twisted as he stared at her. Why was she trying to kid herself? She wanted to be near him.

Needed to be near him.

She was still worried about ending up like her mother, loving a man who was too busy to see her—to love her back. But Eli was busier now than he had been a decade ago, and he'd made time for her. They'd shared tacos, looked at community art, he'd delivered tea to her, and last night when he'd held her as she cried, another bit of the wall she'd built around her heart crumbled.

They were older now, wiser, more sure of themselves.

Maybe a second chance could work between them...*maybe*. Then a little voice prodded at her.

He still didn't know about her double mastectomy, did he?

"Do you want me to make a pot of tea? I also have soda, and I am pretty sure Lizzy wouldn't mind you sneaking some of her milk," Eli said as he set a plate before her and wandered back to the stove.

"Water works." Amara's eyes gleamed. "I wouldn't want to steal milk from such a cutie." She pulled back a stool and sat. "Lizzy really is adorable."

"She is," Eli agreed as he set his plate on the counter and sat beside her. "So, I have an important question."

What did he want to know? Amara's stomach flipped. Once Eli had known everything about her. Did she want him to know everything again? Even the bits she found difficult to talk about?

Yes, maybe, she thought indecisively.

"Ask away."

"Why are you making up a cat?"

She tilted her head as Eli's masculine scent teased her nostrils. He smelled just like she remembered—*like home*. Focusing hard, she stared into his dark chocolate eyes. "I didn't make Pepper up. He was an incredible cat who liked to tip glasses off the counter far too often. I got very tired of cleaning broken pottery, so all my cups are still plastic. But I lost him not long ago."

Amara set her fork down, smiling as she remembered Pepper's antics. "I still tell funny stories about him at work. It helps patients relax—especially children."

Eli gripped her hand. The touch was comforting, but as his thumb rubbed the delicate skin on her wrist, she wanted to pull him close. What would he do if she kissed him again? Really kissed him this time?

Her skin lit up as he held her hand. Such a simple touch, but it made her crave so much more. She'd lain awake last night, replaying those moments. Questioning herself for kissing him. Kicking herself for not kissing him again, more deeply.

Eli's dark eyes were lit with an emotion she wanted to believe was desire. "I was convinced your cat had really destroyed your breakfast by tipping milk into your eggs." Eli chuckled.

Amara laughed too. "That was Pepper's favorite trick. Though I admit that when I'm trying to calm an adult, I change the milk to coffee."

"You actually started drinking coffee? Why have I been bringing you tea?" Eli protested and leaned and close.

If she moved a few inches, she could kiss him again. Was that what he was hoping she'd do? Amara frowned as she pushed back at the desire building in her belly. "Nope. Sorry to disappoint you."

"You could never disappoint me."

His words were soft, but they struck her hard. What would he think of her scars? Would they disappoint him? Worry stabbed at her brain again, and she pulled away.

She cleared her throat, then shrugged. "Coffee works better with adults."

"Because that's what adults drink." Eli's smile wasn't as wide as before, but he didn't release her hand.

And she didn't pull it back.

"How is your mom? There is a specialty grocery down the street, and I stop in to grab naan bread a few times a month. I tried to make her chicken curry once, do you remember? It was a disaster."

Amara swallowed. It was a reasonable question; Eli had no way of knowing how much it would hurt her to answer him. She squeezed his hand, drawing strength from the heat of his body. "Mom passed a little over three years ago." Amara bit her lip as tears coated her eyes. Why was this still so hard for her to talk about?

Eli held her gaze as he reached for her other hand. "What happened?"

"Breast cancer. By the time Mom finally went to the doctor, she was already stage four," Amara said.

"That's why you reacted so strongly to Seth's cancer yesterday."

"Yes."

And no.

She should tell him that she'd learned of her own cancer risk and alleviated as much of it as she could. But she feared he'd look at her like Joe had. Or rather, stop looking at her at all.

The more time she spent with Eli, the more she realized how different she was with him. Relaxed, happy, *ready to love...* But she refused to examine that thought too closely.

"I took care of her. Was there for every step of her treatment and the final decisions she had to make. My father was too busy. Some business deal in California. He barely made it back in time for the funeral and waited less than three months to remarry." She couldn't hide the anger as the words flew from her lips. Amara was surprised by how much she wanted to talk to Eli about this. Joe hadn't wanted to hear it, and she hadn't wanted to share it. But with Eli...

"After she passed, I felt so alone. Then the man I was seeing ended our relationship. Actually, Joe chose someone new before telling me we were over." Amara shook her head. She hadn't meant to lay any of this at Eli's feet. She never usually unloaded on others. Except she always had with Eli.

"I am so sorry, Amara. But you're not alone now," Eli whispered as he held her gaze.

"At least for today," Amara said, trying to find a way to lighten the mood as she skewered a tomato. "Though I could definitely be bribed to return for this."

"Then I will ask Mom for the recipe and practice cooking it whenever I have a chance." His cell buzzed, and Eli silenced it. But it immediately started buzzing again. "Guess Marshall really needs something." Eli squeezed her hand. "I won't be long."

Amara squashed the tinge of worry in her belly. It was just a phone call from his father. Eli was raising Lizzy, and it was obvious from the little girl's smiles that Eli had changed. He spent as much time with her as possible. He made sure to be at his mother's art shows, and he hadn't given in to his father's demands to become a surgeon.

Eli was back in less than five minutes. "Sorry, Amara. Marshall will call or text twenty times a day for a week, then I won't hear from him for a month. Now he's asked me to up my role at the research group. Even though I'm not a surgeon."

"You're an amazing doctor." Amara hated the uncertainty she saw crossing Eli's face.

"Thanks." Eli's lips brushed her cheek as he grabbed the dishes and took them to the sink.

Without thinking, Amara moved to stand beside him and wrapped her arms around him. "I bet you'll do wonderful things for the company. Have you put your notice in at Boston Gen.?" She didn't want him to go, but Eli could do good work at his father's research group.

"Of course not. Marshall still practices several days a week. I can do both. I already have been doing both and raising Lizzy." Eli's brows were knit as he filled the sink with water and dish detergent.

His words sent a flash of concern down Amara's spine. Grabbing a dish towel, she dried the dishes Eli washed. Tapping his hip with hers, Amara said, "You can't do it all, Eli. And that's okay. You're already remarkable, you know."

"Remarkable?" Eli raised an eyebrow. "If you keep those compliments coming, I may never stop smiling."

Amara shook her head. She was glad the statement made him happy, but if he was doing so much, something would break.

And then he'd blame himself.

"I'm serious."

"I know. But it's only part-time, Amara. Mostly I'm reading research grants on my couch. I'm not sleeping at the office, I promise. But I don't want to talk about Marshall anymore."

Amara let out a sigh and laid the towel on the counter. "What would you like to discuss?" She'd come to talk about the health fair, after all.

"Do you ever wonder what would have happened if I hadn't let you walk away?"

"What?" *Yes.* That's what she should have said, but that word was caught in her throat.

"Do you ever think about us? Wonder what-if?" Eli's words were soft as his eyes raked across her face.

"All the time." The truth finally slipped out, and she stepped into his arms. Whatever happened, this was where she wanted to be right now.

The smell of his cologne cascaded over her. His head lowered. His kiss was soft, not demanding, but a part of her heart knit together as he held her. This was where she'd belonged so long ago.

Wanted to belong again.

Eli broke the kiss and pushed a bit of hair away from her cheek. "I should have promised you what you needed then. I wanted to, but I was too caught up in the lure of being like Marshall. *Better.* I still want Boston General to be in the national rankings, but I don't need it like I did. Give me a second chance, Amara. Give us a second chance. Please."

What was she supposed to say? So many thoughts were running through her mind. "What if you never make the list, or if Boston Gen. doesn't?" She loved their hospital, but its administration wasn't interested in courting editors to achieve rankings.

"I want to tell you that it won't matter, but I suspect it will always sting a bit. But I'm not going to give up time with Lizzy, and hopefully, you, to chase that dream. Life is too short, and these last few weeks, I realize how much my life was missing something. It was missing you."

Eli ran a hand through his hair. "Lizzy and I are going to the zoo day after tomorrow. Want to come with us?" He reached for her hand. "It'll be fun and probably a little crazy with a toddler in tow." Eli shrugged. "It could be a date or just…"

Amara dropped a light kiss on his lips. "It's a date. What time?" Maybe she was being reckless with her heart, but she didn't want to tell him no. There'd also been a hole in her life since she'd walked away from Eli. It disappeared when she was with him, and Amara didn't want it to reopen.

A brilliant smile spread across Eli's face. "How about I pick you up at nine? That way, we're there when the zoo opens and can see a good portion before Lizzy needs her afternoon nap."

"Sounds good."

"I just need your number." He laughed, "That sounds so weird." He ran his hand through his hair again.

Amara lifted her cell and opened her contacts. "Have you changed yours since college?" She'd never been able to delete his number.

Despite their parting, the thought of severing that final connection to Eli had always made her cry. He was too important to just wipe away forever. She'd looked at it multiple times, almost dialed it a few times too. Which was why DO NOT CALL was written in the Business Name section under his name.

The expression in his eyes sent a thrill down her spine. "Nope." He grabbed his own phone and sent a text that immediately pinged on her phone's screen.

She stared at the silly emoji. "Guess we're good then." Amara's heart leaped as she leaned toward him; Eli hadn't deleted her number either.

"We're home," Martha called.

Amara jumped back.

His mom's eyes flicked between Eli and Amara, and she winced. "Sorry. Lizzy was falling asleep in the swing. I didn't…"

"It's fine," Amara squeaked. "I needed to get going anyway. We can discuss the health fair after the zoo. Or at the hospital." She hesitated only a moment before dropping a light kiss on his cheek. "Thanks for lunch, Eli."

CHAPTER SIX

ELI PULLED AT the collar of his shirt for the sixth time. He'd changed once already and was feeling more ridiculous by the minute. There was no reason to feel nervous; it was just a trip to the zoo, wasn't it?

He shook his head. Dating jitters had never plagued him before. Except, this wasn't just a date with Amara.

Today could be the start of a new chapter for them. And Eli was going to make sure Amara had a great time.

His phone buzzed with a text from Marshall, and Eli sent a quick response. He waited a minute and then added a note that he'd be at the zoo with Amara and Lizzy and unavailable. He wasn't sure Marshall understood what that meant, but his father's texts and calls had been never-ending the last two days. However, today Eli was just going to enjoy the perfect weather outside with Amara and Lizzy.

Amara's text pinged into his phone.

Want me to pack any snacks?

Nope. I got this!

He could balance everything. She'd see.

He smiled as she sent back a thumbs-up icon. The connection he felt with Amara hadn't been present with anyone else. Eli had always assumed his memory was mistaken and had reinforced an ideal that hadn't existed.

But it wasn't.

"Momma!" Lizzy screamed as Eli grabbed her diaper bag and picked her up.

His heart broke as Lizzy looked at the door. Eli kissed her cheek and redirected her attention. "We're going to see monkeys." Eli tapped her nose to make her laugh. "We just have to stop and get Amara first."

Lizzy's small face puckered as she stared at him. Eli knew she didn't completely understand what he meant, but he sighed in relief when she snuggled against his chest. He'd never realized how much parenting was flying by the seat of your pants, doubting easy choices and gathering as many snuggles as possible. It was exhilarating, exhausting and perfection.

Ruffling Lizzy's curly dark hair, Eli tried to calm his nerves. The weather was perfect, and Amara was coming. Today was going to be fun.

Eli's skin tingled as his eyes landed on Amara. She was dressed in a lightweight gray tank top and blue shorts, and her dark hair was pulled into a side braid. She waved and he grinned.

Amara hustled to the car, giving him a quick kiss before turning to smile at Lizzy. "Hi, cutie!"

Her cinnamon and tea scent flooded his senses. "We would have come up to get you," Eli said. "You didn't have to wait on the sidewalk for us. Or are you hiding something in your apartment?"

Amara shook her head. "Not hiding anything. I'm just excited to go to the zoo."

He saw her cheeks heat as she returned Lizzy's wave. She was obviously just as excited as he was for today. "I'm really looking forward to it too." He laid his hand on her knee before brushing his lips against hers, relishing the moment.

"Monkeys!" Lizzy screamed from the backseat.

Amara's fingers rubbed her lips as she stared at him. "I think someone wants to go see the monkeys."

Lizzy clapped her hands and shouted, "Monkeys," again.

Perhaps a zoo date with a toddler hadn't been such a great idea. But Eli wanted Amara to get to know Lizzy. Wanted Amara to see that *he* understood the importance of family now.

"Monkeys, here we come." Eli exclaimed as they headed out.

They were on a date...

And a light kiss, barely more than a peck, was enough to make her blood sing. She'd thought of kissing Eli nearly every free minute of the last two days. That should thrill her.

But she was still hiding an important part of herself. Amara wasn't ashamed of her new body. It was healthy, and her reconstructive surgeon had done an excellent job, but she still looked different. It had bothered Joe so much. He'd looked at her like she was broken when she'd healed, then found comfort with another woman. If Eli ever looked at her that way...

Amara knew she should tell him—wanted to tell him. But the words had never found their way into any of their conversations. The everyday banter they'd shared had been easier. *Safer.*

This might not be a traditional date, but here with Eli was right where Amara wanted to be. She couldn't seem to stop smiling. Lifting Lizzy, she held her up to see the monkeys, careful to keep her far enough away from the glass that she couldn't bang on it.

"Monkeys," Lizzy squealed and laughed as Eli snapped a few pictures.

"You're going to fill up your phone with pictures of her." Amara grinned as Eli snapped a few more. The happiness in his eyes was contagious.

"Not just of her." Eli showed her the screen. He'd caught an image of Amara laughing with Lizzy and a monkey watching them in the background. "Hard to tell who's having more fun. Lizzy, you or the monkey," Eli teased.

Then his phone buzzed, and Amara saw him immediately shift from Eli back to Dr. Collins. She'd watched her father do that too, whenever his work called. But they weren't on call this weekend, and her phone was still blessedly silent. "Everything okay?"

"Marshall's texting. He wants me to go over some documents later."

"Really?" She tried to keep her voice light. Amara had known when she'd agreed to this date that Eli was already splitting his time between so many projects. It would be disingenuous to complain now. "Hopefully, it's nothing urgent."

"It's always urgent. At least, according to Marshall." Eli winked and then made a show of turning his phone off. "But I'm off the clock today."

Amara's heart raced as Eli placed the phone in his back pocket. Her father had turned his off. He'd barely ever looked away from it. Her mother used to say that if she needed to speak to her husband, she had to video call him—even if they were in the same house.

Her mom had laughed, but Amara had seen the hurt behind it. Eli putting away his connection to the outside world for a few hours meant more than he realized.

Amara was glad Marshall, or anyone else, couldn't interrupt them, but Eli's phone was also a camera and she didn't want him to miss out any memories. "What about taking more pictures of this cutie?"

Eli looked at his niece. "Today, we'll just have to rely on our memory—like in olden times." He laughed. "Perhaps it's time to invest in an actual digital camera, though. Then I can fill up my phone's memory card *and* the camera's memory with pictures."

Amara grinned as he made faces with Lizzy. Even with his overloaded schedule, Amara doubted Eli would forget Lizzy's birthday or miss every dance recital like her father had. Eli was a committed dad, but would he be as committed to her?

Her heart wanted to believe it, needed to believe it, but her brain still urged her to be cautious. This was, after all, only one perfect day in a few weeks of good times. What would happen in a few months or even years? Particularly if neither he nor Boston General received the recognition he wanted?

Lizzy gripped their hands as they walked toward the prairie dog exhibit, and Amara looked at the little girl. "Want us to swing you?" Amara laughed as Lizzy looked at her with surprise.

"I used to love it when my grandmother and mom would swing me when I was little, in grocery store parking lots and even at the zoo. If my fuzzy memory remembers right," Amara explained. She winked at Eli before looking at Lizzy. "Just hold on tight."

As Lizzy's peals of laughter rang out, his gaze bored through Amara. Her skin tingled, and her heart pounded so fast, she thought it was trying to fly from her chest. This was the definition of happiness. This was the life she'd always wanted, the life she'd craved.

With Eli.

"Again!" Lizzy shouted.

"That does have a tendency to happen," Amara said as Eli's eyes sparkled. He was an incredible dad and an amazing doctor.

He was just perfect.

Lizzy clapped as they walked into the petting zoo, then yawned. The day had been lovely, but the little one was quickly losing her ability to stay awake. Amara suspected the toddler would be asleep before they got to the parking lot.

"I'm going to buy some food," Eli said. "Then, we can feed the goats."

"Why don't we see how she does with the goats first?" Amara suggested. "We can always bring her back another day…" Amara made the offer without thinking; still, it felt right. She'd come to the zoo with Lizzy and Eli anytime he asked.

But Eli had already started toward the small hut where a bored teenager was handing out cups of goat pellets. Amara grinned. Eli was having just as much fun, if not more, than his niece.

He was a natural at parenting, even if he overthought birthday cakes. Her heart pounded as she stared at him. If they worked out as a couple this time, would he want more children?

That thought sent a blast of panic through her. Eli had been back in Amara's life for a little over a month, and she was already thinking about family. Wondering what if… Because that was what Amara had always dreamed of.

A family.

But happy families took work and time. Still, Eli had promised he would put them first. *No*, she remembered. He'd promised he could balance his responsibilities perfectly—his patients, his work for the Collins Research Group *and* his family. Could he keep that promise? If he didn't, was she strong enough to demand it, or walk away?

Biting her lip, Amara held Lizzy as she studied the goats. *Stop worrying*, she ordered herself.

Before she'd passed, her mother had warned Amara that constant worrying wouldn't stop the future from happening and only resulted in regrets. Amara wanted to live life without fear, but what if she made the wrong choice and got hurt...again?

Eli's arm slid around Amara's waist, and some of her worry fell away. Eli was here now; that's what she should focus on. As he held up the cup of pellets, his warm gaze pushed the last of her doubts to the back of her mind.

They entered the goat pen, and Amara barely managed to control her *I told you so* when Lizzy refused to get down. The little girl wanted to see the goats but had no desire to pet one. Or use the goat food that Eli had purchased.

"It will be fun." He held up the cup and tried to coax Lizzy to take it.

"No!" Lizzy shouted before she buried her head in Amara's shoulder.

"Want to watch Daddy feed the goats?" Amara suggested and was rewarded with a nod.

Lizzy's giggles were contagious as Eli marched over to the biggest goat. The goat grabbed for the cup, and Eli jumped as the animal quickly gobbled everything in sight.

"Well, that went fast. I'm going to find a trash can," Eli said as Lizzy yawned—again. "Then we should probably head home."

Amara leaned against the petting zoo fence as she held Lizzy. With Eli gone, the goats quickly lost the last of their appeal to the toddler. After a few minutes, Amara turned to look for Eli. The sun was bright, but she could see a trash can less than thirty feet from her.

Where was he?

"Charles Xavier!" The mother's screech tore through the petting zoo. "Get back here!"

Before Amara could react, a young boy bowled into them as he rushed toward the goats. She gripped Lizzy to her chest but couldn't keep her balance. Pain ripped down Amara's left arm and stars danced in her eyes as Lizzy screamed. Despite the pain, she managed to control her fall enough to blunt any injury to the little girl.

"Amara! I'm so sorry." Eli was suddenly next to her, reaching for Lizzy.

Tears stung her eyes, and her derriere was more than a mite sore from the tumble. And her arm burned. As Amara touched her shoulder, she was surprised when her fingers came away covered in blood.

The cut ran from the top of her shoulder to an inch above her elbow. Amara stared up at the fence and glared at a nail she hadn't noticed. She had landed just right to catch the stupid thing. This was not the way she'd wanted the day to end.

Breathing through the pain, she let Eli examine her arm while she kissed the top of Lizzy's head, trying to comfort her as well as she could with one hand.

"I think you need a few stitches." Eli pushed his hand through his hair. "I'm so sorry," he repeated.

"Did you push us?" she asked.

Eli's mouth fell open, but he still looked worried. "What?"

Why did this bother him so much? It was an unfortunate accident that no one could have foreseen. "You've apologized twice for a kid getting excited and accidentally pushing us over. Or are you apologizing for my unluckiness to catch a barely exposed nail just right? This is as far from being your fault as possible."

His eyes shifted a bit as he brushed a loose piece of hair from her face. "You'll need stitches and a tetanus booster."

"Eli." Amara pressed her closed fist to his shoulder, trying to offer some form of comfort without getting blood on him. "I'm going to be fine. I promise."

Eli pulled a T-shirt from Lizzy's diaper bag and pressed it against the wound. "Guess it's a good thing I always pack a change of clothes in case she gets messy."

"Yes." Amara winced as she held the shirt against her shoulder. "Hopefully, this isn't a favorite outfit."

"Nope," Eli stated as he helped Amara to her feet and picked up Lizzy. "We need to get you to Boston Gen."

Amara flinched as another bout of pain shot down her arm. "Not an ideal way to end our date."

"The next one is going to end better," Eli promised.

Next one.

Amara sighed as he wrapped an arm around her. "You're getting blood on your shirt."

"I don't care." Eli kissed her forehead as Lizzy reached for Amara.

The toddler's small demand made her want to beam with joy. Despite their tumble, Lizzy was fine and still wanted Amara to hold her. She'd enjoyed their zoo date, even if it was ending with a few stitches.

"Amara hurt her shoulder, sweetheart. We have to go get her looked at." Eli frowned as they walked from the petting zoo. "I really am so sorry, Amara."

Since she was holding Lizzy's shirt against her arm, Amara couldn't hold his hand, but she leaned her head against his shoulder. "Don't worry."

Eli couldn't believe he was sitting in Boston Gen.'s waiting room with Amara. Technically, he knew he wasn't responsible for the accident. But if he'd just dumped the cup in the trash and come right back, they'd have been halfway to the car by the time the other child had reached the petting zoo.

Instead, he'd stepped away and checked his phone.

After he'd made such a big deal about turning it off.

And then he'd sent a handful of texts back to Marshall.

He probably shouldn't care what his father thought. Eli knew that, but after years of almost no communication, he wanted to help Marshall now that he'd asked for Eli's assistance. To prove to him that he was a great physician. If he never made the rankings like Marshall had, knowing his father respected him would be enough.

When he'd heard Lizzy scream, Eli had raced back and felt his stomach drop at the blood traveling down Amara's arm. "If they'd just let me put a few stitches in your arm, we'd have been out of here hours ago," he grumbled. At least his mother had picked up Lizzy.

He sighed as Amara leaned her head against him. If they were pretty much anywhere else but here, this would feel perfect.

"You're not on the clock. I'm sure Griffin or one of the other doctors will be free soon." Amara pecked his cheek. "Patience is a virtue."

Not one he'd ever excelled at.

"How is it feeling?" Eli asked.

"Like a nail cut into my skin." Amara sighed. "Sorry, Eli. I know you're upset, but at least we have a fun story to tell."

"A fun story?" He raised his hands and gestured to the gray walls of the waiting area. "Not sure this really counts."

"Sure, we can tell people how I saved Lizzy from a rampaging goat, while you were off scouting a long-lost trash can."

Her laughter was contagious, and Eli joined in despite

the guilt racing through him. "I don't think that's how it happened."

Except for the part where he'd been too far away to help.

"When you told me that Lizzy hated going to sleep, I thought you were kidding. She really is passionately against bedtime," Amara said. They'd picked Lizzy up from his mom's apartment on their way home from Boston Gen.

Despite the seven stitches in her arm, Amara wasn't sure she'd change anything about today. Spending the entire day with Eli had quieted most of her worries. She was glad they'd had the health fair to discuss because Amara hadn't wanted their time together to end. She wasn't sure she'd ever get enough of spending time with Lizzy and Eli.

"Lizzy lures you in with her cuteness, never showing the monster beneath it—until bedtime," Eli teased and dropped a light kiss on her lips as he passed her a grilled cheese sandwich.

Her heart felt like it might explode. The kiss wasn't enough. Amara wanted more, so much more. But their stomachs growled, almost in unison, and she laughed. There would be plenty of time for kisses later—*there would*.

"I think all toddlers are tiny adorable monsters." Amara sat next to Eli on the couch, enjoying the warmth coming off him.

He took a few bites of his sandwich before wrapping an arm around her shoulders—careful to avoid the line of stitches. "No, but she does have a stubborn streak. Reminds me of my brother." Eli chuckled.

"So, you and Sam had the same stubborn streak?" Amara asked as Eli put his hand over his heart, pretending she'd wounded him.

Eli nodded. "I prefer to think of the quality as 'determined' when it's me."

"Determined?" Amara whispered, enjoying the slow smile spreading across his face. If she kissed the delicate skin along his collarbone, would Eli still groan and pull her close? Amara felt her cheeks heat as she stared at his lips. They were so near.

"Should we discuss the health fair?" Eli asked huskily. "Or, is there something else you might like do?" His finger slid along her jaw.

As his gaze swept her body, panic raced across her skin. She still hadn't mentioned the scars across her chest. Or the reasons she'd elected to have a preventative double mastectomy. She needed to…and now was the perfect time. Or at least as good as any. But as the memory of Joe's reaction danced behind her eyelids, the words refused to materialize.

"Health fair," she squeaked, hating the touch of anxiety racing through her.

"Oh…right," Eli said before withdrawing his arm and grabbing her empty plate. "Just let me get my notes."

Amara took several deep breaths, trying to calm the rush of emotions tumbling through her.

I had a surgery that drastically changed the odds that I'll get breast cancer despite my genetic markers. But it means I look different from the last time we were together.

Those words should be so easy to state. Eli was a physician, he'd understand. But Joe was a doctor, as well…

Eli returned with a giant binder and laid it out on the coffee table. Amara hated that she was grateful to have a reason to put off the conversation a bit longer.

"This is what I've done for the last few years. Each year

the booth is different, so we need to pick a theme and then look for a giveaway and…"

The binder had more tabs in it than most patient folders. Amara stared at it. When he'd mentioned that he'd won each year, she'd hadn't realized Eli was planning a major event. "Woah…wait, I thought we'd partner with a local health agency like the American Cancer Society or the Red Cross."

"The health fair draws attention to Boston General. The better the booths, the more attention, and the better chance someone nominates us for awards," Eli stated as he flipped through the binder, not looking at her.

Grabbing the binder, Amara laid it in her lap. "That is a lot of pressure to put on a health fair."

On himself.

"And unrealistic to boot!" Eli hid his insecurities better than he had years ago, but they were clearly still there—bubbling just under the surface.

"No, it's not." Eli's voice was tense. "Community involvement might be one of the criteria for getting on the list." Eli pushed his hand through his hair as his eyes held hers.

Amara wished there was a way to make him see himself, truly see himself. He was a great doctor, no matter what a stupid list said. Stroking his cheek, Amara took a deep breath. "You don't know the criteria for the thing that you're chasing after? That's a bit crazy, Eli."

"I've tried to figure out the criteria for years, but it's been a bit elusive." Eli gripped her hands and added, "I even asked Marshall, since he's been on the list a dozen times. But he just said someone nominated him." Eli smiled.

It was so close to a grimace, Amara's heart shook. Eli was chasing a goal with no known path to success. That could drive anyone to madness.

Shifting the conversation, she asked, "What did you do with all the extra vacation days you won?"

"What?" His eyes roamed from her to the closed binder. "Why?"

His defensiveness worried her. He was requesting shifts off to see his mother's art shows. Surely Eli was taking his vacation days? He reached for the binder in her lap, but she held it tightly.

Eli raised an eyebrow as he reached around her. "Come on, Amara. Let me have my notes."

She stood and moved to the other side of the room. "No. Not until you tell me what you used your extra vacation days for last year. Did you go to Rome or Scotland? What about California or Hawaii?"

Eli's lips turned down, and she wanted to shake him. "Did you go skiing? Or hiking?" She knew the answer, but she hoped she was wrong. "The beach? A resort? Eli?"

When he still refused to say anything, Amara dropped the binder on the floor, ignoring the thump it made. "What did you do with the days you earned by putting so much effort into your booth for a grand prize you might never get?"

He looked away. "Nothing. At the end of last year, I had ten unused vacation days that I forfeited. Are you happy now?"

The dismal statement broke her heart. Why would he ask her that? "Of course not."

Amara returned to the couch and wrapped her arms around him. Her breath hitched as his fingers ran along the back of her spine. She was not going to let his soft touch distract her.

"We used to talk about traveling all the time. Remember those silly guidebooks?" Amara grinned as a bit of the tension eased from Eli's features. "Now you're earning extra vacation days and not using them. You're following your father's path, but don't have the map."

Amara put her finger over his lips before he could interrupt. "You are one of the top doctors at Boston Gen. You could work anywhere. You're a wonderful, attentive father, an impressive doctor and gorgeous. You do not need to be on some artificial list to prove your worth. You can chart your own course now." Amara gripped his knee. "You *are* enough, Eli." It was the truth.

If only she could make him see it.

"Gorgeous?" Eli asked and raised an eyebrow.

"All the compliments I give you, and that's the one you focus on." Amara playfully rolled her eyes. Her chest tightened as Eli leaned toward her. He was so close, and she'd missed him so much. Her heart pounded as she stared at his full lips.

Eli pushed a lock of hair behind her ear, his fingers lingering just a bit along her jaw. "If we win, I promise to take a vacation this year."

"If we win, I'll make sure you do," Amara whispered. Her stomach rolled with desire, nervousness and hope. "A real one. With no cell phones, research papers. No work!"

"I missed you so much," Eli stated simply, and her world came undone.

She kissed him then. He still tasted of honey, sunlight, comfort and longing.

Her Eli...

They'd once felt like two halves of a whole. Could they again?

Her fingers ran along his shoulders as he pulled her closer, as if Eli couldn't accept any space between them either. This was the kiss Amara had wanted for days, weeks...years. The one that spoke of all their mutual longing. The kiss that demonstrated how much passion they still felt for one another. It was everything.

Eli's fingers dipped along the side of her breasts, and she froze. If they didn't stop now, where would the night lead? The thought tore through her as she pulled away. "I should leave."

"Amara." Eli took her hands. "Stay…please."

She wanted to, desperately. But staying meant so much more than planning for the health fair. Kisses, promises… maybe the hope of forever clung to Eli. She wanted all of it, but the fear that he'd look at her differently once he found out about her surgery clung to her too. Fear that this happiness could evaporate in an instant ripped through her. She just needed a bit more time.

Amara removed her hands from his, stood and reached for her purse. "I'm going to brainstorm some themes for our booth."

"Can we discuss the health fair over dinner tomorrow?"

Amara shook her head. "We're on shift tomorrow evening."

"I know. But if there's a break, we are having dinner. I'm not sure what happened just now…"

"Eli." Amara frowned.

"It's okay." He stood and pressed his lips to each of her cheeks before lightly kissing her lips. "Whenever you're ready, you'll tell me."

Her eyes clouded with tears. "I'll see you tomorrow." It was a promise, and behind it lay so many more. Amara grabbed her keys and barely kept her feet moving forward.

CHAPTER SEVEN

AMARA WISHED SHE hadn't panicked last night as she walked through the doors of Boston Gen. the next morning. That she'd found the right words to tell him about her surgery. Eli wasn't like the other men she'd dated since her double mastectomy. But she couldn't stop the fear.

Amara had stood before a mirror last night and stared at the scars across her chest. They'd faded in the three years since her surgery. The skin was still tucked, and the nipples she'd had tattooed on would never look exactly like her previous ones had. The memory of Joe's averted gaze threatened to overwhelm her.

It didn't matter now, she tried to tell herself.

She automatically performed a quick search for Eli, but he wasn't in the hall. She'd figured out what they should do for the health fair, laid out some plans, grabbed him a coffee and now she just had to find him.

"Are you doing okay with Eli and the health fair?" Susan asked as she followed Amara into the lounge.

Amara was surprised by the look of concern on Susan's face. "Still planning, but I want to focus on healthy eating and do a cooking demonstration." She just needed to get Eli on board. This idea was different from any he'd ever done, but she was almost certain he'd like it.

Almost...

"Well, I'd do the cooking demonstration. Eli likes to joke that he really shouldn't be allowed near a stove. Though he does make a very passable grilled cheese." Amara chuckled as she leaned against the locker, memories of last night making her smile.

If only she hadn't run.

"He'll probably try to convince you to hire a celebrity chef." Susan's brows furrowed as she stared at Amara.

A celebrity chef for the health fair? That seemed over the top, even for Eli. "Why would he do that?" Amara asked as she placed her stethoscope around her neck.

"To draw attention to Boston Gen." Susan shrugged.

"I know he wants people to see this hospital for the fine institution it is, but a celebrity chef is ridiculous for a community health fair." Amara knew Eli wanted outside recognition. But she still hoped that he didn't *need* it like he once had. After all, he seemed happy with his life now.

"I'm not so sure. He's done a lot for this place in the last six years, but we will never be Massachusetts Research." Susan sighed. "That place chases awards like it's their job."

Amara nodded. "That's true." She'd worked there for nearly a decade. But she knew why Eli cared about those accolades so much. It made her heart ache that he clearly still wrestled with stepping outside of his father's shadow. And Marshall didn't make his son's struggle any easier. He asked Eli for help, called and texted at all hours, but never offered a thank-you or told Eli he'd done well. As soon as one task was completed, Marshall focused on the next, barely seeing the people around him. Eli was chasing an approval Amara feared was never going to come.

"I paired you with him because I figured he would just take over." Susan shrugged. "I assumed Eli would handle everything, and you'd get a few extra vacation days. I know the hospital doesn't offer great starting packages, even for nurses with your résumé. Instead, it appears you've helped him take a desperately needed chill pill. I'm impressed."

Amara swallowed. "I have?"

Susan winked. "This time last year, half the nursing staff wanted to murder him. He and Dr. Stanfred kept goading each other. The fact that Eli never uses the vacation days he wins drives Griffin insane."

Leaning against the locker bank, Susan studied Amara. "You're a calming influence on him." Adjusting her purse, she patted Amara's arm. "Now, if you'll excuse me, my very handsome dinner date is waiting for me."

Eli stepped into the lounge and waved at Susan as she walked out. His dark hair was a bit mussed, but he looked amazing. His eyes met Amara's, and light danced across them.

She'd never get tired of that reaction. *Never.* Amara handed him his coffee. "I know what we should do for the health fair." She knew it was a good idea, but Susan's worries had crawled into her head.

"I think we should do a cooking demonstration." She grabbed her notes and passed them to Eli. She kept talking as he looked over the stack of recipes she'd compiled last night. "I pulled my mom's old recipes. They're healthy, most are vegetarian, so that cuts out the cost of meat, and the rest of the ingredients are inexpensive staples. We can hand out samples and a pamphlet with the cooking instructions."

She held her breath. Amara knew this wasn't a fancy booth like he'd planned before. "I can handle most of it— you'll just show up as my helper." Eli kept his focus on the recipes. "I know this is different—"

"It's perfect," Eli interrupted.

His broad smile sent waves of hope and happiness floating through her. He was letting her take over the booth, and she could cook her mother's recipes. Her mom would have loved that—basked in the glory of it even. "I do need one thing, though."

"What? If it's in my power, the answer is yes."

"I haven't cooked these dishes in a while, and I need to adjust the recipes so I can make larger batches…"

"You need my kitchen." Eli's eyes darkened with desire as they looked at her lips.

"Yes," she whispered. If she was over at his place, they'd kiss again. She wanted to, so badly, but anxiety knotted her stomach once again. "I'd need to be there several times a week to get all the recipes perfected. I don't want to impose."

Eli gripped her hand. "That sounds very much like the opposite of imposition to me. I want you to visit."

The sounds of sirens echoed in the hall, and Eli put his coffee on top of a locker. "Duty calls."

They moved together toward the bay, and Amara barely managed to contain her surprise as Marshall stepped out of the back of the ambulance. She heard Eli's intake of breath, but he didn't hesitate like she did as the paramedics lowered the patient from the ambulance.

"What happened?" Eli asked the paramedic.

"Gillian found Tabitha passed out on the floor, her face slack," Marshall answered.

Stroke… The word raced through Amara's head, and she saw Eli nod.

"The mobile CT scanner is in trauma 2," Eli called. "That's where we're headed, people."

"You need to remain here, Dr. Collins." Eli's voice was tight as he followed Amara.

"Like hell, I will!" Marshall exclaimed. "Tabitha's been

with The Collins Research Group for almost two decades. She'd want me—"

"She's coding, Eli!" Amara pulled out the shock paddles and started to pass them to Eli, but Marshall was in the way.

Eli reached around his father and grabbed the paddles from her. "You don't have visiting physician rights at Boston Gen., and you're impeding the treatment of this patient. I need to get Tabitha stabilized. If you don't leave, I *will* have security remove you."

Amara knew that despite their differences, Eli would hate to call security on his father. She motioned for Eric, another nurse, to take her place. "Come on, Marshall. I'll show you where the waiting room is."

"I know where to go," Marshall barked, and pulled his arm from hers.

Many people responded to stress with anger. Amara had calmed hundreds of angry relatives and friends of patients over the years. Lowering her voice, she said, "Eli is one of the finest emergency room doctors in the state."

Marshall nodded but didn't say anything as he finally started walking toward the waiting room. "I'm sure he's more than adequate. Like this hospital, really—better than most just not great."

Amara knew her mouth was hanging open, but she was stunned. *And furious.* How dare he? How could Marshall just ignore his son's accomplishments? How could he not look at Eli and see what she saw? "Why don't you respect emergency medicine?" Amara hadn't meant to ask that, but she wanted Marshall's answer. Maybe it would help her with Eli.

"Respect?" Marshall rubbed his chin as he stared at her. "What I do is like fine art, delicate, intricate, exclusive." Marshall shrugged. "Emergency medicine has its place. But it's not surgery."

She wanted to shake him. How many of Marshall's patients had been saved by an emergency room doctor or nurse first? Hundreds. They were the ones who stabilized so many of his patients, often more than once, to make sure they had a chance for a successful transplant or heart surgery. "Eli is a better doctor than you."

Amara turned on her heel before Marshall could offer a rebuttal. She didn't care if he didn't believe it. She knew it, and she'd find a way to make Eli accept that fact too. He didn't have anything to prove to his father.

Eli wiped the sweat from his brow as he watched the intensive care team race Tabitha upstairs. The mobile CT scanner had identified a clot in her brain, the reason for her stroke. She'd stabilized after Eli had ordered an injection of tissue plasminogen activator. But her recovery was still uncertain.

Eli made his way to the waiting area to find Tabitha's husband. He was stunned to see his father sitting next to the worried man. He'd assumed Marshall would have headed back to the office by now or to his own hospital. He'd never known his father to take an afternoon off.

"Sir…"

"Mark," Tabitha's husband said. "How is my wife?"

"We managed to get her stabilized, Mark."

The man's gaze shifted between Eli and Marshall. "What does that mean?"

Eli hated this part. There was never a good way to tell someone that their life was changing. Even if their loved one recovered. "They're running some tests now. Your wife had at least one stroke."

Mark's eyes filled with tears. "But she is going to be okay, right?"

"Of course," Marshall stated.

What was his father doing? There was no way for him to

know that. "Dr. Collins, that may not be true." Marshall's eyes flashed, but Eli ignored it.

Directing his attention to Tabitha's husband, Eli started again. "She coded once today. She was breathing on her own when we transferred her upstairs, and that is excellent. But if she makes it through this, your wife will have a long recovery."

Mark flinched. "Can I see her?"

Eli nodded. "Of course. I'll have someone take you to her shortly."

Eli waited until Mark had gone before rounding on his father. "You might not like telling Tabitha's husband that she has a difficult road ahead, but it wasn't appropriate for you to say she's going to be fine. You're not her physician, and you have no idea what her medical prognosis is at the moment."

Eli was shocked by his own sharp tone. The only other time he'd stood up to his father was when he'd chosen not to become a surgeon. Marshall hadn't spoken to him for years after that, but Eli would not allow his father to offer poor medical advice in *his* hospital. Patients deserved the truth, no matter how much it might hurt to hear. He'd have thought his father understood that.

"I hate the family and patient interaction part," Marshall grumbled. "Easier to cut out the problem and replace it than talk to the family."

Eli wanted to shake his father. The patient and their family were the reasons Eli practiced medicine. To help people live their best lives.

For a man who always told his family that it was the patient who came first, Marshall often seemed more concerned about his success rate. He just saw the problem he could fix, not the whole person.

But he saved lives too, Eli thought, *a lot of lives.*

Eli was different from his father, but their reasons for practicing medicine were the same.

Save as many people as possible.

If their approach differed, did that really matter?

"Amara told me you were a better doctor than me." Marshall's statement broke through the rapid-fire of Eli's thoughts.

Eli's soul felt a bit lighter as he continued down the hall. She'd defended him to his father.

Of course she had.

Amara had always believed in him. If he hadn't already thought she was perfect, that would have done it.

"That's absurd, of course." Marshall chuckled. "And I have the stats to prove it."

"The stats?" Eli laughed.

"I've been ranked one of the top surgeons for the last decade. The last time I checked, neither this hospital nor you have ever even been in contention."

The twinge of inadequacy Eli always felt around his father sharpened. *It didn't matter. Shouldn't matter.* Marshall was tired, frustrated and concerned about a colleague. That was why he was lashing out. Eli had dealt with this many times during his career.

"I know you're worried about Tabitha." Eli kept his voice low and controlled. He could offer his father comfort. It was what he did every day of his working life.

His father's eyes shifted, and he sighed. "She's worked for me for a long time." Marshall's eyes swept over Eli. And for the first time in forever, Marshall really seemed to see him. "You did a nice job tonight. You might make that list one day too."

The tiny compliment struck him, and Eli hated that he couldn't stop his smile. Marshall hadn't complimented his career in any way since he'd gone into emergency medicine. What would he think if Eli managed to get Boston General in that report?

He'd have to respect him then.

"Eli?" Amara's voice carried down the hall.

He walked up to her and pulled her into a deep hug. "Thank you."

"For?" Amara's eyes slid to Marshall as he exited the hospital.

"For believing in me and telling my father I was a better doctor than him. It's a bit of a stretch, but I appreciate it." Eli hadn't meant to say it was a stretch out loud. But he couldn't withdraw it now.

Amara frowned. "I don't think it's a stretch."

No, she probably didn't. And that shot of acceptance made Eli feel so alive. "Amara, I—"

"Dr. Collins, there you are!" One of the med techs rushed toward them. "Dr. Stanfred asked if you'd take the elderly woman in room 2." The tech was gone before Eli could answer.

"Duty calls—again," Eli stated. "It's going to be one of those nights."

An older woman was clutching a man's arm and clearly in pain as he tried to help her walk from the bathroom to the bed in room 7. Amara and Eli raced for the couple. As Amara got her arm under the woman's shoulder, she was struck by the heat radiating off her chest. Eli's glance told her that he felt the same thing. The woman was burning up.

"What seems to be the problem?" Eli's voice was steady, comforting, as he helped the woman settle into the bed. Amara had meant what she'd told Marshall. Eli was an excellent doctor, calm in emergency situations, reassuring with his patients, always in control.

And Amara thought Marshall knew it too. Was maybe even a bit jealous of his son. Not that he'd ever admit it.

"I think my surgical incisions are infected." The woman's voice was ragged.

"Betty won't let me see," her husband added as he held his wife's hand. "But she has a fever, and she's changed her surgical dressings three times today."

"I—I—" Her throat was choked with tears as she looked from her husband to Amara. "I look so different, Harry."

"It doesn't matter, sweetheart. I love you." Harry stroked his wife's arm. "In sickness and health, remember."

Amara recognized the woman's meaning. "When was your mastectomy?" She ignored the tilt of Eli's head as she grabbed a pair of gloves and moved toward the bed.

"Two weeks ago."

She would always look different—Amara knew that. But judging her body two weeks postsurgery wasn't fair either.

"We need to look at the incisions, Betty." Eli's concerned tone raked over Amara. "I promise they're not nearly as bad as you think."

The kind statement sent a wave of hope pulsing through Amara. She patted her arm. "I know it's scary, but it *does* get better."

Eli's gaze flicked from Betty to Amara.

Would Eli tell her that her scars weren't that bad too?

Amara pushed the thought away as she looked at Betty. "In a few months, the scars will start to lighten. I promise. They go from red to pink, and eventually, they just become part of you."

"And you're beautiful, no matter what," Harry insisted as he stared at his wife. "But if you want me to leave the room, I will."

"Stay." Betty's chin wobbled, but she started to unbutton her shirt.

The redness along the scars sent a shiver through Amara. Betty needed intravenous antibiotics to get the infection under control before it spread.

As Eli explained that they needed to admit Betty for a day or so, Amara slipped from the room. She needed to get Betty's transfer paperwork done, so they could free up the room, but she had to get away from Eli too.

Every doctor and nurse knew that the scars would lighten, but by the look on his face when she'd explained that to Betty, Eli had known Amara was speaking from experience.

She was almost certain.

It didn't matter; she'd already decided to tell him. *Show him.* And he'd been kind and supportive of Betty. It was going to be fine...*it was.*

So why were her hands shaking?

CHAPTER EIGHT

ELI SAW AMARA start to climb his steps carrying bags of groceries and rushed to open the door. "Why didn't you beep the horn or let me know you needed help with a mountain of vegetables?" he asked as he grabbed two of the sacks from her hands.

Amara had disappeared after they'd worked together on Betty last night. Her response to their teenage patient Hannah's fear that her boyfriend would dump her over a scar, and her reaction to Betty made him almost certain that she'd also had surgery, likely a mastectomy. But he was worried that if he asked, she'd shut him out. Amara was beautiful, every inch of her. Nothing could change that.

The procedure she'd had didn't matter to Eli. But it had obviously mattered to someone else. And he hated that she'd been hurt.

His phone buzzed, and he barely controlled the urge to roll his eyes or answer immediately. Part of him wanted to be able to do both. Marshall had texted about The Collins Research Group all morning and called twice this afternoon. Amara was here, so Eli silenced the alerts from Marshall.

Tonight was all about Amara, Eli reminded himself. If their second chance was going to succeed, any work needed to be on mute when he was with her.

"It's okay if you need to answer that." Amara kissed his

cheek as she put a few things in the fridge. "I know your work is important."

Her offer was sweet, but Eli shook his head. "Lizzy is staying with my mom, so all we have on the agenda tonight is cooking."

"That's all?" Amara's eyes widened.

Eli stepped next to her and ran a finger down her cheek. "We can do whatever you want, Amara. Anything or nothing."

"Eli…" She suddenly closed the distance between them.

He captured her lips and felt her body mold against his. Her arms wrapped around him as her lips parted. The world righted when Amara was in his life.

Eli lifted her onto the counter, and his heart raced as her legs wrapped around his waist. He let his fingers run through her long dark hair. He'd come to life the first time they'd kissed. Spending time with her now was heaven. Her fingers sent flames of longing running down his spine as she held him.

The oven dinged to indicate it was up to temperature, and she pulled away. "If we are going to eat dinner, I should…" Her fingers brushed her swollen lips as she gestured to the bags of groceries.

Eli pressed his head against her forehead. "Or we could order a pizza and cook tomorrow?"

Amara stared at him. "I…" She wanted to agree so badly. She'd hidden last night after treating Betty because she hadn't wanted to have this conversation at the hospital. Hadn't wanted to have it all, but if he couldn't accept her as she was, then it was better to know now. Actually, it would have been better to know weeks ago before she'd gotten close to him again. But Amara couldn't change that now.

"Pizza." Amara wrapped her arms around Eli's neck,

and before she could get another word out, he kissed her. She wanted to kiss him forever, wanted to stay in his arms now and always, but he had to know.

"Eli," Amara murmured as she pulled back. His eyes were dilated with passion and need. She swallowed the last bit of her anxiety. Amara had to trust him.

Eli's fingers traced along the edge of her thigh as he watched her. "Amara, I want you. Need you, but if you aren't ready, I will wait as long as you want."

She took a deep breath. "I don't look the same." Her whispered words echoed across the kitchen. "I…" Amara paused, suddenly feeling sick.

"Had a mastectomy?" Eli asked as he kissed her forehead.

She blinked as he traced her jaw with his thumb. Sparks of need and hope lit up her body. "How do you know?"

"I wasn't completely sure, but you pull away any time my fingers move toward your breasts. You couldn't tell Hannah that her boyfriend wouldn't dump her over her scar, and you talked to Betty with such understanding."

She didn't think the look of desire in Eli's eyes had changed, but he hadn't seen the actual scars—yet. "I had a preventative double mastectomy three years ago. I took the genetic test after Mom was diagnosed. I was BRAC1 positive. I'm sorry I didn't tell you. My surgeon did a great job on the reconstruction, but… I was worried that it would…" Amara's voice died away as she stared at him. She didn't know what else to say, so she closed her eyes and waited.

His heart melted as her bottom lip quivered. "Amara, look at me." Eli kissed her cheek then waited for her to open her eyes. "You are gorgeous."

"I wanted to tell you weeks ago," she stated. "I kept meaning to. But I was scared it would make you look at me differently." Her voice quavered.

So other men hadn't been able to see past the scars. He

hated that. Placing his palms against her cheeks, Eli kissed her deeply. "You are perfection."

Once again, her legs wrapped around his waist. But she folded her hands across her lap, looking everywhere but at him. "Not exactly perfection. The scars are lighter now, but…" Amara shrugged.

"Can I see them?" Eli asked. Until he saw them, she'd worry. And whatever they looked like—he didn't care. Amara was here, with him. Nothing else mattered.

Amara hesitated, then she started to unbutton her blouse. His body raced with desire as she slid the shirt off her shoulders.

She was so lovely.

Eli didn't say anything. He let his hands rest on her knees. He couldn't imagine the emotions rolling through her right now, but Eli could see what a struggle this was.

Her hands shook as she reached to unclasp her silky blue bra.

"Let me." Eli kissed the top of her ear. "You are so beautiful."

"You don't know that."

Eli unclasped her bra and slowly slid it down her arms, but never broke her gaze. Then he deliberately dropped his eyes to her chest.

"Amara." He ran his hands along the edges of her breasts, noticing each place where her breath hitched. "Your scars don't define you, love." Her lip trembled, but he didn't stop. He was not going to let her doubt how much she turned him on. "They show the strength you have, and that makes them part of the tapestry of your beauty."

Stepping back, Eli held her hands as he stared at her, all of her. The long reconstructive scars across each breast didn't diminish her at all. He couldn't imagine the strength it had taken to make that choice. She was amazing.

"You are kind, intelligent, sweet and damn sexy." Eli held his breath as the ghost of a smile tripped along her lips.

"Sexy?" Her eyes held his. Hope hovered there, but Eli also saw the worry.

"Unbelievably so. Come to bed with me, and I will spend the rest of tonight showing you exactly how much you—*all of you*—turns me on." As soon as she nodded, Eli picked her up. Tonight, Amara was going to have no doubt just how much Eli wanted her.

And only her.

Eli's strong hands laid her on the bed, and Amara tried to calm her mind. He'd looked at the long scars, kissed her and told her how beautiful she was. Amara hadn't realized how much she needed to hear those words until Eli spoke them. She wanted to remember everything about tonight.

Eli's fingers ran along the top of her blue jeans, and she sucked in a breath as he undid the buttons and slid them down her hips. She was suddenly acutely aware that she was nearly naked, and Eli had yet to shed a stitch of clothing. He pulled away as she reached for his shirt. Self-consciousness flashed across her body. "Eli?"

"If I start stripping, I don't trust myself to savor tonight." His fingers traced lines of fire along her bare skin. "I've dreamed of touching you again for years, honey. Tonight, I'm going to worship every inch of you."

"That is quite the promise." Amara sighed as he stroked the inside of her thighs. Shivers of delight erupted along her body as his lips glided along her belly. Need poured through her as the stubble on Eli's jaw raked along her sensitive skin. She'd imagined being in his arms for weeks—years. Amara wasn't sure she could stand being worshipped. She needed him...now.

Eli kissed the base of one breast, and Amara gripped the sheets.

She could do this.

The scars were just scars. They didn't matter to him.

He paused. Raising his head, Eli trailed kisses along the edge of her jaw while his fingers moved over the scars on her breasts. "Honey, every inch of you is gorgeous to me—*every single inch.*"

Drawing a breath, Amara released her grip. She didn't have much feeling in her chest. More ghost sensations, but with each of Eli's gentle strokes, her body burned. "Eli." her voice shook as she delicately kissed his lips.

"I…" Under his watchful eyes, she grew bold. There was no room for doubt when she was in Eli's bed.

Grabbing his hand, she guided it lower. "I want you here." Her breath caught as Eli's fingers slid under her cotton panties.

His thumb stroked her as his lips traced the outer edges of her breasts, where the sensation was still the strongest. Each caress sent her soaring a bit higher as Eli worshipped her.

Cool air hit her bottom, and Amara shuddered as Eli trailed kisses lower. His tongue licked the sensitive skin along her upper thighs. She was heady with need as Eli slowly made his way to where she wanted him. Her back arched as his tongue darted across her most sensitive spot. The sensation was too much and not enough. "Eli!"

"You still taste sweet." Eli gripped her buttocks and held her as he drove her closer to pleasure's edge.

When Amara grabbed the sheets this time, it was with need. "Eli!" she moaned as he slipped a long finger into her. He stroked her slowly as he feathered kisses where they were most needed. Energy spread through her, as Amara finally gave herself over to pleasure.

Amara's release nearly sent Eli over the edge himself. Dropping his clothes to the floor, he slid back into bed with her.

Tracing his hand along her hip, Eli swept a line of kisses along her shoulder.

Amara's delicate touch sent a scorching line of need across Eli's soul. Her fingers slid slowly up his back, raced across his stomach, caressed his chest as if she was trying to memorize him too.

Capturing her mouth, Eli drank her in. "Amara…" Her name fell from his lips. He doubted that heaven could be any sweeter than this.

"Eli, worship me later," she gasped. "I need you." Her hand stroked his shaft. "All of you—now!"

The demand sent his heart soaring. *Amara…* Grabbing a condom from the nightstand, he quickly sheathed himself. Amara's lips pressed against his collarbone as he slowly entered her.

His body screamed with desire, but Eli was determined not to rush this. He'd waited too long for her. Dropping his head, he placed deliberate kisses along the base of Amara's neck as she wrapped her legs around his waist. Pulling him closer, deeper.

Drawing his lips to hers, Amara met each of his strokes. Nipping at his ear, she ran her nails lightly across his back. "Eli…" she moaned as her body convulsed around him.

Her next climax undid him. Eli drove into her. Amara gripped his shoulders, holding him, loving him. As his name fell from her lips, he let himself crest over the edge into release.

Eli relished the tender moments afterward, as their bodies lay tangled together. Home, she was home.

His Amara.

Rising, he quickly disposed of the condom and then rejoined her in bed. Running his fingers along her stomach, he cradled her beside him. Amara, in his arms, was the definition of heaven.

CHAPTER NINE

ELI WANDERED OVER to the nurses' station and handed Amara a cup of tea. Her smile sent a thrill through him.

"And here I was afraid you might stop bringing me tea, once we'd been dating a bit." Amara winked as she took a long sip.

"Was that an option?" Eli teased as she rolled her eyes. "I missed you last night." Her dark eyes caught his, and he felt like the luckiest man in the world. Amara was working beside him, staying at his place at least a few times a week and generally just making everything better in his world.

The radio by Amara's hand crackled to life. "Boston Gen.," she answered. "Repeat. Over."

"Male, midthirties, car accident. Inbound in three. Over."

Amara stood and followed Eli toward the door. "It doesn't sound critical." She moved, rubbing the back of her foot with her ankle and crossed her arms.

Preparing.

Eli nodded as he stood in the ambulance bay with her. Preparing was what emergency personnel did. Prepare for the worst, hope for the best. The paramedics hadn't indicated critical, but he'd seen minor injuries turn life-threatening in minutes.

Seconds changed lives.

A young woman climbed out of the ambulance and lost

her balance. She caught herself on the door and frowned. "Sorry." She stepped to the side as the paramedics lowered a man from the back.

"Julian. I'm here." She followed a few feet behind the gurney as they walked toward trauma room 3.

"Crashed into the side of a tree. Driver's side door crushed against his shoulder," the paramedic stated as he walked beside the bed.

"The roads are wet," Julian explained, but Eli kept his focus on the paramedic.

"Airbag deployed, burns on the wrist and he hit his head." The paramedic checked a few items on the paperwork before handing it to the admitting nurse.

"This feels like an overreaction," the patient complained as he pulled at the collar around his neck.

"Julian, let them look you over." The tall blonde slid into a chair and closed her eyes. "It will make me feel better."

"Were you in the car too?" Amara moved toward the woman.

"Passenger side. No damage. My husband, though..." The woman's words died away.

A look of concern crossed Amara's face as she caught Eli's gaze. He raised a brow, and she nodded toward the passenger and tapped her own head. "Can you tell me your name?" Amara asked.

"Kelly." The woman's voice was quiet.

Turning to Julian, Eli ran through his concussion protocols as Amara did with Kelly. Julian had a minor concussion, and his burns from the airbag were superficial. Overall the man was going to need to take it easy for a few days, but then he'd be fine.

"Eli!"

He hit the alarm by Julian's bed before racing to Amara's

aid. Eli barely managed to help Amara catch the woman as she fell out of the chair.

"Kelly!" Julian yelled and started to sit up.

"I need you to stay where you are until I clear you," Eli ordered.

"My wife…"

"I understand, but stay there. Please." Eli wished there was a way to alleviate the man's panic. But Julian had a minor brain injury. The last thing they needed was two patients on the floor.

Griffin and Susan were by their sides in a matter of moments.

"She almost fell getting out of the ambulance with her husband. Her movements were slow and exaggerated, and I think the lights in here caused her pain, though she didn't tell me." Amara recited the issues as they led Kelly into her own room.

Eli rubbed the back of his neck as he walked toward Julian's room. His wife's CT scan had come back indicating a crack on the right side of her head. She'd probably hit the window, and the small bleed hadn't impacted her for over an hour.

Amara staying by Kelly's side while he examined Julian had kept the woman from further injuring herself. Amara's instincts had been spot-on. Working with her, being beside her, made every day better.

Julian needed to be careful, but they were going to release him so he could go upstairs with his wife.

"It happened so fast." He heard Julian's voice echo through the open door. "The road was slick. Kelly seemed fine. The paramedics looked her over at the scene."

"The symptoms with a brain bleed can be difficult to spot immediately. But your wife has some of the finest physicians in Boston watching over her," Amara responded. Of course, she'd checked in on Julian when their shifts ended. It was what Eli was about to do.

Eli saw Julian lay a hand across his head. "Last time I checked, I was at Boston Gen., not Massachusetts Research." Julian stopped. "Sorry, no offense meant."

He saw Amara offer Julian a patient smile. "I used to work at Massachusetts Research. If you need open-heart surgery or orthopedic care, there is no better place in the state, maybe the country." She stood and patted the side of Julian's bed. "But this *is* the top ER in the city. The staff here handle more trauma cases than any other. We just don't advertise it as well as the other hospitals." Amara winked. "Too busy focusing on our patients. Get some rest."

Eli stepped into the room. "I've come to spring you." He gazed at Amara. Every word she'd spoken had been true. This was the best ER in the city, and they *should* do a better job of advertising that fact. "You need to be careful, monitor any headaches, and if you have family nearby, it would be helpful if someone could stay with you while your wife is here."

"Thank you," Julian murmured.

"Someone will be in with your discharge paperwork shortly." Eli motioned for Amara to follow him. "You're extraordinary." He leaned as close as was professionally acceptable, enjoying the grin twitching on her lips. He didn't think he could ever tire of seeing her happy.

"Thank you." Amara gripped his hand briefly. "We make a great team."

We do.

"And you gave me the best idea for raising Boston Gen.'s profile. We need an advertising campaign highlighting the work here."

Amara blinked a few times. "Eli, that isn't your job. Focus on the patients. Boston Gen. does great work. That's all that matters."

"We do exceptional work. And that should be publicly recognized." Eli folded his arms.

Why didn't she see that?

"It *is* recognized." Amara shrugged. "Maybe not by national magazines, where most of the votes are bought with fancy dinners, tours and things that have nothing to do with patient care. Where did the paramedics bring Julian and his wife? Here. You, Griffin, Dr. Jackson and Dr. Carmichael each get asked to give presentations at conferences every year. You were the keynote speaker at two separate conferences last year. Recognition comes in many forms. The most important kind doesn't have a trophy."

"And that is?" Eli raised an eyebrow.

She laid a hand on his arm. "The recognition that you are enough. The only person that can give that to you is yourself. But—" Amara gave him a pointed look "—there are no fancy banners that come with it."

She looked down the hall and placed a quick peck on his cheek. "I know you want this place to be nationally ranked. Want people to identify us as a first-class institution—but we already are that. We just need to fix our staff retention issues," Amara said as she headed back to the nurses' station.

Eli looked around the halls. He'd loved Boston Gen. since the day he'd walked in. Amara was right—this was a first-class ER. But she was also wrong about the rankings. What people thought, or believed, was important too. And ratings affected that. It helped with funding and would solve at least some of the retention issues. Eli was going to find a way to make sure everyone else knew how great *his* hospital was.

* * *

Amara grabbed Lizzy's cup of milk and looked toward the stairs. Eli was going over a stack of papers that Marshall had dropped off last night. Eli had promised to come down for breakfast. If he wasn't down here in a few minutes, Amara would go looking for him. She frowned.

Over the last week, there hadn't been a single day when Eli hadn't gotten a request from Marshall or worked on some project for Boston Gen. He was burning his candle at both ends and down the center. He surely couldn't keep this pace up. At least she was in charge of the health fair booth.

He trusted her with the booth, though he was still joking with Griffin that they were going to win the extra vacation days. Amara's focus was on providing good information, not winning. Cooking her mother's dishes had brought her a sense of peace. In the kitchen, cutting up vegetables, prepping the recipes, she felt closer to her mom than she had in years. Amara hadn't bought a bag of salad on any of her grocery runs this week—and she wasn't going to.

Her mother would have loved having her recipes tasted by hundreds of people. If only a few visitors to the booth made her food afterward, that would be enough. This felt like a beautiful way to honor her mom.

Lizzy laughed as she tried to pick up Amara's bag. Amara walked over and grabbed her. She'd spent the last three nights at Eli's, and she needed to run back to her apartment today. At least to get her mail and pick up a few more clothes before coming home.

Home.

Amara's feet faltered as the word struck her. Her apartment had never really felt like home. It was just a place she'd picked when her life had fallen apart. The rent had been in her price range, and Amara hadn't even bothered to redecorate the place to her taste. But here she felt different. *Loved...*

She hadn't worked up the courage to say those words to him. Amara loved Eli; a part of her had never stopped. But she couldn't help still worrying that he might drift away. He hadn't said that he loved her either. She looked toward the stairs and wondered again where he was.

She bit her lip and tried to ignore the tiny remnant of fear pressing against her. Eli wasn't her father, and he wasn't Marshall, but what if he always persisted in chasing this dream of seeing his hospital on the national rankings—*his own name, too*?

No! She was not going to let fear of what-if stop her from enjoying the here and now. Amara had spent years away from the one person who'd looked at her and seen Amara, no matter what. That was precious. She could share his attention with his work—all his work. And whatever accolades came his way.

But their second chance still felt so new to utter the words "I love you." They had all the time they needed to get to that place. Now, if he would just come down for breakfast. As she stepped away from the counter, Eli walked into the kitchen.

"I was starting to worry you were going to spend the day in your study." Amara gave him a little finger wag.

"It's only been an hour." Eli tapped his watch as he bent to kiss the top of Lizzy's head. Then he gave Amara a much longer kiss.

His hand was warm against her back, and Amara couldn't think of a better way to start her day. "Well, an hour is a long time." She gave him another kiss before he released her.

"My apologies." Eli laughed. "You look beautiful this morning."

Amara picked up her teacup. "What is your father having you work on?"

"The Collins Research Fundraiser." Eli poured coffee into a mug and took a sip. "Guess he's been more impressed by my help than I thought."

"Well, you *are* very impressive." Amara squeezed his hand. She wished Eli didn't need to constantly prove himself to Marshall, but she was determined to tell him how proud she was of him, as often as possible. Maybe then, Marshall's opinion wouldn't carry so much weight. "Time for some breakfast."

Eli set down his mug before picking up Lizzy, taking a seat at the table and settling her in his lap. He shifted a few cut-up grapes around on the plate in front of him. "I admit that I thought he was kidding at first. He never let Sam and me help before."

"Did you want to?" Amara asked. He'd always complained about the fundraiser in the past. She'd thought he hated it.

"No." Eli shook his head, but his eyes gleamed. "But this year Boston Gen. is the focus."

Lizzy looked at Eli and popped a cut-up grape into her mouth, laughing as it squished between her lips. When he didn't react, she frowned.

To distract her, Amara sat down, then lightly bopped Lizzy on the nose before popping one of the grapes in her own mouth. Lizzy's peal of laughter echoed throughout the kitchen, and the toddler focused on making faces at Amara.

"Really, Marshall chose Boston General?" Amara was stunned.

What did Marshall want in exchange for such a prize?

Amara hated the unkind thought, but it wouldn't stop hammering inside her head.

Eli's eyes shone with excitement, and Amara tried to ignore the twinge of unease she felt. It would be fine. *It would.* Eli was committed to Boston General, and he'd been a physician for years—he wouldn't consider an unwanted surgical residency just because his father demanded it of him.

Amara pushed the past away. Swallowing, she tried to keep her voice level. "Has Marshall ever chosen a local hospital before?" Amara guessed the answer, so she wasn't surprised when Eli shook his head.

"Which is why this needs to be perfect. If Boston Gen. can get a large cash infusion, think of all the hospital can do. We can highlight everything it does well, maybe get on that national ranking list." Eli pushed a hand through his hair.

Amara shook her head. "You don't even know the criteria for that list, and this is a fundraiser. It has nothing to do with patient care," she countered. When Eli shrugged, the touch of worry grew in her heart. Marshall was dangling a huge prize in front of his son. Acceptance.

Or the illusion of it...

Ignoring the wave of panic washing over her, Amara tried to focus on the positive. "Will our hospital get much from the fundraiser?" She put a few more pieces of grapes on Lizzy's plate. She might just squish them, but at least it kept her occupied.

"Last year, Clean Water for All took home a little over fifteen million."

"Fifteen million?" Amara felt her eyes widen. How could anyone raise that much money, particularly with one event?

Eli's eyes were bright as he took a bite of his muffin. "The lowest amount Marshall ever managed to raise with the event was just under ten million. I bet we can break the record this year. Marshall told me to shoot for twenty million."

Told him?

Amara tried to focus on the positives. With an additional twenty million dollars, Boston Gen. could fund several new projects.

"I spent this morning writing up a list of sponsors to contact and investors to reach out to. Marshall's always focused on the East Coast, but there are some new medical start-ups in California and one in Nevada that are doing some amazing things too." Eli was thrilled.

"How much of this event did Marshall turn over to you?" Amara asked, dreading the answer.

"He said I could run it." His grin sent a shiver down her spine. "We could make a real difference." He took out his phone and started typing furiously.

"*If* you do this and Marshall still doesn't respect you, what will you do?" She kept her voice level. She hated asking the question, but she needed to know the answer.

Eli's brows furrowed, and he let out a deep breath. "But surely he would…" He paused and closed his eyes.

"He might not." Amara's stomach clenched as she watched Eli shoulders tense. He'd always wanted Marshall's acceptance. But he had to understand that his father might not ever give it—he might not be able to. Maybe it wasn't fair to push this, but even though the fundraiser was months away, this project would steal away Eli's time.

All of it, if Marshall had his way.

"Then I'll try again next year." Eli shrugged. "Marshall will eventually…" He clamped down on whatever he was going to say.

But Amara understood, and frustration rippled through her. Taking a deep breath, she reined in her emotions. "Are you going to work for Marshall full-time then?" Amara knew the answer to that, but she wanted Eli to say it out loud.

"No."

"So, you'll still have your work at the hospital." Amara

swallowed as Eli nodded. "What about Lizzy? What about me? What happens to us, if you spend the next eight months spending the very little free time you already have proving to Marshall that you can host a great fundraiser? Something you didn't ask for. What do you get?"

And what do you risk losing?

She didn't say those words, though. Amara had thrown down that gauntlet years ago, and he'd let her walk away. She'd let her fear that he'd work so much that he forgot his family rule her. Eli had needed to be challenged back then just like she was doing now, but walking away without giving him a chance to think about it and change his mind had been wrong.

And cost them both.

She wouldn't do that again. Eli had promised her he could balance his work and home lives, and Amara would help him do it. *She would.* Even if that meant forcing him to acknowledge that his father might be using him.

"You're right," he said quietly. "Marshall might never see me as an equal—probably won't." Eli's hands shook, and Amara's heart broke for him. "And I never wanted to run the whole fundraiser. I can help him smooth a few things out, but…" Eli smiled, but it didn't reach his eyes.

If only she could wave a magic wand to make Marshall see the man she saw. "You are more than enough for Lizzy and me, Eli. No matter what the rankings say, or your father thinks. You are extraordinary."

Eli gripped her hand. "That's all that matters." He kissed her cheek, but his shoulders didn't relax.

She wasn't sure he really believed her, but Amara didn't know what else to say. She slipped an arm around Eli and held him, trying to let all her feelings flow into him.

You are enough… I love you…

* * *

Amara leaned her head against the tile as the hot water slid over her skin. Her relationship with Eli was going to work this time. She wanted so badly to believe that, but the despair in his eyes racked her with guilt. Maybe she shouldn't have said anything. But what if Marshall never came to his senses? And what if Eli continued to chase after him?

Her father hadn't even called her since he remarried. It hurt, but Amara knew her father wasn't going to change. Amara doubted Marshall could really change either.

Sighing, she slid her hand along the side of her breast and performed her regular check. She'd gotten into the habit during nursing school. If she was going to remind women to check their breasts every month, Amara felt she should do the same. Now she followed the instructions her breast surgeon had given her after her double mastectomy. Even though her surgeon had done her best to get all the breast tissue, there was a small possibility with skin-sparring mastectomies for a bit of residual breast tissue to remain.

Her routine was interrupted as a small lump ran under her fingers. Taking a deep breath, Amara washed her hair and forced herself to finish her shower. She might have imagined it, or maybe there was a bit of scar tissue she hadn't noticed previously. Before shutting off the water, she performed the self-check again. The pea-size lump was still there in the same spot.

Her body was numb as she turned the water off and wrapped the towel around herself. She'd done everything her genetic counselor, ob-gyn and plastic surgeon had recommended. *Everything*. And still there was something there.

She tried to convince herself that it was just a cyst or scar tissue as she pulled a brush through her hair. Amara stared at the clothes she'd laid out on the bed. Just getting dressed suddenly seemed like too much effort.

What if she had...?

Amara couldn't bring herself to even think the word.

Bowing her head, she dialed Susan's number. Amara wouldn't be able to focus on her patients tonight, and a distracted nurse was dangerous. Susan answered on the third ring. Amara choked out an excuse about not feeling well, which wasn't really a lie. Susan wished her well before hustling off the phone to find a replacement.

Leaning her head against the wall, Amara called her doctor. She was lucky; another patient had canceled, and they could fit her in tomorrow afternoon. Twenty-four hours and then more waiting.

Again, she looked at Eli's number, her finger hovering for a moment before she laid down the phone. He needed to work tonight, and she'd already upset him today. Plus she wasn't ready to verbalize her fears. It might be nothing.

It had to be nothing.

But when the tears started, Amara let them fall.

"What's up with Amara?" Griffin said, slapping Eli's shoulder.

"Why?" Eli asked, and immediately looked toward the nurses' station. She wasn't there. This morning, when she'd pressed him on the fundraiser, it had hurt to hear that she thought Marshall might never accept him.

He'd reluctantly agreed not to take over the whole fundraiser, though. Amara *was* right about that. Eli had never cared about it, and Boston General would make a good sum from it no matter what.

It was a considerable time commitment. And Eli didn't want to spend that much time away from his family.

His family.

That word sent a thrill through him. He loved Amara. Had always loved her. It was her soft voice repeating that he was enough that kept him grounded, even during the years they'd spent apart.

"She called in tonight, less than two hours before her shift." Griffin looked at his hospital-issue tablet and swiped a few times.

"Why?" Unease trickled down Eli's spine. Was she more upset than he'd realized this morning? She'd held him, reassured him. But Eli was suddenly very aware that he hadn't asked her how she was feeling. He'd been too focused on himself.

"No idea." Griffin raised an eyebrow. "Maybe Susan knows more."

Eli fell into step with the head nurse. "What's wrong with Amara?"

Susan didn't pause as she walked to the door of room 3. "Don't know. She said she wasn't well and sounded…not like herself. She was…" Susan let that thought die away, and her blue eyes tore through him. "Quiet," she finally added.

Eli pulled his cell out and dialed Amara. The phone rang twice before going to voice mail.

Maybe she was sleeping.

If she'd come down with a virus in the few hours since he'd seen her… Still, Eli couldn't shake the feeling that something was really wrong.

Eli raced up the stairs in the old luxury home that had been turned into a set of apartments. According to his phone, Amara had read each of his texts, but she hadn't responded. He needed to see her, hold her, to calm the racing thoughts streaming across his brain.

She'd called in sick and hadn't phoned him. That stung. They were supposed to be partners. True, they'd had a tense discussion, but Eli hadn't considered it a fight. Certainly not one that necessitated her staying off work. That couldn't be why she wasn't at the hospital.

Eli had run through a litany of possibilities on the short drive from Boston Gen., each making his blood run cold. Amara had to be all right.

She had to be...

She didn't answer his first knocks. Eli ran his hand through his hair. He didn't want to make a scene in the hallway, but he needed to see her. "Amara, honey. Open the door." Eli raised his voice and then knocked on the door twice more.

His cell buzzed, and he frowned at the screen—now she answered his texts! "Amara, I am not leaving, so either text me the location of the spare key or open the door." Eli knocked again. "Let me in, love. Whatever's wrong, I can help." His voice faltered as he leaned against the door. "Please..."

His phone buzzed again, and he straightened up. This was not how he wanted to communicate with the woman he loved. She just needed to answer the door.

Spare key under the green flowerpot.

Eli heaved a huge sigh of relief.

The small living room and galley kitchen were empty. The door to Amara's bedroom was closed. Pushing it open slowly, he saw her sitting in an oversize chair by the window.

"You're supposed to be at the hospital." Amara's voice was small and husky with tears.

His heart stuttered as she kept staring straight ahead. "That was nine hours ago."

What was going on?

"Susan and Griffin send their regards." Eli pressed his lips to her forehead as he slid down beside her.

He wrapped an arm around her shoulders, and they sat in silence. Eli felt her tears fall against his collar but still didn't speak. Whatever was wrong, she'd tell him when she was ready. The important thing was that Amara knew he was here. *No matter what.*

After a few minutes, he kissed her cheek and squeezed her hand. "I'm going to make you some tea." Her near-catatonic state was terrifying him.

Amara nodded as she grabbed a towel and headed to her bathroom.

Eli watched the clock. If she didn't emerge by the time her tea was ready, he was going to go and get her. He set the mug on the small counter just as Amara came out.

"Thank you, Eli." Her voice was stronger but still sounded far away. "Everything is fine."

"That is a lie." He folded his arms and looked at her. "We're a team now. Whatever's wrong, I'll help you fix it."

Tears flooded Amara's dark eyes as she lifted the mug to her lips. "You can't fix this, Eli. I... I..."

She bit her lip so hard, he feared she was tasting blood. "Amara?"

"I found a lump when I was in the shower." Her whispered words stole the air from the small kitchen.

Eli's stomach dropped, but he forced his face to stay neutral. Amara was understandably scared, but he needed to be her rock right now. If this was more than just scar tissue, a cyst or...his brain forced the words away. *If* it was cancer, he'd break then, and not in front of her.

"Okay. Have you set up an appointment to have it checked?" Handle the issues you could first. That's what he always told his patients.

"Tomorrow..." Amara said as her fingers shook.

"All right." Eli took a deep breath. "If, and it's still a big if, it's cancer, then we will deal with it together."

"Together?" Amara picked up the mug and took a sip of her tea as her eyes watered.

"Of course." Eli put an arm around her. How could she even ask?

Because her father hadn't helped her mother.

The truth struck him like a blow.

Amara wasn't sure that he'd stay with her. He tried not to let that hurt. She would always come first with him—*in sickness and in health.* They may not have said those vows to each other, but Eli wouldn't walk away from Amara—ever.

"I just feel so hollow. So scared." Her voice wavered, and she sucked in a deep breath.

"That's to be expected." Eli pressed a kiss to her temple. "I've never lived with the fear of Damocles' sword falling." Amara's lips turned up just barely, but it gave him a bit of hope.

"Ancient Roman parables about death hanging above you? Really, Eli." Amara's dark eyes held his.

"It's the one thing I remember from your Ancient Roman History class. That and the pile of note cards you had all over the apartment. You must have studied those myths for months." Eli took the tea mug from Amara and set it on the counter before pulling her into his arms.

"It was six weeks, and keeping all those gods and goddesses straight was hard. Worst elective ever!" Amara let out a light chuckle. "How can I be laughing right now?"

"Because life can be funny and tragic at the same time. But you can't enjoy life if you're constantly worrying about what might go wrong. You'll go nuts." Eli wiped away a tear from her cheek.

Amara shook her head as she looked up at him. "My

mom used to tell me that." She choked up again, and tears streamed down her cheeks.

Eli's heart broke at the loss in her eyes, and the worry that she'd face the same terrible diagnosis as her mother. Fear pressed against his belly, but Eli pushed it back. Whatever she faced, she'd face it with him. "Well, your mom was right. But no matter what, I'm sticking around. We're partners, Amara."

Eli stroked her arm as she leaned her head against his shoulder. He needed to touch her, to reinforce that he was there—and was staying. "No one gets promised tomorrow, Amara. *No one.* The best any of us can do is enjoy the present. Fill it with laughter, love and hope."

She wrapped her arms around his waist and let out a soft sigh. "Thank you, Eli. I should have called you, or at least sent a text."

"Yes, you should have," he agreed as he ran his hand along her cheek. "But I understand. Now, let's get you packed."

"Packed?" Amara blinked.

Eli felt his cheeks heat as he stared at her. He'd meant to ask it as a question. "I think you should stay with Lizzy and me for a bit, at least until after your doctors' appointments."

"Eli…"

Before she could offer any well-reasoned argument, he added, "You were already with us several nights a week. If you stay here, you're just going to worry. Besides, when raising a toddler, you're often too tired at the end of the day to think straight." Eli winked. He wanted her to stay with them…*forever.*

"Your toddler is adorable." Amara sighed.

"Yes, she is. But don't change the subject. I promise the time will fly by faster if you're with us." Eli threaded her fingers through his.

"I appreciate the offer, Eli. I do. But I can handle this myself. I can." Amara's lips trembled, but her shoulders were straight. The strength running through her was impressive, but she could lean on him too.

"I know you can," Eli stated. He thought Amara might be able to handle anything. "But you don't have to handle it alone. I'm here. Let me help." He squeezed her hand. "Please."

Amara's lips pursed, and she nodded. "Thank you."

Eli's heart soared as she started toward her bedroom. Relationships weren't just the good bits. Real relationships were built in the times like now, when tomorrow looked less than rosy. When life shifted the balance of everything, you shifted with it.

CHAPTER TEN

AMARA WAS SITTING behind the nurses' station, going over a few records, trying to focus. Her brain kept wrapping around what might happen. No matter how much she tried to calm the what-ifs. It was a mental reel that she hadn't been able to shut off for days while she waited for her test results.

At least being at Boston Gen. helped. This place was special. Time passed faster when she was here.

And sped by when she was with Eli.

She smiled as he turned the corner and offered her a short wave.

"My wife needs help!" Amara heard the scream, grabbed a pair of gloves and raced toward the emergency room entrance.

Outside, a young, heavily pregnant woman was lying across the backseat of a car, her breaths coming fast. Amara wasn't surprised when Eli arrived by her side and started putting on gloves.

"How far along is she?" Eli asked as he motioned for a gurney.

"Thirty-nine weeks. We were at the doctor's yesterday, and he told us we still had time."

"Well, babies have their own schedule," Amara stated

as she bent to do an initial medical examination while Eli finished getting gloved. "What's your name?"

"Nicole."

"Well, Nicole, I'm Amara." She'd helped with a few emergency deliveries over the years. "I'm going to lift your dress and see how you're progressing, so we can let the maternity ward know. How far apart are your contractions?"

"They are…" Nicole flinched and let out a low groan.

Adrenaline spun through Amara. The baby was already crowning. "Eli!" Nicole was not even going to make it into the ER.

Amara exchanged places with Eli and headed to the other side of the car. Climbing into the backseat, Amara helped Nicole sit up a bit.

While Eli adjusted Nicole's legs, Amara looked at the frightened woman. "You need to try not to push, okay?"

"I have to," she whimpered. "I can't stop. My body…" Nicole's words were lost as another contraction hit her.

Eli looked over his shoulder. "We can't move her. Get OB here now! The baby is coming."

"Breathe, Nicole." Amara kept her voice calm as the woman stared up at her. "You're going to be a mom soon, but right now, we need you to breathe."

"When the next contraction hits—"

Another contraction came, and Nicole pushed before Eli could finish his statement.

"You're doing great, Nicole," Eli offered encouragement.

The world disappeared around them. Eli, Nicole and Amara focused on the messy miracle of childbirth —in a less than ideal place. New life was coming, no matter the setting.

"You're almost there." Another contraction and the baby slipped into Eli's arms. The little boy started crying straight away.

Amara let out a breath she hadn't realized she was holding as Eli accepted a suction bulb from a person behind him and quickly cleared the baby's airway. *He was perfect.*

"You have a beautiful son," Eli announced. "And you are going to have quite the story to tell."

A maternity nurse arrived and took the baby from Eli, and Dr. Mengh, the senior obstetrician, shifted places with him. "Nice job, Dr. Collins."

Amara looked over at Eli and grinned as he gave her two thumbs-up. They'd worked as the perfect team, and she couldn't stop the glow of warmth spreading across her as she stared at the small child and his mother being wheeled into the ER. *Could she have that with Eli?* For the first time in days, hope for the future replaced the dread in Amara's heart.

Eli stared at Amara through the doorway of Nicole's maternity room. Little Kellen was wrapped securely in Amara's arms. She was beautiful, and his heart felt like it might explode.

Her health was still uncertain, but Eli couldn't stop the image of her holding their own child. She'd be a wonderful mom. Amara was a natural with Lizzy. He wanted a family with her.

He wanted everything.

"There you are." Marshall suddenly popped up beside him, frowning. "Why are you in maternity?" His father motioned for Eli to follow him.

Pushing away from the door, Eli caught Amara's gaze. *You okay?* she mouthed, and he nodded.

And he was.

"What do you need, Marshall?"

"I sent you a list of questions about Boston Gen. this morning for the fundraiser," Marshall stated expectantly.

Eli shook his head. "I've been at work, and those questions you asked should be directed to Human Resources anyway."

"They take days to respond." Marshall's eyes heated as he stared at Eli. "You should have been able to answer them in no time."

"Well, they're busy, and so am I." Eli shrugged. It was the truth, but it felt good to just state it. "If I have a chance, I'll look over them later."

Marshall's eyes narrowed as he looked back toward the room where Amara was. "Do you remember what I told you? You can be a great doctor…"

"But not a great spouse." Eli finished the sentence, believing that had cost him Amara years ago. But Eli wasn't sure he believed it anymore. What he did know was that he didn't want to be like his father. Angry over an unanswered email on an issue that didn't need to be handled immediately.

"I think I can do both." His father just hadn't tried hard enough. Eli could succeed where Marshall had failed.

"Something always suffers," Marshall stated. "Ms. Patel wasn't willing to stand beside you as you chased your goals last time. Think she'll do it now?"

"Yes." Eli was surprised by his confidence Because a decade ago, Eli hadn't been chasing his own goals.

He'd been chasing Marshall's.

They were partners, cheering each other on, supporting each other. Marshall was right. That meant some things might have to suffer, but it wouldn't be Amara, Lizzy or Boston Gen.

"If you don't push yourself, you're never going to make it out of this place." Marshall folded his arms crossly.

Make it out of Boston Gen.?

His father's statement struck him. How could Marshall

think he was stuck here? Boston Gen. was where he belonged. He thought he'd made that clear—except Marshall hadn't been listening.

"You're right; I do need a change." Eli let out a deep breath as a weight lifted from his chest. "I'll send a formal response to the board, but please consider this my resignation from The Collins Research Group." Amara was right, Marshall was never going to respect him, and Eli was done searching for his approval. *He was...*

Before Marshall could respond, Amara exited the room and walked toward them. "Good afternoon, Marshall."

He didn't acknowledge her as he stormed past Eli.

"Was it something I said?" Amara looked from Marshall's retreating form to Eli.

"No. It was something I said." He grinned as Amara raised an eyebrow. "I resigned from The Collins Research Group."

"What?" Amara's eyes widened as she stared at him. "Eli, are you sure?"

"Honestly? No," he admitted. "But it felt right in the moment. Still feels right." He swung an arm around Amara. "Let's go home."

Cutting up a lemon, Amara tilted her head as the tart citrus juice fell into the pan she was heating. She'd practiced each of the recipes she was making for the health fair. Tonight was lemon rice, Eli's favorite.

He'd been in good spirits since telling Marshall he wasn't going to work part-time for The Collins Research Group or serve on its board anymore. But Amara still worried that Eli might change his mind. Or doubt himself.

It had been such a sudden decision. What if he regretted it? Or felt like she'd pressured him into it? That hadn't been her intention when she'd challenged him about the fundraiser.

But what if...?

The lemon scent wafted over her, and Amara let the worry go—mostly.

She'd grown up helping her mother in the kitchen and knew these recipes by heart. As each day passed with no test results, Amara found herself yearning to talk with her. If the veil between worlds could fall for just one day...

As the scent of lemon and spice cascaded over the kitchen, Amara felt her soul relax a bit more. Her mother would have loved that she'd reconnected with Eli. She'd have cheered them on and been first in line at their health fair booth. Particularly since they were serving her recipes.

"That smells delicious," Eli stated before dropping a soft kiss on her forehead, as Lizzy waved at him from the floor. "Tell me that's lemon rice."

"Right now, it's just boiling water, lemon and spices. But yes, it will be lemon rice in about twenty minutes." A yawn stole through Amara, and she saw Eli's eyes fill with concern.

"If you need to rest," he offered, "I can order us takeout. Or we can finally fix that frozen lasagna."

"We are never going to eat that thing!" Amara laughed and then yawned again. She appreciated all of Eli's concerns. She really did, but it was just another reminder that everything might be changing before they'd properly got started on their second chance. "I'm fine. Just tired."

His arms wrapped around her waist. "Do you need anything for the booth? You don't have to handle it alone."

"I've got it," Amara promised. She didn't need help. She was fine.

"Are you—" A loud bang interrupted them, and Eli laughed. "Lizzy's a drummer."

"Yep." Amara had flipped over three pots and set them on the floor before giving Lizzy a spoon. Lifting her head,

Amara kissed him. The worries that hadn't quieted in over a week almost disappeared as she stared at Eli and Lizzy.

"This was how my mother kept me occupied until I was old enough to help in the kitchen." Amara frowned as she yawned again.

"If the health fair is too much, Amara, I can help. In fact, I—"

"No!" Amara interrupted. "I'm fine." If she said it often enough, Amara hoped the mantra would be true.

Her heart raced as Eli bent and patted a few of the pots with Lizzy. This was what a perfect life looked like. Cooking, laughing and turned-over pots.

"If you need anything, will you tell me?" Eli asked before making a silly face for Lizzy.

"Of course." Amara thought her heart might explode from happiness as Lizzy grinned and handed him the spoon. Eli hit the pots, but not hard enough for Lizzy, and soon she was reclaiming her spoon.

"I guess I need my own spoon," Eli said.

His smile was contagious as he stood, and Amara let the worries slip to the back of her mind.

Amara rolled over and sighed as Eli's arm slid around her waist. Lying next to him made the late nights with little sleep pass quicker. His breath was warm against her neck as she snuggled close, enjoying the soft sighs he made. Rubbing her hand along his muscular chest, Amara placed a light kiss just above his heart.

Eli had been her rock. Whether they were at his place or Boston Gen., Eli had kept her sane over the last week and a half. He tasted every meal she'd cooked and finally thrown out the stacks of frozen dinners with more freezer burn than she'd ever seen.

When she'd held baby Kellen, Amara had caught Eli

staring at her. Was he thinking about their future too? She wanted a life with him. But what if the lump she'd found was cancer?

Eli had said he'd stand by her, and she desperately wanted to believe him. But she'd helped her mother throughout her cancer battle. Amara had been stunned by the number of relationships she'd seen that hadn't survived a diagnosis and treatment. For better or worse was a nice sentiment, but in reality it wasn't always possible.

Eli was keeping himself busy since resigning from The Collins Research Group. Amara wasn't sure he knew how to be still. He'd spent all his free time investigating how to get Boston General into next year's Best Hospitals and Physicians edition of the *US News & Reports* magazine.

He'd pored over research and websites that claimed to know what was on the surveys they sent out. Eli asked her opinions and threw stats out in regular conversation, but she was terrified that this could become an obsession. *Already was.*

Worry niggled at the back of her brain, and Amara couldn't quite push it away. She shook herself. Eli had done nothing to make her doubt him. She was letting what-ifs get in the way again, but she couldn't seem to stop them late in the night when sleep eluded her.

What if Eli never found peace? What if he always chased the rankings or some other accolade to prove to himself that he was worthy? Would it be a never-ending cycle of behavior? What if nothing she, or anyone else, did filled the hole that growing up in Marshall Collins's shadow had created? What if eventually, no matter how much she loved him, Eli followed the same patterns as her father?

Amara sighed. She was looking for things to worry about besides the potential time bomb in her body. She knew it but couldn't quite manage to force her brain to be quiet. Leaning over Eli's shoulder, she glared at the clock. Just past three.

Once again, she was going to be operating on only a few hours of sleep. It wasn't ideal for the health fair, but she'd find a way to manage. Cooking all day was easier than work. And being on her feet would keep her from falling asleep.

Soft lips pressed against the base of her neck. "Trouble sleeping?" Eli's words were husky with sleep.

Amara lightly kissed his cheek. "I'm fine. Go back to sleep."

Gentle hands ran along Amara's belly. When Eli's fingers hovered just above her panty line, she let out a light groan.

"I don't think you really want me sleeping," Eli whispered against her ear as his hand slid along the side of her breast. Then he started dropping kisses across the top of her shoulder. Gently pulling the thin straps of her tank top down, he sighed as her breasts rubbed against his hard chest.

Eli had lovingly explored her body over the last few weeks, memorizing each spot where Amara responded. He used those touches with ruthless abandon now, to drive her close to the precipice of need. She arched against him, but he held her firmly in place.

Amara felt his growing need rise against her. Rubbing her hand along the ridge of his arousal, Amara let out a soft plea. "Eli, now…please."

His hands cupped her butt, before pulling her underwear off. Eli kissed her deeply while he twisted to grab a condom. Lifting her leg over his, Eli pushed against her.

"Eli," Amara cried at his maddeningly slow pace.

His lips lingered against the sensitive skin beneath her ear as his fingers pressed against her swollen bud of pleasure. "If we're up hours before everyone else, then we have no reason to rush, Amara."

He teased her with his fingers, while his lips traced tantalizing kisses along her burning skin. Each caress drove her closer to the edge, but never over it as he continued his slow pace. It was heaven, hell and everything in between.

Gripping the sides of his face, Amara placed kisses along his jaw, quivering with need as Eli slowly drove into her—it wasn't enough. Finally, she locked her leg around his waist, her body rocketing into oblivion as he slid all the way into her. "Eli…" Amara sighed as he held her tightly.

He was hers. All the worries and doubts receded into the calm night as she claimed him. For tonight that was enough.

Eli looked at the clock on the nightstand. They needed to be at the hospital in less than two hours if they wanted to have their booth prepared for the start of the health fair. That meant they needed to be up, getting Lizzy fed and ready to go to his mom's fifteen minutes ago.

But Amara looked so peaceful for the first time in over a week. Eli ran a hand over her shoulder. Her training as an ER nurse was probably the only reason she was still functioning on so little rest.

Every time her cell rang, Eli watched her tense. And every time she saw it wasn't her doctor calling with the test results, he saw fear, hope and fatigue play across her face as she made another forced joke. He couldn't take any of her worries away. Eli was completely helpless to make this better.

His phone dinged as an email popped in from one of the hospitals he'd reached out to about their national rankings. It didn't have much information, but neither had any of the others. He just needed one look at the criteria they were being judged against. Which was beginning to seem as elusive as the pot of gold at the end of a rainbow.

Figuring out how to get Boston General on the ranking list had kept his mind occupied while they'd waited for her test results. And Amara's too. She'd looked over the stats and agreed that it seemed more like a popularity contest than it should. She'd listened to his theories. And even offered a few of her own.

Doug Jenkins, the head of Boston Gen., still wasn't sold on focusing on rankings. In fact, he'd told Eli that the only metrics he cared about were shorter ER wait times, staff retention issues in the ER, and better long-term results in the oncology department. Doug didn't consider the rankings a priority compared to providing care to the local community. And he'd flat out refused to direct personnel and resources toward winning over a bunch of journalists.

But he'd agreed to look at whatever Eli found. And Eli was determined to deliver. It would help everyone see Boston Gen. for what it was—a great hospital.

Worthy of recognition.

Amara rolled over and laid her hand against his chest. Eli smiled as she let out a soft moan, she was so content. He couldn't wake her. Sliding from the bed, Eli kissed her temple, and she didn't stir. That made the choice easy. She needed to sleep more than she needed to do the health fair demonstration.

Waiting until he got downstairs, Eli grabbed his cell and placed a call. As a precaution, he'd hired Pippin Werth, one of Boston's premier chefs, the day after Amara found the lump. Eli had tried to tell her about Pippin repeatedly. But every time he'd mentioned helping with the health fair, Amara had interrupted him. And he hadn't wanted to admit that if they got bad news before the fair, she might be unable to do it.

It had felt too much like tempting fate.

Light kisses pressed against Amara's temple. "Amara, love..." The words floated just above her consciousness. Eli's fingers ran along her side, and she moaned, not ready to start the day. How long had it been since she'd been able to sleep until the alarm went off?

Alarm...

That word finally pierced the fog, and Amara sat up. "Did I oversleep?" She rubbed her eyes and then stared at Eli, holding out a cup of tea.

"Nope. You're waking right on time."

She looked at the nightstand, but the clock was turned away from her. She shot a glance at Eli, but he didn't seem to notice. "I need to grab a folder from the office."

Lizzy wailed as Eli moved off the bed. "I put her in the Pack 'n Play while I came to wake you up. She still hates that contraption."

He'd woken Lizzy and got her ready to let Amara sleep. That was sweet, but it had to mean they needed to get moving to make it to the fair on time. "I'll get the folder if you'll tell me where it's at."

Eli hesitated for a moment, but Lizzy let out another scream.

"If one of us doesn't get down there, she is going to tip it over." It had never happened, but Amara had watched the angry toddler rock it before, trying to find its weak spots. It was only a matter of time before she figured out a way to escape.

"Top drawer on the right," Eli stated as he rushed out of the room.

Amara washed quickly, brushed her teeth, pulled her clothes on and pulled her hair into a ponytail. It was nice of Eli to let her sleep in, but she hated feeling rushed.

She hurried to his office and pulled the drawer open to grab the only file inside. The words "Pippin Werth" were scrawled across a Post-it note attached to it. Why did Eli have the name of one of the top chefs in Boston?

The clock on the wall started to chime, and Amara felt her blood chill as the clock struck nine. They'd needed to be at the hospital by seven to ensure the booth was set up. The health fair opened at nine. *Now! The fair was opening right now!*

Flipping the folder open, she stared at a check made out for more than her monthly rent to Pippen Werth. The memo section held Eli's scrawled note: *Health Fair.*

At least she knew why he hadn't bothered to wake her. Pain rippled through Amara as she struggled to catch her breath. After all the work she'd done.

Her mother's recipes... Amara felt her heart crack. *Why?*

When Susan had joked about him hiring a celebrity chef, it had seemed so ridiculous. Apparently, his promises to let her run this on her own meant nothing. Had he not trusted her to do it right?

"We need to get moving," Eli stated as Amara entered the living room.

"Why?" Amara folded her arms and leaned against the door jamb. "Pippin Werth must have the booth under control. No doubt that's what you're paying him so handsomely for."

Juggling Lizzy, her diaper bag and her favorite stuffed animal, Eli swallowed as he saw the hurt hiding behind Amara's fury. "I'm sorry."

Setting Lizzy's bag down, he handed the squirming toddler her stuffed doll and set her at his feet too. If she tried to wander, he could put her in the play yard, but he'd prefer not to have this conversation while she screamed.

"I didn't mean to hurt you, honey. You've barely slept since…" He let the words die away. They never talked about the lump she'd found. Eli tried again. "The health fair didn't need to be one more worry for you."

"That wasn't your decision!" Amara snapped, and he saw her flinch. "*You* decided I couldn't do this? And you didn't tell me! I'm supposed to be your partner. You promised that. Or did you figure you couldn't handle it if I lost? If your famous winning streak came to an end." Her eyebrows rose, but her voice was even.

"That's not fair," Eli protested. "You were exhausted and you needed to rest." Opening his palms, he said, "Partners help."

"Partners tell each other what they are doing," Amara countered.

Pushing a hand through his hair, Eli stared at her.

She was right.

But it was fear that had driven this decision, not pride, though the results were still the same. "I should have told you. But if Dr. Henricks…" Eli let those words die away too. He was a doctor, but the word cancer still got caught in his throat.

"Yes, you should have." Amara's lip wobbled. "There were other options, Eli. I mean, we could have asked one of the other doctors to cover for us. We could have canceled or just shown up late. There are almost thirty booths this year. It would have been fine…"

"Channel 4 is covering the event." Eli hated himself as the words slipped out of his mouth. This wasn't about better coverage for Boston General. *It wasn't.*

"So, you hired a ringer to ensure that if I wasn't *per-*

fect, a local news channel wouldn't see one empty booth?" Amara wrapped her arms around herself.

Tears filled Amara's eyes as she stared at him, and Eli's heart broke. "I'm sorry, Amara. I should have found a way to tell you, but I tried to talk to you about it several times. You wouldn't let me help with the fair once you took this over. Other than taste-testing duties."

"Because I had it handled." Amara's shoulders shook.

"Or because you didn't want my help? Because you still think you might have to do everything by yourself eventually? That I won't follow through on my promises." He held his breath as he stared at her. He wasn't going to walk away from her. But Amara had to believe it too or their relationship was never going to work.

"I don't need to win this year. I want the fair to be successful, for Boston General, that's all. But I also needed to help you, Amara." Eli stepped toward her.

Amara's shoulders loosened, but her jaw was still tight. "This wasn't about adding to your personal stats or Boston General's?"

Personal stats.

That jab hurt.

"No." Eli wrapped his arms around her, grateful when she didn't pull away. "I've laid beside you for the last week. I know how little sleep you've gotten. I've heard you crying in the shower."

"I didn't want to upset you," Amara whispered.

Eli lifted her chin. "I can handle the upset, Amara. My feelings for you are not so fragile that they'll be broken by a few well-deserved sob-fests."

Amara's dark eyes shimmered as she squeezed him tightly. "Sorry I didn't ask for help."

"Well, we both have things we can help each other with. Deal?" Eli dropped a kiss against her cheek. Amara bit her lip as she stared at him, and worry churned in his stomach. Could she not accept his help?

"I'll try." Amara smiled, but it didn't quite reach her eyes.

Eli kissed her cheek. "I messed up. I did it because I…" *Because I love you.*

Those weren't words he wanted to fling at her at the end of an argument. She might think he was just trying to distract her. "I did it because I was trying to take care of you—but it was still wrong."

The rest of the tension finally started to leak from Amara. "I know the last few days haven't been easy, or fun."

"I've been with you and Lizzy, so they've been darn near perfect." Eli meant those words. He'd loved every second she'd been with him. Even this morning's argument had brought them closer.

"When we get to the health fair, I am taking over," Amara stated. "I'm cooking my mom's recipes."

Eli agreed. "I wouldn't have it any other way."

"Eli." Amara grinned.

"What do you need me to get?" After thanking Pippin for getting everything set up and serving the first rounds of visitors, Eli had been Amara's runner for most of the day. Their supplies were nearly exhausted. There wasn't really time to run to the store to pick up anything. If they needed to shut the booth early, that was fine.

"My phone." Amara wiggled her butt and laughed. "It's been ringing for the last hour. Can you see who keeps calling?"

Sliding his hand into her back pocket, Eli grabbed the phone. Staring at the list of missed calls, he felt his heart drop. It was Saturday, but Dr. Henricks had called three times.

If he was calling on the weekend...

"Dr. Henricks?" Amara's voice was tight as she handed a sample to a customer.

Eli nodded as he stepped up to the booth. "I'll handle things here. Take as long as you need."

Amara swallowed and looked at the small line of people waiting. "I think I made enough for everyone."

"If not, I'll start a final batch. I've watched you most of the day. Pretty sure I can follow the recipes."

"And if not?" Amara pursed her lips as she passed out another sample.

"Then, everyone will get to taste what happens when Dr. Eli Collins burns a recipe," Eli said, trying to pretend that his insides weren't turning to liquid. He too was terrified of what Dr. Henricks would say, but waiting, even an hour, didn't seem possible. Amara needed to know now.

They needed to know now.

"Go," Eli insisted. "I can't mess things up here too bad."

"You'll do fine." Amara's voice wavered a bit, but he knew it wasn't because of his cooking abilities. He'd do anything to be able to take the fear away from her.

The line of people happily accepted their small cups of curry and took the packet of recipes Amara had made. All blissfully unaware of the turmoil swirling through Eli. As the final person stepped up, he turned to look for Amara. He didn't know where she'd gone, but he needed to find her. *Now.*

Eli hastily wrote out a sign and placed it in front of the cooking station, then ducked out of the tent. Amara was sitting on a bench overlooking the small garden Boston Gen. maintained. Her head was buried in her hands, and her shoulders were shaking.

God, no...

Despite the fear almost paralyzing him, Eli forced his feet to move. Amara needed him. He sat beside her and wrapped his arms around her shoulders. When she turned and pressed her lips to his, he felt the wetness along her cheeks.

Amara pulled away and smiled. "It's only scar tissue."

Eli felt his mouth fall open. Part of him had been preparing for the worst for the last ten days. He wanted to jump up, to shout with joy, to take her home and make love to her all night, to cry... All the emotions poured through him. "I... I..." Eli wiped a tear from his cheek as a chuckle escaped his lips.

"I know. Dr. Henricks apologized for scaring me. He went into the office after attending the fair and saw the results. He thought I might not want to wait until Monday to hear," Amara whispered. "I've been sitting here laughing and crying for the last few minutes. I'm just so happy."

"I love you." The words were quiet in the garden. "I never stopped loving you, Amara, and you know it wouldn't have mattered what Dr. Henricks said. I—"

Amara placed a finger against his lips. "You're rambling."

"I know. I've wanted to say those words for so long, but I probably could have planned a better time." Eli placed his head against her forehead. She was healthy and here with him.

Amara sighed as she leaned into him. "I love you too."

Eli kissed her hard, then spun her around. "Should we go finish the last bit of the fair? Or do you want to cut out early?"

Amara grabbed his hands. "Let's go finish this thing!"

CHAPTER ELEVEN

"SORRY WE LOST, ELI. Although your winning streak was bound to end eventually," Amara said as she held up her ice cream cone. After a long day behind the stove, Eli's desire for ice cream had sounded delightful.

"I did win." Eli's lips were sweet as he kissed her. "You love me. *And* I got to enjoy some amazing culinary delights. Most importantly—" he squeezed her tightly "—you're healthy. That definitely warrants an ice cream celebration."

"I love you, Eli—I may never tire of saying that." It was such a cheesy statement, but she didn't care. She loved him, and he loved her, and for once, all Amara's worries and doubts seemed to have evaporated.

"I hope you don't," Eli whispered as he closed in for another kiss.

"Dad!" A scream erupted from the front of the restaurant.

Eli pulled back, and they moved together toward the commotion. An older gentleman was lying on the floor, surrounded by people. Amara tapped the counter and forced the employee to look at her. "Call 911. Now. Tell them that a person has collapsed, and there's a doctor and nurse onsite." She waited just long enough for the teenager to nod and grab the phone before turning to another employee. "Do you have a defibrillator?"

The teen blinked at her, and Amara grabbed his shoulders. "Do you have a defibrillator?"

"I'm the manager. There's one in the back," a woman called as she raced to the rear of the restaurant, away from the chaotic scene.

"I need everyone to move back," Eli shouted before leaning over the man.

Amara moved beside him and felt for a pulse. *Nothing.* "I can't find a pulse."

"He's not breathing. I'm starting compressions," Eli stated.

Where was the defibrillator?

Amara had listened to many health professionals discuss the different public crisis situations they'd found themselves in. She'd been grateful to never have anything to add to the discussion. At the hospital, she had options for helping a patient, machines that spit out readings. Here there was nothing but their training and hope to rely on.

"Switch out with me," Eli instructed as he counted the compressions. It was standard training. If there was more than one person, it helped to rotate compressions to avoid fatigue.

"Found it!" The manager dropped beside Eli and handed him the box containing the automated external defibrillator as Amara continued compressions. "Sorry, it was plugged into a back outlet in the office. I don't know that I've seen it in years. This place is constantly putting stuff in odd places. I once found a—"

"Thank you. Can you give us a bit of room?" Eli was polite but firm. Many people got overly talkative in crisis situations. Amara had seen more than one doctor or nurse in the hospital snap at a bystander. It was a natural response to stress, but Eli just asked her to step away. His tone was kind but authoritative, and it worked.

Dust covered the top of the AED pack. Amara managed

to keep herself from cringing. Would the device work? Her arms were starting to get tired, but she kept going while Eli prepped the machine. It booted up, and she saw his shoulders relax a bit. He obviously hadn't been sure it would function either.

Amara moved her arms while Eli cut the man's shirt and placed the shock pads against his chest before resuming compressions. Then she lifted her arms as the AED ordered the shock. *Please*...

The man's son let out a moan as the AED failed to register any heartbeat following the shock, and Eli took over from Amara.

She strained her ears and heard a siren in the distance. Time raced ahead as the AED set up its next charge. Following the second shock, it registered a heartbeat, and the relief among the restaurant patrons was palpable.

Amara and Eli didn't shift their positions. They needed to be ready if his heart stopped again.

When the ambulance finally screeched to a halt outside the building, Amara felt her insides begin to relax. She and Eli stepped back as the paramedics raced in. Eli quickly relayed what they'd already done before stepping away to let them work. The paramedics nodded to Amara and Eli as they prepped the man for transport to the hospital.

The man's son hurriedly offered Amara and Eli a thank-you before rushing after his father. "You're welcome," Amara called, though she doubted he heard her.

She sighed as Eli wrapped an arm around her waist. She stared at the departing emergency vehicle as the bystanders started to go back to their seats. At least they'd been able to give the patient a chance.

"Thank goodness you and your wife were here." The manager beamed as she stepped in front of them.

The assumption surprised her, and she looked to Eli

while letting out a soft giggle. Shaking her head, Amara said, "Nope. We're not married."

But maybe one day.

The thought brought another smile to her lips. Eli was the one she wanted to spend all her days with. He belonged with her.

And she with him.

"Oh." The woman looked at Eli's arm around Amara's waist and blushed. "You just work so well together. Of course, colleagues," she muttered before wandering off.

"Colleagues?" Eli laughed and shook his head. "I feel like there are half a dozen terms I'd use before that."

Amara's stomach danced as her lips touched his cheek. "Such as?"

"Let's see, partners, lovers, my…"

A young woman tapped his arm to grab Eli's attention. "You're Dr. Eli Collins, right?"

Eli nodded. "Yes. Sorry, do I know you?"

"I'm Lia Trupee, a reporter with Channel 4. I saw you at Boston Gen.'s health fair. Can you give me a brief rundown of what happened here?" The blonde nodded to Amara but kept her focus on Eli.

After giving a brief statement on the events in the restaurant and refusing to comment on the likely outcomes for the patient, Eli transitioned the conversation to some of Boston General's perks. Amara beamed as he talked about what the hospital had to offer and the expertise of its professionals. She wasn't sure Lia would use any of his additional commentary in the article, but the pride radiating off Eli was contagious.

"Look, Boston Gen. is in the paper!" Susan handed a copy to Eli and Griffin.

"I didn't realize people still bought the paper." Griffin smirked as Susan glared at him. "They do when their friends and hospital make the news," she told him.

Griffin frowned as he turned the paper over. "Do you mean the small paragraph on page six regarding Eli and Amara stabilizing a heart attack patient who didn't even arrive at our hospital afterward?"

Amara had followed up on the man they'd treated in the fast food restaurant. Mr. Thomas March was recovering well at Marshall's hospital. Eli had tried to follow up with his father too, but all Marshall had said was that the patient was in the city's *best* hands. Eli hadn't responded to the not so subtle insult.

But it still stung.

"Very funny." Susan slapped her copy of the paper against Griffin's arm. "We rarely see our hospital or its employees in the paper. Lighten up."

Eli read over the small paragraph. He knew that all his comments regarding Boston General couldn't have made it into the local paper. But it would have been nice if they had mentioned just a few of the hospital's selling points. Would it have killed the paper's bottom line to praise the hospital where the "heroic medical professionals," of their article actually worked?

"Eli." Amara stepped beside him. "Mrs. Delgado's daughter is here."

"Did you see the article?" Eli asked as they walked back to the room.

"I think Susan has shown it to everyone. Don't tell her, but I think 'heroic medical professionals' is a bit much." Amara rolled her eyes before crossing her arms. "A warning— Mrs. Delgado's daughter isn't happy."

Eli paused a few steps from the door. "Why?" Dealing with difficult patients and their families was unfortunately common in the ER.

The woman's mother, Helen, had a bad chest cold, and as a precaution, she had been brought in by one of her nursing home's caregivers. Mrs. Delgado had just had her ninety-first birthday, and most of her issues were age-related. Eli had recommended rest, fluids and monitoring. He'd just started the discharge paperwork when Susan brought the newspaper over.

"Not sure. She wanted to talk to a doctor. Not just some nurse." Amara sighed, but he could see her frustration.

Nurses were the lifeblood of any unit. But many people saw them as unimportant assistants to the doctors. He'd explained to more than one patient that he hadn't run an IV since his last year of residency, but that most of the nursing staff could do it in under a minute with their eyes shut.

"I'm sorry, Amara." She was one of the best he'd ever worked with, and it was a shame that anyone would question that.

"Thank you. But it's nothing I haven't heard before." She waved her hand. "Just annoying. By the way, the daughter's name is Sylvia Mora."

He was in awe of her as they walked into the room. Amara was certain that she was a good nurse. She never doubted that she did her job well. Never let the cutting statements of others touch her. If only Eli could figure out how to let the jabs roll off him too.

Sylvia Mora was pacing back and forth, barking into her phone. As her eyes latched on to them, she hung up without saying goodbye to whoever was on the other end. "Have you done blood work on my mother?"

The tiny woman in the bed let out a soft snore, and Eli sighed. "Your mother has a chest infection. It will clear with a few days of rest and fluids. As we age, our veins weaken. If we take her blood, which I assure you will not give us a different answer than chest infection, we run the risk of her veins blowing or collapsing. That is painful, and she'll have bruises for at least a week—probably longer. I don't want to put her through any unnecessary discomfort."

Mrs. Mora glared at him. "Have you taken a chest X-ray?"

"No. I listened to her lungs," Eli explained.

"She could have pneumonia," Mrs. Mora shouted. "And you are refusing to do your duty." Her screech echoed in the small room, and still, the woman in the bed didn't stir.

Eli took a small step toward Mrs. Mora and offered a reassuring smile. No medical intervention could stop the passage of time. But many people often weren't ready to accept the inevitable end, and Eli understood that too.

Keeping his voice level, he started, "When people hit a certain age, they're—"

"So, because she's old, you think you can be lazy. Why on earth did her nursing home bring her here? Worst hospital in Boston."

"No, it's not," Eli argued. He was stunned by how much that cut. Mrs. Mora was worried about her mother, but her perception was wrong. *Very wrong.* Boston General had some of the finest physicians and nurses he'd ever had the opportunity to serve with. Including the one standing next to him.

Amara gripped Eli's arm before addressing Mrs. Mora. "Your mother is resting comfortably, and her chest infection will clear in a few days on its own. Any other hospital would tell you the same thing."

Mrs. Mora held up her phone and started scrolling through a website. "Really, would Dr. Anderson at Massachusetts Research tell me that? She has a five-star rating on RateMyMD.com."

What was RateMyMD.com? Eli had no intention of asking Mrs. Mora that question, but he promised himself that he would investigate it later. "Yes," Eli replied, "She would tell you the same thing." He was certain of his diagnosis, and no amount of blood work or chest X-rays would change it.

Mrs. Mora turned back to her phone and furiously started typing before holding up her phone again. She grabbed her purse. "You only have three and a half stars, so you'll excuse me for wanting the best for my mother."

Three and a half stars?

Eli knew it was ridiculous to care about ratings on an internet app. It didn't mean anything, but a niggle of uncertainty bit into him.

Who had found his care lacking?

"Dr. Collins is one of the top ER professionals in the state. He speaks at conferences and is well-respected by his peers." Amara leaped to his defense, but Eli waved her down.

"Your mother's discharge papers will be ready shortly. Her chest infection *will* clear in a few days, and she'll be fine."

"You're right—she *will* be fine." Mrs. Mora picked up her purse. "Because as soon as we leave here, I'm taking her to Massachusetts Research."

Eli nodded but couldn't force out any words. If Mrs. Mora wanted to take her mother for a second opinion, that was her right. But he wanted to know what RateMyMD.com was saying about him...and Boston Gen.

"It looks like a star-based system, where patients rate their experiences," Eli stated.

Amara looked at the lines drawn across his forehead

and gripped his hand. "Eli, these sites pop up and go dark all the time. It's strangers making random complaints."

Eli nodded, but he continued to flip through the reviews. "I know that, but several doctors have updated their own profiles in here to indicate they were nominated for the annual report."

If Amara could discontinue that report, she'd do it in a heartbeat. It was useless, but Eli was still obsessed with it. She frowned as he showed her the stats for two other Massachusetts Research doctors.

Grabbing his cell, Amara stared at it. "These apps don't matter." Amara read out one of Eli's five-star posts. "'Dr. Eli Collins is one of the best! He joked with my son and kept him entertained while putting a cast on his ankle.'"

Amara pulled up another.

"'Dr. Collins is responsible for my father being alive at Christmas. He realized his headache was a brain bleed.' You can't hear those words and think you aren't great."

If he wanted acceptance from strangers, why couldn't Eli focus on *these* reviews?

Eli shrugged. Pulling up a few of the one-star reviews, Amara glared at them. Most were complaints about wait times. One woman complained that the food in the cafeteria was cold. They had nothing to do with Eli. *Nothing!* "Everyone gets a bad review. It doesn't mean anything. I love you, so shall I leave you a five-star review?"

"I love you too, but if you want to leave a review…" Eli sighed as he grabbed the next chart. "I'm kidding. You're right, Amara, of course. It's just a dumb app."

Except that she wasn't sure he believed that. Or believed in himself. Eli patted her hand, and Amara wished there was some way she could silence his inner critic.

"You're right. Love you. Thank you for keeping me grounded." He smiled, but the cloud of uncertainty still hovered in his eyes.

* * *

"I think we should look at vacation spots for next year." Amara slapped an Italy tour guide on the stack of papers in Eli's lap.

He looked up as he set his papers on the coffee table.

Next year...

Those two words sent a thrill through him. "You pick the date and place, and I'll be there."

"It's more than picking a date and a place," Amara said. "Half the fun is planning the adventure. Poring over research—" she eyed his papers "—planning out schedules to see all the sights. Then ripping the schedule up and sleeping in late!"

Amara beamed. "I bought two more guidebooks today too. Figured we might want to plan based on the season. The winters in Boston can be pretty icy. Do we want to escape then? Or spend a week somewhere cool in the summer?"

"Two more?" Eli laughed, "Are we going to own every guidebook ever written?"

"Maybe." Amara tapped his nose.

Eli pulled her into his lap. His lips captured hers. He sighed as Amara's fingers ran through his hair.

"You're trying to distract me," Eli accused as Amara grinned.

"Guilty." She glared at the stack of papers next to him. "You're still wrapped up in the national rankings. You've been digging through apps, ratings and survey criteria for over a week. You even slept on the couch last night. You need a break, Eli."

"It's interesting." He kissed her, hoping it would erase the tiny downward turn of her lips. "Some people argue the rankings are the thing that defines an institution. Others claim the rankings are bought. What no one discusses is how to get on the survey. And that's the key. If you don't get on the survey…get your hospital on the survey," Eli corrected. "Then you can't be on the final list."

Eli tapped the stack of papers. "But I am going to find out. Boston General is at least going to be nominated this year."

Amara's frown deepened, and his heart clenched. He'd been so focused on these apps and ratings that he hadn't been very present this week. And that wasn't fair to his family. Eli grabbed for the guidebook in her lap. "But tonight, none of that matters, because we are talking about vacations."

Her eyes lit up as she flipped to a few pages that were already dog-eared. Her enthusiasm was contagious. It almost made Eli forget the stack of papers and research beside him.

Almost.

"Are you coming to bed, Eli?" He hadn't come up to bed with her in several nights, but she wanted to believe tonight would be different.

Please.

"What did you say?" Eli asked without looking up from the couch.

Amara was trying not to be jealous of the various papers and folders spread across the living room. It was ridiculous to compete with his research. But it was hard when those items seemed to be able to hold his attention far longer than she could.

How could this have happened so quickly? How could he slide away from her so easily? She knew this was important to him, to what he wanted for Boston General. But what if this was only the first of a lifetime of important projects?

Amara tried to push that fear aside as she watched him furiously write out notes as he scrolled through another web page. "Are you coming to bed?" she repeated.

Eli blinked as he turned to face her, and then he rubbed his eyes. He smiled and winked, but Amara saw his exhaustion. "I'll be up in ten minutes, honey. Fifteen tops."

"Promise?" Amara asked as she walked over to drop a kiss on his lips.

"I promise," Eli stated, but his eyes were already focused on the screen in front of him.

"I love you," Amara called as she started for the door. She paused for a moment, but Eli didn't answer back. It was fine, she promised herself. But it was worry that carried her off to sleep—alone.

CHAPTER TWELVE

ELI WAS LATE for their date—again. Twisting the fork around on her plate, Amara glared at the hands on her watch. If she'd wanted to eat alone, she could have gone back to her apartment and done that.

They'd planned to meet before each of their shifts for the last week. Eli had gotten progressively later every day— at least she hadn't waited to order today. Yesterday, Eli had been so late, they hadn't managed to eat anything. She wasn't going to arrive at Boston Gen. hungry again.

Irritated but not hungry.

Boxing up the sandwich she'd ordered for Eli, Amara hated the tears hovering in her eyes and the fear that was increasingly wrapping around her heart. He was pulling away from her. Slipping into work and letting his family slide— just like her father had. What if she wasn't enough compared to apps and rankings and his desire to be the best?

Eli checked his email first thing in the morning, and it was the last thing he looked at before bed—when he made it to bed. Last night was the third time this week that she'd come downstairs to find him asleep on the couch. And it was only Wednesday. She'd woken up holding his pillow this morning, and it was a poor substitute for the man she loved.

Eli had spent weeks outlining plans, making suggestions

and contacting anyone he could about getting Boston Gen. on the annual survey to determine the nominations. Even the head of their hospital was finally on board with Eli's plans. Though Amara wasn't sure that Doug really thought of it as anything more than a useful staff retention tool.

Amara thought there were better ways to recruit talented medical professionals. Over the last three months, they'd lost fewer personnel. Eli had also told her the numbers had been trending down. So the hospital had already been doing the right things.

Still, she'd tried to help, but Eli had been distant.

No, that was unfair.

He'd been focused. Amara understood his need to prove what all the long-term employees of Boston General knew. But he'd pushed everything else aside in order to do it.

After they put Lizzy to bed, Eli spent at least a few hours going over statistics about other ERs, and how Boston Gen. was better. Or how he thought the hospital could improve.

When Amara had pointed out that her former hospital was in those rankings, and she didn't think that it had added much to the patient care, Eli pulled out an entire folder marked *Massachusetts Research*. He'd pulled papers out and gone over three years' worth of data. She didn't think he'd even heard her when she'd told him good-night and finally gone to bed.

Alone—again.

Her lip trembled as she stepped from the small sub shop into the afternoon heat. Checking her phone one last time, she sighed at the lack of text messages and voice mails. Eli wasn't coming.

He'd promised her balance, and for a while he'd delivered. Though for the last few weeks, while his body had been present, his mind had been elsewhere. Maybe she'd been kidding herself that they could have a future together. If someone you loved was so easy to forget…

"Amara!" Eli's voice was ragged as he ran toward her. "I'm so sorry!"

Her heart clenched as she stared at him. Trying to lock her hurt away, she took a deep breath. Maybe there was a good reason this time.

Eli dropped a swift kiss to her lips. "I lost track of time. But I found it!" Eli gripped a folder. His grin was huge, but it looked too forced. It was a look he'd worn so often since they'd found out about the RateMyMD app.

Eli's cheeks heated as his eyes cut to the box in her hand. "Any chance you ordered me a sandwich?"

Handing him the box, Amara asked, "What was so important that you missed lunch? Again."

He pulled out the sandwich out and took a giant bite. "You are the best. What would I do without you?"

You'd get by.

The phrase struck Amara's heart with a resounding crash. Without her, Eli would get by. He'd focus on Boston Gen. and Lizzy. Find a new project to tackle and be okay.

But what would she do without him?

Amara opened the folder and tried to make sense of the numbers and random pie charts on the pages. She raised an eyebrow. "What am I looking at, Eli?"

"The criteria for the annual report. Or at least part of the criteria." He took another bite of the sandwich as they walked toward the hospital.

"So, I got stood up for a bunch of graphs, charts and statistics?" Fury spun through her. He'd chosen a stack of paper over lunch with her.

"I mean, no. It's just this is what we've been looking for."

"What *you've* been looking for, you mean," Amara bit out.

Eli nodded, flinching as he met her angry gaze. "Yes. What I have been looking for. But it helps everyone. Ensures Boston Gen. gets the credit it deserves." He tapped the papers in the folder.

"Or the credit *you* deserve?" Amara sighed as she handed the folder back to him, suddenly too exhausted to be angry. "All this because one patient decided to take her mother to a different emergency room—for a second opinion. It was a fear-based reaction on her part, and your ratings on that app don't mean a thing."

Eli halted beside her, but Amara kept walking. They needed to get to work, and she didn't want to hear any more about stats, rankings or apps. Not today, at least. Amara went through the ER's front doors, Eli close on her heels.

"Amara, honey, I'm sorry. I should have called."

"Yes. You should have." Amara walked into the staff lounge, pulled open her locker, deposited her purse and then faced Eli. "I know you're super focused on Boston General's rankings right now. I know you think that it is some magic pill or something, but you've become obsessed. You have to focus on other things too."

"There were two articles about our hospital in the news this week, Amara," Eli told her. "My plan is working."

"I know!" Amara slammed her locker shut and winced as the noise reverberated around the room. "I know how many articles there were. I know what our stats look like. I know what Massachusetts Research's stats look like. I know the stats for six hospitals in California because I love you and have listened to you going on about it, am still listening to you. But you promised me balance. You told me you loved me."

"I do love you," Eli insisted.

She hated feeling like an afterthought. "This week, you have been late to every date, and even when you arrive, your focus isn't on us. You stood me up today without even so much as a text message for a folder full of papers. I deserve to be remembered. To not take second place to an award." Amara bit her tongue as Griffin walked in.

"I have to do the research, Amara. It's important, so important." Eli's voice was tight as he gripped the folder.

"Research that is more important than your family? Than me?" Amara's voice was hollow as she stared at Eli. "Do you even hear yourself?" He sounded so much like Marshall and her father that Amara's heart tore.

She couldn't stay here. If she didn't leave, she was going to say something she'd regret, or start crying. Neither option would make her feel any better. "I need to get to the nurses' station." She didn't look back.

Eli leaned his head back against the lockers as Amara's words washed over him. He'd never meant to make her think that this project was more important to him than her. It wasn't. But he'd done a poor job of showing that. Eli knew he was focused, knew he seemed borderline obsessed. He didn't know how to explain the emotions rolling through him to Amara. This was a desire she couldn't understand.

After all, she never doubted that she was a good nurse. If she'd received a one-star review, she'd write it off as a disgruntled patient and move on. Eli wanted to do that, but his brain spun around the numbers and the fear that they meant he'd failed his patients. When people made comments about Boston Gen., she ignored them, secure in her knowledge that those opinions didn't matter.

But she was wrong; opinions mattered to most people. That was the argument his brain kept screaming, and rankings and awards elevated opinion. Which helped with staff recruitment, retention and fundraising. It wasn't Boston Gen.'s primary focus, but fundraising helped provide the newest technology at a lower cost. That helped their patients. After doing a bit more research, he was certain that Boston General could be considered for the list this year.

That he could be...

Amara was right, too; he hadn't been present enough lately. He'd let his need to prove that this hospital was great, to show it off to the community overtake him. Amara deserved better. He loved her, and Eli never wanted her to doubt that. He was going to make this up to her.

Amara was at the nurses' station, going over paperwork when Eli exited the staff lounge. Her eyes were hooded with exhaustion. Was she having a difficult time sleeping too? They were going to bed at different times lately. Or more accurately, he was falling asleep on the couch.

"I'm sorry I stood you up, and I am sorry that everything has been so crazy. I almost have everything under control." Eli placed a cup of herbal tea on the counter and offered her a small smile.

"Do you?" Amara blew a piece of hair away from her eyes as she stared at him. "Do you even know what you want, Eli?"

Fear slipped down his spine as she refused to acknowledge the tea. Had he done more damage than he realized? "To be recognized." Eli shook his head "For Boston Gen. to be recognized," he corrected.

"And if it's not?" Amara pressed. "What if you can't figure out how to get the hospital on the rankings list? What if they reject you for a survey?"

"Then, we keep trying," Eli stated. His stomach sank as Amara looked away.

"Amara?"

She leaned forward, her eyes clear as she met his gaze. "Eli, if you want to work at a nationally ranked institution, then maybe you should take a job at Massachusetts

Research or one of the others on the list. Your résumé is impressive. I am sure any of them would be thrilled to employ you. If recognition will make you happy, will make you realize…" Her voice caught, and she swallowed hard.

Her words felt like a knife twisting through his side. This wasn't about working at a nationally ranked institution. It was about their hospital getting the recognition it already deserved. How could she not see that? He wasn't doing this for himself—well, not only for himself anyway.

"Amara, I don't want to work anywhere else. They've been calling and sending me letters for years and I've always said no." Eli looked over her shoulder at the emergency room.

This was where he was meant to be. He'd known that the first day he'd walked through the door. Boston Gen. did good work. Important work. And the doctors and nurses here deserved that recognition.

They'd earned it.

Eli was tired of explaining why he never took the positions that were offered from other hospitals. Tired of defending his ER. Tired of people disregarding it.

Amara took a folder from one of the techs and stood up. "Hospital accolades are not going to make you feel whole. And they won't matter to Marshall."

"It's not about that," Eli bit out.

"Are you sure?" Amara raised an eyebrow.

Eli wanted to say yes, but his tongue refused to produce the word.

Why was she bringing his father into this?

"Let me make today up to you. How about we go out tomorrow? A real date? I'll pick you up, and we'll go anywhere you want." Eli frowned as Amara looked at the papers in her hand instead of at him.

Her eyes were shiny when they finally met his. "I don't

know, Eli." She crossed her arms. "I want you to succeed, I really do, but your family can't trail after you on the path of life."

The hurt hovering in her eyes made Eli flinch.

He'd done that—again.

Eli's chest ripped open. He couldn't lose her; he couldn't. "I love you. I do. I know things have been hectic, and I have been more than a little distracted. I promise you it won't keep happening. You and Lizzy are the most important things to me. I swear. Where do you want to go—name the place and time, and I am there. No distractions!"

Amara's teeth dug into her lip, but she nodded. "I want to go dancing. And I am going to hold you to your promise of no statistic discussions."

"Dancing?" Eli asked.

"Dancing," Amara repeated. "The two of us together, close to each other, swaying to the music." A tiny smile touched her lips as she looked at him.

Eli's heart started beating again. She wasn't walking away. He hadn't lost her. He just needed to refocus. "I'll make sure that my shoes are shined."

Big news! Can we reschedule dancing? I'll call soon.

Amara read the text and looked down at the black dress that she'd picked for this evening. The V-neck cut was lower than anything she'd worn since her double mastectomy. But she'd gone back to her apartment tonight, pulled it out of the closet and slipped it on, excited to see Eli's reaction. If they'd gone dancing, it would have spun beautifully.

How many times had she'd seen her mother waiting on her father? Listened to the voice mail apologies that they'd need to reschedule something while he chased his dreams.

Her mother always believed he'd come, but with each new round of success, his family slipped further away.

It'd started with missed dinners and dates and ended in a lifetime of loneliness. Amara couldn't do that—wouldn't. Her breath was ragged as she grabbed her keys, but she forced her feet to keep moving.

If she didn't end this now, she was worried that she'd never work up her courage again. She couldn't be an afterthought to her partner for the rest of their lives. It was better to be alone than plan events the person you loved didn't attend.

Her heart bled as she walked to her car. The tears started, but Amara didn't bother to push them away. After all, her makeup didn't need to be perfect for a night out anymore.

Eli raised a glass with Mr. Jonah Richards. The researcher responsible for sending out surveys was in his home. The surveys determined who made the US News & Reports rankings. Victory was so close.

The front door opened. "Eli?"

Eli blinked as Amara's voice carried down the hall. What was she doing here? She was supposed to be getting ready at her apartment tonight. He'd sent her a text. Told her he'd call soon. He hated that they'd had to reschedule their date, but when he explained what this meant, he was sure she'd understand. She wanted him to succeed—she'd said it herself only yesterday.

"We're in here, Amara," Eli called. "I'm glad you came. There's someone I want you to meet."

Her eyes were red from crying, and ice slid down Eli's spine. It was his fault. But there had been a good reason.

A great reason.

"This is Jonah Richards. He's responsible for the annual report." Eli smiled and tried to catch her eye.

"Well, I help organize it. We're actually starting this year's interviews and surveys next week. Very good timing on your boyfriend's part."

She crossed her arms and raised an eyebrow at Eli. "Not sure about that," Amara stated bluntly. "I just need to get a few things."

As Amara headed for the stairs, she nodded to Jonah. "Nice to meet you. For the record, I think Boston General is a wonderful place to work."

He'd hurt her—again. But Eli had gotten their hospital included in the survey. Amara would celebrate with him.

She would.

Eli's heart clenched as her tearstained face floated before his eyes.

Wouldn't she?

Eli nodded toward Jonah. "Just give me a few minutes."

Jonah's eyes had followed Amara's departure. "I need to be heading out anyway. My wife will be wondering where I am. We'll be in touch, Dr. Collins."

Eli accompanied Jonah to the door and said good-night, then hurried upstairs.

"Amara," Eli choked out as he saw her picking up her book from the nightstand and grabbing all the clothes that she'd kept here over the last month. "I'm sorry. He called and had some urgent questions. I had to—"

"I understand, Eli." Her words were barely audible.

For a moment he could breathe again. Amara understood. So why was she still packing her things? When she finally looked at him, the sorrow in her dark eyes broke him.

"I'm sorry, Amara. We can go dancing now," Eli suggested. "To celebrate! Your dress is gorgeous; you are gorgeous. I'll change right now. Lizzy's already at Mom's."

Her eyes flashed, and she shook her head. "So, you got

us approved for the survey." Amara zipped up the bag and put it over her shoulder.

"Yes," Eli said, but he was suddenly terrified of what it might cost. "Please." He swallowed hard. How had he let something come before her again? *How?* "Stay."

"I want to." Amara touched his cheek. "I do."

"But you're not going to." Eli's heart was shattering as he stared at her.

Amara sighed. "I've spent the last several weeks waiting for you. Waiting for you to come to bed, only to finally sleep alone. Waiting at lunch, waiting tonight. I warned you I wouldn't compete with statistics and accolades. Tonight was supposed to be our night, ours. No matter what. You promised me. And yet—work came first."

Amara sucked in a deep breath, but she kept her eyes focused on him. "Did you consider rescheduling with Jonah? Setting up a time to see him tomorrow?"

"No." Eli realized what he had done, but he told her the truth. He'd been so excited that he'd texted the quick note to Amara and invited Jonah to his home to talk immediately. "It won't happen again."

"I want to believe that." Her voice broke, and Amara visibly tensed before continuing. "But you promised me the exact same thing yesterday. And in less than twenty-four hours, something else took priority over our plans. I want to be a partner, a wife, a mother. And I want a man who comes to bed with me, wants to raise our children together, arranges dates and then actually goes on them with me."

She added, "I want to be someone's priority. Maybe that is selfish, but I want to know that I come before a building or an organization that can't love you back."

You do. Eli wanted to scream those words, but his mouth refused to open.

Her hand laid against his cheek for just a moment longer.

"I hope that one day when you look at yourself, you'll see what's really there. And I hope you accept that man whether he's won countless awards or none." Amara dropped her hand and headed for the door. "He's truly exceptional."

Eli felt his soul crack as Amara walked out the door. She'd told him what she wanted in a partner, and Eli had sworn to be that man. It had been in his grasp until he'd gotten distracted. He'd chased someone else's acceptance when he'd always had hers. She'd walked away from him—again—and he totally understood why.

Pulling out the drawer on his nightstand, Eli lifted out the small ring box. He'd chosen it weeks ago and planned to ask her... *When?* He'd been too busy to make the time.

He groaned. When he'd finally finished with his plans for Boston Gen.? He'd put off asking the love of his life to marry him because he was too busy chasing stats and interviews.

The cup of tea was still warm as Amara sat behind the desk. It didn't have a note; none of the others had either. She and Eli hadn't been on the same shift all week. He'd effectively removed himself from the schedule any time she was on it. Without the pain that still radiated through her body, Amara might believe the last few months had been the best and worst dream.

"The surveys from *US News & Reports* arrived today." Griffin laid the envelope on the nurses' station and walked away. She contemplated throwing it in the trash, but if Eli had managed to get Boston General nominated for the list, she felt honor-bound to fill out the staff survey.

"Look!" Amara heard one of the nurses let out an excited squeal. "This is so exciting."

Holding the envelope in her hand, Amara stared at the staff around her. They were all excitedly holding their surveys. Congratulations, smiles and laughter dominated the ER floor.

Over just being nominated...

Amara felt her insides chill. Eli was right—the staff had wanted that recognition. And he'd given it to them. She'd been so worried about being left behind that she hadn't considered others wanted it too.

A pit formed in her stomach as she ripped open the envelope. Eli should be here to see the people he usually worked with celebrate. Amara's fingers were numb as she stared at the list of hospitals and practitioners. Dr. Carmichael and Griffin were both listed as potential candidates. Where was Eli's name after all the work he'd done to make this happen?

Amara marched toward Griffin, shaking the survey paperwork. "Where's Eli's name? I know the hospitals get to nominate their physicians. Where is it?"

"Is it me or Dr. Carmichael you think doesn't belong?" Griffin held up his hands as Amara glared at him.

"Eli turned down his nomination." Griffin sighed. "Happy?"

No. "He…he…" Amara felt her insides shake.

Had her fears cost Eli his dreams?

Her heart raced as she stared at the list. She'd challenged him to put her first, but Amara hadn't meant to make him give up on the accolades completely.

Or had she?

Heat engulfed Amara's skin as she stood among the celebrating staff. Was that the only way she'd think he was putting his family first? She wanted to say no, but the truth floored her. Had her love really been that fragile?

Amara crumpled the sheets of paper and then started straightening them out. Eli had worked hard for this. She couldn't just throw it away.

Like she'd thrown their relationship away...

Amara forced herself to breathe. Despite everything he'd done, Amara had played the what-if game and only focused on the negatives. What if this was enough for Eli? What if seeing the staff at Boston Gen. happy was all he'd really wanted? What if she'd been willing to reschedule a dancing date or waited for him to call? What if she could have had everything she wanted, and Eli could too?

Lizzy was playing on the floor while Eli downed another cup of coffee. He hadn't managed to get much sleep since Amara left. But he'd taken a cold hard look at himself, and Eli had not liked the image in the mirror.

He'd been chasing recognition for so long. First from Marshall and then from a stupid survey for an accolade that didn't matter. It was ridiculous. When he'd decided to give it up, Eli had spent an entire day thinking about what *he* wanted, not the script he'd tried to follow since birth. What were Eli's true measures for a successful life?

The answer had been easy to see with the gaping hole left in his heart. And it had nothing to do with ratings, apps, or the opinions of others. Eli was a good doctor—a great doctor already—awards or no awards. What Eli wanted was a happy family, a long life full of love, good work and adventures. Everything that Amara wanted, and he hadn't even realized it was the real prize.

Eli had had that life too. For a few blessed weeks, he'd had it. Until he'd let a simple comment by an irate patient's relative be the final thing that sent him spiraling out of control. It wasn't Mrs. Mora's fault. Eventually, his father, Griffin, a nurse, or some other stranger would have said something that made him want, so desperately, to prove them wrong.

That was what Eli had done so many times. He'd gone into emergency medicine because he'd felt it was his true calling. Then he'd immediately let Marshall's digs cause him to chase an acceptance that he doubted his father was capable of ever giving. Marshall's desire to be the best would always keep him from accepting a competitor for that title. Even if it was his own son.

The one person who'd never questioned his choices had been Amara. She'd offered him acceptance ten years ago and again when they'd reconnected. He'd never had to earn it—so it hadn't felt real.

That was the truth that burned him the worst. He'd thrown away the most real thing in his life. He'd always love her.

Always.

The doorbell rang, and Eli pushed his hands through his hair. He wasn't really presentable, but he doubted that was going to change anytime soon. "It's open," Eli called, not caring if the person on the other side of the door came in or left.

"Why is Griffin Stanfred's name on this survey and not yours?" Amara's voice was tired as she walked into the kitchen.

Eli shook his head and tried to figure out why Amara was here. His arms ached to pull her to him. To hold her, just one last time. It would never be enough, but he'd give almost anything for one more hug.

One more kiss, one more tomorrow.

Sucking in a deep breath, Eli shrugged. "The hospital could nominate two physicians from every department. When I talked to Doug, I suggested that we put at least two names down in every category. Just being nominated is something that Griffin and the others can put on their résumé."

"That is not what I asked, and you know it." Amara scowled. "Why did *you*, Dr. Eli Collins, withdraw your name from contention? Was it because of me?" Her voice wobbled. "Were you punishing yourself?"

"Oh, honey. No." Eli stepped around the counter, but he still didn't reach for her. If he did, and she moved away, he wasn't sure he could survive that. "I did it for me, and for Griffin."

"For Griffin?" Amara blinked. "I don't understand."

"Griffin is looking to advance his career in a year or so. I'm not planning on leaving Boston Gen." Eli hesitated. "Unless you want me to?"

"No," Amara whispered.

That simple answer sent hope cascading through Eli's heart. "The nomination means more for him than for me."

"But it means the accolades, the acceptance, go to Griffin too." Amara walked toward him. "You needed those."

Eli sighed. "No. I wanted them. So badly that I looked past the one person's acceptance who mattered most. And I lost her."

He took a chance and reached for Amara's hand. "I don't need to chase awards, love. I promise if any drop into my lap, I will happily accept them. But I want what I had and got too busy to enjoy. I want zoo days and dancing dates, vacations, morning snuggles and weird tea in the cupboard. I want all of it. And I will spend the rest of my life trying to show that to you if you will just give me a *second* second chance."

A tear slipped down Amara's cheek. "I never wanted you to not get all the awards." She hiccupped. "Or maybe I did. Because I was scared. I was so afraid that I'd get left behind that I never considered running beside you. That we could chase all our dreams together. I almost let fear chase away our happily-ever-after."

"Oh, honey—"

"No, let me finish, please." Amara wiped a tear away.

"My father chased success, and my mom was alone, but that was her life. Not mine. I have been playing what-ifs for years. I thought it was so I could protect myself." She choked back a sob. "But I refuse to let fear cost me everything."

She put her hand on his cheek as she continued. "I want you to have every accolade, Eli Collins. And I want to be by your side as you collect them. I want to be your partner in everything. I love you."

"I love you too," Eli replied as his heart soared. His world righted as she held his gaze. This was life's top prize.

EPILOGUE

"It's hot!" Lizzy complained as Amara held her hand.

"We'll be done soon," Amara promised. The head of the hospital stepped to the podium, and Amara smiled. Doug had sworn this would take no more than fifteen minutes.

"Up!" Lizzy said.

The three-year-old was having a rough time understanding why her constant growth spurts and Amara's growing belly meant that Amara couldn't hold her as long anymore. But she was being so patient today.

Just as she bent down to pick Lizzy up, Eli joined them. "Why don't you let me hold you, sweetie?" He kissed Amara's cheek as he lifted Lizzy.

Amara leaned her head against his shoulder and grinned. "Not that I'm complaining, but I thought Doug wanted you front and center for this?"

Eli laughed as he pulled at the collar of his shirt. "I told him I wanted the best seat in the house and standing back here is that location." He dropped a kiss across Amara's lips. "Besides, we'll see the banner better from here."

The *US News & Reports* team had sent banners to all the hospitals listed in the annual report. Amara had joked that it was a great marketing campaign for the magazine, and Eli had agreed. But it was a nice perk.

As the banner unrolled down the side of the hospital,

Amara looked at Eli. It had taken a few years, but he'd made this possible. Her heart was full. "Happy?"

Eli stared at her and placed his free hand on her stomach, where their son was restless in the heat too. "Incredibly so." He kissed her before nodding toward the banner. "And it has nothing to do with that."

Amara laughed and gestured toward the bright blue words acknowledging Boston General as one of this year's Top-Rated Hospitals. "It's a nice bonus, though."

Eli chuckled. "It is."

* * * * *

COMING SOON!

We really hope you enjoyed reading this book.
If you're looking for more romance, be sure to
head to the shops when new books are
available on

Thursday 17th September

To see which titles are coming soon, please visit

millsandboon.co.uk/nextmonth

MILLS & BOON

Coming next month

SECOND CHANCE WITH HIS ARMY DOC
Charlotte Hawkes

'Kane?'

Kane stopped, paused, then swivelled around to stare back down the corridor to where Mattie was standing immobile, as though rooted to the spot, and ignored as something kickstarted deep in his chest.

'It is you,' she muttered, and even from a distance he could see the stunned expression playing over her striking features.

Suddenly, his hands itched to smooth them away and he had to clench them into fists and punch them down, deep into his pockets in a very non-military way.

Thank god he wasn't in uniform.

'Hello Matz.' The name that only he had ever used for her. He couldn't help himself. 'It's been a while.'

'Fourteen years,' the words were clipped, sharper.

As though it still mattered.

Kane hated that his heart twisted in some perverse hope. Of course she didn't care, she was just surprised, even shocked, and he was just reading into it what he wanted to see. He had no idea how he managed it when so many emotions were charging through him right at this second, but he folded his arms across his chest and affected a lighter air.

'What are you doing here, Kane?'

'Just visiting…someone,' he didn't think she detected the momentary hesitation where he'd stalled. Wanting, for a split second, to tell her more.

Suddenly needing to unburden to someone – he refused to admit it was only because it was her – that he was here visiting a former army buddy. The only other survivor of a mission gone wrong a few years back, and who was only in this hospital now because he'd let the guilt of it eat into him.

Kane slammed the shutters in his mind in an instant. He had no intention of following his old buddy down that dark path. And baring his soul to Mattie wasn't going to help anyone.

'Which ward?'

She bit her lip, her brows furrowing together in a hint of irritation which was so painfully familiar that it caused a sharp band to tighten around his chest. Still, he was fairly certain her question had slipped out before she could check herself and it felt as though there was some comfort to be drawn from that.

Still, saying anything to her about his visit was bound to have her demanding to know how he – army-hating as he had been as a kid – had even come to sign-up. And then he'd have to tell her where he'd disappeared to all those years ago. And why.

Continue reading
SECOND CHANCE WITH HIS ARMY DOC
Charlotte Hawkes

Available next month
www.millsandboon.co.uk

WE'RE LOOKING FOR NEW AUTHORS FOR THE MILLS & BOON MEDICAL SERIES!

Whether you're a published author or an aspiring one, our editors would love to read your story.

You can submit the synopsis and first three chapters of your novel online, and find out more about the series, at **harlequin.submittable.com/submit**

We read all submissions and you do not need to have an agent to submit.

IF YOU'RE INTERESTED, WHY NOT HAVE A GO?

Submit your story at:
harlequin.submittable.com/submit

MILLS & BOON